Sons Of The Red Dragon

MARDI LYNN ROSELIUS

D1444509

Island Girl
Publishing

AN IMPRINT OF PAIGE TURNER INTERNATIONAL

NEW YORK·LONDON·SARASOTA

Island Girl
Publishing

Sons Of The Red Dragon
by Mardi Lynn Roselius

This book is a work of fiction. Names, characters, locations and events are either a product of the author's imagination, fictitious or used fictitiously. Any resemblance to any event, locale or person, living or dead, is purely coincidental.

Cover Designer: Mardi Lynn Roselius
Cover Technical Consultant: Yvonne San Luis
Interior Design and Formatting: Deborah J Ledford

Issued in Print and Electronic Formats
Trade Paperback ISBN: 979-8603383583

Manufactured in the United States of America

Sons Of The Red Dragon

MARDI LYNN ROSELIUS

DEDICATION

To Sherry, for believing in me and every dream I ever pursued.

PROLOGUE

Bainbridge Island, Washington
Late December 2012

MY FOOTSTEPS THUMPED the wet pavement as I glanced over my shoulder, searching the darkness that swept the rural road. No headlights. No sign I'd been followed. Faded yellow centerlines became a blur. My mind fought to maintain focus as I struggled against fatigue. I blinked once, twice, raised an arm, swiped my eyes with the back of my hand to remove the sting of sweat. My breath came heavy. A muscle spasm developed in my calf as pain and fear compelled me to keep running, knowing, if they caught me they'd kill me.

A black mass of clouds had settled over the area, a storm spinning in from the Pacific. The front promised discomfort, but adverse conditions that would provide a measure of cover.

Subtle whiffs of saline, the scent of ocean air, alerted me to the nearness of the shoreline. As I rounded a curve, the undergrowth disappeared and my sprint to safety ended against the sharp edge of Puget Sound.

Stopping beneath an evergreen rising from the perimeter of the concrete boat ramp, I bent over, pressed my palms against my knees and hung my head. Sucking deep breaths, the warm air from my lungs released white puffs into the cold air.

I kept an anxious watch on the road where it emerged

1

from a thin curtain of young spruce. This narrow entrance wound its way into the vacant parking lot, bathed in the soft illumination of a single streetlight. Droplets breaking out of the night sky glistened, a shower of slivers in the glow of the lamp as they splashed against the pavement and reflected in puddles on the uneven surface.

Sweat combined with the cool mist created a chill that penetrated to the bone. I tugged on the forest green parka Sarah insisted I take, pulled it tight, hunched over and jammed my hands into my pockets. My jeans clung heavy, damp. Sneakers, speckled with droplets of mud, squished, oozing wetness as I shifted from foot to foot.

Where was Barry?

I checked my watch. I'd only been waiting fifteen minutes. Seemed longer. The strap on the satchel holding my laptop dug into my shoulder as if I'd dragged a mainframe. It slid down my arm and rested at my feet, balanced atop a fallen limb.

The rain continued. Accumulating in the canopy above my head, the heavy droplets created a staccato rhythm against my parka as I listened for the distant whine of a small marine motor.

How had they found me? How is it they seem to know my every move? It was apparent I had hit a nerve with more than just *our* government. But it was impossible to tell the good guys from the bad.

Though I recognized the danger I would face, I decided to push on. Yes, there would be risk. I knew that. But I had been through too much. This was a risk I had to take.

Across Elliott Bay, the lights of Seattle shimmered and a mirror image danced across the ripples of Puget Sound, a false recital of tranquility. A silhouette of skyscrapers, tall and compressed; an industrial forest of glass and steel.

A city I once thought safe.

A city I now feared.

2

PART ONE

THE IMMIGRANTS

CHAPTER ONE

Northeast China
Spring 1950

THE BOY HAD celebrated his thirteenth birthday, a significant milestone that came with a great amount of responsibility. In the Liaoning province in Northeast China a boy became a young man at this tender age. He would be expected to learn his father's trade because one day, it would be his own. When that day came, being the oldest of four children, it would fall upon him to run the family business. To manage over two thousand acres of fertile farmland of rice and vegetables, worked by peasants who labored for food and shelter for their families. He would oversee expansive holdings that consisted of a chicken farm, pigpen, bakery, and herds of milk cows and goats.

The farm provided a good life for the boy's family. He and his siblings had tutors who taught them the Mandarin of their fathers and the mathematics necessary to run the family business. He had warm clothes during the cold winters and a house heated with wood fireplaces. He had slight understanding of the suffering that existed around him.

Early one crisp spring morning, he awoke to the rumble of motorized vehicles and the shouting of angry voices. A swarm of heavy footsteps raced up the steps and across the slatted wood floorboards of the front porch. They clattered and reverberated like hooves of cattle. Fists pounded the front door. He heard his father's voice amid a wave of shouts. Still in a daze from a deep sleep, he sat up in the bed he shared with his younger brother, confused, the words coming to him jumbled and unintelligible. He heard his mother scream, her bare feet slap against the floor as she rushed down the hallway. The front screen door slammed shut with a loud crack, his father's pleas barely distinguishable above the shouting and chaos.

The boy bounded from his bed, raced to his mother's side and stood with her in the doorway. "Mother! Mother! What is happening?"

He watched as soldiers brandishing weapons scuffled with his father in the dirt. He saw a rifle lifted above a soldier's head, the barrel pointing skyward, then dropped with a sharp thrust, the butt making a sullen thud. It rose again, then again.

"What are they doing to father?" He wrapped his arms around his mother as she pushed her way through the door. His three younger siblings had gathered behind them. She pushed them back, "Shut the door! Stay inside!"

She turned to the soldiers. "Please! I beg of you." She cried as she held on to her son with a tight grip. Her fingers dug into his side. Two soldiers stepped in, rifles crossed, and held them back.

Amid the dissipating dust in front of the house, three government vehicles idled as exhaust fumes choked the air. Soldiers shuffled across the yard in a pack, dragging his father through the dirt by his weakened arms as his shoes left a trail in the soft soil. Soldiers kicked and spat upon him as he passed. The boy looked for help, but saw only two men dressed in the clothing of the Revolution standing by a black sedan watching with stone faces.

His mother pleaded, "Please, don't take him!" One soldier clenched the shoulder of her garment, hate in his eyes as steel muzzles of long rifles stared mother and son in the face. Terrified and in tears, they huddled together.

Soldiers bent over and grabbed hold of his father's loose fitting clothing. Their arms strained as they pulled the fabric tight, lifted and tossed his limp body like a bale of hay into the back of the canvas covered truck with a bright red star on the door. The soldiers leapt over the tailgate into the darkness. Outstretched arms reached up and yanked the rolled canvas flap. It tumbled downward and they disappeared behind it.

His mother screamed, then bolted from the soldier's grip and the boy's arms, only to be dragged down from behind, her sleeping gown ripped as she collapsed in the dirt. Her cries of anguish pierced his ears. Having been knocked back against the door, he jumped up and ran down the steps, throwing himself upon her, holding her tight as sobs choked his throat and tears flowed down his cheeks. She reached out for her husband, her arm outstretched, fingers finding nothing but swirling dust.

The boy watched as the vehicle rumbled off, a cloud in its wake that soon dissipated, leaving an empty road over-shadowed by trees with ghostly trunks and barren limbs.

An unarmed soldier wearing a different style cap shouted commands as he approached the boy and his mother. "Gather clothes for you and your children. One small bag for each family member." He smiled, not of warmth and compassion, but of vengeance and cruel pleasure. "Prepare to leave immediately."

The boy looked to his mother for assurance, her dust-covered face streaked with tears, and heard her ask in a broken voice, "Where are you taking us? What of my husband?"

The leader said nothing, only grinned with yellowing teeth,

turned and flipped his hand in the air, a silent order the soldiers were eager to follow.

* * *

AFTER LONG HOURS in the back of a truck, bouncing along unfamiliar back-roads, the boy found himself in Shenyang, the capital of the province. Tired, hungry and still in shock, he, his mother, his brother and two sisters joined others collected from the countryside in a similar manner, sharing stories of comparable anguish. The events of the day had begun to sink in, and the boy began to understand. Life as he knew it would never be the same.

After subsisting for thirty days in a small room of a guarded building, the family was sent to a re-education camp in the countryside. The children attended a school administered by the Party while their mother worked twelve-hour days in a collective camp factory, then spent two hours each evening in mandatory lectures.

Their mother did her best to hold the family together, to provide the love, attention and guidance necessary with an absent father. Combined with her obligations in the labor camp, this was a heavy burden on her shoulders, a responsibility she had never expected to take on alone. The strain of the new life subjected her to physical demands and emotional pressures she had never known. Awakened many late nights by the sound of his mother's cries, the boy buried his head in his blanket to muffle the heartbreak, vowing one day he would provide the support she needed.

Two years later, at the age of fifteen, the boy was sent to a school in Shenyang, to begin preparations for a career in the People's Liberation Army and instructed in the ideologies of the Communist manifesto. He did well and prospered in a world altered by a radical hand. He looked forward to his new responsibilities and embraced his future, but he never forgot his past.

At thirteen the boy's life changed in the most dramatic of ways. He saw his father for the last time. The sight of his father beaten and dragged away would remain with him forever. A place, a time, a horrifying image burned into his memory that would never be forgotten and that he swore to himself, would one day be avenged.

CHAPTER TWO

Central China
Spring, 1987

WUNG HU WAS accustomed to the heavy traffic and slow commute to his factory on the west side of Tannanu, where he served as production line manager for the Yanghu Manufacturing Company. Through the open window, he remained conscious of the sounds and smells of the city. The late spring air felt cool but tainted with pollution because hot summer winds had yet to engage the central plains.

The high-pitched whine of two-stroke engines from an army of small scooters pierced the air. A swarm of bicycles, rickshaws, pedi-cabs, buses and automobiles joined him to create a river of noise and dust that wound its way through the streets and boulevards. The clamor of a densely packed city reverberated up the sides of high-rise apartment buildings as the light of dawn parted the early morning darkness and awakened the street-level shops and markets he passed twice each day.

At age twenty-nine, Wung Hu was fortunate. Educated at Wujung People's University with a degree in industrial management, he had begun his ascension in the business world of Tannanu, with a responsible management position in a state-run manufacturing company.

His family was respected and had a long history of political involvement. His grandfather fought with Mao Tse-tung during the Chinese Civil War against Chiang Kai-shek, marching with Mao in the historic Long March, six thousand miles through China's most rugged terrain. His grandfather had witnessed the onset of the Chinese Revolution as Mao Tse-tung proclaimed the People's Republic of China in Beijing on October 1, 1949.

Wung Hu's father, a retired Major in the People's Liberation Army, had become a district representative of the Wujung Province People's Party. Like his father and grandfather before him, Wung Hu was an active participant in the Chinese Communist Party and hoped one day to hold a position of importance himself.

Wung Hu had a dutiful and caring wife, Li Chen, a young woman with delicate features and skin as smooth as the silk gowns she often wore. Her eyes were large and unusually round, exhibiting an ever-present sparkle. The daughter of a party official who had worked with Wung Hu's own father at party headquarters, she had been introduced to Wung Hu nearly seven years earlier. Their union seemed a perfect match.

Wung Hu and Li Chen had one child, a daughter, Sung Wi, named after her maternal grandmother. At six years old, she was the flame that warmed her father's heart. She had begun her formal school training, proud she could dress herself each morning in her uniform of red bib trousers, tan-colored long-sleeved shirt and red cap.

Wung Hu placed all his hopes and dreams in Sung Wi. Since the government had enacted the "One Child Policy" to slow the rapidly escalating birth rate and burgeoning population of China, there would be no more children in the Hu household. Throughout China, for couples who started their families after that socially significant date, there would be only one child. Yet, as much as Wung Hu loved his daughter, he longed for a son.

Despite the rapid changes in the cultural tapestry of China, there was still that deep-rooted tradition that said the young shall take care of the old. Every family with a son took great comfort knowing their son would be there for them when the day came they could not care for themselves. Wung Hu had to put his faith and trust in his young daughter. He had to believe that she might someday be capable of taking care of her aging parents, but this was a developing concept in Chinese family dynamics. Thousands of years of Chinese culture mandated that sons would be the ones to maintain the household, the family, and raise a new generation of sons to follow in their father's footsteps. Wung Hu, being a devoted party member and staunch supporter of the government, had resigned himself to his single-child parenting status...one that did not include a male child.

Wung Hu turned left when he arrived at the intersection that led to Yanghu Manufacturing Company. He continued past a row of factory buildings and pulled up to the entrance gate. The security guard glanced at his credentials and waved him through.

The factory occupied an austere three-story, gray concrete-block structure. A simple steel door with a small window at the top served as the entrance. A facility constructed for the mass production of plastic consumer goods, it afforded an environment indifferent to the comfort of workers. Wung Hu's office on the first level was separated from the factory floor by a single door that reduced the thump and whine of factory machinery but did not eliminate the sounds or obnoxious smells of manufacturing.

Production reports, order forms and supervisor schedules covered his small metal desk, waiting for his review before being filed in thick three-ring binders. His assistant kept a tidy desk against the opposite wall and pounded with feverish abandon on a manual typewriter to deliver the many forms and reports that filled those binders.

Upon arriving on Friday morning, Wung Hu received a message telling him to report immediately to the conference room on the third floor. This was not unusual. He had often been called on to address the management team concerning production schedules, but he had no such presentation scheduled for today.

They must have information to give me regarding a contract with a new Western company, or a new product we will soon be producing, he thought as he climbed the stairs to the third floor. Reaching the conference room, he knocked twice.

The door swung open. A man Wung Hu recognized as the assistant to Mr. Jiang, the head of the management team, faced him. Both men bowed slightly from the waist. "Please step in," the assistant said.

As Wung Hu entered, an uneasy feeling overcame him. The air in the room felt charged with a sense of gravity. He glanced around, unsettled by those he saw seated at the table. This was *not* a normal meeting of the management team. His anxiety rose, his attention drawn to the two men in dark business suits sitting on either side of Mr. Jiang. Team members sat rigid, hands clasped in front of them. Their familiar faces stared back unsmiling, eyes focused on Wung Hu. He looked for any encouraging sign. There was none. The two businessmen scrutinized him. He recognized one from photos, a high-level official of the local Tannanu Chinese Communist Party. The other he did not know.

Intuition sent his body warning signals. He tensed, expecting an accusatory blow. Nervous thoughts raced through his mind—*Why are these men here? What do they want with me?* He glanced from one to the other. A party official did not seek a meeting with a simple production manager unless there were issues to discuss that were important to the State. Wung Hu knew he had been a good party member. He had done nothing that would have brought attention to himself. To his knowledge, he had not violated any rules that deserved a visit from Party headquarters. So what did they want with him?

As Wung Hu stepped forward, Mr. Jiang rose from his chair. "Mr. Wung Hu." He then turned to his left and gestured with an open palm of his left hand. "This is Mr. Choi Yengtze, deputy director of the Tannanu Chinese Communist Party." He paused, then turned to his right and gestured with the open palm of his right hand. "And this is Mr. Lu Yapp, director general of the Department of Emigration and Resettlement for the Chinese Communist Party. He is here on very important business." Mr. Jiang eyed Wung Hu a moment before proceeding.

"He has come from Beijing to discuss a serious matter with you."

CHAPTER THREE

WUNG HU COULD not hide his concern as he stood facing the Party official from Beijing. The room closed around him, sucking the air out, leaving him breathless as heat surged through his body. Thoughts rushed through his mind—the safety of his family, the security of his job.

Following the lead of the two government officials, everyone rose. Pointing to an empty chair, Mr. Jiang asked Wung Hu to be seated. "Mr. Wung Hu," he began. "Mr. Lu Yapp has come from the Department of Emigration and Resettlement to meet with you on some important Party business. It is imperative that you listen carefully to what he has to say."

Wung Hu squirmed in his seat, he nodded, a knot in his throat. His hands in his lap, his feet planted flat on the wood floor, he moved his eyes from Mr. Jiang to Mr. Lu Yapp.

"Mr. Wung Hu," the government official began as he stared across the table. "I am here to discuss a program whereby we assess worthy candidates to join a historic and monumental endeavor. It is a program as important to the future of The People's Republic of China as the Long March was to the beginning. We are looking for young men who have proven their loyalties to the Party to join us in an organization known as the Sons of the Red Dragon."

As Mr. Lu Yapp spoke, Wung Hu watched his lips move, attempting to grasp every word. They came with alarming speed. *The Long March? Join them? Sons of the Red Dragon?* Wung Hu did not want to miss a single thing. His heart raced, rushing blood to his head. His body wobbled.

Mr. Lu Yapp continued. "I knew your father well as we served together many years ago in the People's Liberation Army. He is a good man and a good party member. We believe you are, in that respect, like your father. We are looking for young married men such as yourself, who have a strong family line of unswerving dedication. Young men who have put the Party first, above all else."

Wung Hu felt the intense gaze of Mr. Lu Yapp burning into him, but he knew not to stare in return, as that would seem a sign of defiance to one of high authority. He lowered his eyes to the top of the polished wood table, where he watched the animated reflection of Mr. Lu Yapp, and tried to retain his composure. He felt moisture on his brow and wished to reach for the handkerchief in his trouser pocket, but feared to make a move.

"You are a family man?" Mr. Lu Yapp asked.

Wung Hu shuffled his feet in an unconscious spasm. "Yes, Mr. Lu Yapp." He clasped his hands and strummed his interlocked fingers with a silent nervous motion.

"We know much about you," Mr. Lu Yapp said. "You meet our profile objectives. Especially since you have a daughter."

A puzzled look fell across Wung Hu's face and he felt a greater sense of alarm. He thought back to what Mr. Lu Yapp had said, the Sons of the Red Dragon. *What does this have to do with my daughter?*

"Have no concern regarding your daughter," Mr. Lu Yapp said. "We know she is very important to you. That pleases us." Mr. Lu Yapp rose from his seat and stood erect, his hands by his sides. "We must continue to discuss our program and your place within it, but not here, not today. Tomorrow I will see you at the Office of the Director Political, at eight a.m. We will outline our program to you in great detail." He glanced around the table. "Let me remind everyone…this conversation is the proprietary business of the Party. There will be no further discussion outside this room. Mr. Wung Hu, until we meet tomorrow morning, do not discuss this with your wife, Li Chen. We do understand each other, do we not?"

Each person nodded. Wung Hu rose from his chair, once again bowed with respect, and as Mr. Jiang's assistant opened the door, backed out into the hallway. He hurried down the hall, stunned and confused.

What could they possibly want with me, he asked himself again. *I do not know how I can be worthy of this most important program. And my daughter? What does she have to do with all of this? A mere child. What is this program, Sons of the Red Dragon? What will I be asked to do?*

Tomorrow Wung Hu would find out. But today he knew he would not be able to concentrate on his job and the work at hand. And tonight, he knew he would not sleep.

* * *

WUNG HU RETURNED home that evening and made an effort to act his normal self, but the meeting earlier in the day made that impossible. He slumped into his chair, lifted his daughter Sung Wi and hugged her against his chest as the thump of her heartbeat raced against his own. Tears welled in the corners of his eyes and rolled down his cheeks. He wiped them away so Li Chen would not notice. He sat and said little as Sung Wi played and Li Chen prepared the evening meal.

"You do not eat," Li Chen said. "Do you not enjoy your meal?"

Her words startled Wung Hu. His mind had drifted. He stared at the rice, fried pork belly and medley of green vegetables, as he rearranged them on his plate with a delicate touch of his polished wood chopsticks. "Yes. It is a fitting meal. But tonight I do not feel an appetite." He looked at Sung Wi who had raised her plate, her tongue licking the last of the soy sauce, her face masked in a brown stain. Wung Hu forced a smile. "Sung Wi will have to make up for my deficiency."

"Sung Wi!" Li Chen scolded. "Where are your manners? This is not proper behavior for our table."

Sung Wi looked to her father for support, but tonight she found none.

Wung Hu stared off in a vacant gaze as Li Chen cleaned the kitchen. She prepared Sung Wi for bed, then busied herself in their bedroom.

When she returned, she placed a hand on Wung Hu's shoulder. "It is time for bed."

He reached up and stroked her hand. "You go. I will be along soon."

He sat motionless at the small table, his mind playing games, as much as he tried to push these thoughts away. Eventually he laid his head on his folded arms, exhausted and fraught with fear of the unknown.

* * *

WHEN LI CHEN arose the next morning to heat water for their morning tea, she found Wung Hu where she had left him the night before. It was not like Wung Hu to sleep at the table, but she had sensed something was worrying him. His mind was elsewhere. He had not stopped by the market on his way home to purchase the bok choy and chicken she had requested. To forget was not like him. He had not acted his normal self the previous evening, and she knew not to pry into his deepest thoughts.

She nudged him as she passed. Startled, Wung Hu jerked. He reached out, pulled her to him and gave her a warm hug.

She set a cup of tea in front of him. He smiled but did not speak. Li Chen loved Wung Hu and she knew he loved her, but she wished he would open up to her when he was troubled. He never did. She believed it to be her husband's way of protecting her, keeping the weight of responsibility on his shoulders, but she wished Wung Hu would share his burdens with her, as they shared their life in every other way.

* * *

PRECISELY AT EIGHT A.M., after Wung Hu had located the compound of government offices reserved for party committees and the chairman, just off Tinglee Square, he knocked on the door of the Office of the Director Political. He was led to a room in the back. Seated at a table facing him were Mr. Lu Yapp and the same Mr. Choi Yengtze he had met the day before.

Both stood and all three bowed. Looking for any sign of reassurance, Wung Hu noticed Mr. Lu Yapp offered a slight smile of greeting.

"Mr. Wung Hu," Mr. Lu Yapp began. "Thank you for coming. I know we did not provide you with any details during our brief meeting yesterday morning. I hope today we can ease any concerns as we explain our program fully. As I mentioned, this is most vital. There will be a lot for you to comprehend, so please feel free to ask questions as we proceed."

Mr. Lu Yapp motioned toward the empty chair and Wung Hu seated himself, keeping his eyes on the two men. He did not know what to expect. What he had heard the previous day made him apprehensive yet anxious to hear what Mr. Lu Yapp had to say.

"Yesterday I talked of the Sons of the Red Dragon, a program for dedicated party members like you. As I said, it is most important that those selected have a history of support and dedication to the principles of the Party. A deep devotion bred from the roots of the grandfathers and fathers and sons of the revolution. You are a son of a son of the revolution. But you do not have a son of your own. You understand the Party position on that sensitive but imperative issue. You have supported this important policy of the land. It is nondiscriminatory, but may appear more fair to some than to others. Those to whom I am referring are those with the good fortune to have fathered a son."

Wung Hu swallowed, understanding fully.

"Now, Wung Hu, would you like to have a son of your own?"

Wung Hu looked at Mr. Lu Yapp, unsure he had heard him correctly. He lowered his head. "Respectfully, sir, I have a daughter. I love my daughter and would not trade my daughter for a thousand sons." Wung Hu had heard stories of parents who had found ways to rid themselves of their baby girls, in a most appalling and unspeakable manner, in order to try a second time, for a son.

"You do not have to give up your daughter," Mr. Lu Yapp replied. "Yet you can have a son...two or three if you wish. Participants in our program, the Sons of the Red Dragon, as it implies, may have many sons."

"But...but how can this be?" Wung Hu asked. "I do not understand."

"If you live in America, you may have as many sons as you wish."

Wung Hu stared at Mr. Lu Yapp. Puzzled, confused, his thought process teetered, about to fall into a pit of complete incomprehension. His mind suffered a disconnect between the words he heard and his sense of reason. He had been programmed since a child to be a good citizen of China, loyal to the Party and the doctrine of Communism.

A few moments passed before Wung Hu responded. "Did you say, 'If I lived in America?'" He paused, not certain he had heard himself ask such an absurd question. "I could have as many sons as I wish? I do not understand. I am a simple factory worker. I live here in China with my family. This is my country. My home. The home of my father and his father and a hundred fathers before him. I do not understand what you say."

Lu Yapp stood up, pushed his chair aside and clasped his hands behind his back. He walked a few steps then turned and looked down at Wung Hu.

"I am sure you were not prepared for this, Mr. Wung Hu. One never is. So let me explain the grand plan the Party has for you and your family."

Wung Hu squirmed in the hard chair. His mind wanted to race ahead, anticipate what terrible thing Lu Yapp would tell him next, but he forced himself to stay focused.

"Those of us in the Department of Emigration and Resettlement help families emigrate from China to the West. America, if you will. There are many tens of thousands of Chinese immigrant families living in America. Most have rejected their homeland, rejected their history, their heritage and their culture to live among the white Europeans and the black Africans who settled there. Our purpose is to select honorable Chinese families with strong ties to China, and relocate them. Young families who will keep the love of China in their hearts and in their minds, even as they live in a cultural abyss such as America. Families who would put China first, above their adopted home. Families such as yours."

Wung Hu listened in stunned silence. He heard the words, but they were difficult to fathom. In his wildest imagination, he never expected his beloved Party to ask him to leave the land of his birth, the land of his forefathers. To live his life and spend his last years on soil foreign to him.

Wung Hu had never questioned authority, but now he could not hold back. "Why did you select me?" he asked in a pleading tone. "I am sorry for my reluctance to embrace your words with the enthusiasm that I should, but I did not expect you would ask this of me. I am a good citizen of the Party, loyal and devoted to my country, which I love. I know no other place than the place of my birth."

"I understand," Mr. Lu Yapp said as he returned to his seat, leaned over and studied Wung Hu. "Because you *are* so loyal to the Party and devoted to your country, you *are* the perfect one. You are educated from the University, so the American immigration officials will look favorably on you."

"You said my family would come with me?"

"Yes, your wife and child will go with you, but no one else. You must make a new home in America. The purpose of sending you to America is to father sons, to raise them as Chinese-Americans. Sons with an umbilical cord to China, with a strong sense of their Chinese heritage, and who will maintain a love for their ancestral home. Chinese-Americans who would be Chinese first—Americans second."

Wung Hu shifted and glanced at Mr. Choi Yengtze. The Party official nodded his head, affirming his approval.

"We want you to raise your sons to be loyal, dedicated to the ideals of our Chinese homeland. We want them to understand the Western culture but never forget the culture of their ancestors. To study the policies and politics of the Western world at the American universities. To become politically active. To rise through the world of politics to the highest levels of American government. They will be leaders in America, but must maintain loyalty to the land of their fathers." Mr. Lu Yapp touched his forefinger to his temple. "To rest their heads in the bed of America," he then pointed to his chest. "But keep their hearts pumping the blood of China.

"Your country has selected you, Wung Hu, to serve China at a sacrifice unheard of in the many centuries of our fathers. You are among the chosen few. An elite group of loyal and dedicated families. An army without arms. An army with strong hearts and sound minds. The hearts and minds of China."

Wung Hu struggled to keep his concentration. With so much startling information he had to hold off the urge to let his thoughts drift, to think of the many consequences of what he had heard. *A life in America? What about my family? My father? My job? My life in China?*

Mr. Lu Yapp continued. "There is much for you to know. You will attend orientation classes to prepare for your journey. And when you arrive in America, you will have a contact, a man of China such as yourself, who will see that you succeed."

"What of my father?" Wung Hu asked. "He will need someone to care for him. It is my duty to be there in his final years."

"Your father is an honored veteran of the People's Liberation Army. He will be well cared for. He is no longer your responsibility. Your responsibility will be to raise your own sons."

Wung Hu let out a deep breath. He hung his head, stared at the floor, his forearms resting on his knees. He clasped his hands, finality sinking in. The great Party had decided the destiny of a simple factory worker and that destiny now lay across the ocean in a new land. Although he felt great anxiety, the last sentence Mr. Lu Yapp spoke continued to resonate in his mind. Five simple words that made his eyes moist and his heart pound.

At the conclusion of the meeting, Wung Hu returned to his office, his mind swirling with disbelief and apprehension. Gathering his thoughts, he reflected back to the message this astounding meeting had brought. His lips dry, he mouthed those five words that made his heart race, repeating them over and over, again and again—*to raise your own sons!*

CHAPTER FOUR

THAT EVENING WUNG Hu returned to his home and told Li Chen of the events that had transpired over the past two days.

"This cannot be true," Li Chen cried out. Tears rolled down her cheeks. She dropped to her knees. Her body quivered, her hands covered her muffled sobs of anguish. "I cannot leave my home. Tell me this is not true."

Wung Hu bent over and lowered himself to the floor. Their knees met as he pulled her close to him, wrapping his arms around her as she rested her head on his shoulder. His eyes were moist, his heart broken, believing he had failed his family. Failed Li Chen. "Yes, it is true. I wish it were not, but the Party has directed. I go tomorrow to Beijing. By months end we must leave for America."

Little Sung Wi, at her tender age, did not understand. Upset over the sight of her mother's pain, she ran to her and held her as tight as her arms would allow, her tiny tears leaving stains on her mother's cotton blouse.

Wung Hu cupped Li Chen's face and looked into her deep black eyes. They were puffy and moist but still the most expressive eyes he had ever seen. "Li Chen. I have you by my side and we have our beautiful Sung Wi. I could not make this journey by myself, or with any other soul. We will make this journey to America as a family. It will be good for us. It will be good for China. We will prosper in this new land and we will bear many children. Our new home will be filled with the love of family and the love of Chinese ways."

He wiped her tears with his thumbs. "We will not leave our life in China behind, buried and forgotten. We will take our cherished memories to our new home and share them with our children. And most importantly, we will be together."

Li Chen looked up at Wung Hu and nodded as he held her face in his cupped hands. He knew the crying had not ended. There would be many more quiet moments when Li Chen would cry for her lost home and her family left behind. Their life as they knew it would soon be ripped away. They would be pushed toward a new and strange life by a brown sleeve bearing a bright red star.

* * *

THE FOLLOWING DAY Wung Hu traveled to Beijing to apply for emigration to the United States of America, to fill out legions of official forms and documents and be further advised of the Sons of the Red Dragon program. For three weeks he received intense orientation in the doctrines and dogma of the Chinese Communist Party. He was schooled in the history of America and America's relationship with China over the past two hundred years—a woefully short account considering the great and colorful history of his own native land. He also received refresher courses to bolster his English classes from earlier school days.

When he completed his indoctrination and all documents had been approved and duly authorized, he prepared himself for his life-changing journey.

Friends and family gathered. Goodbyes were said and tears flowed once again. Wung Hu and his family, each carrying a small suitcase, waited for the car provided by the Party to drive them to the train station. From Tannanu they would travel to Shanghai where they would board a cargo ship bound for America.

As they closed their door for the last time, Li Chen turned and took one last look at her home. Wung Hu stopped to give her a moment, then tugged at her sleeve. Under her arm she cradled a small cardboard box wrapped with string and tied with a tight knot. Inside, a small porcelain tea set had been packed with care for the journey. Given to her by her mother as a wedding present, this gift would be the only memento of her home she would take to her new life. As they waited, two black government vehicles approached in a cloud of dust and pulled to a stop. The door to the first car opened and Mr. Choi Yengtze, from Party headquarters, stepped out and approached.

"Mr. Wung Hu. The Party would like to thank you for the sacrifice you and your family are making for your country. You will have difficult days ahead, but we know you will succeed and be an honorable envoy for your country and your Party."

He handed Wung Hu a small wood box wrapped with a band of thin bamboo, a wood button held it secure. Wung Hu unbuttoned the band and opened the lid. Inside a brass medallion sparkled as it caught the morning sun. In the outer ring an embossed inscription read, THE PARTY, THE COUNTRY, THE FAMILY. In the center, a thin clear glass vial held a small amount of dark, black soil. The soil of China.

Again tears welled up and Wung Hu brushed them away. He bowed with respect and without a word, led his family to the waiting vehicle.

* * *

AFTER FOUR DAYS the seasickness that had gripped the entire family abated. They had been fortunate, the ocean had been calm but the rolling swells assaulted their equilibrium, disjointed their bodies from their mind's sense of balance. Even tremors of frequent earthquakes in central China ran their course after only a few moments. They had never experienced the ground beneath their feet move in such an unrelenting roll as the great Pacific had sent their way.

Their small cabin provided little comfort. The air carried into the lower decks had been fouled by fumes of the working ship, the machinery, the rust, the sanitation. The sweet smell of stir-fry drifting through the corridors had also contributed to the nausea that kept them near the bathroom.

Once able to stand and move about, the family surfaced, took a firm hold on the steel handrails and gazed out into a sea of whitecaps. Wung Hu breathed in and filled his lungs with fresh air. He licked his lips and tasted the sea salt that swirled in a fine mist. The horizon moved and dipped, first at one angle, then another. But this was the first time he had felt alive since they had sailed. He moved closer to Li Chen, squeezing Sung Wi between them, smiling, he spoke. "Li Chen. I believe I would like to eat."

"Yes," she replied. "A hot meal would be good."

They went to the dining room and joined the few passengers and crew for their first meal beyond the shores of their homeland. Their appetites were stronger than their stomachs however, so they ate little. The conversation was welcomed and invigorating. They learned they were traveling among others that shared similar futures and possessed like anxieties.

The days passed without further discomforts and the boring routine of a trans-Pacific crossing settled in. They were limited to their cabin, one area of an outside deck and the dining room. In an ocean of sixty four million square miles, claustrophobia was the last condition Wung Hu had expected to experience. But boredom, monotony and claustrophobia would be the agenda for the next twelve days.

After too many time zones to keep track of and a pass through the international dateline, they arrived at their final destination, Seattle, Washington, the city they would live in and raise their children. The hour of the day and even the day of the week escaped Wung Hu in the confusion of prolonged travel. Passing through immigration and customs, they were finally on firm ground in their new home. With luggage in hand they walked through a set of double doors not knowing what to expect.

*　*　*

WILLIE WONG HADN'T been waiting long. He held a hand-lettered sign in front of him so his new guests could identify him. In Mandarin it simply stated, MR. WUNG HU AND FAMILY.

A distinctive looking Chinese-American gentleman in his late forties, Willie Wong sported premature shocking-white hair with a matching mustache and goatee. He wore a long black overcoat to give comfort against the cold damp air of the Seattle spring.

A young family with a youngster clutching her mother's dress passed through the doors and glanced around. They each carried a small suitcase and the woman held a cardboard box wrapped with string in her free hand. Their eyes finally settled on Willie Wong's sign.

"Mr. Willie Wong?" the man asked as they approached. "I am Wung Hu, and this is Li Chen and our daughter Sung Wi."

Willie Wong smiled and greeted them with a polite bow. He spoke fluent Mandarin and knew he would have to use it to converse with his new guests. "Mr. Wung Hu, it is an honor to meet you." Looking at Li Chen and down to Sung Wi, he continued, "Welcome to America."

Wung Hu bowed and replied, "It is an honor to meet you, Mr. Willie Wong. We are your most obedient servants."

Willie Wong looked at Wung Hu with an understanding borne from having lived in two cultures for many years. "Mr. Wung Hu. I respect your submissive demeanor, and I know you do it with great deference, but it is unnecessary. While we cling to our strong Chinese traditions, class lines have been blurred and left at the gateway to America. The gateway you have just passed through. If we are to succeed and prosper, we must slip into the world of the Americans. To learn their ways. To understand the character and the behaviors of the American. You are a good man, an educated man. It will come quickly to you." He smiled warmly. "Please, call me Uncle Willie."

Uncle Willie took Li Chen's suitcase and led them to a parking lot where he left his SUV. He noticed Wung Hu's eyes light up at the sight of his gleaming vehicle. A vehicle that Uncle Willie knew to be unimagined luxury to his new guest. He drove them to his home, passing through the International District. "This is an area of many Chinese businesses," he pointed out. "Grocery stores, vegetable markets, laundries and import shops." He glanced in the rearview mirror to see Li Chen staring out the window, studying the shops as they passed.

"There are shops here to make you feel at home. Products imported from China or made locally for the growing population of immigrants from Asia. As you can see, the International District is not just a community of Chinese ethnicity, but also home to immigrants from all over Southeast Asia and the Pacific Rim. Japan, Korea, the Philippines, as well as Thailand, Cambodia and Laos."

Wung Hu turned to him with a puzzled look.

"Wung Hu. This may surprise you. In the old countries, these people did not necessarily like each other, and many harbored an animosity or even a deep hatred due to long-standing political or geographical differences. But in America, we live together, in the same neighborhoods." Uncle Willie smiled at Wung Hu's look of disbelief.

Within minutes they pulled up to Uncle Willie's residence,

a rather unpretentious wood frame house on Fifteenth Avenue, near the International District. As they entered, Uncle Willie realized this would be a new experience for Wung Hu and Li Chen. They had never been in a house like this one; a single-family home with two floors, three bedrooms and two baths— Western style baths. He watched their faces, expressions of awe spreading over them as they glanced at the stuffed furniture with silk cushions, Chinese art and beautiful porcelain vases. Although modestly furnished by western standards, to Wung Hu and Li Chen, it would seem quite elegant. Sung Wi plopped down on the floor and kicked her legs in the air as she rubbed her tiny fingers through the soft carpet and giggled.

"Sung Wi!" Li Chen scolded. "You must not behave like this. Stand up."

Uncle Willie grinned, leaned over and tickled Sung Wi. "No, let her play. Let her come to know my home. She cannot do harm. My home is your home." He took their bags and turned toward the stairs. "Come, let me show you to your room."

* * *

TWO DAYS LATER, after much needed rest, Uncle Willie and Wung Hu sat down in the living room to talk while having a cup of green tea.

"I knew your father," Uncle Willie began. "I served under him in the People's Liberation Army, although he was well into his career while I was just beginning mine. He was a fine soldier and a dedicated member of the Party. I never met your grandfather, but I have heard stories of him and his important role during the early days of the revolution. Your family has been a strong limb on the revolutionary tree."

Uncle Willie lifted his cup and sipped. He studied Wung Hu's face. "I understand you must have mixed feelings about your new venture into the Western world. It is natural to be saddened with the loss of your family home. We have asked a lot of you and your family. I will try to help ease the discomfort of the transition. I am not your family now, but I hope you, Li Chen and Sung Wi will come to think of me in that way. We are not of the same blood, but we are all of the blood of China."

Wung Hu looked up at Uncle Willie. "I want to be here. I want to live in America and do my duty for my country and my Party."

"I know you do, Wung Hu. But it is not wrong to have reservations about this new life. In America it is acceptable to think differently. To say what you believe. But you must be strong and remember the basic tenets we grew up with and lived by, as did our fathers. You are a strong man. You will do well."

Uncle Willie picked up the teapot and filled their cups once more. "Tomorrow we will get started with your new life. We will find an apartment, a furnished one, so you can settle your family in. I know a woman, a good friend, who will help Li Chen with her household, to explain to her how to use her new kitchen and show her where to shop. We will find a place for you to live in the International District so Li Chen will be close to shopping for the things she is familiar with. We also need to enroll Sung Wi into school. There is a good one near the District that many immigrant children attend."

"Yes," Wung Hu said. "Her education is very important. It will be good for her to be with children of Chinese families."

Uncle Willie continued. "Then I will introduce you to my business. I have a modest import company and I have a position for you there. It is best you work close to me so I will be available to help you in your transition. You will need to become more fluent in English. It will help you in your new life. Many of your contacts at work, and in the community, will speak Mandarin, but you need to know the language of the Americans. Besides," Uncle Willie gave Wung Hu a grin, "your *sons* will speak English and you will want to know what they are saying."

Wung Hu smiled at the thought.

Uncle Willie moved a little closer to Wung Hu. "Once we have you settled in your new apartment, you must start working on that other part of your mission." Uncle Willie grinned, "Making sons."

Uncle Willie sipped his tea. He felt the hot vapors drifting upwards, filling his lungs. "Life in America will not be as difficult as the life you lived in China," Uncle Willie continued. "There will be time for enjoying oneself, and time for laughter. The Americans have a humorous saying they sometimes use when they have an enjoyable task to do, a task that might be the envy of everyone."

Wung Hu did not speak fluent English, so they conversed in Mandarin. Uncle Willie began, "The Americans say," and to make his point, he switched to English, "It's a tough job, but somebody has to do it." He then translated this American concept to Wung Hu.

"So, Wung Hu, my friend, are you up to the task?"

Wung Hu's eyes glistened, and he allowed a broad smile to make a rare appearance.

* * *

WUNG HU LOOKED up as he exhaled a deep breath, his eyes drawn to the glow through the bedroom window. He could see lights from buildings that surrounded the new apartment he shared with Li Chen and Sung Wi. Li Chen lay beneath him, her eyes closed. His palms pressed against the bed on either side of her warm body as he held himself above her. His nakedness glistened with sweat and his heart pounded from an uncharted run of passionate lovemaking. The first time they had forsaken birth control since Sung Wi had been conceived.

Li Chen's chest heaved, her small firm breasts moved up and down as the filtered light from the window highlighted her nipples, firm and erect from his deft light kisses. She hummed and cooed with each breath, exhaling a sweetness. Wung Hu remained still, his eyes absorbing her beauty. He wished to stay forever inside her warm moistness. If his heart stopped beating tonight he would die a happy man. But he knew he could not. For tonight he was certain he had made a son and he would have to be there for him.

Li Chen opened her eyes as Wung Hu lowered himself, kissed her on her lips and whispered. "Let me stay longer."

Li Chen held his face with a gentle touch, "You can stay as long as you want, for tonight, we have made a son. I know this in my heart. I felt a man inside of me tonight, and a strong little son will come from that man. He is your son, Wung Hu. And I will give you many more."

CHAPTER FIVE

Seattle, Washington
Nine months later

LI CHEN LEANED over and nudged Wung Hu, sleeping soundly by her side. She had been lying awake for hours as the flutter within her grew more persistent. She laid her hand on his shoulder and whispered, "My time has come."

* * *

AS THE NEW dawn broke over the Cascade Mountains to the east, a small infant cry rose above the normal bedlam in the sterile, clinical delivery room. Wung Hu smiled down at Li Chen as he held his son in his arms, a chubby cherub with a head full of jet-black hair that stood up like a stiff hairbrush. The longing and desire of many years rushed through him. His heart filled with joy. Looking into those tiny eyes—eyes that had yet to see a full day in the new world—he knew his son would be special. He pushed back tears and spoke to Li Chen through a choked voice, his eyes fixated on the bundle he cradled.

"Li Chen. My son will be a leader of men and a proud voice for all Chinese. He must have a great name." He paused as he brushed his hand against the infant's hair, tickling his palm. "There is no name more befitting my first son than a name I remember from my American studies, a name that embodies history, leadership and heroism." He looked down at Li Chen. "I will name my son, George Washington Hu."

A smile crossed her face lifting her flushed cheeks, then her eyes closed as she fell silent, exhausted, but content.

CHAPTER SIX

WUNG HU AND his family settled into their new life in America. He embraced his new trade with Uncle Willie and Li Chen busied herself raising their two children. They waited for Li Chen to recover from the birth of their first son before having another child. Li Chen was a strong woman, but the care of a new baby was demanding, although a duty she cherished.

Wung Hu was anxious to have another child, so two years after the birth of their first son, Li Chen delivered a second. A son expected to be no less successful than his older brother and who deserved a name no less fitting than the one bestowed on the first son. Wung Hu went to the history books once again, and decided his second son would be named after another great American, his birth certificate recorded as Thomas Jefferson Hu.

The names Wung Hu had chosen for his sons were not of Chinese origin and did not reflect their Chinese heritage, or honor any of the great leaders of China. He felt the names he had selected would be more advantageous for his sons in their quest for greatness in the political world of America. George and Thomas were names quite common in the West. Strong names that would help them fulfill the Party's grand plan—their ascension to the top of American political influence.

The boys grew and prospered and two years later, Li Chen delivered what would be their fourth and final child, a baby girl they named Angela. Their family complete, Wung Hu felt blessed to have two healthy, beautiful daughters and two strong, energetic sons.

* * *

WUNG HU CONTINUED to work in the export business with Uncle Willie even as Uncle Willie became more involved with his duties as the "sponsor" of a growing number of immigrants who had joined the Sons of the Red Dragon. He saw to it they kept the children in the right schools and that some of their activities included Chinese cultural studies and language classes available at the Chinese Cultural Academy in the International District.

The years passed, and the Hu family thrived and assimilated into the American-Asian way of life. Wung Hu's oldest son George had reached his thirteenth birthday. He had never heard any mention of the Sons of the Red Dragon. Guiding George and Thomas with a very specific structure, Uncle Willie could only hope they follow a path compatible to the program that had been laid out in great detail to Wung Hu before he left China, fourteen years ago.

It was time for Uncle Willie to have a personal meeting with George Hu.

It was time for George to take the next step in his education, development and growth in the Sons of the Red Dragon program.

* * *

YOUNG GEORGE HU rang the doorbell at precisely four p.m. The door opened with a twist of the brass doorknob, and Uncle Willie's smiling face appeared behind it. Uncle Willie had always been kind and gentle to George, and George in turn, loved and admired him.

"George. Come in," he said as he held the door. "Come,

let us be seated in the living room."

Uncle Willie pointed to a cushy sofa with silk pillows. "Please sit down. Would you like something to drink? A Coke or some tea?"

"A Coke would be fine, sir."

Uncle Willie turned to Ki Chung, his housekeeper, who emerged from the kitchen. "Please, Ki Chung, a Coke for George."

Before turning back to the kitchen she peered at George, "Ice with glass, Mr. George?"

George watched her with unease. About thirty years old, she had pale, nearly colorless skin and a scar on her cheek that shone brightly against her thin, sharp features. Her cold, deep-set eyes penetrated right through him. He believed she had an intense dislike for him and had always given him the creeps. "Just the can, thank you."

George studied the room as his eyes danced from one piece of art to the next—paintings, sculpture and vases Uncle Willie had collected over the years. All of it from Asia, most of it Chinese, except two unique items that fascinated George. A large portrait of a frontiersman from the American Indian wars hung on one wall. He wore a buckskin jacket with fringed gloves that stretched to the elbow. He posed with a long barrel rifle and his rugged face displayed a white mustache and goatee much like Uncle Willies. A brass nameplate on the bottom of the frame identified him as Buffalo Bill Cody. On the end table next to the couch sat a sculpture of polished bronze, a cowboy riding a rearing horse, a lariat swirling above his head, a stray calf in his sights. They seemed out of place among the many artifacts of Chinese culture. George had inquired about the painting and the sculpture once before when his family had been invited to dinner.

Uncle Willie had told him he had an affinity for the American West. He loved the idea of the cowboy culture and the art that defined that segment of America's history. He seemed especially fond of his western art.

Ki Chung returned from the kitchen and handed George his drink.

"Thank you Ki Chung, you may leave us now." Uncle Willie watched as she climbed the steps to the upper bedrooms, and disappeared from view.

"George, do you know why I invited you here to have this talk?"

George's fingers twitched as he held the can loosely, turning it slowly, staring at the floor. "Well, not exactly."

"You know your parents immigrated to America before you were born, of course."

George looked up and nodded.

"You have been taking classes at the Cultural Academy, studying and learning many things about your parent's native land, and your ancestral home."

George nodded again.

Uncle Willie leaned forward to study George's reaction. "Well, your father and I have discussed this at length. We both believe you would benefit a great deal by visiting China."

George's eyes lit up and a wide grin showed off his perfect teeth. "Are you kidding me?"

"No, most certainly not. I must go to China on a business trip in June. I would be pleased if you would accompany me. Would that please you?"

"Wow! That would be great. You really mean it?"

Uncle Willie smiled. "Most certainly. You are an excellent student. You have worked hard at your studies and learned much about China from your classes. Experiences you have firsthand will mean much more to you than what you obtain from the printed page. I can arrange for you to meet some very important people. They can tell you many things and instruct you in subjects I think you will find very interesting. We will be gone for two weeks."

George's eyes sparkled, and he almost crushed the can between his fingers. "Uncle Willie. That's really cool. I'd love to go. I've had friends who visited China and they were impressed. Will we go to Tannanu?"

"Not this time. I must return to Beijing for business. And the people I want you to meet will be there."

George looked down and hung his head for a brief moment then sat up and flashed Uncle Willie a big smile. "This is so cool. My father said I can go?"

"Yes, we discussed it in great detail and he is in favor of this trip."

Uncle Willie paused, then continued. "George, this is a special trip. You should feel privileged to have been selected. Not every young man has an opportunity such as this. But you are very deserving. I will be proud to escort you back to your father's homeland."

Uncle Willie and Wung Hu did not reveal to George that this trip had been planned since before he was born—officially mandated for every young boy in the program when they reached the age of thirteen. The administrators of The Sons of the Red Dragon had deemed this age the appropriate time to return their sons to China, to see firsthand the real China, to reawaken their dormant Chinese souls and get the blood of China coursing through their veins. To participate in a comprehensive fourteen-day program to introduce new thoughts, reinforce teachings in politics and Chinese culture, and bolster their young understanding and belief in Chinese Communist theorems.

* * *

GEORGE WASHINGTON HU'S visit to China was an impressionable one for a young mind. The whirlwind tour filled his head with the wonders, ideals and greatness of China, the state and the Party. He met important leaders with impressive credentials; some in distinguished uniforms with ribbons and medals pinned to their chests and offices with large ornately carved desks in rooms overflowing with ancient Chinese art and artifacts. He visited historic buildings that towered over large public squares, majestic cathedrals of political propaganda and was shown monuments and memorials of great importance to the State in official ceremonies of grand magnitude. He was overwhelmed with events and images grander than life, burned into his memory, to be savored for years to come.

After two weeks George had developed a renewed bond to his ancestral home. Imbued with a sense of camaraderie and solidarity, a sense of belonging to something greater than he ever felt before.

George returned to America a young man committed to the land of his ancestors. A young man with new vision. From his home he watched as the evening sun dropped below the Olympic Mountains to the west. He stood in awe as the sky lit up with a warm glow.

The red glow of his true homeland. China.

PART TWO

THE RIPPLE

CHAPTER SEVEN

New York City
Early November, 2012

AS THE CAB pulled out into heavy traffic, I sat back and stared through the side window. A first-time visitor to New York, common street scenes appeared as postcard images. Skyscrapers, popular landmarks, and street corners had become celebrities in their own right thanks to Hollywood and television. Sights I had only seen through a camera's lens, I now experienced with my own eyes as a living, breathing metropolis.

As one block followed another, I promised myself I would return when I had more time—and money—to explore more deeply. A delicious cake, during this short visit I would only sample the icing, saving the triple layers beneath for another time. Buildings of glass and granite lined each street, stacked along city blocks that seemed to never end, stirring visions of home and the evergreen forests that towered over narrow mountain roads.

"Hey, isn't this Times Square?" I asked the driver as my head swiveled to follow the action on a bustling intersection. Turning back to the turbaned cabbie I saw him glance in the rear-view mirror to reveal a broad grin and a gold tooth. I smiled too, having been exposed as a "Big Apple virgin."

Gazing down at my briefcase, I slid my hand across the soft leather and squeezed the handle. My completed manuscript. My first novel. I fought off the apprehension of this initial meeting. I had to be positive. At twenty-nine, this could be my first published book.

The cab darted across two lanes of traffic and slowed to a stop as the tires flirted with the curb. I fumbled with a few bills, settled on a twenty, hoped that covered a New York tip. I hopped out, glanced around, took in the moment. My eyes moved up the stone and glass façade, squinting as the morning light reflected off panes on the upper levels. The chill of goose bumps betrayed my excitement.

Dodging my way through the crowd, I pushed through the impressive entrance—brass, glass and class—doors that swiveled with a smooth touch in spite of their immense size. My new loafers clicked on the polished floors and reverberated off the marble walls of the three-story lobby, joining a chorus of echoes from the morning rush.

In the center of the foyer an information booth attended by an attractive young lady in a gray blazer blocked my path. She wore a bright smile, dark red lips and darker eyes that peered from behind a cascade of long black hair parted in the center. I glanced her way and half smiled as I headed for the bank of elevators servicing the upper floors.

I confirmed again the business card that stated, KALEIDOSCOPE BOOK PUBLISHING CORPORATION, JACK BUICK, ACQUISITIONS EDITOR - 46TH FLOOR. The elevator shot skyward, dispensing businessmen and women on lower levels before gliding to a smooth stop for my exit. I stepped out into a wide hallway that faced the glass doors of Kaleidoscope Book Publishing, pushed them open and approached the silver-haired woman seated at the reception desk. Her concentration fixed on a small pad as she jotted notes and talked on a telephone headset.

She looked up, lifted her index finger and mouthed, "One moment." I glanced around, star-struck by the ambiance of publishing success. Behind her desk sprouted a wall display of large black and white photographs, formal portraits boldly signed in the lower corner. Successful authors of the Kaleidoscope empire, perhaps?

A coffee table with two red couches graced one side of the room. Another wall held a montage of poster-size book covers, some I recognized as best sellers.

"I'm sorry," she said as she caught me staring. "How can I help you?"

"I'm here to see Mr. Jack Buick."

"Your name?"

"Curtis Beecham. I have an appointment."

She glanced down, clicked on her keyboard for a moment, then spoke into the hands-free headset that floated in front of her deep red lips, "Mr. Beecham is here for his nine forty-five."

Receiving directions to Jack Buick's office, I headed back to the elevators and rode up to the forty-ninth floor, clutching my briefcase, anxiety building. I stepped out, located his nameplate, paused, took a deep breath, then knocked three times.

"Come in. Come in," boomed a voice. Pushing the door open I eased in, my eyes making contact with Jack Buick as he walked around a chrome and glass desk, his arm extended as he introduced himself. "Jack Buick." His immense hand swallowed mine.

"Curtis Beecham. Nice to finally meet you, sir."

Of medium height, he possessed a hefty frame that carried more than a few extra pounds. About mid-fifty, he sported a full head of tousled black hair. A thick black mustache divided his round face and double chin. The distinct scent of cigar smoke lingered in the air. Jack turned and stubbed out his smoldering tobacco bomb in an ashtray with remnants of earlier indulgences on the corner of his desk.

"Sorry about the smell." He waved his hand above his head in an effort to dispel any lingering fumes. "What can I say? It's my one and only vice. Well..." He chuckled. "One of many I must confess. But I love a good Cuban. They're on my short list of life's great pleasures, which includes of course, fine aged bourbon and long legs in short skirts. Gotta be careful where you get 'em though." Jack winked. "The cigars, Curtis, *not* the legs. The Feds kinda frown on importing the good ole Havana. They're still pissed off with Castro and his brother, after what, fifty years? Sheesh!" He held his hands out and pointed at his own chest. "I'm telling ya, it's us cigar aficionados bein' punished."

I gave a quick glance around the room as Jack stepped back, lifted one leg and planted his bottom on the corner of the desktop. Daylight from the large expanse of windows flooded in, leaving him in near silhouette. Bookshelves filled with books covered the left wall and to the right, stuffed file folders wrapped with rubber bands were piled on the floor.

An oversized framed painting dominated the wall above the stacks of folders—two crusty looking bulldogs, fawn-colored with black faces, sitting on red velvet-tufted chairs smoking cigars. They held playing cards in their paws and stacks of colorful poker chips towered on the small round table between them.

Jack caught me staring. "Mighty proud of that one. A signed lithograph by C. M. Coolidge. Very rare. Set me back a cool six figures. But I just had to have it."

I nodded. "It's quite a piece."

"Anyway, nice to meet you Curtis. Welcome to New York. How was your trip?"

Jack's casual demeanor put me at ease. Still a little apprehensive, I wanted to make a good first impression.

"Great so far. But I arrived late last night. Haven't had a chance to get a real taste of the city."

"A real taste, huh." Jack grinned. "I'll tell you where you can get some of the best eatin' around here for your money. Food carts." He pointed over his shoulder with his thumb. "Those damn street vendors camped on every corner. Anything from hot dogs to tamales to steaks on a stick. Fast food for fast times, they say. Lotsa congestion around noon." He glanced down and strummed his fingers against his sizeable abdomen as he chuckled. "And lotsa indigestion by afternoon. But, hey, the price is right."

I smiled. "I bet it is."

"Watch out for the goddamn mustard though." Jack winked. "Ya know, those plastic pouches. Last week I passed this hot dog stand and stepped on one of those little bastards. A glob squirted out and hit this guy on his pant leg. Right here." He leaned over and pointed to the lowest spot he could reach. "A real expensive Armani, too." Jack snickered. "He didn't notice. I didn't tell."

I grinned with a hint of disbelief, then anxiously switched my briefcase to my right hand. Jack apparently enjoyed the art of light-hearted conversation, but I was anxious to discuss my manuscript.

Jack continued without taking a breath. "I know you weren't referring to the 'culinary' taste. Just thought I'd throw that in, this being your first trip to the Big Apple and all. But, food carts not withstanding, you gotta see a little of the city before you leave. What's the point of coming all this way and not having a little fun?" Jack slapped his hand against his broad thigh. "Ya know, that 'all work, no play' thing. After all, New York is the greatest city in the world. You can get everything you want, anything you can imagine, right here!" Jack emphasized his point by stubbing his thick index finger against the glass top, just missing his overflowing ashtray.

"I'm sure you're right," I said, as Jack slipped behind his desk and plopped down into his padded chair. "I'll try to catch a few sights before I fly back."

"Good. Have a seat. Seattle, right?"

I nodded and sat down in the chair opposite Jack.

"Never quite made it to that corner of the world. The rain as bad as they say?"

"Can be. The gray drizzle can last for months. We don't call it the 'northwet' for nothing."

"The 'northwet', huh?" Jack scrunched his face. "Sounds like a great place to be *from*! Now, what have you got?"

"The complete manuscript with the changes you requested. They were good suggestions. Made the story stronger. I liked your idea of giving the younger sister a stronger character, a bigger part in the plot, even though she isn't a major player in the immigration program." I reached into my briefcase and retrieved the hard copy printout. "And here's a disk."

Jack nodded as he reached for the two-inch stack of laser-print pages. Removing the thick rubber band, he flipped through them with his thumb, browsing, interspersed with a few grunts. I sat on the edge of my seat and fiddled with my hands. Jack had made me comfortable, but I was still a bit anxious. A meeting like this may be commonplace to Jack Buick and those in the publishing world, but was a momentous occasion for me. I turned to my right, coming face to face with the framed print of the bulldogs. Studying it a second, I glanced at Jack, then back to the print. *Hmmm!* I grinned. *Is there a subtle similarity between man and his chosen breed perhaps?*

"You could have just e-mailed it like everyone else, ya know," Jack said, as he continued to browse. "This is the goddamn computer age, after all."

"Well, yes, I know. But..." I hesitated, not wanting to dwell on my rookie status. "This is my first, and it's...well, it is

New York. I wanted to enjoy the experience in person. And, if I hadn't met you face to face, I wouldn't have known about the great mustard menace." Jack and I shared a grin. "Besides, I wanted to make sure you're a warm body and not just a flat screen and a keyboard."

Jack chuckled. "Well, here I am, in the flesh." He laid the manuscript on the desk and held out his arms, palms up and stared down at his midriff. Looking back up he scrunched his thick eyebrows. "In this business, I have to deal with a lot of interesting characters, as you can imagine. Writers! A weird bunch they are." He paused and eyed me with a sly grin. "You're not, are ya?" I shrugged and met his grin as he continued. "I worked with this one who insisted we only communicate on even-numbered days, some kind of goddamn karma thing. Needless to say he's in the past tense."

Jack's chair squeaked as he leaned back. "Let me take a moment to refresh my memory." He reached for his notes and began reading under his breath. "The Communist government of the People's Republic of China develops a long-term policy of controlling emigration to America by hand-selecting loyal members of the Communist Party to fill immigration quotas. Their purpose of emigrating is to father sons, provide the best education and encourage them to enter politics, developing a core group of 'American' politicians sympathetic to China. The plot line follows one such family and the development of the political careers of their adult children as they move into high political office, culminating with the Presidency of the United States."

Jack looked up. "China's a hot topic. And this plot line. Makes one think." He shrugged. "Who the hell knows?" He set the manuscript on the desk, tapping the cover sheet with a drum roll of his fingers. "Only a few decades ago John F. Kennedy had a hell of a time getting voters to look past his Catholic background when he was campaigning for president.

Imagine, less then fifty years ago the country was hardly ready to accept a goddamn Catholic in the White House. Now, we have an African-American president. Times have changed. But I wonder if the American public would have some hesitancy when the time comes..." He paused a moment. "You know, to elect a Chinese-American President because they may suspect some sort of torn loyalty, as you suggest in your book." Jack seemed deep in thought before he caught himself and continued.

"This is a process. There will be more editing and I'll keep you posted on our schedule. But right now, I'm up to my ass in alligators, and the pressure is on to get something past the formal editing board, so I may not get back to you as quickly as ya might like. Gotta keep the alligators at bay, ya know. Keep the razor-sharp teeth of management from getting anywhere near my ass." Jack eyed me with a bit of a squint. "It's been nice meeting you and getting this personal hand-off, but next time, just e-mail the goddamn thing, okay?" He lifted himself from his chair and extended his right hand.

"I studied Chinese in college," he continued. "Thought I might go into the god-foreign-damn-service or something like that after graduation. It was difficult to read, as you might imagine, but I could speak a little. Comes in handy when I want a table at one of those restaurants in Chinatown. But that's not much of a payoff after spending two years of my life trying to figure out those cryptic little bastards."

I grinned. "Maybe I should submit my next revisions in Mandarin."

Jack raised his eyebrows.

"Just kidding, Mr. Buick. But seriously, I do appreciate everything you've done."

Jack looked straight into my eyes. "There's guys around here that would like nothing better than to kick ole Jack's ass. Remember, it's all about getting books into the consumers' hands—ringing that cash register."

As he concluded, his bear-sized paw had just about fused my hand into a stump with five fingernails. "Yes, I understand. Thank you, Mr. Buick. I'll wait to hear from you." I extricated my numbed digits, turned and twisted the doorknob to let myself out.

As the door closed behind me, I stared at the brass plate etched with Jack Buick's name. I glanced around to be certain I had the hallway to myself, then reached up and swiped my sleeve across it to remove a slight smudge.

I looked at my watch. 9:57. Twelve minutes. I chuckled. A full day to get here. A full day to get home. I'd spent more money than I could afford, just for twelve minutes of my editor's time.

Hmmm…*I just might need to stop by that information booth in the lobby. See if that young lady would be interested in a soon-to-be "New York Times Best-Selling Author." A Northwest novelist who just happens to have an evening free. Maybe she'd be willing to show him a little of the wild side of this big red McIntosh.*

As I rode the elevator I felt at least ten feet tall. My feet didn't seem to have made contact with the floor. Then again, I might have been a little bit full of myself, a temporary indulgence, that for the moment, I just might have deserved. I crossed the lobby and stopped at the information booth, my ego inflated to heights I hadn't known.

"Hi. I'm Curtis Beecham…"

CHAPTER EIGHT

Seattle Washington
Two Days Later

AFTER MEETING WITH my editor, Jack Buick, I was anxious to share my New York experience with my friend, and fellow conspirator, Su Wan Cho. We had worked together a few years back at an advertising agency and remained friends as we struggled to establish our own independent careers: he as a graphic designer, me as a writer. I telephoned the day after I returned from the Big Apple and asked Su Wan to meet me at the Hilltop Coffee Shop in Queen Anne.

As I entered the local purveyor of fine lattes I heard Su Wan call out, "Curtis, over here." I turned and saw him sitting near the window.

"Hey," I hollered. I waved and headed for the order counter. "Be right there."

He raised a hand in acknowledgement.

Su Wan was Korean-American, tall and lanky. His wardrobe consisted of jeans and T-shirts, always black, featuring one rock n' roll band or another across his chest. As his leather jacket gapped open, I noticed the neck of a pink guitar and a few distorted letters of some unidentifiable group.

I slid into the stainless steel seat across from him.

"So, how'd it go?" Su Wan asked.

I smiled, "Well, let's see, the *New York Times* never requested an interview and there wasn't a ticker-tape parade in my honor, but otherwise, I think it went pretty well."

I was messing with Su Wan. In reality, I didn't want to get too excited. I had a long way to go before becoming a published author and Jack Buick hadn't acknowledged me as the next John Grisham. "Buick's an interesting guy. He talks a lot but he knows the business. And it goes without saying, New York was a lot of fun." I grinned and took a swig of my latte before continuing. "Well, in all honesty, maybe his enthusiasm was a little reserved. You know, dealing with new books and writers every day, it probably takes a lot to excite him. He said he wouldn't have taken on the project if he didn't believe in it, so that's good."

Su Wan nodded.

"I left my revised manuscript with him but he said to expect a lengthy editing process. I'm told that's normal. Though I still have a sense the manuscript lacks that one thing to put it over the top. I don't know, more drama, tension, something. Maybe I need to kill somebody off. I'm not sure." I jammed a large bite of chocolate muffin into my mouth, and mumbled, "Want some?"

"Thanks, but no." Su Wan glared at his cup. "Why do they have to make it so damn hot?"

"Hey, the hotter the better. When I'm sitting on my boat and the wind blows across the lake, I want my coffee hot and my insides warm." I took a big gulp, stuck out my tongue and pointed to it. "Carbon steel."

Su Wan curled up his face. "Bet that goes over well with the ladies."

I wiggled my eyebrows. "My secret weapon."

If it hadn't been for a fortuitous encounter Su Wan had had with one of his friends, a drinking party, guy talk, loose ramblings poured from a cold six-pack, I wouldn't be writing this book. It was George Hu who had divulged the strange tale of his parents immigrating to America to Su Wan that had become the basis for my manuscript. Su Wan shared the story with me and I saw the potential for a book. Not exactly the stuff of a thriller novel, but a concept with promise. With a little literary license, I thought I could turn it into a story of mystery and intrigue.

I lifted my insulated cup. "To our success."

Su Wan reached out and we toasted with a light tap as he watched me with an intense stare. "As I see it, the success is all yours."

I leaned in and studied him closely. "Hey man, we're in this together. Without you, I wouldn't have this deal. We're a team. Right?"

"Yeah, but you get all the glory. What's in it for me?"

"Su Wan. You're my research partner. I'll be sure to give you credit in the book. Maybe a whole paragraph. I'll even put in a word with Jack Buick, he might let you design the cover and produce some promotional materials. Before it's over, we'll both benefit from this."

Su Wan glanced away. I waited through a minute of uncomfortable silence, not sure if my reply satisfied him.

"So, what have you heard from George Hu?" I asked.

"Haven't seen him lately."

I hesitated as I took another bite of muffin. "I've been thinking. About George's story." To make sure Su Wan was still with me, I decided to probe. "I want to hear more. Talk to him. See what else you can find out. I have everything about the immigration aspect, but I'd like to know more about how he feels about it. Him and his younger brother. Now that they're older, do they feel the same way? Is he anxious to get into politics? What does he see for his future? You know, that kind of stuff. He still doesn't know about me. I can't ask him myself, but you're his friend, he'll talk to you."

Su Wan hesitated a moment, staring at his coffee, then looked up. "Yeah. I'll give him a call."

"Good." I grinned, teasing Su Wan as I held up a large, moist chocolate chunk. "Sure you don't want a bite?"

* * *

AFTER LEAVING THE coffee shop, Su Wan called George and arranged to stop by later that evening at his apartment, a small one-bedroom in the University District.

Being of Korean heritage, Su Wan Cho wasn't involved in activities in the Chinese community. He had met George Hu in high school where they both participated in the chess club. Su Wan was two years older than George but they struck up a friendship and had remained friends, even though their lives after graduation took them in different directions. Su Wan immersed himself in the world of graphic design, and George, after completing his Bachelor's degree, entered law school at the University of Washington.

Su Wan climbed the stairs to the second floor and knocked on a weathered green door that had begun to flake, revealing a flash of bright yellow underneath. There was no response. "George?" He knocked again, with more force. "George. You there?"

A muffled voice seeped through the closed door, "What! Ah, yeah. Who is it?"

"It's Su Wan. You alive in there?"

"Oh, Su Wan. Yeah, come on in."

Su Wan pushed open the unlocked door and poked his head in. "Hey guy, how are ya?" A strong whiff of musty air, a combination of stale beer and dirty socks, met him head on. He wrinkled his nose and adjusted his eyes to the dim interior, lit only by the open door and streetlights that sent thin beams streaming through half-closed Venetian blinds.

"Ah, good." George responded, without much enthusiasm. "Yeah, yeah I'm good."

Su Wan found him slumped down in a worn overstuffed couch wearing a stained gray Huskies sweatshirt and white boxer shorts. "You okay?"

"Yeah. Forgot you were coming. Can I get ya a beer?"

"Sure." Su Wan held up his open palm. "Don't get up, I'll get it. Mind if I hit the light?"

George nodded.

Su Wan headed for the small refrigerator in the kitchen, separated from the living room by a Formica-topped counter. As he stepped over a pile of dirty laundry he noticed a pyramid of beer cans teetering on the coffee table in front of the couch. An open pizza box sat on the counter littered with half eaten slices. In the kitchen, empty take-out containers—an international assortment of Chinese, Mexican and Northwest—were stacked in and around the sink. A colony of ants had taken advantage of the remaining contents, forming a bustling conga line that disappeared behind the corner cabinet. The refrigerator, empty except for a collection of cold six packs, had sticky food residue dripping across the glass shelf.

Su Wan grabbed a beer, hesitated a second, then turned and picked-up a knotted dishcloth and wiped the bottom of the can. Then for good measure, he wiped the top. Returning to the opposite couch he shoved a stack of magazines and textbooks to one end and sat. He glanced around the apartment. This mess was not at all like the George he knew. George had always been an organized and tidy person. This was out of character.

"So, how's the law thing going?" Su Wan inquired.

"Oh, you know. Studying and studying and more studying. Then, tests and tests and more tests. It never ends."

"Tough program, huh?" He stared over his beer at George, who had barely budged except to lift his own.

"Yep. It's not for the weak." George seemed to be searching for the right words. "You gotta be brilliant and unfaltering in your quest for greatness. Like I'm *supposed* to be." He didn't smile, his eyes betraying a deep sadness.

"Yeah, I can only imagine." Su Wan took a sip. It was still early evening, and George appeared to have been through more than a few beers already. Looking around the disheveled apartment he wondered how often George tipped the can.

"Hey, George. Remember that conversation we had some time ago. When you told me about that program in China that sent your father to America to have sons? You know, you and your brother? All that stuff about entering politics. You going back there when you were thirteen and all? I found that fascinating."

For a few seconds George remained silent. He gave Su Wan an inquisitive stare as he seemed to be searching his memory. He appeared confused. Then his face tensed and he jerked upright spilling beer across his shorts that trickled onto the carpet. "What? What are you talking about? That was bullshit! It meant nothing. Just talk. I had too much to drink…and, and I…" He glanced down and brushed his hand across his wet shorts, pausing a moment, hedging, his voice lower. "Maybe I heard something. I don't know."

He reached up and ran his hand through his hair, then wiped it across his face, rubbing his chin. He mumbled something through his fingers that Su Wan couldn't make out.

George fell silent and stared at the floor. With one bare foot he scuffed at the invisible wet spot, then looked up. "You don't want to know about this." He paused again, glared at Su Wan and spoke with dead seriousness. "Listen, Su Wan. There's more to this than I've told you. It goes deeper than you can imagine. There are people who don't want this known to anyone outside the community. Believe me, it leads down a dangerous path. Just forget you ever heard anything about it."

His head dropped and he stared at the stained carpet, then closed his eyes, reached up and pressed his fingertips against his temples as he let out a long breath.

Su Wan Cho remained silent, sipping his beer, watching George. *What's he talking about? There's more to this? It leads down a dangerous path?*

After a period of uneasy quiet, Su Wan engaged George in some mindless chatter: girlfriends, chess, and the state of Husky football. Su Wan made several more trips to George's refrigerator-turned-beer-cooler and they continued to talk late into the night.

After a discussion that hardly challenged their intellects, their conversation appeared to be running out of steam. George fidgeted with an empty beer can. He stared over the pyramid at Su Wan. His eyes glistened in the glare of the bright ceiling light as he spoke with a soft voice. "Su Wan." He hesitated. "Everything is *not* good." He sighed, and wiped at his cheek. "I'm going to disappoint my father. My grades have slipped. I've been cutting class. Things are not going well right now."

Considering the state of the apartment and George's apparent depression, Su Wan was not surprised by this admission. He knew George had always been an excellent student, taking his studies seriously. Su Wan sensed this conversation had shifted.

"My father has put tremendous pressure on me to do well in school. He pushed me to apply for law school. I do not feel my life is my own. Uncle Willie...well, he's not really my uncle. More of a family friend. He's the one encouraging me...no, more like pushing me and Thomas with our studies at the Chinese Cultural Academy."

"Is that the guy who took you to China when you were thirteen?"

George nodded. "He's put pressure on me to remain close

to my ancestral roots. Follow a path true to the teachings of China. I love China. I know a lot about China, but I love America too. After all, I'm an *American*. This is where *I've* lived all my life. But I'm being asked to choose between my father and the land of my ancestors on one hand...and the country I've been raised in on the other. I'm caught between two different ideologies, each one tugging at me, grasping to grab hold. I can hardly sleep. I dream of battles raging between dragons and eagles. I wake up in a sweat."

Su Wan listened with keen interest but didn't hold a lot of heartfelt sympathy. He wasn't concerned with George's problems. As Su Wan saw it, each person was responsible for his own happiness. George grew up with advantages Su Wan never had. George had a supportive and loving father. Su Wan's father had left him and his mother when Su Wan was very young. His mother had to work long hours in seafood processing plants to support her family, so Su Wan had raised himself. He had no father figure to turn to, to guide him. He knew what it meant to struggle. To take care of ones self.

Now that George was feeling vulnerable and talking, Su Wan would encourage him. He wanted to hear everything George would divulge. Anything George might add that would benefit the book project, and by way of association, benefit Su Wan.

"George, you're a bright guy," Su Wan said. "You always knew the right move to make on the chessboard. If anyone can solve your problems, you can. You're very analytical."

George leaned over and stacked another empty can atop the pyramid. He stared. "Yes. I am very analytical. But this is not a problem of analysis. It's a problem of the heart. It's not something that can be solved using a calculator." George reached out and fingered one beer can from the bottom of the pyramid, sliding it out. Su Wan tensed, expecting the stack to topple, but it remained upright. George's expression remained unchanged.

Su Wan wanted to return to George's earlier conversation. He braced himself for a possible rebuff, but he wanted answers. "You said earlier there was more to this than you had already told me. That this could lead down a dangerous path. What do you mean? What is it you haven't told me? Why is it dangerous?"

George shook his head and glared. "Dammit Su Wan. Why do you keep probing? I've said more than I should as it is. It's family business you just don't need to know about. Let's leave it at that. I meant it when I said there could be dangerous repercussions." George sipped his beer. He kept his gaze on Su Wan. "Trust me. There's shit going on you don't want to know about...and you sure as hell don't want to be involved in."

CHAPTER NINE

ANXIOUS TO HEAR from Su Wan, I called him first thing the next morning. I could tell he wasn't awake yet. "Su Wan, it's Curtis. Get your butt out of bed and get over here."

He grumbled something about the early hour although it was nearly ten, but agreed to meet me at my place as soon as he got himself together.

My place, such as it was. Moorage on Lake Union. A lake fifteen minutes from the downtown core, surrounded by marinas, restaurants and yacht brokers. The north end anchored by Gas Works Park, a knoll of rolling green grass that surrounded the towering remains of an abandoned gas plant built in the early 1900s, a sculpture of rusted iron that served as a memento of industrial development.

My classic thirty-eight foot 1928 Matthews Sedan Cruiser wasn't much to look at, but I called her home—where I hung my assorted ball caps and pounded the keys of my laptop computer. A floating wood tub held together by rust and corrosion. Although I loved her, love alone wasn't enough. She desperately needed a complete renovation. Work I was willing to do if only I had the money. As I glanced across her sun-bleached, once beautiful teak deck, I could easily envision her as she might someday be.

I had named her *Mockaritaville*. An appropriate name

considering her condition and her location in the cold, wet northwest. A true Jimmy Buffett fan, I couldn't embarrass my mentor or sully the image Jimmy Buffet had created in the minds of so many faithful fans. I hoped one day she would earn her place among finer seagoing vessels, and I would be able to power her hull into warm, turquoise waters with white sand beaches and swaying palm trees. Then I would allow myself to pay tribute to her in a proper manner and bestow upon her the honored title of *Margaritaville Too*.

I was on deck hosing off duck droppings when I noticed Su Wan approach the wooden dock. He waved as I jumped over the rail to turn off the spigot and gather in the hose.

"What's this? Two days in a row without rain?" He held his arms out, palms up.

"Yeah, and that leaves me with two days of duck shit to wash down. I don't know what's worse, the rain or the duck shit."

"Just be sure you keep her in running condition for the boat parade on Opening Day. I'm looking forward to another year of cruisin' and boozin'."

I smiled. "Come on. Let's walk." I nodded toward the path that led around the south end of the lake and down a bike trail that lined the Lake Washington Ship Canal: the narrow canal that connected fresh water Lake Union with Puget Sound.

"So how'd it go with George?"

"Strange."

"Strange?"

"Yeah. He's a mess. Emotionally he's a bit unstable."

"What do you mean?" I asked.

"Well, he's in a lot of torment over this whole immigration program. Says he's torn between his father's world of China and his life here in America. Feels like he has to choose between them and it's tearing him up. He's drinking a lot.

Letting himself go. Falling behind in his studies."

I picked up a rock and tossed it into the canal, watched as the ripples grew. "So what do you think he'll do?"

Su Wan frowned. "He'd better get over it. But he's too sensitive. I don't see him snapping out of it anytime soon. I tried to talk to him about the immigration program. When I brought the subject up, he denied everything at first. Said he'd been drinking and everything he'd told me earlier was made up. A bunch of bullshit, he said. As the evening wore on, he drank more. I kept him talking."

As we walked on, a couple of bicycles zipped by, stirring up fallen leaves from the enormous poplar trees that lined the bank. Su Wan continued to fill me in with his take on their late night conversation.

"Don't forget, I get a credit line in the book," Su Wan said. "And the cover design. And some marketing stuff."

I liked Su Wan, but I didn't like the relentless way he was willing to exploit his friend George Hu. From what I knew, George had unwittingly told Su Wan more than he should have, albeit under a little alcohol inducement. If George knew Su Wan was sharing it with a writer, I'm sure he'd be quite upset with Su Wan, his supposed friend. Though I didn't know George, I felt a twinge of guilt. I slapped Su Wan on the back. "Sure. We're in this together. You get your credit line and I'll see what I can do about the other stuff."

"He mentioned something else." Su Wan paused and shot me a serious look that caught my attention. "He said what he'd already told me led down a dangerous path and certain people wouldn't want outsiders to know about it. He said there was more to it, something deeper, more involved that he hadn't told me. I asked him what he meant by that, but he refused to explain. Wouldn't go there. Kept repeating, 'This is family business. Stuff you just don't wanna know about.' He emphasized a couple of times it was dangerous to be involved."

Su Wan paused, then continued. "So afterwards I began to think about what he had said. It's supposed to be a secret program of the Chinese government, right? My guess is, they wouldn't be too happy to see a book about it."

"Well, maybe not," I agreed. "But I'm sure a lot of books get published that *our* government wouldn't like to see in the hands of the reading public."

Su Wan turned to me. "Yes, but we're talking the Chinese government. Where I come from, that's a lot different."

I looked at him and squinted. "I thought you were Korean and came from just over there?" I pointed across the canal.

He grinned and punched me in the shoulder. "Right."

I shook my head, "Well, it's kinda late to stop it now. And don't forget, the book's a novel." I held my hands up, palms out. "Strictly fiction. And what's the chance of any of these 'dangerous' Chinese guys ever hearing about or even reading this book?"

"Who knows? But remember *The Satanic Verses* by Salman Rushdie. Remember him? He wrote a book that pissed off the Muslims and the Ayatollah Khomeini issued a death sentence against him. If the Chinese get pissed off we might end up in someone's trunk with ventilation shafts through our heads. We wouldn't be the first. Keep that in mind."

We turned around and headed back to the dock. I kept wondering, what was it George had referred to? The part I couldn't shake, when he told Su Wan, "there was more to it, something deeper." So far, he *hadn't* divulged it. Not to Su Wan anyway.

After Su Wan left, I walked to the stern of my boat, leaned against the aft railing and gazed across the lake. We were having one of those brief periods of unusual weather, the air crisp, no wind, a cloudless sky with bright sunshine. A flock of geese skimmed the surface heading for Gasworks Park. I thought about what Su Wan had said. Did I really believe it could be dangerous? Or is Su Wan paranoid? This is America. We do have laws to protect us. Freedom of the press, right? If the Chinese don't like it, so what. What can they do?

* * *

LATER THAT AFTERNOON I drove to my father's house in the blue-collar neighborhood of Ballard, a district of modest bungalow-style homes built to house fishermen and crabbers in the early 1900s. I hadn't checked on my dad for a few weeks and I'd been feeling guilty. Walking up the aged wood steps leading to the front porch, I hesitated a moment, thinking about what I might encounter, then knocked with the brass fish doorknocker. My father answered with the familiar scratchy voice of a long-time smoker. "Yeah. Who's there?"

"It's me. Curtis."

A minute went by and clunky footsteps echoed behind the door. It swung open and my father peered out. I studied him a moment. His health had deteriorated since mom passed away. His face, unshaven. His eyes, streaked with red. His bib overalls and long-sleeve flannel red shirt crumpled to the extent they could have been slept in.

"Hey, Pops. How're you doing?"

"What's it to you?"

"I'm not here to argue, Dad. I'm here to see how you are."

"Since when."

I sighed. "Can I come in?"

Dad studied me a moment, nodded his head then turned and walked toward his recliner. I moved to the couch and sat myself on the worn cushion. I glanced around the room. It appeared just as it had always been when mom was alive, though not as well kept. "So, you doing okay?"

"Good as expected."

I nodded. "Stopped by to see if you needed anything. I'm

sorry I haven't been by lately, but, you know. Been busy."

"Busy?" Dad raised his eyebrows. "Since when? Since you quit that other job? I don't know what they paid you for, but they did pay ya at least. Now all you do is sit on that rickety-ass boat of yours and play with your computer."

"That *is* my job, Dad. I'm a writer. You know that. That's what I love to do."

"I been saying for years, get a real job. I supported you and your mom, God rest her soul, with a real job. Carpentry. A man's job. Sooner or later your momma's money's gonna run out. Then what you gonna do?"

I hung my head, stared at the floor and gripped my hands. I hadn't come to argue, but it seemed every visit turned into an unpleasant discussion about my ability to make a living. I looked up. "I've got a publisher who's interested in my book. This might be the break I've been waiting for. It's real promising."

"Can you make a living off this book?"

"No. Not really. But it's a start."

"A start? You've done a lot of starting in your life. How about finishing something. Your wife left you. You couldn't support her. She had to find work herself. Made more money'n you, you said so yourself."

"Dad, you know she didn't leave me because I couldn't make a living. And writing is a living. It's just not something you appreciate."

"I read a book once. It was fool nonsense. Waste a time." He leaned back and exhaled a deep breath.

"Look, Dad. I know you disapprove of how I choose to make a living. And you don't approve of my living arrangements. We've discussed it. We've agreed to disagree." I stood, shuffled my feet. "I'm going to the store to pick up a few things. Can I get you anything?"

Dad shook his head. I watched him begin to retreat back

into his own deep thoughts. He'd been that way since he lost his wife. I lost a mom, but I knew her death had taken a greater toll on dad. He hadn't been the same since.

Growing up, he'd always been tough on me. Wanted to make a man of me. Dad would have been happy if I'd taken up carpentry, became a plumber or even a crab fisherman, but my interests took me in a totally different direction. A direction my father couldn't understand. I had always disappointed him. Could never please him with my modest accomplishments. I probably never would.

"Okay, Dad. I'd better be going." I walked over, leaned down and planted a light kiss on top of his head. "Love you, Dad."

Dad grunted, his typical response, as I turned and walked to the door. I paused before stepping out, studied him another moment before he looked up with a blank stare. His lips barely moved. "Coffee."

"Ah, coffee? You need some coffee?"

"Yeah. Not that decaf crap either."

I grinned. "Sure Pops. I'll get you some."

CHAPTER TEN

New York City

JACK BUICK SCANNED his desk and his eyes landed on the file with the manuscript Curtis Beecham had left with him a few days earlier. He picked it up, flipped through a few pages in deep thought, then picked up the phone and called his friend Roger Lee.

"Good afternoon, China Gate Publishing. How may I help you?"

"I need to speak to Roger Lee, please."

"And your name?"

"Jack Buick."

After a few minutes delay a voice responded. "Hello, Jack."

"Roger, how the hell are ya?"

"Doing okay. Good to hear from you. Been a long time, my friend. How's it going over at Kaleidoscope Book Publishing?"

"Same old shit, ya know. Been working like hell trying to keep the alligators off my ass." Jack smiled and leaned back in his chair.

"I know the feeling. We have an alligator pond too, on the ground floor. They make us walk a rope bridge across it in the morning as we come in—during feeding time no less—just to see us sweat!"

Jack laughed. "Throw 'em candy. Rot their teeth!"

"Yeah, good idea. I'll pick up a bag of Chinese bonbons." He paused, "Hey, you still getting to the poker table? I know I haven't. My wife put herself on a mission of poker intervention, if you know what I mean."

"Yes—I—do." Jack emphasized each word. "That's why I'm divorced. It was either the wife or the cards. Easy choice. She drew a pair of deuces," Jack said with a chuckle.

"I wish life could be that simple, Jack. I sometimes envy you. You do dance to the beat of your own drum."

"As long as it's not an oil drum on the bottom of the East River." Even as he said it Jack felt himself cringe.

"Listen, Jack. You've got to watch out for those guys. They're serious about collecting their debts."

"Yeah, yeah, I know." Jack put his feet up on his desk and took a puff on his cigar. "I got everything under control."

"You better have. I don't want to read that some vagrant found your body in a dumpster."

Jack shook his head. "Yeah, like I said, everything's fine."

"I hope so. So, what's up?"

"Well, hey," Jack began. "I got this new writer I've taken on. I was intrigued with his manuscript. Has an interesting angle. I'd like to run it past you. Not the whole thing, of course, just the concept, the plot line."

"Why me?" Roger asked. "I'd like to help you out, but I don't consider myself a qualified editor."

"You publish Chinese books, don't ya?"

"Yes, but what we do are translations."

"That's okay," Jack replied. "I don't need you for editing. It's only for the story line, the concept. It has to do with a Chinese family and I want to hear your thoughts. You know, your heritage might be helpful, and I'm guessing you've read a few books on China yourself, given your position with China Gate."

"Well, if you think I can be of some help, run it by me."

"Let me read you the summary." Jack reached for the manuscript notes he had read through when the young writer, Curtis Beecham, was in his office earlier that week. "You know, the kid's a decent writer, but there's a lot of good talent out there. I wanted to see where he was going to take this story. It's an intriguing angle. After reading it, I think it needs something, more intrigue maybe, but I think it shows real promise." Shuffling through the papers on his desk, he located the summary for the book and began reading. When he finished, he waited for a response. There was none.

"Roger, you there?"

"Uh, yeah. I'm here. Just thinking." The phone remained silent for a moment. "Who did you say gave you that?"

"That's not important. What do you think? Is the concept believable? Is it plausible? It's fiction, of course."

Jack heard only silence.

After a pause, Roger spoke, "You said it's a new writer. Is he Chinese?"

"Well, no," Jack replied. "He's Anglo. And pale. He's from the Northwest. I understand they don't use sunscreen up there, they use WD-forty." Jack chuckled at his own wit. "But he said he got the idea for the story from a Chinese-American friend of his in Seattle. He probably has a pretty good handle on the Chinese cultural part of it if it's coming from someone in the Chinese community. But what about the idea? The concept? What are your thoughts?"

Roger was slow to reply. "Ah, well, I don't know Jack. Seems kind of far-fetched to me. I'm not sure what to think. Oh, ah, hey Jack. Someone just came in. Something important. I gotta go. We'll talk later, okay."

Jack heard a click on the other end and stared at the

receiver. He frowned as he held the handset away from his ear. *That was strange. Must have caught him at a bad moment. Damn alligators must be snapping his ass too!*

* * *

ROGER LEE LEFT the offices of China Gate International a few minutes early. His phone conversation with Jack Buick had disturbed him and he wanted to beat the rush-hour traffic. He took the subway to Chinatown and stepped off when it pulled into Grand Street station. Winding his way on foot he passed through a maze of streets crammed with food establishments, fresh markets, tea and spice shops.

It was late afternoon. An eclectic mix of Chinese-American residents, local New Yorkers and out-of-town tourists mingled, carrying shopping bags of fresh produce, market purchases and souvenirs. The streets were crowded and filled with the sounds of traffic—buses braking and automobiles accelerating—as the smell of exotic foods sizzling in thick grease-filled woks drifted through the air. Roger Lee was unfazed by the normal comings and goings in Chinatown. He dodged and pushed his way through the crowd and down the narrow street to his appointed destination, the China Moon restaurant.

He skirted the dining room and passed through the kitchen to a closed wood door marked OFFICE at the very rear. He knocked twice. The door half-opened and Lin Fongyeh peered out, a surprised look on his face. "Come. Come." He gestured with his hand as Roger Lee slipped inside and sat down on a wicker chair. Lin Fongyeh glanced around the kitchen before he closed the door behind him. He sat down very close to Roger Lee, reached over and turned up the volume on a small radio tuned to a classical music station. They leaned their heads together and Roger Lee told Lin Fongyeh about the telephone conversation he had had earlier that day with Jack Buick.

Lin Fongyeh listened with great interest. When Roger Lee finished, he nodded. "You have done well. This is disturbing information. I will get back to you very soon."

CHAPTER ELEVEN

Seattle, Washington

THE PHONE RANG three times before Deng Qin lifted the receiver.

"Yes," he answered in his usual abrupt Mandarin.

"Red Fever Seventeen," the voice on the phone replied, also in Mandarin.

Without responding, Deng Qin hung up the phone in his Seattle apartment. He immediately recognized the code from Lin Fongyeh, his MSS counterpart in Chinatown, New York City.

Leaving his apartment, he pulled out onto Boren Avenue and continued north, checking his rear-view mirror as he drove.

Darkness had long since fallen among the high-rises of downtown Seattle. The rush hour over, traffic had thinned. Streetlights and neon signs from neighborhood businesses reflected on wet pavement, creating an abstract of glassy color that made driving in the incessant drizzle more difficult in the long hours of a Northwest night.

Deng Qin managed the Longzee Import and Export Company, but he answered to the Ministry of State Security for the People's Republic of China. His real reason for living in

Seattle for the past three years was to gather and obtain information, MSS being to China what the CIA is to America—an intelligence gathering organization. He was charged with running clandestine operations in the aerospace industry, as well as within the high-tech world of computer technology dealing with intellectual property.

Deng Qin continued up Boren, then turned off to wend his way through the one-way streets of Pioneer Square until he reached the designated pay phone in the empty parking lot near First and King Street. He dialed the phone number of a public phone booth located in Manhattan that he had committed to memory. His eyes scanned the parking lot as the receiver on the other end picked up. Deng Qin spoke first, "Yes, Red Fever Seventeen."

Deng Qin heard Lin Fongyeh respond. "I had a very interesting meeting with a contact of mine. It is important and disturbing information."

"Yes, continue."

"My contact has a friend in New York. This friend is an editor and works for a publishing company here in Manhattan. This editor is working with a writer who is developing a book. This book details the plans and objectives of the Program. I do not have specific information about the book, but as my contact explained it, it follows a specific family and is definitely about the Program. Exactly as it has been designed and orchestrated these many years."

Deng Qin was surprised, although in his business he had been trained to expect anything. He understood Lin Fongyeh could not say too much over the phone and would not mention any specific names or identify the Sons of the Red Dragon, but simply refer to it as the Program. Deng Qin also knew he would receive a coded message through the mail with more details of Lin Fongyeh's conversation. "The Program? Are you sure?"

"Most sure."

"Did he identify this editor?"

"Yes. Following protocol, I will send you a detailed memorandum that will explain everything we know. This writer is proposing the work as a novel. Fiction. One of those tasteless, paperback novels the Americans are fond of reading. It is not an exposé or a documentary, so I do not know if this is a real family, or if they are from his own imagination."

"This is most serious. We must know for certain if he named any other names." Deng Qin let the seriousness of the situation sink in. "You and I both know the consequences if this goes deeper. We have a much bigger investment, a greater involvement than the Program."

Deng Qin didn't have to say more. Both men worked for MSS. They knew information gathering was more important to China than the pursuits of the Sons of the Red Dragon program. MSS was at the heart of China's spy activity. They ran it, controlled it and because of it, China saw immediate results. The Sons of the Red Dragon was a low level, long-term program of influence development whose effects would not be seen for many years. A program for which MSS had little respect. But there were occasions when participants of the Sons of the Red Dragon would become contacts for agents of MSS, performing double-duty, and those contacts that crossed the lines between the two programs formed the anxiety Deng Qin felt. If this writer had information about The Sons of the Red Dragon, did he also have knowledge of the operations of MSS?

"I understand the importance of finding out more about this book and its contents," Lin Fongyeh said. "I will see what I can do. I will talk further with my contact in the publishing business. But he told me editors do not talk about ongoing book projects. So he wasn't sure how much new information he might get."

"You must find a way." Then Deng Qin asked, "Why did this New York editor call your contact with this information?"

"They are friends. This editor knew my contact worked for a publisher of Chinese books, but they are not competitors in the business world. He asked about the feasibility of such a program, if such a concept made a good story. But I believe this editor may have wanted to know if this program really existed. He may have been probing. Wanted to know if my contact had heard about any such program administered by Beijing."

"And the name of the writer. Do we know this?"

"No. I do not know his name. All I know is that he is not Chinese. He is white, an Anglo, as my contact quoted. He obtained the information to write his book about the Program from a friend of his in the Program who is of course Chinese and who lives in Seattle."

"From a friend in the Program. A Son of the Red Dragon and he lives in Seattle!" Deng Qin said. "Yes, this is very serious. We have many contacts in Seattle. It is a large Chinese community. I will check my sources. Turn the community upside down if necessary to get this traitor that is working with this writer. You work your contact. Let me know when you get further information."

Deng Qin hung up the phone, scanned the parking lot once more then crossed the brick-lined walk to his car.

* * *

TWO DAYS LATER, after receiving the memorandum from Lin Fongyeh that identified Jack Buick and his publishing company, Deng Qin arranged a meeting with Willie Wong. Although Willie Wong did not work with MSS, he had on occasion dealt with Deng Qin, as some members of the Sons of the Red Dragon program had supported MSS in their information gathering process.

To the families and participants of the Red Dragon Program, Willie Wong was affectionately known as Uncle Willie. But Deng Qin preferred to call him by his given name. After all, Deng Qin was a senior officer in MSS, and felt superior to those in the Sons of the Red Dragon program. MSS dealt with more important matters. He knew their contributions to the State were of greater value. They took serious risks. He expected Willie Wong to defer to him. "Uncle" was too chummy a moniker that might work for the relationship Willie Wong must build with his immigrant families, but was not appropriate for the relationship Willie Wong should have with MSS.

They met in their usual remote location outside the city, a place where they would not be seen together by members of the Chinese community, or the FBI. Located on a logging road east of Seattle near the junction of Interstate 90 and the Preston Fall City Road, the abandoned cabin had proven to be a safe place for meeting and passing information. Where approaching vehicles could be observed well before they arrived.

Deng Qin was already waiting when Willie Wong drove up, sending splashes of mud against the undercarriage of his SUV from potholes in the dirt road dug out by heavy logging trucks. Tall evergreens, a mix of Douglas fir, spruce and hemlock rose skyward, all but blocking out any rays of sunlight that might find their way into these remote foothills of the Cascade Mountains. After a cool greeting, Deng Qin told Willie Wong about his phone conversation and the memorandum from his counterpart in New York.

Willie Wong appeared disturbed. "I can't believe it. Who would do such a thing? It has to be someone familiar with the Program. I know these people well. They are like family. I cannot imagine who it could be." He paused, his eyebrows furrowed. "But, I will find out."

"Yes," Deng Qin said, quite annoyed. "We must find out who it is and what they know. Everything they have told this writer. We have much at risk. We must find out how deep this goes." Deng Qin looked Willie Wong directly in the eye as he continued, "This is your Program. It is your people. You must find this person. But I am warning you, go about this quietly. I have been operating for three years, and because I have been prudent in managing my sources, I have never had a problem. I do not need to feel the attention of the authorities." Deng Qin pointed his finger at Willie Wong. "I expect you will tell me very soon you have met with success in this matter. You must find and sever the head of this loose goose."

CHAPTER TWELVE

FBI SUPERVISORY SPECIAL Agent Lou Jengwi was not distracted by the expansive view from his thirty-fourth floor office in downtown Seattle. A wall of windows faced out to the waterfront, Bainbridge Island, Puget Sound, and the Olympic Mountains—a dramatic snow-capped ridge on the Olympic Peninsula in the distance. The cherry-wood desk and office furnishings were government issue, but a nice upgrade from the steel gray office desk he sat behind when he began his career. Behind him on a credenza sat framed photos of Jengwi posing with dignitaries and politicians, and a favorite one of him and a buddy in U.S. Marine Corp combat fatigues gripping M-16's—a few mementos of a long career of service to his country. Fond memories he will take with him when he retires. He had just completed his twenty-third year of service with the FBI and had many successful investigations in his résumé.

Lou Jengwi wanted to close this case, his first assignment in the Seattle District Office, and his last before he turned in his shield. It might be his toughest yet. He could never completely turn off the spigot allowing the flow of America's top secrets across the Pacific, but he was more than willing to put his wingtip across the throat of those responsible. He would do whatever he had to, to crack this case. This one struck at his very heart.

America had given him and his family a wonderful life. He

appreciated living in a free democratic society, a country with rights guaranteed by the Constitution, rights that had never been experienced by his ancestors. Just as he loved America, he despised Communism and the oppressive regime of his ancestral home. His loathing for that ideology was similar to the level of hate often found between a spouse and an ex. A hate born of love, is a much deeper, more intense hate.

A third-generation Chinese American, his grandfather had arrived on American soil an immigrant, with little more than a rice sack filled with a few possessions. But Lou Jengwi had been raised in middle-class affluence, thanks to the hard work and determination of his father. Because of his ethnic background, he had been hand-selected to join the counter-intelligence unit of the Federal Bureau of Investigation. He spoke Mandarin, having been raised in a home of Chinese Americans. His heritage would allow him to get close to the Chinese community in Seattle—the first step he would take on his last walk down the path of federal investigations.

On his desk was his assignment, a thick file looming like a plague, an epidemic sweeping down on Seattle's aerospace and high-tech industries. Carefully studying the documents detailing Chinese spy activity over recent years, he had begun the arduous task of familiarizing himself with ongoing operations.

Jengwi's previous experience had been in bank fraud and kidnapping so he had never been involved in an investigation of Chinese espionage. He knew this particular assignment would pump the blood through his veins a little faster. The knowledge that those who shared a common ancestry, had come to America to enjoy a life of freedom and were willing to betray the hand that fed them, was enough to put a sharp edge on his sword. He had no feelings of dormant loyalty to his grandfather's homeland, only a staunch patriotism to *his* own country. He had no compassion for Chinese Americans with divided loyalties. They were traitors. This was the case he had waited for his entire career. This is where his legacy would be made. A bulldog, Jengwi would dig his teeth into this one and not let go.

A hard knock on the door startled him. "Come in," he said, as he removed his readers, placing them on his desk.

Special Agent Skip Chouw poked his head in. "You wanted to see me?"

Skip Chouw had been born and raised in Seattle and knew the local Chinese community intimately. He had most recently been attached to the Portland office, but had been reassigned to the Seattle office to work Chinese espionage. He was of Chinese descent, fluent in Mandarin and had twelve years experience with the FBI.

Jengwi watched as he entered. Agent Chouw displayed a waistline pushing the limits of Bureau guidelines. In a career that left little time for sit-down dinners, he exhibited a fondness for fast food. Chouw himself had confessed that fellow agents often teased him regarding his personal eating habits. They were fond of saying, no matter how busy Agent Chouw might find himself, he never "skipped chow."

Jengwi gestured at the chair in front of his desk. "Yes. Have a seat. I was just going over the 'Bamboo Water Drip' files. I need to be brought up to speed as quickly as possible. I know you've been working this, so I want your input." He leaned back in his padded executive chair, and got right to the point. "Operation Bamboo Water Drip? Who's idea was that?"

"Just a little inside humor. You're familiar with the Chinese method of extracting information from prisoners, 'Chinese Water Torture'?"

Jengwi nodded, his curiosity piqued.

"Well, as you've probably read in the reports, the most common espionage technique used by MSS is a slow methodical one. They have hundreds of sources gathering classified information one little bit at a time. To the Bureau, it's like facing an episode of Chinese Water Torture. You know the method, a prisoner strapped down on a table, unable to move while water drips from above, striking him on the forehead. He soon reaches near insanity." He paused a second. "That's how we feel."

Jengwi didn't smile. The insinuation that the Bureau was nearly powerless disturbed him. "We see ourselves as impotent?"

Agent Chouw shifted in his seat, and looked a little uncomfortable. "Well, no, not entirely. We've had our successes. But it's a drop in the bucket." Chouw cringed, his discomfort obvious to Jengwi.

Jengwi frowned but ignored the unintentional pun, moving on. "So tell me about this 'quansi' I've read about."

"Yeah, now *that's* something we didn't learn about in the Academy. MSS is not as sophisticated in their methods as our Russian friends, but they're just as determined, if not more persistent. The very nature of quansi makes identifying agents and sources very difficult, let alone apprehending *and* convicting them. Even when we've done our job, we've not had a lot of success prosecuting them."

Jengwi rocked back in his chair. "This quansi? It's more of a friendship? A relationship?"

"Exactly. Quansi is the Chinese method of information gathering based on friendships, relationships, contacts and persuasion. They've been using this process for over four thousand years. Instead of sending trained agents to infiltrate our aerospace and high-tech industries, they use home-grown ethnic Chinese living and working in the community."

Jengwi asked for clarification. "You mean Chinese Americans employed by these same industries?"

"Yes. They're sources of information. They're not spies as such. But spies nonetheless. Untrained. But effective. And like I said, difficult to expose."

Agent Chouw continued. "Here's how it works. The trained MSS agent develops a relationship within the Chinese community, a friendship with someone who works in a position of importance in a targeted industry. They build a trust, and a dialog eventually develops between them that produces information. Many small bits of knowledge are obtained from those many contacts, then MSS compiles them until eventually they have the full picture. No one person has to provide a whole masterpiece, he only has to supply a few brush strokes."

"Yes, I remember reading that," Jengwi interjected. "I liked the comparison someone made. They said if the Russians wanted to determine the content of the sand on our beach, they'd send a submarine with a few armed agents to Waikiki. In the middle of the night they'd paddle ashore in rubber rafts and dig up bucketfuls, killing everyone who got in the way. On the other hand, the Chinese would send a hundred families to have a picnic on the beach, each would discreetly scoop up a handful, then send it back to China through the U.S. mail."

Jengwi rested his elbows on the arms of his chair, his fingers resting against his bottom lip, his mind reminiscing. "This is quite different than the tactics used by the KGB during the Cold War. I suppose our methods are different too. This may be a softer and gentler war, but a war nonetheless."

"You bet," Chouw continued. "The Chinese also exploit opportunities available during cultural exchanges, trade shows and technology conferences, where information is freely and openly discussed."

"Yes," Jengwi thought out loud. "There was that case out of the New York office. A Chinese delegation touring the Kodak plant in New Jersey was caught dipping their ties into vats of processing fluid so they could take it back to China and have their laboratories determine the exact chemical mix Kodak was using."

"That's it exactly," Chouw said. "Low-tech espionage. In that case, it almost worked. And we have no idea how often they're successful. It's scary. I hate to think, but someday our military may end up facing weapons systems built and constructed in China, but designed and developed in America."

Jengwi nodded. *Yes, a sobering thought.* "How successful is MSS at recruiting agents?" Jengwi asked.

"Like I said, these contacts aren't considered 'agents'," Chouw continued. "They're not paid. And they don't think of themselves as agents. To MSS, they're sources. They may meet in a Chinese restaurant, having tea. They speak in their native tongue, and exchange stories of their families in the old country. They get comfortable. They are told America is a great and wealthy country while China is poor and backward. A little harmless information would be helpful and shows gratitude toward their ancestral home. And the reason they're so hard to uncover is because this relationship between the Chinese intelligence service and the source is nearly invisible. It's a personal relationship between two friends. The source doesn't think of himself as an employee or a contractor. He only thinks of himself as helping out a friend or a colleague."

"It's all very simple," Jengwi mumbled. "Too damn simple."

Chouw appeared more relaxed as the discussion continued, crossing his leg over his knee. Jengwi noticed Chouw's shoe had become untied, the shoelace dangling in space as he bounced his foot. Chouw went on. "And if a source has family remaining in China, the obligation could be extorted to a greater extent. For example, if an MSS contact told his source that his ailing aunt in Beijing had been moved from a fourth floor apartment to a first floor unit and been given special care, the source would feel even more indebted."

"I'm sure if one has family remaining in China, the use of threats would be very effective too," Jengwi added. "As an incentive to obtain information from sources over here, it's not beyond them to use threatening means against family remaining back there. We *are* in a war. Not a true Cold War, but a war that's getting colder by the day. And it's on our turf."

Jengwi sat contemplating for a minute. He thought of his career and his early Marine Corp training that was a part of him still. He felt a rush of adrenalin and a twinge of excitement, his body's normal preparation when beginning a new mission. He smiled, eager to tackle the challenge, but aware of the immense battle this was going to be.

"Okay, thanks Agent Chouw. That's all for now."

Skip Chouw stood to leave. As he did he tucked in his shirt. Jengwi caught a flash of bulging midriff and made a mental note to have physical fitness requirements posted throughout the office.

As Chouw turned toward the door, he pulled a spiral notebook from his shirt pocket and began flipping pages. He hesitated then spun around. "Almost forgot. Got a call from OPUS."

Jengwi looked at Agent Chouw, somewhat annoyed. *Almost forgot! OPUS. OPUS. Where have I heard that?* "Fill me in," Jengwi scowled.

"Yeah, OPUS. Ah, two years ago we developed a relationship with an asset within the Chinese community. Calls himself OPUS." He gestured over his shoulder. "I'll see that Bernadette gets you a copy of his file. He's provided information from time to time. Some valuable, some not. It's an unusual relationship. No one's actually met him, but he's passed on numerous tips we've found to be accurate."

"What do we know about him?"

"Not much. I don't know if we can ever fully trust him, but he may prove to be valuable. He's never demanded money or payment for services, so his motive for passing information is unknown."

Chouw shifted. "He called in on the same line as before. Confirmed his pass code." Jengwi nodded as Chouw continued. "Said he had information about someone writing a book on a Chinese immigration program. Has to do with immigrants being sent to the States, in a program controlled and run by the Communist Party."

"You mean MSS?"

"No. I asked him. He specifically said it wasn't MSS."

Jengwi nodded and waved his hand for Chouw to continue.

"As he tells it, the purpose of immigrating is to birth children, sons in particular, and raise them in America, you know, native-born Chinese Americans. Their plan is to guide these children through the American education system, into universities, then as they move into adulthood, direct them into politics, creating a whole army of American politicians with sympathies to China. Congressmen, Senators and the like. And, OPUS says it's more than just a plotline in a book. It's not a coincidence. The Chinese have an ongoing program whereby they're doing this." Chouw paused and looked down at his notes. "Of course, there's nothing illegal here. We've heard rumors over the years, but never followed up on it. Didn't seem to be of any immediate concern. Our investigations of active spy activity are more important, certainly, then a bunch of Chinese American babies."

Agent Chouw closed his note pad and slipped it into his shirt pocket, then interjected his own personal opinion. "Sounds to me like a long-range plan to influence our politics. It would be just like them to try to stack Congress with a bunch of Communist sympathizers to get their hands on Taiwan."

Jengwi held up his arms, palms out. "Hold on now. Let's not promote a wave of paranoia. Remember your history. We don't want our investigation to smack of McCarthyism. Let the bureaucrats hang themselves on *that* rope. If all they wanted was Taiwan, they'd implement this same immigration program there, without our help. And they probably have. No. They don't *just* want Taiwan. They want America."

Chouw frowned and nodded his head. "Yeah, the domino theory goes West."

"Well as long as I'm here I'm going to see that doesn't happen." Jengwi studied Agent Chouw, digesting the information. "Is that all OPUS gave you?"

"No. He gave me a name. Jack Buick. He isn't the writer though. He didn't know the name of the writer, just that he lived in Seattle, and wasn't Chinese."

This caught Jengwi's attention. He sat back in his chair and blew out a long breath. "He's not Chinese?"

"No, he's Caucasian. And as I said, we don't have his name. The Jack Buick guy's his editor. Works for a publisher in New York." Chouw pulled his notes back out of his pocket and flipped a few pages. "Kaleidoscope Book Publishing. Other than that, there isn't much, but thought I'd keep you updated. I'll file a contact report."

"Yes, do. But I wonder if there's more to it than what OPUS is telling us?" Jengwi clasped his hands behind his head, interlocking his fingers, and closed his eyes as if reading from a script inside his eyelids. "First we need to know who this writer is. What are the facts, if indeed they are facts, he's based this book on? How much is drawn from his imagination? And does he know more than what he's writing about?"

He opened his eyes and looked at Chouw. "If this immigration program exists, and this writer is not Chinese, who's his source in the Chinese community? Where's he getting his information? If OPUS thought it was worth passing on, maybe it's something we should look at more closely. He *says* it's not MSS behind this, but we don't know that. There could be more to this. They could be involved. See where I'm going? This could be a seemingly unimportant tip, but who knows, it could lead somewhere. Any information we can uncover may prove to be an important link to something bigger."

Chouw nodded.

"Plus we have valuable contacts and sources of our own we need to protect," Jengwi continued. "Maybe this book, this writer, has information that could put *our* people in danger. That's not acceptable. I don't like loose ends. I want to know what everyone else knows. Including this damn writer."

Jengwi leaned forward and tapped the desktop with his index finger. "I don't want any damn book hitting the best-seller list exposing our investigation while it's still ongoing. Find out who this writer is and what he knows."

Chouw stood up straight, lifting his hunched shoulders. "Gottcha, chief. I'll get on it right away." He turned to leave, but Jengwi hadn't finished.

"Hell, we have a hard enough time controlling the flow of information passing through the Pacific pipeline. The damn government isn't helping. Every time they let a delegation of businessmen into our country for a tour, those guys end up returning home with a suitcase full of secrets."

Jengwi reached across the desk for his readers.

"Our damn State Department isn't doing their part. If they did, they'd keep our door closed and padlock it. Cultural exchanges my ass!" Jengwi never expected a response, as Agent Chouw slipped out the door and pulled it shut. Jengwi glanced down at the desktop and fingered the troubling document. He took a deep breath, the outrage within him boiling. He adjusted his glasses and continued reading, the magnitude of involvement growing with each page. He had only a limited number of fingers to plug the many leaks the Chinese had created in that Great Wall. He sighed. *Chinese water torture my ass!*

CHAPTER THIRTEEN

THE KITCHEN FILLED with the chatter and bustle of two generations of women of the Hu family. Li Chen and her two daughters, Sung Wi and Angela each tried to out-talk each other as they conspired to coordinate six hands and as many pots, on one stovetop with four burners. The scent of Chinese spices and traditional cuisine filled the room, seeped through the open doorway and drifted through the house.

It would be a rare gathering at the home of Wung Hu and Li Chen, as their four children joined them for a family dinner, celebrating Thanksgiving, Chinese style. Now that the children had become young adults, they kept themselves busy in pursuit of their careers or furthering their educations and rarely had the opportunity to sit at the same table, as they had in earlier years. To Wung Hu this was not the way of the traditional home in his native China, where the family gathered to share meals, to talk and discuss issues important to one another. Then again, they often lived together, one family, multiple generations, in the same house. Yes, it was different in America. And it was not *all* for the better.

Their chatter abated when the women, carrying platters of pineapple chicken with sweet and sour sauce, beef and peppers in black bean sauce, crispy noodles with vegetables, and fried rice joined the men at the dining table. The meal commenced and conversation continued amid the rhythm of clicking chopsticks. Afterwards the men adjourned to the living room while the women cleaned the kitchen and washed the dishes—a custom common to both cultures. Sung Wi brought a fresh pot of hot tea and filled the empty cups.

"I am so pleased to have my family here with me today," Wung Hu began. "It is much too infrequent an occasion." He sipped from his cup, peering at his sons over the delicate porcelain rim.

"Yes, father," Thomas spoke up. "We enjoy spending the holidays with our family. It certainly beats cafeteria food."

George sipped and nodded in agreement.

Wung Hu had looked forward to having this opportunity to catch up with his sons. They hadn't talked as often as Wung Hu would have liked. Uncle Willie had told Wung Hu this was not unusual behavior from young men immersed in the hectic life of academia.

He had noticed that throughout the evening George had been especially quiet and reserved. "George, my son the lawyer, you seem to be weighed down, a heavy burden upon your shoulders. I see in your eyes a deep troubling, a weariness in your spirit. Is there something you would like to share?"

George shifted. He seemed a bit uncomfortable. "No, Father. It's school. My studies take a great toll on my energy." George dropped his eyes. "This second year of law school is very demanding. I don't know what a social life is anymore." He looked up with a half smile. "But, I *am* doing fine. And Father. Please. I'm not a lawyer. Not yet."

Wung Hu studied his son. He knew him well, even though he had not lived at home since he had enrolled at the University of Washington. His son had a deep spirit. A complex thinker, he processed information in a methodical, thorough manner, often keeping his thoughts private, closing that door to his inner self. Wung Hu was not convinced

George was fine, but he replied with a thin smile. "Yes, I know you are doing well. I am proud of you. But I am your father, and I am here if you wish to talk."

"Yes, Father." George did not look up. He leaned his elbows on his knees and stared at his teacup, his nimble fingers turning it in his hands.

Wung Hu let his eyes follow the contour of his eldest son as he slumped, searching for truth. He knew his firstborn son was a troubled young man. This was a burden on Wung Hu's heart.

Wung Hu kept his focus fixed on George for a moment, then shifted his attention to Thomas. His heart felt lighter, his face lit up. Thomas was the yang to his older brother's yin. Outgoing, energetic, he was quick to make friends. Had an enthusiasm he couldn't cap, an optimism that never waned, and was without doubt more athletic than his older brother. Wung Hu believed his son's involvement in athletics helped him keep his mind sharp and his spirit strong. "Thomas." Wung Hu smiled. "My son. You look fit and of good health."

"I'm doing well, Father. I'm enjoying my senior year, especially my business classes, but as you know, I *looove* my baseball." He put his hands together gripping an imaginary bat and gave a mock swing, his mouth lipping, *"Kapow!"*

Wung Hu sat back, relaxed, enjoying the moment as he crossed his leg over his knee and sipped his tea.

Thomas continued. "The university team doesn't begin spring practice for a few months yet, but I attend workouts every week. I want to be prepared for my final season. Every year we begin with great optimism, you know. Maybe *this* year we can bring home a PAC-12 championship." He smiled and winked at his father.

Wung Hu leaned over and placed his hand on his son's knee, a glint in his eye. "Yes, I am certain you will."

Wung Hu knew both his sons had done well at the

university and he was a proud father. He knew they were busy with their studies, but he still encouraged them to continue to attend classes and social activities at the Chinese Cultural Academy—their link to their ancestral home.

Wung Hu saw Sung Wi through the kitchen doorway. He lifted his cup. "Ah, Sung Wi. May we have more tea?"

Sung Wi, at age twenty-nine, still lived at home, the first-born and the last to leave. She worked at a neighborhood market, satisfied to remain with her parents, helping her mother prepare the family meals. Wung Hu and his eldest child had a special bond, a bond endowed by sharing a common birthplace, the ancient land of his forefathers.

Angela drifted into the living room, twisting a dishtowel as she dried her hands. Wung Hu's youngest child at nineteen, she had grown into a woman and embraced her American lifestyle. "My dear Angela," he said. "That was a wonderful meal."

"I can't take the credit, Father." She gave a shrug and a look of consigned resignation. "Mother and Sung Wi are the cooks in this family. I'm more comfortable at the clinic than in the kitchen."

"Yes. I know. You should go to the university, finish your studies, get your degree and become a veterinarian."

"Yes, Father. Maybe someday."

Wung Hu knew she said this to appease him. He knew she had always tried to please him. She was a warm and sensitive young woman and in Angela, he could find no fault.

"I love my work at the clinic," Angela said. "Caring for the animals. And Dr. Jessica let's me do stuff, you know, like vaccinations and blood tests. It's totally fun."

She smiled, then leaned over and kissed her father on the forehead. "I'd better get back to the kitchen and help Mother and Sung Wi before they start talking about me." She took the dishtowel and playfully slapped George's knee, as she turned and left the room.

Wung Hu glanced from one son to the other, "Uncle Willie tells me you haven't been going to the Cultural Academy like you once did."

"Father, our studies tie us to our books," Thomas said, pleading his case. "We'd like to spend more time at the Cultural Academy, but there's not enough hours in our day. I know you want us to do our best in our university studies."

Wung Hu nodded, but it saddened him. He could not push his sons too hard. He had been instructed by Uncle Willie to use gentle persuasion. He was told that to force his sons would only make them reject the goals of the Program. He knew if he were a young man, he would find the time. Young men today spent too much time playing, and not enough effort on their cultural studies.

Wung Hu slowly rose from his favorite chair, carved from the thick limbs of Chinese Elm, hand painted by artisans from the old country. The backrest displayed a delicate scene of traditional costumed figures, bordered with ornate designs and patterns outlined with a thin stroke of decorative gold. With a hard flat wood seat and a curved back, it was not built for comfort, but Wung Hu treasured it. Uncle Willie had given it to him, a gift, years ago.

He walked over to a cabinet, opened the top drawer and removed a small box wrapped with a band of thin bamboo. A wood button held it closed. Wung Hu carefully cradled the box in his hands and returned to his seat. Li Chen appeared through the kitchen door, walked up behind his chair and laid her hands on his shoulders. He looked up and placed his hand on hers, feeling her warmth.

He unbuttoned the band and opened the lid. Inside, a brass medallion lay nestled atop an indented red-velvet cushion. Shiny from frequent polishing, the light from the lamp reflected in a small burst as he held it up for his sons to see. Embossed lettering in Mandarin filled a border within the outer ring. Wung Hu watched his sons as their lips silently formed the words, THE PARTY, THE COUNTRY, THE FAMILY. In the center a thin clear glass vial held loose soil. George reached over and slid his finger down the flat face of the glass. Wung Hu had showed it to his sons once before, but they hadn't seen it for many years.

"Yes, Father," George said. "It's a wonderful memento."

Wung Hu noticed Thomas glance at George. A strange exchange took place between them that Wung Hu did not understand. His son's eyes met for a moment, then Thomas turned back to his father. "Your country honors you with this gift, Father."

Wung Hu hesitated, looking at his sons, then glanced down at the medallion once more. This token had traveled with him from his ancestral home and held great meaning. For the love of his homeland, he revered this cherished possession and wanted to share it with his sons.

He looked up again, studying the young men carefully for a moment, then returned the medallion to the box, slipping on the band of thin bamboo, closing it with the wood button. He had done everything he could to guide his sons toward the goals of the Program. But he had noticed they had become very American in their ways, in their actions, and maybe even in their thoughts. Had they accepted their part in the Sons of the Red Dragon as they should? Or had they, behind the mask of love and respect they held for their father, abandoned the ideals of *his* homeland. Had they tossed aside the Party plan as they embraced their American life? If this were true, then Wung Hu knew he had failed his Party, his country, and even his family.

CHAPTER FOURTEEN

New York City

CONCENTRATING ON A manuscript, Jack Buick jerked when the phone rang, pulling him out of a tense moment of a serial murder. He pushed the receive button on the speakerphone. "Yes."

"Mr. Buick. There are two gentlemen here to see you. They say they're with the Chinese-American Trade & Cultural Exchange Commission. They don't have an appointment, but asked if you would have a few moments."

"Ahh, well, shit. Okay. But let them know I'm up to my ass in alligators and keep it short." He heard a chuckle on the other end, then a click.

A few minutes later Jack responded to a gentle knock. Two men in business suits entered. "Sorry, I've only one chair," Jack said. "How can I help you?" The men remained standing, one holding a black leather briefcase.

"Mr. Jack Buick. I am Sing Hon and this is Ji Chen. We are with the Chinese-American Trade & Cultural Exchange Commission. We understand you are quite busy, so we will be brief. We have an interest in all things related to China. We deal in many areas that effect the relations of our two countries. We wish to continue to build trust between us. If I may come straight to the point?"

Jack nodded his head as he rocked back and forth in his leather chair, the weight of his elbows indented the padded arms as he locked his hands together beneath his chin.

"We understand you are to publish a book about China," Sing Hon said. "This interests us."

Jack studied the two gentlemen. They exhibited Asian features, had clean-cut haircuts, wore dark suits with white shirts and conservative ties. He was a bit perplexed. "I don't know what you're referring to," he responded, as he glanced from one to the other.

"Ah, yes. Let me explain. It is not exactly about China. It is about Chinese immigrants. A Chinese family that came to America. Raising a family here, I believe. We would like to meet the author. Perhaps we can be of some assistance."

Jack immediately knew what they were referring to. He was not pleased. Nobody outside the publishing house should know about current projects. *How'd they find out about this book? Why are they interested in it?* He stared at them. "Sorry, I can't discuss any project I may or may not be involved in. Even if I were involved in such a project, I wouldn't discuss it with you. What I'm working on is my own damn business and no concern of the..." he paused. "What'd you call yourselves?"

"The Chinese-American Trade & Cultural Exchange Commission."

"Yeah. Well, there ain't no trading or exchanging going on here, you can bet your ass on that. And the name of the author is none of your business. So if that's all you're here for, then I guess we're done." Jack lifted himself from his seat, and leaned on his desk.

"I am sorry you see it that way," said Sing Hon. "We could be of some service. Because you see, there are people who are very interested in the progress of this book. In fact, there are people who wish to see that this book does not make any progress at all. So you may need a friend. Do you understand?"

Jack felt his blood pressure rise and anger build. He stared at them. "Is that a threat?"

"Like I said, we could be a friend. You might need one in the future."

"I certainly don't need *your* kind of friend," Jack said, jamming a finger toward the first man. "There's the door. Things don't work the same way around here as they do in China. You can't just walk in and order people to do your bidding. That's bullshit! I ain't having none of it."

"I hope you will reconsider, Mr. Buick. Please think about what we have said. We will contact you again, after you have had time to think it through."

"Don't bother. I'm not interested!"

Jack was pissed and wanted to tell them in such a way they would not misinterpret his feelings. As the first man reached for the doorknob, Jack blurted out a phrase in Mandarin he had learned in his Chinese language studies. With an accent right out of the Bronx, he barked his best Mandarin slur.

The two men turned and stared, surprised to hear him speak in their native tongue. Their perplexed looks changed into insolent smirks as the first one cocked his head and motioned with his thumb toward Jack. They turned and left without another word.

Shit! Jack pounded his palm on his desktop. *Damn, they must think I'm an idiot.* In a fit of anger, the first thing that came to his mind was the only Chinese phrase he had spoken since college. What he intended to say was, "I'd like to throw the two of you out the window!" What came out of his mouth was, "I'd like a table for two by the window."

Jack sat down and tried to calm his anger. He thought for a minute about the brief and hostile meeting he had just engaged in. *Strange. Who were these guys? How'd they know about the damn manuscript?* He pulled out his computer keyboard and went to Google, typing in CHINESE-AMERICAN TRADE & CULTURAL EXCHANGE COMMISSION. Instantly his monitor displayed the first page of listings. In all, Google identified over three thousand sites related in some way to the title he had input, but there was no match for the name he was given by the two men on any of the first six pages. In fact, as he thought it through, he realized they had never given him a business card or presented any form of identification. Jack leaned back and stared at the computer listings. *Two Chinese guys just threatened me. Who the hell are they?*

CHAPTER FIFTEEN

Seattle, Washington

SSA LOU JENGWI left the downtown FBI office, headed across the floating bridge spanning Lake Washington and continued into downtown Redmond, an eastside suburb of Seattle and a major high-tech corridor. There he joined Special Agent Skip Chouw handling surveillance of a suspected Chinese agent.

The suspect, Tai Kang, was Chinese-American and a computer engineer employed by WUZ-Tech. He had been identified by in-house security as very active in downloading sensitive files, including over twelve thousand technical documents from the company's electronic library. Although he had authorized access, his downloading activity was sixteen times higher than the next highest user. WUZ-Tech had under development, among other things, a small electronic sensor that had commercial, as well as military, significance. This sensor worked under extreme heat as well as under great pressure. It had the potential, with modifications, for use in sophisticated military applications.

Jengwi located Chouw's vehicle and pulled up beside him in the employee parking lot. He parked his car, acknowledged the second agent sitting in the passenger seat, then stepped out and opened the back door of Chouw's sedan and slipped in. "Anything?"

"Nope. He should be leaving shortly. Our team's ready to go through his computer as soon as he leaves."

The three agents kept an eye on the throng of employees as they scattered throughout the parking lot, heading for their vehicles.

"I don't want Tai Kang to know we're sniffing around."

"He won't. Our guys are good."

Jengwi pulled out a pack of cigarettes and retrieved one. He lit it, inhaled and blew a gray cloud out the open window. They sat in silence for a few moments.

WUZ-Tech International had contacted the FBI, informing the Bureau of their suspicion that had brought this suspect to Jenwi's attention. The FBI, as part of it's program to crack down on espionage in corporate America, had met with CEO's and security personnel of target corporations within the communities surrounding each of their fifty-six field offices. In the Seattle area, SSA Lou Jengwi had met with ten major corporations, including WUZ-Tech International. Although much of the information sought by the Chinese was not classified, it was still sensitive, proprietary technology that could be crippling and devastating to the economic security of American companies. With China's low labor costs, Chinese industry already had an advantage over U.S. companies. If they could neutralize America's technological advantage through the theft of homegrown technology they would easily leapfrog their American rivals.

"Anything more on the book thing?" Jengwi asked. "The guy writing that book."

"Nope. I checked my contacts. No one seems to know anything. We're still working it."

"How about that guy in New York? The publisher guy. What's his name?"

"Jack Buick."

"How about having New York check his phone records? See who he's calling in Seattle."

"They're on that right now. Should have something soon."

"Good. I need to find this guy."

They sat in silence, kept their eyes on the parking lot and a vehicle two rows away belonging to Tai Kang, while Jengwi smoked his filter tips. "The wiretap?"

"We got the court order. Should be in place tonight."

A few minutes later Agent Chouw spotted a tall thin man carrying a briefcase as he walked across the parking lot and headed toward the second row of cars. "There," he said.

"Got him." Jengwi opened the door and slipped back into his own vehicle.

The FBI didn't believe Tai Kang suspected anything and their information suggested he was an amateur—a contact recruited by a pro. They wanted Tai Kang, but they wanted Tai Kang to lead them to his handler.

Surveillance was a slow, long drawn-out affair, but so was the traffic during rush hour in the Seattle metropolitan area. Both agents followed Tai Kang in separate cars as he led them back across Lake Washington to his home in the Wallingford area of Seattle.

Chouw and the second agent took the first shift that night as Jengwi drove on. Camped in their rather plain, gray, government issued sedan, one agent whiled away his time with a few magazines stashed under the front seat as the other agent provided the eyes.

* * *

AGENT CHOUW MET with Jengwi in his office the next morning. Jengwi sat back in his chair and sipped on a steamy cup of fresh coffee. "How'd it go?"

"Never left his house," Chouw replied. "Our guys went through his office and his computer last night. His office was clean, as we expected. His computer had a lot of information and they're still sifting through it. His email was clean. Any contact he makes is probably in person, or on a safe phone. I don't expect him to leave us a nice neat trail."

Jengwi nodded and rocked back in his chair, warming both hands with the cup. "Keep that tail on him."

"I do have something on the writer." Chouw reached into his pocket and pulled out his notebook. "We believe his name's Curtis Beecham. He was the only contact that editor Jack Buick has had in Seattle over the past two months. They've talked four times. I have his phone number and an address. It's a pier on Lake Union. Must be a boat of some sort. Likely a houseboat, there are a lot of them around there."

Jengwi smiled. "Good. Let's pay him a visit."

* * *

I WAS IN the galley, finishing up a late breakfast of cold cereal when I heard someone call my name.

"Hello. Mr. Curtis Beecham?"

It came from topside, on the dock. I set my empty bowl in the sink, picked up my coffee cup, and climbed the stairs leading to the cockpit. I poked my head out the doorway and saw two men standing on the dock dressed in dark suits and ties, both of apparent Asian background. One was in his forties, average build, the other a little younger, with a shorter, wider physique. They seemed too old for missionaries, but I eyed them suspiciously. "Yeah."

The two men approached, holding up their open wallets to display their credentials. "I'm Supervisory Special Agent Lou Jengwi. This is Special Agent Skip Chouw," the older man said. "We're with the FBI."

FBI! Are you kidding me? I leaned across the port side and scrutinized their very official looking badges, then stepped back, shielding the morning glare with my hand. "What do you want?"

"We'd like to talk for a minute. May we come aboard?"

I didn't know quite what to say. "Ah, well, yeah. Watch your step."

The two agents eyed the high railing, then turned and walked toward the gangway.

I watched them with reservation. "Down here." I pointed at the steep steps that led down into the salon where a wrap-around settee surrounded a small dining table.

I nodded for them to sit and watched as they slid in, facing me. Their dour faces stared back.

The agent who identified himself as Lou Jengwi, glanced around the cluttered salon. "Nice boat."

"Thanks," I replied, knowing he didn't mean it. A lot of comments had been tossed around concerning my boat, *nice* wasn't one of them.

He continued, "Let me come straight to the point. We understand you're writing a book. A book about Chinese immigrants coming to the States, raising families."

I stared at him, shock registering on my face. *He knows about my book? How'd they know about my book?* I immediately felt uneasy.

"We'd like to know where your information to write this book came from. Who are you talking to in the Chinese community? And, we'd like to see a copy of the manuscript."

"How'd you know about my book?" I asked, my anxiety growing.

"We have sources." He kept a straight face. "Which we can't reveal, of course. I'm sure you understand."

Sources? Shit! What sources? My mind raced. Only a very few people knew about my book project and all of them were involved in it in some way. None of them would have talked. Certainly there would be no reason to talk to the FBI.

I glanced from one to the other, feeling their glare. "Why

are you so interested in my book? It's just a story I made up. It's fiction." My voiced cracked a little. I lifted my hand and adjusted my ball cap. I had a sense of preservation that told me I shouldn't say any more than I had to. In fact, I wasn't sure I had to tell them anything. They'd need a warrant, wouldn't they?

"We know your book's not based on fiction, but on actual activity in the Chinese community. We know you're working with someone. Someone's helping you, feeding you information."

My mind continued to put the pieces together. *Shit. How'd they know this? Do they know about George?*

The agent continued. "We believe there's a connection between your story and a more sensitive issue. We need to follow up on it. We have investigations ongoing, and we need to know everything you know. You've talked to someone, and you know something. We want to know who it is and what you know."

"What do you mean a connection between my story and a more sensitive issue?" I asked. "What are you referring to?"

"I'm not at liberty to say. Bureau business."

My book is Bureau business? What's this connection to a sensitive issue thing? My mind was spinning with questions. It was apparent these guys weren't giving answers.

The agent's eyes shot past the galley behind me to the front stateroom where my computer sat on a table. "That where you do your writing?" He rose and stepped away from the table, staring down the short corridor.

"It's my private office." I scooted to the edge of the bench seat. "I thought you just wanted to talk?"

He sat back down and folded his hands on the table. "We need to look into everything and anything that comes to our attention during an investigation. Your name came up. Your book came up. We need to gather any-and-all information into our case files. Significant or not. Government bureaucracy at its best, you know." He smiled a weak smile in a feeble attempt to put me at ease.

The heavier agent flashed a sly grin and quipped, "We get paid by how much paperwork we generate."

I didn't think it was amusing. I remained silent.

"Mr. Beecham. We know you didn't come up with this idea by yourself," the older agent said. He stared as if checking out every feature of my Anglo face. "*You* certainly wouldn't have any first-hand knowledge. We know you have a source. Who is it? A friend? A Chinese girlfriend maybe?"

A bout of annoyance began to set in. The salon was normally stuffy, but with two unwanted visitors sitting across from me sucking the air out of the room it was getting uncomfortable. Worse, that distinct odor that follows in the wake of a smoker began to irritate me.

"Look, no one's in trouble here." The heavier agent forced that phony smile again. "We just need to talk to them. You haven't broken any laws. At least not yet." He paused, waiting for my reaction, then leaned in closer. "Ever heard of aiding and abetting, investigative interference, or withholding evidence?"

I squirmed. The bench seat seemed hard and suddenly uncomfortable. *Why is this book so important to them? Hadn't they heard of freedom of the press? It's fiction, even if it's based on a true story. Even so, it's not an illegal activity. They're fishing, and I'm not taking the bait.*

The older guy spoke with an added edge to his voice. "We need to know who your contacts are. These people may be dangerous, or in danger themselves. You don't know what you're getting into." Looking around the salon, he continued, "You're a sailor, you should recognize when you're in deep water. You're in over your head."

I looked down, breaking eye contact and fiddled with my

coffee cup. *These guys are threatening me? Damn. The FBI is now threatening me. This is the second time the phrase "dangerous information" has surfaced. What's so important about this book? There's gotta be more to it.* I looked up hoping these guys would give up and go away. I figured if they had a search warrant they'd have already played it.

"Think about what we've said, Mr. Beecham. Call us when you decide to talk. We'll find out one way or another, but it'd be better if the information came from you." The two agents stood up and the older one dropped a business card onto the table. "I don't suppose you'd like to share a copy of your manuscript?"

I shook my head.

"Call us. Remember, I've got the life preserver. We're on your side. There are those who aren't. When they find you, their message won't be very subtle."

They stood and found their way out. I followed and watched them climb the steps, walk to the back of the boat, step across the gangway and head up the dock. I went back inside, picked up the business card from the table, studied it a moment, then tossed it next to the keyboard and sat down on my bed, my stomach churning. I looked over at my computer sitting on the small table. It seemed to have eyes. It stared back. *This is getting a little too serious. The damn FBI! Shit! I gotta find out what has everybody spooked about my book. What is it that George knows and I don't?*

For the time being, I knew I wouldn't be productive. I needed to relieve some tension. Emerge from my stuffy cabin and fill my lungs with fresh air. I decided to break out the kayak. Circle the lake and the finger piers that embraced the houseboat community and chase down a few mallards. I enjoyed watching them scatter like leaves blowing in the wind, a little revenge for the droppings they frequently left on my deck. My kayak was my gym. It worked me hard, helped me clear my head and relieve my stress. I had the only kayak in Seattle with an outrigger. It forced double takes and smiles from passing cruisers. I needed a few smiles.

* * *

AS AGENT CHOUW drove back to the office, Jengwi sat in the passenger seat, reflecting on their brief conversation with Curtis. "He knows more than he's telling us," Jengwi said. "I'm not having any upstart son-of-a-bitch writer meddling in my investigation."

"Yeah, he's involved. I could see it in his face."

"We've got to get his contact." Stopped at a red light, Jengwi turned, looked out the window and watched as a wild-eyed member of Seattle's homeless community attempted to repack his already overloaded grocery cart. "Check his phone records. He might not have a landline. But we know he has a cell phone. And for the time being, put a tail on him."

Jengwi pushed in the cigarette lighter on the dashboard while retrieving a pack of cigarettes from his pocket. "He knows something and he's not gonna talk without a little persuasion."

Chouw glanced at Jengwi.

"This guy's not a pro," Jengwi continued. "He's a fucking writer. We should be able to open him up like a can of sardines. He needs to be convinced it's best for his own health and welfare to be more forthcoming."

Jengwi held the red-hot coil to the tip of his cigarette and took a few quick puffs. "And I know just how to do it."

CHAPTER SIXTEEN

UNCLE WILLIE ARRIVED at the indoor practice facility as the downpour continued to puddle in the parking lot. He pulled his coat tight and held a firm grip on his fedora, shielding his face against the driving rain as he quickened his pace along the walkway. After passing through the aluminum entrance door, he stood off to the side to observe a handful of ball players as they participated in infield drills while others took turns in the batting cage. The ting of aluminum bats against baseballs echoed in the cavernous facility as ground balls were scooped up, released and found the deep pocket of a teammate's glove with a loud slap.

Thirty-five minutes later a shrill whistle sounded and players began to jog off the field toward the dugout. Uncle Willie waved his arm and caught the attention of Thomas who altered course and headed in his direction.

"Your glove looked sharp out there today, Thomas."

"Thanks," Thomas grinned. "But I missed one. Did you see it? Bad hop. I should've blocked it with my body."

"Good practice, Thomas." A man in a ball cap and a gray jogging suit hollered as he passed.

Thomas turned. "Thanks, Coach."

"Tomorrow. Three o'clock."

"I'll be here," Thomas hollered back.

Thomas turned back to Uncle Willie. "So, Uncle Willie. Have you talked to George?"

"No. I plan on dropping by Saturday morning. He won't have classes. I can catch him then."

"I'm a little worried about him," Thomas said. "Like I told you on the phone, we don't see each other much anymore with our schedules as they are, but he seemed a little depressed the last time we talked. And he's drinking too much. Even for a college kid. Know what I mean."

"Yes. That is not good."

"Hey, Thomas," a teammate hollered from a crowd of young men. "Your ride's leaving."

"Be right there," Thomas yelled back.

"Hey, Uncle Willie. I gotta run. Got some papers due tomorrow. It'll be a late one." Thomas smiled as he back-peddled then turned and jogged off.

"I'll call you later," Uncle Willie hollered after him. He waved and smiled as Thomas joined his teammates. Uncle Willie smiled outwardly, but inside he felt a concern building for George and a bit of anxiety about Saturday morning.

He felt a responsibility for George, having watched him grow from a newborn into a promising young man. George Hu was family and Uncle Willie felt himself the most suitable person to make an evaluation. Wung Hu's sons were just two of the young men among many in the Sons of the Red Dragon program, but two he was especially fond of.

* * *

UNCLE WILLIE KNOCKED and waited for over five minutes. When George opened the door, Uncle Willie's eyes fell upon a young man in disarray. George's hair, which had always stood straight up, was greasy, matted. His eyes were puffy, red and barely open. His pajamas, wrinkled, stained and buttoned in the wrong holes, fell over bare feet.

An invisible cloud rushed out of the house, stale air infused with the stench of dirty laundry, body odor and bad breath. Uncle Willie clenched his jaw and without a word pushed past. He glanced around the filthy apartment, turned back to George and shook his head. Disheartened, he walked to the couch, cleared off a section, took a seat and unbuttoned his black trench coat in concession to the warmth within the room.

"George," Uncle Willie began. "I am saddened to see you like this. You have always been a young man of great promise. A man with tremendous intelligence and self-respect. There must be some reason you have allowed yourself to come to this. Tell me what is troubling you. Is it school? A romance gone bad?"

George hung his head and stared at his feet, shifting with discomfort, but remained silent.

"I am worried about you. If your father saw you like this he would be very upset. He has tried to give you everything, to help you in every way. What has gone wrong? How can I help?"

George did not look at Uncle Willie. He rubbed his fingers through his hair then walked over to the kitchen table and sat down, resting his head on his arms. He did not respond.

Uncle Willie rose and crossed over to the table. He stood next to George, put his hand on his shoulder and gave him a pat. He then cleared the trash—empty fast food containers and magazines from the table and the wood chair across from George—and sat down. He leaned in close to the young man, searching for answers.

George raised his head, blinked and wiped moisture from his eyes. "I know I've disappointed you and Father. I've disgraced my family's name. I've wronged you. I'm so sorry. I've been under so much pressure from everyone. My mind is spinning. I feel like I'm bouncing on a roulette wheel, and I don't know if I'll land on the Dragon or the Eagle. Which way do I go? I hear many voices, but I don't know which one to follow. I know I cannot fail either."

Uncle Willie listened with compassion. He understood the young man's torment. It was a reaction not unheard of from young men of immigrant families, those who struggled with the difficulties brought about by a divided household. A home that by its very nature created divided allegiances and sent conflicting messages—a division between immigrant and native born. A crack in the Sons of the Red Dragon program that many fell into. Uncle Willie had seen it before.

"You do not have to choose between your ancestral home and the home of your birth. You must be true to your heart. By doing so, you do not fail your father or yourself. You know much of your father's homeland. You know much of the country you have been raised in. You cannot be expected to choose between them." Uncle Willie reached out and laid a hand on George's arm.

"They both have a place in your heart. Embrace your heritage. Embrace your homeland. You are an American. But it is good you love the land of your father as well. At the very least we expect you to love and respect your ancestral home, keep it in your heart and share it with the people of America."

George looked up. Uncle Willie saw pain on his face.

"Uncle Willie. You've been very good to my family. You've trusted me. We've shared many things." George paused and he dropped his eyes. "But I've betrayed you."

Concern burrowed deeply into Uncle Willie's brow.

George continued. "I've been drinking too much." He hesitated as if the words had trouble passing his lips. "And I've been talking too much. I've told a friend all about the Program. About father. I needed to talk to someone. I needed to share my guilt, release my anguish. I know it was selfish. I thought it would lighten my heart, but it didn't. It made my heart heavier.

I beg your forgiveness."

Uncle Willie stiffened. He blinked his eyes and stared at George. The words had cut through him like a sword from an ancient warrior. George had talked. George Hu was the loose goose. The cause for all the anxiety MSS had expressed over the writing of this book had originated right here, in this very room. From one he thought of as a son. This was not what he had expected to hear or what he wished to know. He spoke, an edge to his voice, his compassion waning, his agitation increasing. "You told this friend about the Program! You told him everything?"

"I think so. I'd been drinking...depressed. I don't remember all I said...but I...I think so."

Uncle Willie reached out and gripped the sides of the table, his knuckles turned white, his temperature rose. He stared at George, his eyes burning. George hung his head. The silence of the room replaced by tension.

"Who is this friend?"

"A friend from high school."

"I want his name."

"Su Wan Cho."

Uncle Willie took a moment to put his emotions in check. He pulled a handkerchief from the pocket of his overcoat and wiped his face then cleared his dry throat. "George, look at me." George lifted his head. "You must not tell anyone of this. Do you understand me? This is important."

"Yes." George's eyes watered. "I'm ashamed. I won't speak of this with anyone ever again."

"Su Wan Cho is his name?"

"Yes."

"That is a Korean name."

"Yes, he's Korean-American."

Uncle Willie thought for a moment. *No wonder we could not find him. He is Korean, not Chinese. The contact feeding the Anglo writer is not from the Chinese community.*

"I want you to forget we ever talked of this. Do you understand?"

George nodded.

Uncle Willie swept his arm around the room. "Clean up this mess. Get your life back on track. I know you and your family too well, George. You have strong values from your father. Now that you have removed this burden from your heart, it is time to begin the healing process. I will come to see you again. If you need to talk, you do so with me. Do not discuss this with anyone else."

Uncle Willie thought for a minute while he studied George, hoping to see a burden lifted, a stronger resolve. He pushed his chair back, raised himself up as he leaned over the table, his hands holding a loose grip on the edge. In a soft voice he said, "Remember, say nothing to anyone. No one."

Again, George nodded.

Uncle Willie straightened up. "I will see you in a few days. Your father does not need to know that I have come to visit. You have fallen into a dark hole. Only you can pull yourself out. You have made a mistake. You are shamed. Now, you must do something to help yourself."

Uncle Willie crossed the room, opened the door, took one last look at George, then shook his head. He pulled the door closed, descended the steps and buttoned his coat. He stuffed his hands in his pockets and stared down at the cracked sidewalk as he strolled to his car, his mind racing through the impact and potential consequences of this meeting with George.

He now knew George Hu was the loose goose. He had talked to the Korean-American, Su Wan Cho, the writer's contact. Now Uncle Willie had to decide what to do with this information. The game had changed. He had to decide how he wanted to play it. How would this new twist affect his exit strategy?

* * *

I RECEIVED A notice from the marina office advising boat owners that beginning the first of the year they'd be charging a fee to park in the lot adjacent to our moorage. I had two vehicles. My Jeep Cherokee—my everyday car—and a 1937 Ford woodie wagon. The woodie had been my dad's. He'd had it as long as I can remember then gave it to me a few years ago, after mom died. Said he wouldn't be driving it anymore. I knew he had a lot of memories tucked behind those wood panels. So did I. I've cherished it. Though, like my boat, it needed some major work.

I drove it to my dad's house. He had a stand-alone garage in back. Had no car, so it wasn't in use. I'd hoped to keep the woodie there for the time being. Save me the cost of paying to park two vehicles.

I rumbled up a driveway that consisted of two cracked concrete pads surrounding a patch of overgrown weeds that ran beside his house, parked, walked up to the door and knocked.

"Yeah. Who's there?"

"It's me. Curtis."

After a moment the door opened.

"Hey, Pops."

"Whatda ya want?"

"I need a favor."

He stared with a blank look.

I pointed off to my right. "I need a place to store the woodie. They're gonna charge me to park it down at the marina. I know you're not using the garage anymore, so I thought..."

Dad stepped out onto the porch and glanced to his left. A slow smile crept across his face. "You still got her? Thought you'd sell her."

116

I loved the woodie. I knew the old classic meant a lot to my dad, was part of my family history, memories, and therefore was important to me. "Are you kidding? I only wish I could afford to fix her up."

Dad's smile faded. "What's that damn thing on top?"

"A surfboard."

"What in hell's that for?"

"For looks. You know. Every woodie needs a surfboard."

Dad turned to face me. "That's a family car. Not some hippy love wagon."

"Has nothing to do with hippies, Dad. It's for style."

"Style my ass. I shoulda known you'd find a way to mess it up."

I sighed. "I never imagined you'd take offense, Dad. I love the woodie and I cherish those fond memories I have when I was a kid and we went riding up to Snoqualmie Falls. And Mount Rainier. Remember that. We'd always stop for ice cream. You wouldn't let me eat it in the car. I never understood. Now, of course, I do."

A slight grin returned to my dad's face. "You know I rebuilt all that wood paneling. Your mother had a fit. Thought I spent too much time and money."

"You did a beautiful job, Dad. The wood has held up better than the metal body. I sure hope I can restore her someday."

Dad shook his head and mumbled under his breath, "A lot of work. A damn lot of work."

I gave him a moment before bringing up the garage again. "Dad. About storing the woodie in the garage. Are you okay with it?"

He hesitated. Looked again toward the woodie, nodded his head and turned back toward the door. "Garage is open."

CHAPTER SEVENTEEN

THE TWO SHADOWY figures would not be noticed at this late hour in the dark calm surrounding Lake Union. Dressed in black, their faces smudged with black powder, their hands covered by thin black gloves, they moved down the pier. Their soft-soled shoes cushioned their steps against the thick wood planks as they scurried with purpose, yet extreme caution.

The aged boat creaked as it rocked in the gentle swell and strained against the taut ropes that tethered it to the pylons. They crossed the gangplank, then crept across the deck and knelt down by the locked wood entry door. Within minutes the first figure had disengaged the locking mechanism and crept down the stairway. The second figure handed a black duffle bag down to his outstretched arms, careful not to hit the walls of the narrow passageway.

They did not talk, but communicated with simple hand signals. They entered the salon and went straight to the forward stateroom, searching with flashlights, looking for a computer, disks or flash drives. They found none. They returned to the salon. Directing the beam of a small flashlight, the first figure located the distinct pattern of a panel door flush against the floor. He knelt down and pulled on a brass ring that lifted it, exposing the mechanics that powered the vessel. The second figure began to empty the contents of the bag on the scuffed flooring. Within a few short minutes they had attached thin wires to a black box with a small dial on top. A low clicking sound broke the silence as they set the timer for twenty minutes.

The two figures gathered the duffle bag and the few hand tools, then ascended the stairway. Surveying the surrounding area, they observed no person or moving vehicles in the vicinity. They closed the wood hatch, re-crossed the deck and the gangplank, headed up the pier and disappeared into the night.

* * *

THE 911 CALL came in at 3:17 A.M. The caller reported a boat fire on Lake Union, off Westlake Avenue, a small marina next to the Aurora Bridge. Fire department vehicles responded and arrived on the scene within minutes, although too late to save the burning vessel. The marine fire patrol was contacted but would need time to maneuver through the ship canal that connected Elliott Bay with Lake Union.

The force of the small explosion obliterated whatever had not burned. All that remained were small, unidentified pieces of charred wood that floated in the dark water and a burning oil patch that would soon drift under the dock. The dock was blackened where it had been touched by flames and a gaping hole appeared where the boat had been tied up. There was little smoke but a strong scent of fuel and burned debris lingered in the air.

The red lights of the emergency vehicles flashed across the neighboring boathouses and reflected on the calm lake surface as firemen sprayed foam on the burning oil. There wasn't much to be done. The oil slick was small. Apparently there hadn't been much fuel in the tanks, and most of it was incinerated when flames ignited it. Fortunately, there was no other boat moored in close proximity to the ill-fated vessel.

Crews would soon begin the clean-up process and divers would be sent down into the dark depths to search for any human remains.

Lieutenant Sam Watkins of the Seattle Police Department stepped out of his white sedan and scanned the area. Emergency crews were still cleaning up. Red spinning lights created a sense of urgency, although it was apparent, the emergency was over. There wasn't much to see. The few neighbors, awakened in the middle of the night by the sound of the explosion and the subsequent sirens, had dispersed to the warmth of their own beds.

Watkins walked down the dock and approached the firefighter. "What can you tell me?"

The fireman glanced at Watkins then looked down to the wallet the lieutenant had flipped open, exposing his police investigators badge.

"What you see is what's left of a boat. A fire. An explosion. It went quick. Apparently an old wood structure. We've got a team on the way so we can begin our investigation. Guy over there," the fireman turned and pointed to an older man standing two docks over, "said he heard a roaring, crackling sound and got up to investigate. He saw a glow and within seconds saw and heard an explosion. Blew shit everywhere. Wasn't much left after that. He can probably help you."

"Anybody on board?"

"Not sure. Haven't found any bodies or signs of human remains. The old guy said a young man, about thirty, lived here alone. Name of Curtis, so he says. Didn't know if he was here last night or not. Didn't see him or anybody else around the boat after the explosion."

"Arson? Accident? Got a theory?"

"Not yet. But it did burn quick. And, if nobody was on board?" He shrugged. "I'll keep an open mind. It's not my call. We'll see what our guys say."

"Okay, thanks. I'll talk to the witness."

Watkins crossed over to the second pier and walked up to the older man standing beside a creaky houseboat, wearing pajamas and a thick plaid robe. "Lieutenant Sam Watkins, Seattle Police. You live here?"

"Yes. I'm Walter Philstrom. Lived here for twelve years now. Never saw anything like it. It's our worst nightmare, you know. Fire on a boat. Worse thing that can happen to a man."

"Do you know if anybody was on the boat at the time?"

"Nope. Like I told that gentleman over there," he pointed to the fireman, "a young fellow name of Curtis lived there, but don't know if he was here last night or not. He comes and goes a lot. He's a writer." He looked down at the pier and shook his head.

"How 'bout a car?" Lieutenant Watkins took a quick glance around the gravel parking area near the docks. "What kind of vehicle does this Curtis drive?"

"Oh, yeah. He has an old station wagon of some kind. Has that wood paneling on it, you know. From the old days. He kept a surfboard on the roof. Imagine that. A surfboard. Don't know what he'd use that thing for around here." Walter looked around behind him. "Nope. Don't see it. He usually parks it over there." Walter pointed to an area at the end of the parking lot. "Told me he doesn't drive it all the time though."

"Does he have another car?"

"Couldn't say. Never noticed. But that old station wagon of his. You can't help but notice that one."

"I'll need you to come to the station later this morning and make a formal statement. Can you do that? Just need you to tell us everything you saw or heard tonight. Anything about this Curtis guy and anything else you think might be helpful."

"Do you think this is, well, like a crime? Somebody do this on purpose?"

"It's all part of the investigation. I gotta make my boss

happy. Dot the eyes and cross the tees. Now before I go, I do need to get this guy Curtis's last name. And could you give me an address. What would it be? A pier number, a slip number?"

"Sure. Let me get something from below. He gave me a card that had his name on it and I can figure out his slip number by counting, starting with mine. Let me jot it down. I'll be right back."

* * *

THE PHONE RANG six times in the parlor of the red-brick Tudor on top of Queen Anne hill, nestled between Lake Union and downtown Seattle. Shelly Beecham had just returned home after a long day at her office. "Hello," she answered out of breath.

"Is this Ms. Shelly Beecham?"

"Yes, it is."

"This is Lieutenant Sam Watkins with the Seattle Police Department."

Shelly interrupted, "I'm sorry. I don't respond to fund raising solicitations on the phone, but if you want to send—"

"No, Ms. Beecham, you misunderstood. I'm investigating a fire. A boat on Lake Union burned last night. It was registered to a Mr. Curtis Beecham."

Shelly gasped, placing her hand on her chest as she caught her breath. "Oh, my God! Is he all right? Where is he? Is he okay?"

"Sorry I have to break it to you like this. We don't know where he is. We don't know if he was on the boat last night or not. We haven't found a body. But we haven't located him either. That's why I'm calling. Do you know where he is or where he might be?"

"No. I don't. Oh, my God! He might be dead?" she cried out. Her eyes moistened and she leaned over the kitchen table, placing her hand on it for support.

"We don't know that, Ms. Beecham. Again, I'm sorry to

have to tell you this. But I have a few questions. You *are* divorced?" Watkins asked.

"Yes."

"Do you see Mr. Beecham often?"

"Yes. We have two children. He's close to them. Sees them a lot."

"Have you seen him in the past twenty-four hours?"

Shelly pulled out a dining chair and sat down, resting her hand against her forehead. "No."

"How about girlfriends? Does he have a woman he sees? Maybe stays overnight at her place?"

"No. Not that he ever mentioned. Then again, he probably wouldn't say anything to me about that. But the kids never mentioned it, so I don't believe he does."

"Okay. How about anyplace else he might be? Someplace he might have gone that would require an overnight?"

Shelly thought for a minute. "Yes. The cabin. He sometimes goes to his cabin to get away, get out of the rain, do some writing."

"Where's that?"

"Eastern Washington. Lake Chelan. It was his parent's cabin. His Mom died a few years ago and his dad stopped using it. Gave it to him."

"Yeah. I've been to Lake Chelan. It's a big lake. Do you know where exactly?"

"No. I've been there but I don't know how to tell you where it is. I don't have an address, but I do have a phone number. He sometimes calls the kids from there."

"That's good. I can start with that."

Shelly retrieved the phone number from her directory in the desk drawer and gave it to Detective Watkins, then asked, "Should I call him to see if he's there?"

"No. I'll be calling that number as soon as we hang up. Thank you, Ms. Beecham. I'll be in contact. I'll let you know if we find out anything."

Shelly hung up the phone and stared out the window, holding back tears. She and Curtis were divorced, but there wasn't any hatred between them. It wasn't another woman on his part or another man on hers. She just couldn't live with him.

He had never focused enough on his career. Got distracted, liked to play too much. His life was too disorganized, and he was perfectly content living on a run-down leaky old boat. A bit of a dreamer, he saw himself living the good life on some fancy yacht, moored in a secluded bay of some tropical island in the Caribbean. He preferred to ignore reality, and the fact he lived smack dab in the middle of the cold, wet northwest. For a divorced couple, they got along well. The hot embers of an earlier love hadn't completely burned out. And she knew he loved the kids. So if something had happened to Curtis, she and the kids would be devastated.

CHAPTER EIGHTEEN

Lake Chelan, Eastern Washington

I GRABBED THE phone on the umpteenth ring, having retrieved it from under a stack of papers and magazines piled on the small table. I dashed in from the back deck where I'd been working on my laptop. For the past few days I'd been writing in the peace and tranquility of my lakeside escape. Without cell phone reception on this side of the mountains, my communication with the rest of the world required a landline.

"Hello," I said lifting the phone.

"Mr. Curtis Beecham?"

"Yes."

"Mr. Beecham. I'm glad I've located you. This is Lieutenant Sam Watkins with the Seattle Police Department."

"Yes." I hesitated. "How can I help you?"

"Well, Mr. Beecham. I'm sorry to have to tell you this. I'm investigating a fire. Your boat moored on Lake Union caught fire early this morning. It's a complete loss. There was an explosion. It was completely destroyed."

The words hit me like rapid punches from a heavyweight champion. I stood stunned, unable to believe what I was hearing. It took a second to sink in. "What are you saying? My boat caught fire? It was destroyed?" My knees buckled and I slumped down onto the couch. "No! Don't tell me this!" I grimaced, closed my eyes tight, and gritted my teeth, distorting my face as physical pain raked my body. "My boat caught fire?" I repeated with disbelief. "When did this happen?" I still couldn't accept the words I heard. "It's gone? The *Mockaritaville*'s gone?"

I rocked back and forth, pressing my head against my knees. A pain shot up from my chest and my temples throbbed.

"Early this morning. Your neighbor, the old fella, let's see, yes, Walter Philstrom. He called it in to nine-one-one around three this morning. It burned quick. There was an explosion. We don't know what caused it but we're investigating."

I heard the detective's voice, but his sentences were a mumbled blur of noise, until the last word broke through my numbed state. "Investigating? Is there some reason to investigate?"

"Normal procedure. There's a fire. Loss of property. We thought you might have been on board. You're lucky you weren't. Could have had a loss of life."

Lieutenant Watkins continued, "I know this has come as a shock, but I need to talk to you in person. How soon can you be back in Seattle?"

He rambled on, but I concentrated on a tiny fragment that wrapped itself around my throat, putting me in a choke hold. *Loss of life? That's my life he's talking about. Holy shit! I could have been there! Asleep.* My mind raced. I tried to calm down and think rational. Take one step at a time. *There must be an explanation. An electrical fire maybe. It was an old boat. A wire might have gone bad or something. Surely that would explain it. Don't get too excited. Calm down. But Jesus, how can I, my boat's...gone!*

"Mr. Beecham, how soon can you be back in Seattle?" he repeated, breaking through my consciousness.

"Ah, umm, I...I'll get there as soon as I can."

"Call me. Downtown precinct. Here's the number."

I grabbed a pencil and note pad from the table and jotted down the details.

The Lieutenant continued. "I need to talk to you further, get your statement."

"Ahh. Sure. Okay."

"And, Mr. Beecham."

"Yeah."

"Glad you're okay. And from what I gather, your ex-wife and kids will be very relieved to hear this too. I just talked to her. Give her a call. I think she'd appreciate it."

I walked outside and collapsed into a deck chair, my mind filled with flashes of *Mockaritaville*. She was more than a boat. She was my home. My lifestyle. My sanctuary from the cold, the wet, and the dreary. My retreat from the insanity and craziness of life in a busy congested city. I couldn't replace her. I had no insurance.

I stared at the lake. A lake view always had a calming effect. I needed to be calm. I needed to think. I needed to grieve a loss.

* * *

SHAKEN BY THE burning and sinking of the *Mockaritaville*, I had been hanging around the cabin, depressed, trying to come to grips with the tragedy. I needed time to think before I headed back over the Cascades to Seattle. I didn't know if my manuscript had anything to do with the loss of my home, but it preyed on my mind. Until I had information to the contrary from the Fire Marshall's investigation, I'd remain concerned. I decided to give Jack Buick a call.

Jack picked up on the first ring.

"Mr. Buick. This is Curtis Beecham."

"Curtis. I've tried to get hold of you. Left messages on your cell."

"Oh, yeah. I'm in Eastern Washington at my cabin. I don't get reception over here. I have to use my landline."

"You staying dry?" Jack chuckled.

"Well, yeah, I am. But my boat's not. In fact, what's left of her is sittin' on the bottom of Lake Union."

"What do you mean?" Jack asked, his voice filled with alarm. "She sank?"

"She burned, exploded. Went right to the bottom."

"My God. You weren't on it were you?"

"No, luckily I was here at the cabin. Came to do some writing. Get away for a while. So I do have my computer and all my work."

"Holy shit! It exploded? What was it? A gas leak or something?"

"It could have been, or maybe bad wiring. I really don't know yet. She was an old boat. The police are investigating. Should know in a week."

I hesitated for a minute, but knew I had to mention the FBI visit to Jack. I wanted to get his reaction and advice. "On the other hand, Mr. Buick, I did get a visit and an implied threat from the FBI a couple of days before the explosion."

"Shit!" I heard Jack choke and the sound of liquid spewing. "The FBI! What in hell'd the FBI want to see you for?"

"That's kinda why I'm calling. They came to talk to me about my book. They knew all about it. Said it could endanger ongoing investigations and put people at risk. Their people. And *me*. And that's what has me concerned. If the Seattle Fire Marshall's investigation determines my boat was arson, I'll know someone's really serious about silencing me."

"That's impossible," Jack said. "How did the FBI find out about the book? No one knows about it but you, me and a few here at the office. And your contact. How the hell'd they know? And how'd they find out about you?"

"No idea. They just showed up at my boat and started asking questions."

"You sure they were FBI?"

"Their credentials looked authentic, I guess. I'd never seen FBI credentials before, but they looked genuine. Two Asian guys in suits. They wanted to know who my contact was and wanted a copy of the manuscript. I didn't tell them anything. And I didn't give them my manuscript. They had no warrant. They left me their card so I could call them if I changed my mind."

"Damn!" Jack responded.

"I know. I don't like it either."

"No. Not that. I had a visit from two Asian guys in suits too. That's why I tried to call you."

I sat up on the couch. My pulse quickened. "What!"

"Yeah. About a week ago. Said they were from some kind of Chinese thing. Here, wait a minute, I wrote it down." I could hear Jack fumbling through the drawer of his desk. "Here it is. The Chinese American Trade & Cultural Exchange Commission, whatever the hell that is. I went on the Internet to find out more about them, but I couldn't find anything. They didn't leave business cards either."

"That's too strange. What'd they want?"

"They'd heard about the book. Damn if I know how. That's the bizarre part. Anyway, they said they were interested in helping, from a cultural standpoint, whatever that means. Said there were people who may not be happy to see this book published. Sure as hell sounded like a threat. They pissed me off. I threw them out on their ear."

I could certainly imagine Jack doing just that. "Shit, Jack. Ah, sorry, Mr. Buick. But, damn. That's outrageous. What's going on?"

"Like I said, they didn't leave a business card, and I couldn't find anything on the Internet, so I just don't know."

"Were they FBI?"

"I don't think so. They would have said so instead of using that fake Chinese cultural thing."

"Think they were serious?" As I allowed the words to escape my lips, I realized how naive that sounded. Someone might have blown up my boat. *That's* serious.

"Well, maybe I do. Let's wait until you get word from the fire department investigation. See what they say."

"Yeah, I will. But, let me ask you something. Has anything like this happened to you before? Can the FBI threaten me like that? Don't I have the right to write a book? You know, freedom of the press and all that."

"Yes, Curtis, you do have the right. Can the FBI threaten you in some way? Well, not legally, unless you've done something wrong, and you haven't. Can they make you uncomfortable in order to get what they want? Yes. Sometimes they see it as the end justifying the means. They play on a playground with dirty guys, and sometimes I'm sure they get a little dirty too. That's just my opinion. I'm no lawyer, but I think we have to watch our backs."

"Yeah, you're probably right. I'm gonna head back to Seattle in a few days. I'll contact you as soon as I hear the results on the investigation. I'm not sure where I'll be staying, but I'll let you know."

I hung up, my mind swirling. This was making me feel real uneasy. And I wasn't sure what my next step should be. I only knew, I'd have to be more careful.

CHAPTER NINETEEN

Seattle, Washington

A FEW DAYS later, after accepting the hard fact that my home and my life as I knew it were gone, I drove back to Seattle in my Jeep Cherokee. The thought of what happened to my boat scared the hell out of me. Did somebody blow it up? Was it a warning? If so, who was responsible? Did they know I wasn't home or did they think I was? Either way, I could be in great danger.

I needed to know what happened. Was I becoming paranoid? I didn't know. But I was going to be cautious from here on out. I wouldn't be taking chances.

I checked into a low-budget motel on Aurora Avenue, about a quarter-mile north of the bridge. Also known as U.S. Highway 99, it was the principle four-lane route on the Pacific coast before they built the Interstate Highway System. It stretched from Canada to Mexico, connecting thousands of small towns from Washington to California. Typical of these thoroughfares, it was lined end to end with cheap motels, fast-food restaurants, liquor stores, taverns, and tacky strip malls.

It was a good place to hide, with a constant parade of traffic passing north and south, continuing through most of the night. Some of it rumbled by on four wheels and some of it strutted by on six-inch heels, a short miniskirt and long legs in black fishnet stockings.

My obscure hideaway, with the distinct regional name of the Pink Salmon Motel, smelled a lot like its namesake. Though tackier than my deceased boat, it would do for the short term. I checked in using an alias, and surprised the clerk by paying cash for three days. Most guests paid by the hour.

Under these circumstances, I decided to put my freelance writing business on hold, even though I had access to my computer. But it hardly mattered. Over the past few months as I worked on the manuscript in earnest, I had pretty much ignored that part of my working life, depending on a modest inheritance I had received from my mother to support my humble lifestyle. Money wouldn't be an issue for a while, considering the favorable rate accorded by the Pink Salmon.

I pulled out my cell phone and began to dial Su Wan Cho, but quickly closed it. I sat on the stained bedspread, and thought for a minute. I needed to keep out of sight. I figured it might be better if I didn't use my cell phone, or the phone in the room. I grabbed my keys and drove north on Aurora Avenue.

I found a diner about two miles away with a pay phone in the back hallway by the men's room. Dark and dingy, it provided the perfect spot for a discreet conversation. Smoking had been prohibited in eating and drinking establishments for a few years now, but the stale smell of old tobacco still permeated the place. I gave Su Wan a ring.

"Su Wan. This is Curtis. Got a minute?"

"Sure. Just on the computer. What's up?"

I filled Su Wan in on the events of the past few days.

"I can't believe this," Su Wan said. "If I couldn't tell by the tone of your voice, I'd say you were bullshitting me. But you're serious, aren't you?"

"Serious as hell. I wish I weren't. I'm not even using my

cell phone. I'm at a pay phone. I'm not taking any chances until I know more."

Su Wan spoke up. "Remember what George Hu said? This information could lead down a dangerous path. We blew it off, but there might be something to it."

"Well, let's not get too carried away quite yet. I need to know the results of the investigation before I go there. But it's on my mind. Meanwhile, I'm staying at a little motel on Aurora. I'll keep a low profile until I find out." I flipped open the coin return out of habit, but found it empty. "Hey, what about George? Maybe you should talk to him again. Feel him out. See if he's heard about any threats. Don't tell him anything though. Keep it close to the vest. See if he knows anything that might be helpful."

"Yeah, I suppose I can. I'm not sure he'll be willing to talk though. But...I'll get back to you. Hey, how do I do that? Get back to you I mean."

"I'll call in a day or two."

CHAPTER TWENTY

"CAUSE OF FIRE, arson."
The words cut through me with the precision of a fish carving knife. Stunned, I had tried to prepare myself for the worst, while my inner-self kept telling me things were not looking good. Too many incidents had occurred to be mere coincidence. As Lieutenant Sam Watkins read through the report I sat numb, slumped in the straight-back wood chair that faced the police investigator's desk.

Watkins removed his glasses and looked up, his expression sober, his demeanor stern. "Arson is a serious crime, Mr. Beecham." He studied me, his eyes reading my every twitch. I could see where he was going. In his mind I was as good a suspect as anyone.

He continued. "To lose a home is a tragedy, in any sense. To lose a home in an arson fire is more tragic still. Like suicide. A senseless loss. Know what I mean?"

Still in a state of shock, I could only nod.

"Sorry, but I gotta ask these questions." The Lieutenant grabbed his glasses once again, glanced at his report then looked up. "According to your statement you left for Lake Chelan early on Friday. Around nine in the morning. The fire broke out, or at least the nine-one-one call came in at three seventeen Monday morning. You were in Lake Chelan when the fire broke out. Correct?"

"Yes, sir."

"Can anybody verify your story? Anybody see you?"

"I picked up some groceries at a little market. I probably have a receipt back at the cabin. I don't know if anybody would remember me coming in, though. A lot of people come and go in that market."

"Okay. It would be good if you can produce that receipt. As I said, the fire started with a rapid spreading igniter, and there was a blast of some magnitude from an incendiary device. We found fragments of material that wouldn't normally be found on your boat. The evidence points to this being a professional job. Someone who knew what they were doing. They wanted total destruction. At this point I don't know if you were the target, or just your boat."

Lieutenant Watkins leaned back in his chair and stared at me while tapping a yellow pencil against the padded arm of his seat. About fifty years old, his eyes were clear and sharp with crow's feet making an appearance. Slightly balding, he wore a long-sleeve shirt rolled up at the sleeves and bright red suspenders held his pants over his paunch. As he continued the interview I remained on edge, my fears growing by the minute. My mind raced. *A professional job? Was I the target?*

"So, Mr. Beecham, I have two theories. My first theory is you hired someone to do your dirty work. You needed the insurance money. You were tired of the old nag and wanted to put her out of her misery. Probably costs a bundle to keep a classic old boat afloat, doesn't it? I would hate to think you'd do something like that, but you do have a very convenient alibi, being out of town, yet within a three-hour drive. I've been in this business long enough to know the Pope himself is not above suspicion. Get my drift?"

I sat up straight and despite my nervousness, responded with a firm voice. "I had no insurance. There was nothing to collect. I loved that boat. Anybody can tell you that. It was my home. I had dreams tied to her. Plans that…" I choked and swallowed hard. "Now, will never be fulfilled. I'm just sick about this." I paused to regain my composure. "I stand by my statement. I had nothing to do with it."

Lieutenant Watkins remained quiet a moment, stared, tapped his pencil. I sensed he was trying to see into my head. Use his intuition from years of interrogating suspects to determine if I was telling the truth. I had seen enough cop shows to know he was testing me.

"Okay," he finally said. "That brings me to my second theory. Someone has an issue with you. Got any enemies? Know anybody who might want to get even? Maybe something in your past? Somebody that might even want to kill you?"

I cleared my throat. Just the sound of that word unnerved me. I could hardly say anything of my suspicions when in fact I had no evidence. He'd never believe a crazy story about some Chinese guys not wanting me to publish a book? And the FBI? I still couldn't imagine they had anything to do with it, but who knew? Anything's possible and everyone's a suspect. Someone did blow the hell out of my boat. And they may have wanted to see me and my Hawaiian shirt and flip-flops scattered in small pieces around Lake Union in the process.

"No." I hesitated. "I don't think I have any enemies. I can't imagine anyone would do this."

"You gamble? Play the horses? Owe money to somebody?"

"No. Nothing like that."

"Well, here's my problem," Lieutenant Watkins continued as he stared at me. "People don't just blow up boats and try to kill someone without a reason. There has to be a motive. So if you tell me you had nothing to do with it, then who did? Somebody had to do it. And they had to have a reason."

Watkins looked down at his file and tapped it with the

back of his open hand. "You have no record, no serious debt, nothing that makes me believe you might be involved, but somebody has a grievance. It's best we find out, for your sake. The sooner the better."

I understood what the Lieutenant meant. I was determined I wouldn't make it easy for them to get a second chance.

He closed the file and leaned back. "Call me if you think of anything, or anyone, who might have had something to do with this. Where you staying?"

"A motel on Aurora." I decided not to disclose the name to the Lieutenant. After all, motels on Aurora had names that were hardly unique or memorable, much like the names used by their registered guests. "The, ah, the Sunset Motel," I blurted, coming up with a creation of my own. The Aurora motel scene was the definition of transiency. It wouldn't matter where I stayed for a few nights.

"We'll keep in touch. I'll let you know anything we uncover that I think you need to know. And Mr. Beecham, if my first theory is correct, don't leave town. And if my second theory is correct…be careful."

* * *

I HEADED TO the diner to call Jack Buick and Su Wan Cho with this latest news. As I drove down Aurora Avenue I felt a tightness in my chest. I thought it might be the seatbelt, but then realized my own apprehension was squeezing the air out of me. Somebody had tried to *kill* me. And they would probably try again. Who was it? Was it some Chinese cultural group or our own FBI?

What was it that George Hu hadn't divulged? On the surface what he had confided seemed harmless, hardly illegal. The facts surrounding this family immigration program did not justify murder. There was something else behind it.

I turned into the diner. I had to get to the bottom of this. I had to confront George Hu myself. A cold shiver shuddered through my body. A voice inside screamed, "Somebody tried to kill me." I thought once again of George's words of warning, "This leads down a dangerous path. Something you don't want to know anything about."

CHAPTER TWENTY-ONE

KI CHUNG LEFT Uncle Willie's house at 6:00 P.M. Her housekeeping duties completed, she hurried down the front steps to the waiting cab, slipped in and asked to be taken to Occidental Park on the corner of Occidental and South Main in Pioneer Square. Within twelve minutes she had paid her fare and swung the door shut on the bright green taxi. Let off near the middle of the block, she crossed the brick-paved commons to a bench beneath a small leafless oak.

As she waited, a curious squirrel approached, raised itself on its hind legs and gave a beggar's glare. A quick stomp of her shoe on the brick pavement sent it scurrying for safety as four sets of nails scratched against the bark of the tree and the pest disappeared. She checked her watch. 6:15. She was early. Deng Qin would be here at 6:30. She scanned the park, watching. Three derelicts huddled against the façade of a brick building sharing the neck of a bottle exposed from a brown paper bag. She frowned as she recognized the source of the stench of urine that lingered about the park.

A middle-age couple traversed the brick plaza with a brisk step, holding hands, gripping shopping bags, heads down, winter coats pulled tight against the chill. Daylight had begun to abandon the city earlier in the afternoon as clouds sealed the sky with the threat of the ever-pervasive drizzle.

Ki Chung crossed her arms, wrapped them around her thin frame to fend off the cold evening air. A silk scarf tied under her chin covered her head, and large buttons fastened her knee-length gray wool coat.

She had left a message for Deng Qin in a sealed envelope with the designated RF12 scrawled across the back. She had given it to Yung, the headwaiter at the Lotus Blossom Restaurant on Jefferson Street, as she had been instructed. She waited anxious, eager to pass on a conversation she had overheard from Uncle Willie. Eager to show Deng Qin she was a valuable asset. As Willie Wong's housekeeper, Ki Chung had been approached by Deng Qin and asked to watch and listen and report back anything she thought of importance. She had been told it would be a good gesture toward her native China. It would make China a safer place for her family that remained in the old country and the government would look favorably on them if they wished to immigrate to America.

After what seemed a long fifteen minutes her attention was drawn to the Waterfront Streetcar as it rumbled up South Main. She spotted her MSS contact approaching from that same direction. A black trench coat draped his broad shoulders and a wide-brimmed wool hat covered his head. His eyes darted left and right in continual surveillance as he walked with a purposeful gait. He stepped up and stood beside her for a moment, staring off into the shadows, then settled next to her on the slatted wood bench.

She glanced at him, but he stared straight ahead. "Deng Qin. I have information. Most important for you." He nodded. Encouraged by even this slight recognition, she continued. "I hear Mr. Willie Wong on telephone. He think nobody here. But I here. I not gone. I no have umbrella. I go back for umbrella. I hear Mr. Willie Wong in kitchen. He talk on telephone. He not see me. I listen. Him say you do very bad thing for family. Him say you talk too much. Him say now you no tell no one. Tell no one about talk. Tell no one about Program. I know this Program. I hear him talk before. I think you want know this. Yes, Mr. Deng Qin?"

Deng Qin continued to stare straight ahead. "Yes, Ki Chung. I do want to know this. This is good. Do you know who he was talking to?"

"Him talk to Mr. George."

"Do you know this Mr. George he talked to?

"Oh, yes. This Mr. George Hu. Son of Wung Hu."

Deng Qin nodded, his facial expression acknowledging he recognized the name. "When did you hear this conversation?"

"Mr. Willie Wong him talk three days last. He no know I hear. I leave message Mr. Yung at Lotus Blossom."

"Yes. You have done well. I need you to continue to watch Mr. Willie Wong closely. I need to know who he is talking to and what he says. Anything you can find out. You must keep me informed."

Ki Chung grinned. She rocked back and forth, pleased with herself. Mr. Deng Qin said she had done well.

CHAPTER TWENTY-TWO

I WALKED TO the back of the diner and dialed Su Wan.

"Oh, hey Curtis. Find out anything?"

"Yeah. I just met with Lieutenant Watkins of the Seattle PD." I took a deep breath. "It was arson."

"Oh, shit! I can't believe it. What'd he say?"

I turned and scanned the diner, a little paranoid. Satisfied nobody appeared to be paying attention, I continued. "He said it looked like a professional job. Somebody wanted to take me out, or scare the hell out of me. And they have. Look, we should meet. We don't really know what's going on yet, but it's gotta be more than just this immigration and making babies thing. Have you talked to George Hu yet?"

"Not yet, but I'm seeing him this afternoon. He said to stop by around four."

"Good. I want to come."

"What!"

"What have I got to lose? Don't answer that. Yes. I need to confront him myself. I need to find out what he knows." I paused, as something occurred to me. "Wait. Do you think George could possibly have had anything to do with my boat? He doesn't know about the book, does he?"

"No. I never mentioned the book. I'm afraid that might put him over the edge. He was reluctant to divulge anything, and then, only after he'd been drinking and a bit depressed." There was silence for a moment. "You know, I'm not so sure this is such a good idea."

"Maybe not, but I need to meet him. Somebody tried to kill me. I gotta find out who. At this point, it's my only defense."

"What about the cops?"

"I didn't tell Lieutenant Watkins about the book or the visit by the FBI. It just doesn't make any sense. I couldn't tell him I suspect either the FBI or some Chinese guys tried to kill me because of some book I'm writing. He'd think I was a whack job. And the visit those two guys made to Jack Buick's office? I, I just don't know. We don't have all the pieces. *I* need to talk to George. But, if you go with me, I'll be dragging you into this. You realize that, don't you?"

"Ah, yeah. That's okay for now. I'll hang with you until I feel the heat. Then don't be surprised if I check out. But I need to be there when you talk to him. He trusts me, or at least he did. He has a small apartment in the University District, not far from you. I'll pick you up about ten to four."

I returned to the Pink Salmon Motel with a lot on my mind. I had talked to Jack Buick, and Jack was equally shocked. It didn't make sense that the Chinese community or the FBI would find this book so threatening that one of them would go to such extreme measures. I hoped that by talking to George Hu, I would be able to shed some light. I also knew I might be putting myself and my friend, Su Wan Cho, into greater risk.

* * *

AS WE TROMPED up the wood steps to George's apartment, thoughts raced through my mind. He may be Su Wan's friend, but I expect George will not be too happy when we disclose the book project. I imagine he's going to feel blind-sided, even betrayed, and I expect this will be anything but a friendly little chit-chat.

The door opened and George acknowledged us.

"George, this is my friend Curtis." Su Wan nodded in my direction. "We used to work together before we both left to work for ourselves. We've been harassing each other ever since."

I smiled and threw out a cautious, "Hi."

George nodded. His eyes twitched and his focus seemed to be elsewhere. He held the door and swung his arm in a half-hearted gesture. "Welcome to the lair of dragons and eagles."

In George I saw a scruffy looking young man, Asian features with a slight stubble, and hair that stood straight up on his head. He smiled but seemed a little reserved. As I entered, a woodsy pine smell lingered in the room, the kind of scent dispersed from a can of bathroom air freshener.

George cleared the couch of a brown corduroy coat and a stack of textbooks and notebooks, piling them in a corner, and gestured with his hand, "Have a seat. Beer?"

"Sure," Su Wan replied.

I looked at Su Wan and shrugged my shoulders. "Yeah, sure."

George stepped over a pile of laundry stacked against the wall, skirted the pass-through counter and retrieved three beers from the fridge. I glanced around and my immediate impression confirmed what Su Wan had said earlier. Though I'd never met George, this guy in the sweatshirt and baggy jogging pants appeared a little out of sorts. Not the sharp, well-put-together kid Su Wan had described from his school days, but rather the depressed young man fighting his own demons Su Wan had reported more recently.

George handed out the beers and we sat down. "What's up?" he asked. "You guys working on some kind of design thing?"

I exchanged looks with Su Wan. George seemed to be

attempting to mask his apparent melancholy mood with perky conversation, but the words were slow and drawn out. His faint smile seemed forced. I waited for Su Wan to speak up.

"Come on," George prodded. "What's up? A new logo for Microsoft or some big corporate somebody? What do you call that?"

Su Wan popped the top on his beer. "Corporate Identity."

"Oh, yeah. Corporate Identity. Microsoft. Now that'd be a nice account for the two of you."

I took a sip. "Sure, if you want to work against crash-and-burn deadlines and make a ton of money in the process." I grinned, hoping to cut through the thick aura of pine-scented air. "Yeah, if we could be so lucky."

George pointed a finger. "I'll put in a good word for you, next time I have Bill Gates over for a formal dinner party."

"You do that." I lifted my beer in a mock toast.

Su Wan looked over at me, turned to face George, then in a somber tone began to move the conversation in the intended direction. "George, we need to talk. It's rather serious."

George leaned up from his slouched position but did not reply.

"Remember when I was here before?" Su Wan continued. "That night we had those beers, and we drank and we talked. When you first told me about your family and that program that brought your father to America from China. The immigration thing." Su Wan paused, glanced at me, then back to George. "I told Curtis about it."

George's body tensed. His jaw tightened and his eyes narrowed, but he remained silent.

"I thought there would be no harm in it," Su Wan continued. "It's a great story. Curtis thought so too. In fact, Curtis thought it would *make* a great story. He's a writer, and he's been developing a manuscript based on our conversations. It's fiction of course. Kind of a suspense novel. And now, a publisher is interested."

George slammed his beer can against the arm of the couch, squeezing it with a tight fist as he jumped to his feet. Contents from the can exploded, sending liquid spewing. "What!" He stared down at Su Wan, his eyes penetrating. "What in hell are you talking about? He's writing a goddamn book about my family?" He glared at me. "And you're gonna publish it!" He threw his crushed can against the door. It clattered and toppled onto the carpet. "I can't believe this!"

George stepped over to the counter, stood there facing the wall, mumbled, "Fuck!" then struck it with a swift kick, crushing a hole through the wallboard. I hung my head and stared at the floor, regret slipping in. "You son of a bitch!" He took his hand and swept the counter, scattering newspapers and sending beer cans and a dirty plate crashing to the kitchen floor.

Su Wan fidgeted with his can of beer, watching George's reaction. I kept an eye on him, tried to measure his anger. He was pissed and I didn't know if his fury would escalate to violence.

George spun around to face Su Wan, pointing a finger that shook with rage. "What the hell were you thinking?" he screamed. "I told you that's my family's business." His nostrils flared with his rapid breathing and veins on the side of his head throbbed from his rising blood pressure. "You had no right to talk about this." He smacked the wall with the side of his closed fist. "I can't believe you did this. What's in this book? Is it everything I told you?" His dark scathing eyes settled on me. "And you're writing about this?"

I nodded.

George turned and slammed his palms on the counter as he leaned his head back and stared at the ceiling. "I've never told *anybody* about my family. Nobody." He looked back at Su Wan. "But I told *you*. You were supposed to be a trusted friend. And now this guy's putting it in a fucking book? I can't believe you'd do this to me. Why, Su Wan? To make a buck? Is that what this is all about? Is that what a friend does? Take advantage for profit. Drag his name and his family through mud. This is fucking un-believable."

George looked down at the counter and shook his head, the sound of his heavy breathing cut through the silence. After a few moments, he calmed, spoke up in a more controlled, subdued tone, but his face didn't hide his angry demeanor. "You know what this means? Do you have any idea what you're getting into?" His eyes darted from me to Su Wan. "You have *no* idea." George shook his head, his face acknowledged the inevitable. "Well, if you think I'm unhappy about this, you can't imagine how my family and the Chinese community will react. I told you before that this was a dangerous place to go. Apparently, you didn't listen."

Su Wan spoke up. "George. I know you trusted me. We'd been drinking and maybe you wouldn't have told me if you hadn't been. But you did, and it's out now. I'm sure you weren't the first to discuss this with outsiders. This could be a good thing."

George glared at Su Wan. "Are you serious! Good for who? You and your damn writer friend? If he goes through with this, you'll find out soon enough it's not such a good thing, for me or for you." His eyes flashed back to me. "And especially him."

I swallowed. My stomach tightened. *What does he know?*

George leaned over the counter and braced himself with his arms. He glanced to his left, and stared at a beer can that had survived his assault. He shook his head, then buried his face in the crease of his folded arms.

"Really, George," Su Wan continued. "You're my friend. Have been since high school. But I never knew about this. This is a great story."

I could see that in his exuberance, Su Wan might be adding fuel to the fire. I thought it best to show empathy. "We never meant to hurt you or your family," I said. "I guess I didn't realize how this would affect you. Believe me, if I'd known, and I'm sure Su Wan would agree, we never would have pursued it."

Su Wan quickly added. "But it's a done deal, George. We can't go back."

George turned away and walked down the hall. A door closed behind him. I looked at Su Wan. Su Wan stood up and walked to the counter, leaned back and rested his elbows against it. He looked at me, shrugged his shoulders and stared up at the ceiling.

Within a few minutes we heard the toilet flush, George returned to the room and sat down on the couch. He rested his head in the palm of his left hand, while he ran the fingers of his right hand through his prickly hair.

"This whole damn program has been tearing my life apart. I'm being pulled in two directions. Something *you'll* never understand. I've been going through great pain. Now this pain is going to be out there for everyone to see."

We had to make peace, if we expected George to help. "Listen, George. This book is not about your pain. It's a novel. Total fiction as far as anyone is concerned. In reality, for it to be a successful novel, I have to embellish the story. Make it much more than it is. It will barely resemble your family's life. It's a fictitious story that has more to do with politics than anything."

I sipped my beer and let a calming silence fall over us for a moment before continuing. "I can only imagine what you're going through. Yes, it's true I'm using details about the immigration program, but the characters are from my imagination. I'm not out to expose your struggle or reduce your feelings to ink on paper. You're more than that. So is your family. I only hope the characters I create will be as strong as you, have as much family honor as you."

Having spent his anger, George looked at me, nodded, then stared at the floor. "I still can't believe you're doing this. Believe me, someone's gonna end up paying."

I swallowed hard.

Su Wan cleared his throat. "Listen, George, I know this came as a shock. We had our reasons to tell this story, and, well, maybe some of them were selfish. But there's something else. There's another reason we came to see you." George shifted his gaze to Su Wan, probably expecting another bombshell. Su Wan paused. "Somebody tried to *kill* Curtis."

George's eyes widened. He stiffened. "What do you mean, somebody tried to kill him?"

"My boat was set on fire," I said. "It sank. It's a..." I struggled with the words. "It *was* a houseboat on Lake Union. I lived there. Had my office there too. Just a little more than a week ago. I wasn't on board. I was...well, I was out of town. If I'd been there I wouldn't be sitting here now." I studied George's facial expression, wondering if at this point, he might have been glad if that had happened. To see if his face showed he knew more than he would admit.

George didn't betray his inner feelings. "Yes. I remember seeing that on the news. That was your houseboat?"

I nodded.

He shrugged. "You're saying someone tried to kill you?"

"Yes, the police said it was arson. Some kind of explosive device. The investigator said it looked like a professional job."

George looked at me, paused, than glanced at Su Wan. "Wait. You...don't think..." he stuttered. "That's why you're here. Isn't it? You think this has something to do with me. Don't you? That's the only reason you came, isn't it?"

I waited a moment to answer. "You told Su Wan the information could lead down a dangerous path. Knowing about the Program. You said we didn't know what we were getting into. There was more to this. What did you mean?"

"Who knows about this book?" he asked, avoiding my question.

Su Wan and I exchanged glances. "We don't know for sure," I said. "We think the FBI, and it seems someone in the Chinese community." George's face revealed fear and deep concern, as I continued. "And of course my editor in New York."

"The FBI! Someone in the Chinese community. Shit!" George dropped his head back into his hands and stared at the floor.

"We don't know how the FBI found out, and we suspect someone in the Chinese community knows, but we haven't a clue how, or who," I continued. "Do you have any information that might help? I know I'm asking a lot, but you're my only hope. If my life's in danger, I need to know who's behind it. I need to find a way to protect myself." I studied George, knowing we had wronged him and he had no reason to be sympathetic. I pleaded, "Do *you* know who would try to kill me?"

CHAPTER TWENTY-THREE

Atlantic City, New Jersey

JACK BUICK PRESSED his polished Gucci loafer on the accelerator. The speedometer indicator drifted past ninety as the rented Town Car sped down the Garden State Parkway heading for Atlantic City. He had not been to the tables for weeks and he had the itch. This *would* be his lucky day. His hometown team had clinched a playoff spot, one of his authors landed atop the New York Times Best Seller list and he had gotten laid the night before at the discount rate for repeat customers. Life was good. He was certain his luck would be too. It had to be. He was due. Fortunes were certain to turn and this had to be the day for turning. Smiling, he flipped the automobile's turn signal on and off, as he flew down the freeway.

The car stereo belted out a classic Frank Sinatra tune. *Now there's a guy who knew all the right people.* A prophetic omen maybe? Jack wished he'd had the comfort of a few good connections himself. But when it came to cards he was forever the optimist. This *would* be his lucky day.

He pulled into the underground parking lot of Harrah's Atlantic City Hotel & Casino, pushed through the doors and rode the escalator to the main floor. The sights and sounds of the casino made his fingers twitch. Lights flashed on every surface from over-stimulated slot machines. Rowdy cheers resonated from the craps tables and rolled like a wave through the casino. He passed a roulette table where the black ball bounced and clicked, sounding like a tap dancer as it spun around the rim of the wheel, slowing down, dropping toward the center, igniting the crowd as a chorus of screams drowned out one or two groans. A cocktail waitress with the long legs and short skirts Jack was fond of passed by, balancing a tray of cold beer and glasses of whiskey. The ice glistened and tinkled as the small cubes knocked against each other like the overflowing breasts in her skimpy pushup bra.

As Jack walked through the casino he grinned, he was comfortable, but recognized something amiss. Had been for the past few years. The sound of winning from a bygone era had disappeared as casinos upgraded slot machines into electronic gamers—issuing paper receipts rather than coins. Jack liked the incessant jingling of coins as they dropped into polished metal trays, a sound that threw his competitive desire into a fever pitch and quickened his gambling adrenalin. Jack missed that.

But the slots were not Jack's game. His game was chips. Poker chips. And the hundred-dollar table beckoned. You could win a fortune in mere hours. Unfortunately for those *other* unlucky souls, you could lose a fortune just as quickly, if not quicker. But that would not be the case today. Jack would bet on it.

"Another bourbon, rocks," Jack said as the waitress leaned in, her tray hidden beneath two jiggling mountains of flesh. He wasn't distracted. His cards, and those of his opponents, kept his attention. He twisted a hundred-dollar chip between his fingers, tapping it on the soft green felt, contemplating his next move. He had been sitting in this exact spot for over two hours and his pile of chips had grown and shrunk more times than the dress size of a celebrity spokesperson for a diet food plan. He had been up, in his estimation, nearly ten thousand, but for the past half-hour had been sliding on a rough patch. All he needed was a couple of good hands and he'd be back. He tipped the edge of the first card up, cupped his hand and peered at it, placing it face down with a slap.

"I'd fold if I were you," came a whisper.

Jack jumped as he felt a warm breath tickle his ear. He jerked his head to the side and turned to see a stranger leaning over him, inches away, an unrecognizable face with piercing eyes, a sharp nose and shaved head. "Ah, do I know you?" Jack asked, quite annoyed.

"No, you don't," the stranger said. "But you will."

"Look, this is not a good time. I don't know who the hell you are, but obviously, you can see I'm in the middle of a fucking card game here." Jack turned his attention back to his hand, but noticed the eyes around the table, including those of the dealer, fixed on the stranger. Jack began to sense this was not some wannabe enamored with the big-stakes table.

"As I said, I'd fold if I were you," the man repeated.

As Jack shifted to face the stranger again, his mouth dropped open, his face froze. His blood ran cold, his breath caught.

"Hi, Jack," said a second man as he stepped from behind the stranger. "Having any luck?" He had a full head of silver hair, parted near the middle. About sixty years old, he had deeply tanned skin that showed the effects of time in the sun. The man spoke with his hands, his manicured nails indicating his days had been spent in leisure. His deep voice continued. "A nice day like this Jack? Come on. You should be outside enjoying the weather. It's stuffy in here. Why don't you join me for a little vitamin D. You look a little pale. It'll do ya good." He stepped back, leaned forward and waved his hand in a gentle arc toward the front entrance, the black mink trim on the sleeve of his cashmere coat catching air.

Looking back at the table, Jack's eyes caught more than a few nervous glances. With his fingers he pushed his cards together, scooted them to the side and picked up his remaining chips. He stood up, stuffed the chips in his coat pocket and glanced at the stranger with the shaved head. The Cashmere Coat had walked away, and the stranger, his hands stuffed in the pockets of his overcoat, stepped back and nodded his head in that direction. Jack glanced from side to side then dropped his eyes and followed the Coat through the casino to the front entrance. The sounds of the casino faded away until all he heard was the soft thump of his shoes on the embroidered carpet, his heavy breathing, and his pounding heart.

He glanced around and noticed a security guard by the door. He passed him, kept his head down as he shuffled through the entrance, trailing the Coat.

A black limousine pulled up as the tires turned and squealed on the polished pavement of the curved driveway. The stranger opened the door and stepped back. The Coat stepped in and the stranger motioned for Jack to follow. Jack slid around and sat facing both men. The limo drove off, moving without urgency. The stranger opened a mirrored cabinet and pulled out two crystal glasses and a bottle of bourbon, then began to pour. He handed the first glass to the Coat.

Jack's eyes darted from one man to the next. His chest pounded, the throbbing echoed in his ears, his stomach was a knot.

The stranger reached out and handed him the other glass. With Jack's eyes fixated on the Coat, he accepted the drink with some reluctance.

"To your health, Jack." The Coat gave the glass a gentle swirl, then took a large swallow. "Ah, fine bourbon. Had

Vincent here pick it up special, just for you, Jack. Can't say I'm not a good host."

Jack lifted the glass to his lips, afraid to drink, afraid not to.

"But, Jack," the Coat continued. "I haven't seen you around lately. Where've you been hiding? I miss your company. When my friends don't come by and show their appreciation, I get offended. You don't want to offend me now, do you, Jack?"

Jack couldn't speak. He shook his head.

"That's good, Jack. I want my friends to have a clear understanding of where we stand. I want my friends to know when they have offended me. You see, Vincent here, he don't like it when someone offends me. He takes it personal-like. Know what I mean?"

Jack choked. His throat, despite the bourbon, was dry and began to constrict. He looked at the stranger, who now had a name. Vincent. This time, Jack nodded.

"I'm glad we understand each other, Jack. You're a nice guy. You got a good life. Working in that fancy office tower in Manhattan. Nice apartment in the village. Don't spoil it." The Coat leaned forward and drove his piercing eyes into Jack's. "Don't offend me, Jack. Do the right thing. And do it in ten days." He sat back, smiled and took another drink. "Oh, yes, I nearly forgot. I've added a small late fee. Not much. But my girlfriend, well, her birthday's coming up and she's got expensive tastes. She'll be twenty-nine. That's a big one, you know. I can't disappoint her." The Coat leaned over and gave Jack two light taps on his cheek as Jack winced. "Hey, I'm a sensitive guy, Jack. Just like you."

The Coat winked as Vincent raised his hand and tapped his knuckles on the tinted window between them and the driver. The vehicle pulled to the curb. Vincent opened the door, stepped out and signaled for Jack to follow. Jack planted his Gucci's onto the cracked sidewalk of a rather undesirable neighborhood and Vincent handed him an envelope. He leaned over and whispered in Jack's ear, "Ten days, Jack. I'll be in touch. Don't offend him."

CHAPTER TWENTY-FOUR

Seattle, Washington

I SAT BACK on my bed in the "Presidential Suite" at the Pink Salmon, leaned against the headboard, stared at the wall and wondered who did the interior decorating for motel rooms. Whoever it was, they always followed the same annoying pattern. One too-small-picture on one too-big-wall hung at the eye level of a seven footer. I guess I shouldn't expect too much care to be taken in the hanging of the picture when the picture itself is part of a one-piece molded plastic frame. But the big screw driven through the middle of the frame where it attached to the wall offended even my somewhat unrefined palette.

I thought of my Dad. I couldn't bring myself to tell him about the loss of my boat, knowing I wouldn't find any empathy there, then I reflected on my conversation with George Hu. I had become more disturbed after talking to him. He was quite upset about the book, but what seemed to worry him more was the backlash he expected from the Chinese community. He wouldn't tell us why he was concerned, but the fear I saw on his face sent chills up my spine. I still didn't know what the danger was or where it would be coming from. The information George hadn't shared came hand-in-hand with this dangerous threat. That didn't make me feel any better. I didn't know where to turn. I'd been rolling it over in my mind and sleeping on it for a week, on that same set of thin sheets provided by the Pink Salmon Motel. I decided to call Su Wan, as promised.

I went back to the diner and headed straight for the payphone near the men's room. "Hey, Su Wan. It's me."

"Hell, Curtis, where ya been? I needed to get hold of you."

I could sense his urgency. "Why? What's going on?"

"It's George. He's gone. Disappeared. I got a call from his sister, Angie. She knows I'm a friend of his and she's been calling around trying to find him."

"What do you mean he's disappeared?" My mind raced. "How long has he been gone?"

"She thinks about a week. I told her I had talked to him last week but hadn't seen him since."

"You didn't tell her anything, did you?" I asked.

"Hell, no. I don't want to go through that again. She's been trying to reach him. He hasn't been at his apartment. She can't find any sign of him."

I paused in thought. If he's disappeared, it might have something to do with the book and the information he'd given us, but I didn't want to mention my concerns to Su Wan just yet. "Well, what do you think?" I asked.

"He's either in trouble, or he's bailed. You saw him. He was pretty upset about the book. Add that to the unstable condition he was in, and, well, anything's possible."

"Yeah. Anything's possible," I admitted. I thought for a moment. Now George is missing. Not that I had any hope he would help, but his unexpected disappearance adds more questions. I needed answers. An irrational thought crossed my mind. "Let's go see this sister of his, Angie. Talk to her. See what she knows."

"Are you crazy? Been there and done that with George.

No way."

"Just listen for a minute. George was our best hope of getting to the bottom of this. Now apparently he's gone. Even if he weren't, I doubt he'd help us. We still don't know the real risk or where the danger's coming from. We have to dig deeper. She may or may not be able to help. But it's all we've got right now. Come on, Su Wan. I need you to do this one last thing."

"It's crazy man. We'd just get someone else pissed off. What could she know?"

"She may be part of the emigration program," I said. "I know she's a girl, you know, a daughter and not a son, but we don't know every aspect of the Program. She could be involved in some way." The phone remained silent. "Look," I pleaded my case, "this is the last time I'll ask you to do anything. The last favor. After this you can get out. I won't pressure you again." More silence. "Su Wan? You there?"

"Yeah." There was a long pause. "Okay. But it's against my better judgment. And if things get tense, I'm outta there. I've done all I can do. All I wanna do. You got that?"

"Yeah. Got it."

"Call me back in an hour." He sighed. "I'll see if I can catch her and set something up."

"Thanks." I hung up the phone and looked at my watch. Eleven-thirty. I scanned the diner, then sat down at a booth, an hour to kill. How about a cheeseburger in paradise? *Paradise!* I tried to force a chuckle, but it caught in my throat as if I'd swallowed a giant jawbreaker.

* * *

AFTER TORMENTING MY stomach lining with a greasy patty of suspicious brown-round, I called Su Wan. He said Angie was anxious for any assistance she might get in helping locate her brother, so she agreed to meet at her place, around six p.m. Su Wan had told her he would be bringing a friend.

Later that afternoon Su Wan picked me up and we headed for the International District. Within fifteen minutes we pulled into a pot-holed asphalt parking lot in front of an austere two-story apartment building. Su Wan pointed to a door on the second level, "That's her apartment there."

It had an open stairway that led to an exterior walkway and four dark-orange doors. It reminded me of some of the motels on Aurora Avenue, without the hookers. We climbed the stairs and Su Wan knocked three times.

The door opened and an attractive young Asian girl, about twenty, greeted us. In her arms she held a thick gray fur-ball with a fluffy tail that twitched back and forth in a state of mild agitation. Behind her stood a young Asian man about the same age. She smiled, but beneath it, I detected a look of concern. "Hello, Su Wan," she said. "Come in."

Su Wan turned to me. "This is my friend Curtis." I returned her smile and extended my arm. Her slim hand had a warm touch and met mine with a light handshake, more like a quiver.

"I'm Angela. But my friends call me Angie." She had smooth soft features, a heart-shaped face with full lips, and long jet-black hair that draped her shoulders. Petite and thin, she appeared fragile, but through her steady dark almond-shaped eyes, I imagined a strong will. She wore a white pantsuit like a nurse or a lab technician.

"Su Wan, you know Thomas," she said. Thomas stepped forward.

"Yes." Su Wan reached out to shake his hand. "Good to see you, Thomas. It's been a while." Su Wan turned to me. "Thomas is George's brother."

I was surprised to see Thomas, although I had no reason to believe he wouldn't be here. He would have information about the Program, even if Angie didn't. But it remained to be seen if he'd be more forthcoming than George. He was shorter than George and a bit stockier, with an athletic build. He wore a baseball cap—purple with a gold University of Washington "W" embroidered on the front.

"Hi. Nice to meet you, Thomas." I took his firm handshake.

Angie led us to a modest seating area that barely cleared the front door. We sat and she offered bottled water or hot tea. We declined.

As Angie seated herself, the fur-ball leaped from her arms and disappeared down the hallway. "What can you tell me of my brother?" she asked.

"I wish I knew something," Su Wan said. "As I told you, we," he turned to me, "we both met with George about a week ago. Last Wednesday. That's the last we saw or heard from him."

I took the initiative. "When did *you* see him last?" I asked her.

Angie turned to me. "I dropped by on Thursday afternoon. I hadn't seen him since we all gathered at my father's house for Thanksgiving. He seemed a bit depressed then. I've been worried about him. I stopped by with a plate of dinner Mother had cooked. He loves Mother's fried rice. I suppose I should have called first, but I wanted to surprise him. Since then, I've called every day three or four times." Her eyes watered and she wiped at them. "I stopped by a few days later and the food container I left for him was still sitting on his step. A dog or some animal had gotten into it, but the container was still there."

My eyes met Su Wan's then I turned my attention to Angie. "You have no idea where he might be? Staying with a friend? Visiting a relative?"

"No. He would never leave for any extended period

without letting one of us know. We are a close family. George isn't like that. He would have told someone. Besides, he's not answering his cell phone. He's a cell phone junkie. He always kept his cell phone on."

"What about your parents?" I asked. "Your father? Can he do something?"

Angie looked down. "No. They are both very upset and nervous. My father is too scared to ask for help."

"Too scared? You mean he's concerned for George?"

"No. You don't understand. It's different in the Chinese community."

I felt her reluctance to continue, so I didn't pursue that further. "How about the police?" I asked. "Have you contacted them?"

Angie looked at Thomas. Thomas fisted one hand against the palm of the other and looked down. "No. I don't think we'd get much help."

"Why not?"

"Many reasons." Thomas apparently didn't want to elaborate.

I noticed Angie and Thomas pass an awkward glance between them, his face hiding an expression that seemed odd, out of place. He saw me watching and turned away. I wanted them to share any information they had, but it appeared I would have to be the one to share first.

"Do you know why we're here?" I asked.

Angie brushed her hair from her eyes. "I assume it's because I called Su Wan about George."

"In a way it is." I hesitated, then glanced at the brother. "Thomas. We know about the Program."

A puzzled expression crossed Thomas's face.

I continued. "George told us everything about the emigration program. The one that brought your father to America. The Chinese Party plan of fathering sons, their desire for you and George and other young men of the program to enter politics. Even your visit to China when you were thirteen."

Thomas's mouth dropped open and he stiffened. "He told you that?"

I nodded.

"Why?" He glanced at Su Wan. "That's crazy. I can't imagine he would have told you that. Why'd he do it?" Thomas leaned back in his chair and removed his hat. He rubbed his head, then put it back on with a quick flip.

"It's complicated," I said. "But I need to tell you this because there's been some trouble. It might even have to do with George's disappearance, but…"

I waited for their reaction. Thomas sat stunned. Angie looked fearful. Her eyes glistened, then she jumped up and disappeared into the back room.

"Tell me," Thomas demanded. "What does this have to do with George's disappearance?"

I tried to talk in a calm voice with an even rhythm to arrest any anxiety. "That's the reason we're here. We hoped *you* could help us." I nodded to Su Wan, who had apparently decided he had said enough.

"How could *we* help *you*?" Thomas asked.

At this point I wished I'd accepted the offer of water. My throat was becoming a dry gulch. "George knew something. But we don't know what it was. When he found out Su Wan had told me about the Program, that I was a writer, he was upset, said this knowledge would lead down a dangerous path. That there were additional things I didn't know. He insinuated that if we knew what he *hadn't* told us, it could put us in even greater danger. He said there were people who wouldn't want this information getting out." As I talked I studied Thomas's reaction. His face appeared to be stone. He hadn't moved a muscle.

Angie returned with a tissue in her hand. She sat on the

arm of the chair next to Thomas and rested her hand on his shoulder.

"What could George have been referring to?" I asked.

Thomas remained stoic. "I don't know." I could see his mind churning as he tilted his head and glared. "What kind of writer are you?"

"Fiction. A novelist. Or at least that's what I'm striving for. I haven't published a book yet, but I'm working on one." Thomas eyed me with suspicion but I would only divulge what I had to.

"What's it about? This book you're working on."

"It's a fictionalized story of Chinese immigrants in America."

Thomas and Angie both stared at me. "Like us?"

"Yes, like you."

"How much like us?" he asked, anticipating my answer.

I sighed. "A lot. But it's fiction. A novel. A lot of embellishment and exaggeration. Different names, different everything. It's based on what George told us, but I changed the details."

"And George knew this?"

"Yes, he did. He talked openly to Su Wan. He seemed depressed. It helped him to talk. But he didn't know about the book until later. He was upset over that. That's when he told us how dangerous this information is." I took a deep breath. "I know I'm in danger. My houseboat has been destroyed. Somebody has tried to kill me."

Thomas gasped. "Kill you!"

Angie lifted her hand to her mouth, her eyes grew wide.

I nodded. "That's why we're here. We're worried about *our* own safety as well as George's. George's disappearance only adds to our concern."

Angie spoke up in a soft voice, with a slight quiver. "George wouldn't just disappear on his own. It's not like him.

I'm worried something has happened. I need to know where he is. That he's safe." She dabbed her eyes. "And you think this book and the stuff he told you might have something to do with his disappearance?"

"Yes, I do," I said. "It's too coincidental. I need to know what it is that George knew. Whatever it is he hasn't told us. I think that might be crucial. Why he's missing." I had to probe one more time. "You said you didn't know what it could be? You have no idea?"

They both shook their heads.

"Well, as much as I would like to help you find George, I would also like to assure my safety. I think they're tied together. We can help each other. But we need to be honest and pool our resources. You have resources in the Chinese community that I don't. I need your help. Anything you know may be of some value."

At this point I didn't know what else to ask. I sensed they were holding back, but there was nothing I could do. Frustration set in.

Thomas sat silent. Angie rose and walked into the kitchen, separated from our seating area by a wall with an open doorway. With nothing more to say, I stood up and thanked Thomas for his time and asked him to call Su Wan if anything came to him. Anything he thought we should know.

We headed for the door just as Angie reemerged.

"Thank you for coming," she said. "We are worried about George." She looked me in the eye and held out her hand. "Maybe we can help each other." I extended my arm. It wasn't a light feather-touch she offered this time, but a firm grip, and I felt something scratch my palm. She had squeezed something into my hand. She held my grip until I recognized this. My eyes flinched and I curled my fingers around a small piece of paper, making a fist.

"Yes. I know how worried you are," I said. "We are too."

Su Wan and I headed for the car and I slipped the folded paper into my pocket. If Angie wanted me alone to see this, I would wait until I returned to the motel.

I had told Su Wan I would not involve him anymore. I hoped I could keep my word.

CHAPTER TWENTY-FIVE

MEET ME TOMORROW AT NOON. THE
FISH BAR. FISHERMAN'S TERMINAL.

I COULDN'T CONTAIN my excitement. After reading
Angie's note, it was apparent she wanted to talk. And for some
reason she didn't want her brother or Su Wan to know. I could
only hope this meant she had information to share. I needed
something positive to grab hold of. I felt like I had been sitting
around with a blindfold on. Everyone seemed to know what
was going on except me.

Fisherman's Terminal on Salmon Bay had remained an
integral part of Seattle's maritime industry since the early 1900s.
Originally developed as a homeport for the commercial fishing
fleet, it now shared space with pleasure boaters, restaurants and
fresh fish markets. At one end sat a small fish and chips bar
where Angie had intended we meet. I was familiar with the area
since it was located only about a mile down the Washington
Ship Canal from where the *Mockaritaville* had been moored.

I arrived early. I wanted to be there before she showed. I
suppose a little paranoia went a long way, but I wanted to be
sure she came alone. I didn't know what she would be driving,
but I positioned myself so I could see her arrive and determine
if anyone had tagged along.

At about the appointed time, I caught sight of her driving a silver Hyundai. I recognized her long silky hair. She was alone and no other car appeared to be following. I waited until she parked, walked over and sat down at an outside table. She was dressed in the same white uniform pantsuit she wore yesterday. I gave her a few extra minutes, scanned the parking lot, then joined her.

Her back was to me as I approached. "Hi."

She turned and gave me a thin smile. Without saying a word she stood and walked across the pier toward the bay. I stuffed my hands in my pockets and followed, the thump of her rubber sole shoes on the bleached, worn planks of the boardwalk echoed a soft rhythm. She headed for the wood railing that looked out over the fleet. Hundreds of white, but stained crabbing boats bobbed against the piers, their decks stacked with king crab pots—large reinforced steel cages that could hold a sumo wrestler and weighed about as much. A jungle of masts, communication antennas, ropes, lines and pulleys created a hodgepodge of marine paraphernalia against the sky. The smell of sea salt drifted in the breeze as seagulls squawked and dove past to snatch parcels of old bait and fish remnants.

I walked up and leaned my elbows on the rail. "Thanks for seeing me."

"I'm scared and worried to death over George's safety."

"I understand." I got right to the point. "Why'd you want to meet? Can you help me?"

She stared at the fleet, her chin up, gaze intense. "My father's a good man. He's a wonderful father to his children. And I love him dearly." She paused, apparently in no rush. "He was sent to America by the government of China many years ago, as you apparently know."

I nodded as I stared across the bay.

"He had only one child then, my sister, Sung Wi. They

called the emigration program the Sons of the Red Dragon. His purpose in coming was to have sons and raise them as Americans. He had been instructed to be certain they had training, education and exposure to the culture of China and the Communist Party. The Party wanted these sons to someday become leaders in America. They hoped to gain support and sympathy for China's interests through them. There have been hundreds, maybe even thousands of families over the years that have come to America through this program."

An aged gentleman approached, stopped and poked at his shoe with his walking stick. Angie glanced at him and fell silent.

I filled in the gap with irrelevant small talk. "I used to live on a boat."

She turned to me. "Yes. You mentioned that yesterday. What happened?"

"It was destroyed by an explosion. Police said it was arson. They have no suspects. But I have my suspicions." Angie looked at me but didn't pursue it. Perhaps she didn't want to know. "I kept her moored on Lake Union," I continued. "A thirty-eight foot cruiser built in nineteen twenty-eight. She was a bit weathered, but a classic wood-hulled beauty." I snuck a glance over my shoulder and noticed our friend had shuffled on.

Angie continued, "Everything I've told you, you already know of course." She looked up at me. She studied my face and I could see stress lines around her eyes. Her lips began to speak, but no sound emerged. She seemed to be struggling with the words. "Yesterday you asked Thomas and me if we knew what it was that George hadn't told you. We told you we didn't." She hesitated. "But we did. Thomas couldn't say anything. And neither could I, in front of him anyway."

She laid her hand on my arm and glanced around before speaking. "I don't want him or anyone else to know who you heard this from. I'm only telling you in hopes it might lead to finding George. I'll try anything, if I think it might help. You have to promise me this goes nowhere else, though. If it does, I won't be able to help you anymore." She paused and gripped the sleeve of my sweatshirt. "*Nobody* will be able to help you."

I leaned on my elbows and stared out at nothing, my mind spinning, thoughts rushing through my head but unable to identify a plausible explanation for this danger. The tension in my body felt ready to snap the railing. I clenched my jaw.

"There's danger in you knowing what I'm going to say, just as George warned. Are you sure you want to know?"

I nodded, and swallowed hard.

She studied me a moment, then continued. "The Chinese hope to have *some* success with the Sons of the Red Dragon program. But it's not their top priority. In the scheme of things, it's a low level program. A program meant to build support for China in the minds of the American people and in the halls of American government. Essentially, a program of influence gathering. The Chinese though, are more interested in *information gathering*. Sons and even daughters born within the program are often recruited and sometimes used by MSS to gather information."

I gave her a puzzled look. "Gather information? What's MSS?"

"Ministry of State Security. It's the Chinese Communist government's department of intelligence gathering. It's their espionage apparatus. Like America's CIA."

I choked. "Like the CIA? You mean spies? Shit! You guys are spies for the Chinese government?" I suddenly sensed the metaphorical rush of water. It's getting deep and I may be in over my head, just as that FBI agent had said. These guys were professionals. I had read enough paperbacks. Spies don't just steal information, they kill people who get in their way!

Angie displayed a slight smile at her perception of my naiveté. "No. *We* are not spies. Nobody in my family is involved with MSS. But it's not because we haven't been recruited. We know of its existence and we know they'd exploit us if we let them. They're always looking for recruits. Many participants of the Sons of the Red Dragon have provided support to them over the years. It's a fertile recruiting ground, as you can imagine. Most of their recruits work for industries they have an interest in. Aerospace, high-tech, bio-tech, that sort of thing. Anyplace that has information or secrets that would be helpful to the Chinese military or their industry."

Stunned by Angie's revelation, I stared straight ahead. Bobbing masts became a hypnotic blur. A seagull became a little too curious and swooped near my head. I jumped back and swung my arm in a wild arc. He squawked in defiance. My sudden movement reawakened my focus. "You're not a spy?"

"No. Neither is anybody in our family."

"But, the Sons of the Red Dragon is somehow part of this spy program?"

"In some ways. At some times. Although many of the participants are just normal Americans, just like us. Just like you."

I wasn't sure I bought that, at least, not until I learned more. "Then, do you think they might have been pressuring George? You know. To work with this MSS? Or, is George working with them and you just don't know it."

"No, he wouldn't. I know him. But, he had become very depressed. We were very close, but he wouldn't open up to anyone in the family. I wish I knew what was going on in his mind. He's a sensitive guy. A deep thinker. He may have felt under a lot of pressure from Father and Uncle Willie."

"Uncle Willie. He's the guy that runs the Sons of the Red Dragon program, isn't he?"

"Yes. He's like a family member though. An uncle. He's been close to our family."

"Is he involved with MSS? Is *he* a spy?"

171

"Oh, no. Not Uncle Willie." Angie paused and stared down at the water, seeming to be in deep thought. "Uncle Willie would never be involved with them."

We stood in silence a minute, then Angie pulled my arm. "Let's walk."

We sauntered down the boardwalk, heading in the direction of the Fisherman's Memorial, a bronze and stone sculpture with plaques memorializing more than five hundred commercial fishermen and women lost at sea since the beginning of the twentieth century. There were a few bouquets and ceramic containers holding plastic flowers in remembrance. As we passed, I glanced at the brass plates identifying those who had been taken by the sea. Water that ran deep and treacherous. A quick chill rippled down my arms.

"Will this information help us find George?" she asked.

"I don't know. But it's another piece of the puzzle. I understand now why George said it could be dangerous. I had sensed the Chinese knew about the book. It's probably made them a bit nervous. If I'm writing about the Sons of the Red Dragon, they might think I know something about their MSS spy operations, since they seem to be interconnected. Damn. I can see now why they would think that. And that's what made George so nervous. He said he was concerned how the Chinese community would react. He must have meant MSS." I thought back to our conversation with George, and the pieces were beginning to form a picture. An ugly one.

"Do you think they did something to him?" I asked, attempting to confirm my growing suspicion. "Does that really happen?"

Angie looked at me and nodded. "Yes. They can be dangerous. They work outside the law. If something goes wrong, they can easily disappear. Escape back to China. I don't know of any specific cases, but we hear things. You know, in the community. At the Cultural Academy. They aren't people

172

to fool with."

I thought about this for a minute. "Last night I asked why you didn't go to the police. Was that the reason? This MSS connection?"

"Yes. We wouldn't know who to trust. Some of the local police are from the Chinese community. We couldn't take the risk."

"I understand." I looked down at the boardwalk, my mind thinking how different Angie's world was, as I stepped from plank to plank, catching a glimpse between the cracks to the dark water below. "I know somebody. In the police department that is. A Lieutenant Watkins. He was the investigator assigned to the arson fire on my boat. I've talked with him a couple times. He seemed okay. And he's a white guy. Maybe I can talk to him? Have him check with 'missing persons.' "

"I'm not sure." Angie hesitated. "I don't know who to trust."

"Let me talk to him. Maybe he can help. It could be worth a shot." I looked at my watch. "Hey. It's past lunchtime. How about some of those fish 'n chips?"

She smiled. "Sure." We began walking toward the fish bar.

"Tell me. What was the name of your boat?"

"*Mockaritaville*," I answered. Angie shot me a strange look. Memories of my boat allowed me a slight smile. "Every year I powered her down the ship canal in the Parade of Boats celebration on the opening day of boating season. She'd be decked out in the finest 'Parrot Head' tradition. An eight-foot tall plastic palm tree sat on the bow and a giant inflatable margarita glass with a slice of lime sat on the cabin rooftop. Flags and banners flapped from the mast. We cranked the stereo up and blasted a medley of Jimmy Buffett tunes to the delight of boating fans along the bank. We'd deck out in our most colorful Hawaiian flowered shirts, plastic flowered leis, shorts and flip flops while the girls wore grass skirts and coconut bras. Of course, you know what the weathers like the beginning of boating season. We had to add a fleet of propane heaters around the deck to keep from freezing our butts off."

Angie grinned.

"We had a great time though," I continued. "I guess it was my little snub to that highfalutin' yachting crowd that thought they were better'n us. They always dressed up in their proper yacht club finest, starched white pants, white jackets with gold braid and those fake medals."

Angie shared my smile.

I was grateful to Angie. She had taken a risk and provided some incredible information; the Sons of the Red Dragon link to Chinese espionage—a dangerous world of professional spies. Although it terrified me to know what I was up against, I felt the blindfold had been lifted. Now I just had to figure out how this piece of the puzzle would help. Needless to say, this knowledge was unsettling, but I was certain this confirmed link to MSS was at the heart of my problems and related to George's disappearance.

CHAPTER TWENTY-SIX

"WHAT THE HELL do you mean, you don't know where Curtis Beecham is?" Special Agent Lou Jengwi asked Special Agent Skip Chouw with disbelief. Jengwi sat up in his desk chair and shoved his computer keyboard under the desktop. He frowned and his brows wrinkled into a deep furrow.

Agent Chouw dropped his eyes to the floor and shifted his weight to his other foot before looking up. "After we paid him a visit, he disappeared. Gone before we had surveillance in place."

"Shit." Jengwi glared and slapped the palm of his hand against the desktop. He thought a moment before moving on. "What do you hear on the boat?"

"SPD's calling it arson. They say they've found evidence of an incendiary device. Pretty coincidental, after we'd just paid him a visit, don't you think."

Jengwi grinned. "Well, well. Can't say we didn't warn him. Think maybe he's got some enemies?" His eyes penetrated through Agent Chouw.

"Looks like it." Chouw swallowed. "SPD hasn't asked for our assistance, but they'll be sending trace evidence to our lab in Virginia. Explosive residue."

Jengwi sat emotionless, staring straight ahead. "Fine."

"After it went down, he apparently took off. Must have rattled him pretty good."

Jengwi continued thinking about his visit to the boat on Lake Union, as Curtis Beecham had sat in his cabin silent, defying him. This problematic writer could cause Jengwi trouble. Interfere in his investigation. Jengwi was not going to allow that to happen. He blinked and his thoughts returned to the present. "I should hope to hell. But now we need to know where he is. He have a wife? Family?"

Agent Chouw pulled out his notebook and flipped a few pages. "Has a dad living in the Ballard area. Mom's deceased. An ex-wife and two kids living on Queen Anne. No steady girlfriends we've been able to determine. We know his vehicles. One's a thirty-seven Ford woodie wagon. It's a classic collector car. He's parked it in his dad's garage. We talked to him. Claims he hasn't seen his son in about two weeks. Claims they're not close. Don't see each other that often. His other vehicle's a ninety-six Jeep Cherokee. My guess is, he's staying with a friend or relative somewhere but we haven't been able to catch any leads."

"How about his cell phone?"

"Funny thing. There's no record of usage since he disappeared."

"Well, if he's gone into hiding, he probably figured his phone wouldn't be safe. Contact that editor. See what he'll tell you. Let's see if we can get word back to Mr. Beecham through his editor. Let him know we're still looking over his shoulder. Keep the pressure on. Make him think long and hard about continuing with that book." Jengwi moved on. "How about WUZ-Tech?"

"Tai Kang has been active. But still hasn't led us up the food chain. He'll make a mistake eventually. They always do."

Agent Chouw flipped a few pages. "We've got two other situations. Ever since we got the attention of those suits in the corporate world, they've instigated internal reviews. They wouldn't get off their asses until the pencil pushers computed the bottom line, now they see a spook in every corner. But I think we have a couple of live ones. Boudie Aerospace and Microturnkey Technology have both alerted us to potential situations. They seem legit. We've got teams working them."

Jengwi nodded. "I want tight communication with all our people. Find any connection these firms may have between them. Everything gets cross-referenced. Names. Phone numbers. Everything. I want to know if there are any common threads. Any similarities at all. I want to know if their shit smells the same. Got it?"

"Got it, Chief."

* * *

AFTER MEETING WITH Angie at Fisherman's Terminal, I had some serious thinking to do. I now realized there was some heavy crap going on. A Chinese spy ring. International espionage. The book is seen as a threat not because of the immigration program per se, but because of the connection between the immigration program and the Chinese spy program. They were kissing cousins. Somewhat of an incestuous relationship that involved "who knows who" in the Chinese community. This might be more than I bargained for, a little over my head, as I had already been told. But at least I now knew who was playing the game. I knew who the teams were, but I still didn't know the players.

I felt indebted to Angie. She'd gone out on a limb for me, desperate to find her brother, so I followed through on my promise to see Lieutenant Sam Watkins with the Seattle Police Department.

I stopped by unannounced, hoping to catch a meeting with the investigator. Directed to his office, I felt I stood out like a grape in an egg carton as I passed by numerous suited detectives staring at computer monitors or talking on telephones.

I knocked on Watkins's door and through the frosted glass window saw a blurred image rise up from behind a dark shape. "Come in, Mr. Beecham," he called out. I pushed the door open and met him half way. He shook my hand and pointed. "Have a seat."

He returned to his chair, sat back and tapped a pencil on the padded arm, hesitating for a moment, as he stared with an intense gaze. "I don't have anything more for you. They didn't leave a lot of evidence, other than the incendiary residue. Our lab's looking for any match to previous cases. So far they've come up empty."

"I understand," I said. "It's probably a long shot, huh?"

"Yeah. Don't get a lot of cases like this around here. Arson? Yes. Explosives? Rarely. We've forwarded a sample of the explosive residue to the FBI lab. See what they can tell us. But I'm not optimistic."

The FBI lab? Great. For all I know these are the guys that may be behind this. Them or their buddies on the Chinese side of this cat and mouse game. And me? I'm that piece of cheese in the middle waiting for the spring latch to release and my head to snap. I nodded, having heard pretty much what I had expected. I then got to the point. "I really came to see you on another matter. It may be related to the sinking of my boat."

Lieutenant Watkins sat up. I had his attention. So far, he seemed pretty straight. But when I told him what I knew, I'd be laying it all out. I'd be vulnerable.

I cleared my throat. "I met with a friend yesterday. She has an older brother who's missing. She hasn't been able to contact him for over a week now and says that's not like him at all. She can't reach him on his cell phone either. He's just gone. She's panicked, but afraid to involve the police."

Lieutenant Watkins's frowned. "Why's she afraid of the police?"

I glanced around the room then settled my eyes on the Lieutenant. "Do you share information with the FBI? You know, if you heard something you thought they might be interested in, would you pass it on, or bring them in on it?"

Watkins's eyes opened wide then he squinted, flashing a look like I'd scratched a raw scab. "We normally don't share ongoing investigations. We do our job. They do theirs. Unless of course, it's beyond our jurisdiction. We sometimes have to dance together, but never love songs, they're more like tempestuous tangos." He smiled, but it didn't seem genuine.

"So whatever I say here, remains between us," I asked. "It won't be shared with the FBI?" I wanted a firm confirmation, although I knew such a thing probably didn't exist in the world of investigative dealings where information was spent like legal tender.

Lieutenant Watkins placed his thumb and finger together and swiped them across his closed lips. "The case is sealed. Whatever you say is part of *our* investigation."

I sighed and took a moment to reflect back. "This friend of mine, she's Chinese American, was born here, as were her two brothers. Her parents immigrated to America from China years ago. They were sent here as part of a program of the Chinese government to settle in America. I won't get into all of that now, but because of this they have continued contact with the Chinese government." I paused to search for the right words, knowing the next admission would probably skew the Lieutenant's unbiased sentiments. "Although they are aware there is an active program of espionage within the Chinese community, let me emphasize, *they are not spies.*"

I watched the Lieutenant. I knew the mere mention of the words "espionage" and "spies" would raise his interest level. He didn't interrupt, he kept his focus, if not honing it to a sharper plane.

"She's worried this espionage activity may have something

to do with his disappearance."

Watkins waited a second before he spoke. "And why would she think that? You said her missing brother wasn't involved in espionage."

"It's complicated, so I won't bog you down with details, but it begins with the fact that I'm writing a book about it."

Lieutenant Watkins raised his eyebrows as he reached for a ceramic coffee cup and sipped, his eyes fixed on me.

I realized I had better backtrack a bit. "Well, the book's not exactly about espionage, but it's based on the emigration program his family's involved in. It's a novel about Chinese immigrants, and I obtained a lot of my background material from her brother. I believe the Chinese know about the book and they aren't happy about it. I think they believe I've written about sensitive stuff. Stuff they'd rather not see in print. Something I would have gotten from him about their espionage program. He'd be seen as a security leak I guess you'd say. He isn't, of course, because he had never divulged anything like that to me. But they may think he did."

"But if he's not a spy, why would they think he had knowledge of their operations?"

"Through this emigration program his family's been a part of, they hear things. Through his contacts within the Chinese community things become known. Not specific details, but vague inferences and suggestions. Some of the participants of this emigration program *are* involved in espionage, or so I'm told. So they probably assume he knows something, maybe too much, and has passed it on to me. But like I said, he hasn't."

Lieutenant Watkins rocked back and folded his hands under his chin, his elbows on the arms of the chair. "Okay, let me see if I've got this straight. This woman's brother is missing. He's Chinese American. And due to some emigration program he and his family are involved in, he probably knows more than the average Joe about Chinese espionage operations in the area. You say he's not involved in illegal activity himself, to the best of your knowledge, but that the Chinese government may think he's passed on information anyway. Stuff they wouldn't want you to publish. And you're assuming that's why he's missing. You think they're responsible for his disappearance, either to shut him up, or punish him for what they think he's already divulged."

"Yes. Exactly. It may sound a bit far fetched, but there's too much evidence pointing to this."

"What kind of evidence? Real or imagined?"

"Well. I'm certain the emigration program is for real. More than one person has told me this. And his sister has told me in confidence that this program has a link to Chinese espionage. Then there's my boat. Arson. Incendiary. Professional job. Those are your words. Then there's the Chinese guys who threatened my editor, the visit by the FBI and now Geo…ah, her brother's disappearance."

"Whoa! Hold on." Lieutenant Watkins held up his hand and gave me a hard look. "What is this about Chinese guys threatening your editor and the visit by the FBI? I haven't heard this before."

"Yeah, well, the FBI paid me a visit on my boat before it blew up. It wasn't a social call. They somehow knew about the book and basically threatened me. Said it would interfere with ongoing investigations and put agents at risk. I haven't heard from them since, but I haven't exactly made myself available either."

Lieutenant Watkins nodded. "And these guys threatened your editor?"

"Someone did. He had a strange visit by two Chinese guys who claimed to be from some cultural group. Never showed IDs so we're not sure who they were. Said they were interested in helping with the book, but they essentially threatened him. Said there were people who didn't want the book published.

He told them to go to hell. He's that kind of guy."

Lieutenant Watkins shook his head. I suppose I threw a lot at him unexpectedly and he needed some time to digest it.

"So do you think you can help? My friend wouldn't come to the police herself because she's afraid. The Chinese community has long arms. No place and no person are out of their reach. In this particular matter she doesn't even think she can trust police officers of Chinese descent. She's concerned any one of them might have connections to the Chinese community. You know, he may have a cousin who has a friend who knows somebody, and her name may be passed on to the wrong person. That kind of thing."

Lieutenant Watkins smiled. "I'd like to vouch for all our officers. We have a solid and reputable department, but I understand her concerns." He paused a moment. "Tell you what I'll do. I'll ask around. See if I can dig anything up. Keep it off the books for now. Nothing official, but I'll need this missing man's full name."

I hesitated, but I knew without a name, Watkins wouldn't get far. "George Hu. H. U."

The lieutenant jotted the name down then removed his reading glasses. "Okay. Now, your boat. You mentioned there might be a connection between the arson and this book you're writing. Then there's the Chinese, and the FBI. You didn't mention any of this in your earlier deposition. You want to tell me why?"

I had not mentioned this to the Lieutenant in earlier conversations, but now I knew I had to explain myself. "At the time, I somehow suspected there could be a connection between the boat sinking and my book. It *had* crossed my mind. But I didn't find out about the link to Chinese espionage until a couple days ago. Until then, I didn't anticipate the book would be seen as such a serious threat. Because it's a work of fiction, it seemed so unlikely."

"Apparently, someone else sees it differently," Watkins said. "This missing fellow," he glanced down, grabbed his glasses and perused his notes, "George Hu. He may not have thought it was that serious either. But now he's turned up missing."

"Yes, and to be honest, he did warn me. He told me that beyond the facts of the emigration program there was information of another sort that some people would not want to see in a book."

Watkins shot me a look. "He told you that? He foresaw this threat, knew of this danger?" He leaned back and slapped his hands on the arms of his chair. "Okay, now what *else* haven't you told me?"

CHAPTER TWENTY-SEVEN

I WAITED UNTIL after six, then headed back to the diner and the public telephone. I had become pretty comfortable there and had almost begun to think of it as my own personal office. All I needed was a file cabinet and a stereo playing Jimmy Buffet. But this diner was not an island-music kind of place. Judging by the clientele and twangy music seeping out of the dusty jukebox, it catered more to the Jimmy Redneck crowd.

I telephoned Angie and filled her in on my conversation with Lieutenant Watkins.

"Listen, Curtis, I really appreciate you doing that. Maybe this detective can find out something. I hope so anyway." She paused. "I want you to meet a friend of mine. I talked to her a few days ago, and from what she told me on the phone, I think she might have something you'd want to hear."

"Who is she?"

"Well, it's a long story. I don't want to talk about it on the phone."

"Okay. Where?"

"The Bamblue Club. It's a small private club in the International District off Jefferson Street. I'll meet you there. Eight forty-five."

"I'll find it. Did you say Bamboo Club?

"No. Bamblue, like the color blue."

* * *

LATER THAT EVENING at the appointed time, I spotted Angie leaning against a building in the alley, about a block away. She wore jeans and a long coat that hung below her knees. This was the first time I had seen her in something other than her white pants uniform. The alley was dark but a bulb against a brick wall threw enough light in the area to illuminate her. When I approached she pulled me toward her and spoke in a quiet voice. "This is the club." She motioned toward a nondescript doorway to her right.

"Before we go in, I want you to know something. This is a strip club. But not your normal strip club. There could be sexual acts performed on stage. The woman we need to talk to works here. Are you okay with that?"

A little surprised, I glanced at the door and whispered, "In there? There's not even a sign on the door. How'd you know?"

"I've been here before."

I stared at Angie, a little shocked. She did not seem the type to frequent a place such as this. "You've been here before?" At this point I wasn't sure if she meant she had been here as a customer or as a performer. And, I didn't want to know.

"Like I said, it's a long story. I'll tell you later. So, you okay with this?"

"Uh, yeah. Sure. What kind of useful information could we get in a place like this?"

"Just go with it. We'll see."

Angie stepped up to the door and knocked. A face appeared at a small window.

"We're friends of Sayonara."

The door opened and a large Asian man motioned us in. "Forty bucks," he said, his face showing as much emotion as a stone Buddha.

I dug in my pocket and handed him two twenties. This did not seem the kind of place you pulled out a credit card.

The lighting was dim. I had to squint as I allowed my eyes time to adjust. We followed the money collector down the hall toward the muffled sound of music where we approached another door. He motioned for us to enter. As the door swung open the music came alive and shouts and whistles competed to be heard above the din. The room appeared to be the size of the average coffee shop, with a small stage surrounded by a few rows of theater style seating. Stage lighting threw a warm red glow across the room while sultry music reverberated off the red-carpeted walls. A smoky veil masked the ceiling, fed by thin plumes that drifted upwards from tiny burning embers. The intimate setting encapsulated the stagnant air, filling the room with the stale odor of overheated bodies and tobacco. The kind of scent I knew would cling to my clothing and remain for hours. We found two seats against the back wall and slipped in.

On stage a tall Asian woman danced with calculated movements that accentuated her undulating hips. Her red sequined gown with a deep plunging neckline sparkled and glittered against the soft light and a high slit up the sides displayed slender, shapely legs. Red patent-leather platform heels made her six inches taller. Straight black hair cascaded across her shoulders and down the small of her back. Her face displayed full red lips and dark eyes with long lashes. She was stunning.

As I grew accustomed to the darkness, I glanced around. The crowd was a mix of Asian businessmen, gay partners, and suspicious looking women. From the whistles and cheers of admiration, I could tell they were enjoying the show. Angie leaned over and whispered. "That's Sayonara."

Like other customers and fervent admirers, my eyes were

fixated on flashes of movement that shimmered under the light, throwing sparkles from a sequined gown that hugged her sinuous figure and emphasized her sultry moves.

She sang in a husky voice that radiated the primal call of nature. Finishing her song, she began a dialog with the overheated patrons.

"How's everyone tonight?" She called out, her red lips nearly sucking in the chrome microphone. The crowd responded as hoots and cheers filled the small room. "I can see we have an excited crowd out there tonight. How excited are we?" The crowd ignited once again. "Okay! Okay, I get the picture. Is it hot in here or is it just me?" She fanned herself in an exaggerated motion with a small ornate Japanese fan, her long flirty eyelashes skimming the crowd. "Okay guys, settle down. We got *all* night. And I intend to do it *alllll* night!"

The cheers were loud but I hardly noticed the crowd noise as she swept me up in her charismatic hold.

"Okay, simmer down. Let me ask you something. It's kind of personal. You don't mind getting personal do you?" She gave the crowd a coy smile. There was a loud response in various languages, but the meaning was the same nonetheless. "I didn't think you would. So, what is it with you guys? You *men*. You have this infatuation with your penises. A penis addiction *I'd* call it. Yeah. I know. I've been around the block once or twice. But you really do. I've seen you admiring it in the mirror while wearing tighty-whities clinging to your buns. 'Hmmm, don't *I* look good?' You love to talk about your penis. I've even seen you talk *to* it. You call it by name. Some clever pet name you made up yourself. 'Knight Rider', with a capital K. Now aren't *we* proud! 'Lady Charmer'. Give–me–a–break! Then there's 'Pink Python'. How cute, and of course, 'Big Daddy's Pile Driver'. Hmmm, think about that for a minute. And of course, 'The Lovvve Stick'. Pa-lleeaase!" The crowd laughed and cheered.

"Unfortunately—sorry guys, this is the pathetic part—you do most of your *thinking* with it too! That will always land you in deep shit. And God knows, you *looooove* to play with it. What would you talk about, think about and play with if you didn't have that little, tiny pee-pee between your legs to entertain you?"

The crowd continued in a raucous exhibition of unabashed, adolescent behavior. "You're forever looking for anything or anyplace small and tight enough to stick—it—in. And I would guess there's not a one of you out there who doesn't appreciate a *good* blowjob." She paused as the crowd hooted. "Or a bad one!" The crowd screamed and cheered, in profound agreement.

She strutted along the edge of the stage then stared down at one gentleman sitting in the front row. "How about you, big guy? You love your penis? Yeah, you do. I can tell. You'd probably suck yours if you could reach it, wouldn't you? Ah huh. I know." The crowd exploded and the guy next to him slapped him across his bald head. She looked around at the audience and swept her slender arm from side to side. "Don't you all laugh like you hadn't thought about it. I know you *all* would if you could. It's *just* a matter of inches!"

She returned her gaze to the short Asian fellow in the front row. "Hey, what's your name?" She put her free hand to her ear. "What, Hiro? Yeah, you look like a hero to me too, big guy. Here, come on up and join me. Yeah, right up here, next to me. Come on. Don't be shy."

As the gentleman, who appeared to be a Japanese businessman jumped up on stage, Sayonara moved close to him, taking her time to peel off the man's coat and unbutton his shirt and trousers as she sang another tune. His slacks collapsed in a heap on the floor as the nervous—and now reluctant—participant stared straight ahead. "And what do we have here?" Sayonara asked as she rubbed her hand across his jockey shorts. Within seconds she encouraged an erection and the embarrassed gentleman attempted to cover it with his too small hands.

"Just wanted to see if we had any life in there." She spun the man around, grabbed him on the ass and scooted him toward the curtain behind the stage. "Don't finish without me!" she purred to him as he shuffled out of sight.

The audience showed their appreciation with whistles and cheers. She then moved into a groove and sang and pranced onstage through three upbeat song and dance numbers. After the echo faded, the sweet sound of Oriental music rose throughout the calmed room. The slow distinct twang set an enchanting tone. In one subtle move she unzipped her gown. The flowing garment fell to the floor to reveal bare breasts under the red glow of stage lights. They stood firm like pillows as she teased her nipples with a long red fingernail. With one smooth motion she kicked the dress to the side as she continued to sing and move her nearly bare hips to the exotic music. She wore red panties with lace that proved to be thong-style when she turned, exposing a firm, tight derrière. Having commanded and received everyone's attention and having narrowed their focus, the loud rowdiness of previous moments had diminished.

She motioned for a handsome young fellow sitting in an aisle seat to join her on stage, extending her hand for him to grasp. She continued to sing. The young man closed in on her and they moved in unison, shuffling their feet and gyrating their hips against one other. The man had a smooth young face and blond hair that whipped around his ears and the back of his neck. He unbuttoned and removed his shirt to expose two small breasts. *Huh?* A murmur spread among the audience. Sayonara unbuckled his belt, pulled down his zipper and let his slacks drop to the stage floor. Everyone leaned forward and stared, mouths open. He was *not* a man. He was a she. The audience gaped, leaned forward for a closer look. The murmur rose.

The newly revealed young woman slid her hands down Sayonara's waist, moved closer, rubbed her pelvis against Sayonara. Sayonara turned, her back to the crowd. The young woman slipped her fingers inside the band of Sayonara's silk panties, slid them down, released them as they dropped upon Sayonara's ankles. She kicked them loose, and they slid across the polished wood stage.

She held Sayonara tight, her hands circling her waist, as they rotated and Sayonara turned to face the crowd. The crowd shuffled as everyone readjusted, leaning forward toward the edge of their seat and stared. Sayonara had a penis. Gasps were heard and breath exhaled as chatter grew throughout the room. I choked on my dry throat, finding it hard to swallow. Am I really seeing this? But, there they were. The he was a she, and the she was a he.

They continued to dance as the young woman raised one leg and draped it around Sayonara's waist. Sayonara closed in. They continued to move in unison to the slow beat, joined together as they kissed. Caressing each other as they made love in a private but public way.

Sayonara was right. It was hot in there. I sneaked at look at Angie. She caught me.

"She's part of the act," she said. "They're good friends."

I thought to myself, as I adjusted my shirt collar, I bet they are.

* * *

ANGIE TAPPED ON the door with the brass plate that announced, PRIVATE. "Come in," came the response in a raspy voice.

She pushed the door open and stuck her head in. "Hi."

Sayonara turned, saw Angie, and exclaimed, "Oh, honey. How are you? Come in. Come in. It's been too, too long."

Then she saw me behind her. "Oh, yes, dear. Please *do* come in." She rose from her dressing vanity and moved toward Angie, giving her a warm embrace.

Angie grasped my arm, pulling me forward. "This is Curtis. He's a friend of mine."

"Yes, yes. Pleased to meet you, Curtis. Have a seat right here." She pointed to a worn red-velvet tufted couch.

She held both of Angie's hands. "It's so good to see you. How are you sweetie?"

"I'm doing okay. But as I told you on the phone I'm worried about George."

"Yes, I understand. I will do what I can."

I was completely dumbfounded. What am I doing here? How can this lady, ah, guy, or whatever, help me? Or help Angie? This is the last place I expected to find myself today or any day. And the last place I would expect to find help.

Angie sat down next to me while I stared at Sayonara. She sat on her makeup bench, her legs crossed, exposing a lot of thigh through the gap in her red silk kimono. The lights around her dressing mirror highlighted the edges of her hair.

"I told Curtis we had talked recently on the phone, that you had information to share with me. I believe he might find it of interest too."

"Yes, I do. Interesting? Bizarre? It's your call, honey. But you might want to hear it first and then decide." She glanced at me and studied my face. "You saw the show?"

"Yes, it was quite…ah, different." Although I knew shows like this existed, I had never seen one. Yeah, maybe a few titillating strip shows in Vegas, but *nothing* like this.

I felt a little awkward. I had just witnessed what I thought to be a beautiful woman having a kind of sexual interaction on stage with what I thought was a young man. I had been fooled, not once, but twice. I actually thought she was quite beautiful and sensuous. As a man, I began to question my own sexual instincts. I was embarrassed that this person had actually raised the heat of my own sexual thermostat. I continued, "Ahhh, I guess this is kind of new to me. I've never actually seen a show quite like that before."

"Heaven knows, it's not for everyone." She smiled. "As you saw, there's definitely an audience for this, well, what shall we call it, 'burlesque with an edge'? It's a living. And I have to admit, I enjoy the striptease. And as long as my fans continue to show their appreciation, I suppose I feel obligated to entertain them. After all, what else can a transvestite blessed with a sexy voice and beautiful breasts do?" She smiled at me, re-crossed her legs and leaned back in her chair, resting her elbows atop the vanity, which raised her chest like an orca breaking the surface.

I didn't know if Angie had enjoyed making me uncomfortable or not, but she had succeeded. Thankfully at this point she attempted to divert the subject back to the reason we were here in the first place.

"The information you had for us," Angie asked. "What exactly is it?"

"Well, let me begin by saying I don't *just* dance and have sex on stage for a living. I also have private sessions with a few select gentlemen. Men who get off on having sex with a, well, you know. One of these clients is Chinese. I see him about once a month, or more frequent if he's under stress. I've serviced him for about a year now. He's into dominance. Meaning he likes me to dominate him, at least for the first part of our session, then he turns the tables."

I realized I was going to get a real education into some of the more kinky sexual practices found behind closed doors. I stared at Sayonara, seizing on every word as she described in detail this encounter with the unnamed Chinese. I struggled, trying to decide what gender she really was, or should be. As I studied her face, I couldn't get that earlier vision out of my mind—the anatomy between her legs.

Sayonara continued, as she glanced from Angie to me. "He likes to be whipped on his bare buttocks with a sex whip, you know, a wood handle with leather straps. He imagines an imperialist interrogator is torturing him, forcing him to give up state secrets. He always lets a little information slip. And of course, I play the game. I make *sure* he lets a little information slip. When he feels he has successfully evaded all attempts to extract any *worthy* information by the imperialist interrogator, we change roles, and he dominates me. Not with the whip, mind you, but with sex. I'm Japanese, he's Chinese. There's a history of Japanese aggression against China that goes back many years. I suppose this is his way of making up for Japan's bad behavior."

I was speechless as she described these parlor games. My mind struggled to comprehend why anyone would willingly want to have their ass whipped with leather straps.

"What does this guy divulge?" Angie asked. I nodded, anxious to hear this.

Sayonara sat up and braced her hands on her knees. "He's MSS. Ministry of State Security for the People's Republic of China. He's a spy."

My jaw just about dropped to the floor. "Oh shit!"

I looked at Angie and she stared at me, a disturbed look that must have mirrored mine.

Sayonara continued. "He also said he's searching for a traitor. A traitor to China he says. Someone who is writing a revealing book about a Chinese family that had immigrated to America in a secret program." She looked at Angie and sighed, her eyes revealing a deep concern, "Like I told you on the phone, it sounded a lot like your family."

CHAPTER TWENTY-EIGHT

AFTER HEARING THE unsettling news from Sayonara, Angie and I needed to talk. We decided to meet at my place, the somewhat less-than-distinguished Pink Salmon Motel. She followed in her car giving me time alone to digest this new revelation. The memory and the startling visual impression of the stage performance quickly faded with the impact this information brought.

As Angie sat next to the window in the one and only chair, I sprawled across the bed. Raising myself up on my left elbow, I watched her closely. "Okay. First, I need to know the whole story. Begin with how you happen to know Sayonara."

Angie looked down at the floor and crossed her ankles. She remained quiet for a few moments. I feared the worst. Knowing what I had witnessed earlier, too many undesirable scenarios flashed through my mind, none of which I wanted to hear. I studied what I could see of her face. She seemed pained. Could she possibly have a reasonable, rational explanation? I could tell it would not be easy for her, but I had to know before we went further. Based on events that seemed to be unfolding at a rapid pace, I knew Angie and I would be spending time together. I needed to hear her story.

"About two years ago," she began in a soft, wavering voice, "Sayonara saved my life. I was seventeen. I had been at a friend's house, studying, before walking home. It was early evening. I never saw them. Two guys. One grabbed me from behind and covered my mouth with a rag. He pushed me through the doorway of an abandoned building. The other guy was already there, I couldn't see him, and the two of them dragged me into an empty room. They told me not to scream. They slapped me and yanked my hair. I thought they would pull it right out of my head. They ripped my blouse off and tore at my bra. Then they threw me down onto the concrete floor and yanked my jeans and panties off. One guy pulled his jeans down to his knees and knelt between my legs. The other guy held my arms down. To this day I see his face over me. Rage in his eyes, the nasal sound of his heavy breathing."

I had not expected this. Angie looked at me, her eyes moist. Seeing the pain in her face made me feel her torment. I had not known I was asking her to relive a nightmare. To drag up demons I'm sure she had tried to bury and forget.

Angie stepped into the bathroom and returned a moment later with a tissue. "I was so scared. I begged them to let me go, but they slapped me again and groped me. Then without warning, a loud scream echoed throughout the empty building. I turned my head toward the source of the voice. Silhouetted in the doorway against the light streaming into the room I saw a tall figure of a woman."

Angie wiped at her eyes and continued. "The woman wore a short black leather skirt with a split and knee-length black boots. She had her arms outstretched and in her hands she gripped a small silver gun. She shouted again, but I was crying, in fear and in such a frantic state, I couldn't comprehend what she said.

"The two guys jumped off me, scooted a short distance away and knelt, their face down on the concrete. She walked over, stopped behind the one with his pants down and swung her leg back in a swift arc, jamming the pointed heel of her boot between his buttocks. There was a different scream this time. One of pain and agony. He reached down with his hands and I saw blood seep between his fingers."

I cringed, tightened my butt cheeks in reflex and shifted to my other elbow.

"The other guy looked at her, terror on his face, jumped up and bolted for the door. The woman watched him but didn't shoot. She hurried to me, stooped down and cuddled me, slowly rocking me back and forth, cradling my head. She offered soothing words of support. I was terrified and the tears flowed down my cheeks. I couldn't stop shaking. I hugged her in return as I tried to calm myself, knowing she had just saved me from a certain double rape and possible death."

I shifted on the bed, turned, lay face down, my chin on my arms, staring at the floor. I felt guilty about asking her to divulge such an intimate secret, but I knew in order to trust her, I had to know everything. I listened as she continued.

"She helped me into my clothes and supported me as we stepped out onto the street. She took me to her apartment two blocks away. Cleaned me up. I asked her not to call the police. She told me it wasn't my fault. I just happened to be in the wrong place at the wrong time."

She paused. "The woman, of course, was Sayonara."

Angie stood up and gazed out the window through a gap in the curtain. The darkness of the motel parking lot was broken by the harshness of the occasional floodlight attached to the corridor. In the late night a sense of peace and quiet had settled over the Pink Salmon, unlike the lives of most of the guests. She reached up and pulled her hair away from her face then wrapped her arms around her chest.

"I owe her my life. We became friends. She has been a mentor to me. One I could talk to, who would listen. She kept her real life from me, protecting me I suppose, but eventually she knew she had to tell me her story. I don't condemn her for it. There are all types of people in this world, and just because someone is different, doesn't mean they are a bad person." Angie turned back to me. "It's what's in here, that counts." She pointed to her chest. "She's a good person and deserves the same respect as everyone else, regardless of how she lives her personal life."

"Not many people would step into danger to save a stranger," I said. "I understand how you would become close."

"Yes, we have. Over time we have talked often and openly. I shared the worst few minutes of my life with her, so I feel I can share anything. We have talked of our families. I have told of my father coming to America, his having sons, and of Uncle Willie. I have shared everything."

I was both stunned and moved by Angie's confession. I knew for her to tell me such intimate information she must feel she can trust me. That was good. I needed someone I could depend on as well. We both needed someone to talk to. Someone we could share our fears with. Even though we hadn't known each other very long, we seemed comfortable enough with each other to provide that.

After having talked to Sayonara, it was clear she at least wasn't aware of my involvement as the writer. I thought it best to keep it that way for now.

I lay there in silence for a few moments, then rolled over on my back and turned my gaze her way. I reached for her hand. "I know that was very difficult for you. I had no idea what I was asking. I'm truly sorry you ever had to experience that. No one should."

She smiled and gave a light squeeze. I thought how strong she was to suffer through the violence of that despicable act and accept without reservation the lifestyle embraced by her rescuer.

The light from the lamp by the bed threw a warm cast against her face. She was beautiful in a simple, natural way, without aid from the heavy hand of the cosmetic queens. She had removed her coat to uncover a pink tank top that hung loose against her midriff with thin straps that crossed her shoulders. Tight jeans with a trendy worn spot in the thigh gripped her ankles above a pair of stylish black heels—the uniform of the young after-hours crowd. She smelled of a clean freshness, unlike a perfumery, and very unlike the Pink Salmon Motel.

My mind wandered back to the show I had just witnessed. Angie must have read my thoughts.

"Asians are more accepting and tolerant of the public display of genitalia," she began. "Many Asian cultures celebrate the act of procreation in colorful fertility ceremonies and festivals. It's not uncommon for them to observe holidays with street parades consisting of floats with replicas of giant phalluses. Asians are not as shocked as Americans by such an exhibition as we have just seen. It's a part of life. Part of our culture. Although I must admit Sayonara does put her own special spin on it. But she is a true friend. We can trust her."

I thought for a moment, as something had been bothering me. "Tell me. Does she consider herself a girl or a guy? I mean, she dresses like a woman, but in reality she's a man."

She quickly answered. "It depends."

I let her response sink in. "Yeah, I suppose so." I decided to leave this topic of discussion alone for now. Probably forever.

"So this agent Sayonara is seeing," I said. "He seems a bit violent. A dangerous guy. And he's looking for me. And, how'd he found out about the book? First, the FBI found out about it and now we have confirmation MSS knows as well. *No one* should know about it but you, me, Thomas, George, Su Wan and my editor. That still has me concerned. Not one of these people has a reason to talk about it. In fact it would not be in their best interest if they did. I just can't figure it out."

"I agree. This guy does sound dangerous. A man without respect for anyone. Himself included as far as I'm concerned. I'd been worried all along that MSS might somehow know about George, and that might be why he's missing. Sayonara said she would be seeing this agent again soon. Lets hope she can get him to reveal what he knows about George."

"From what I saw of her," I said, "she could make anybody talk. Despite appearances, she's a tough cookie. But I don't think we can wait for her. For George's sake, we have to do something, and do it now."

CHAPTER TWENTY-NINE

ANGIE ARRIVED AT the import warehouse before they closed for the day, hoping to meet with her father and Uncle Willie. She had been in contact with her father over the disappearance of George and he, like everyone in the family, had become very distraught. Her mother, Li Chen and older sister Sung Wi, were terrified for George, but as women, had embraced more traditional roles in the family and felt powerless to do anything on their own.

The Asian Antique Import Company was located in the International District. A wholesaler, they imported merchandise from China and distributed it to retailers and antique shops around the country. The front room offered a small reception area while the administrative staff and sales and marketing department occupied a larger room to the left. Both Uncle Willie's office and her father's were found through a door behind the reception desk. Past their offices and farther down the hall was the warehouse, a large space with a tall ceiling capped by a corrugated tin roof, stacked with containers and crates twenty feet high. As a youngster Angie had wandered among the many boxes, studying the fascinating labels and stickers that had traveled from that distant and exotic land, imagining the many unique furnishings and wildly colorful art to be found inside.

Regina, the receptionist, on seeing Angie enter, pointed toward the door. "Hi Angela. Your father's in his office. Go on back. He'll be pleased to see you."

Angie smiled, passed through the door, took a few steps down the hall, then peered into her father's office. "Father?"

Wung Hu looked up from a stack of papers he was flipping through and smiled a broad grin. "My dear child. What brings you to see me today?" He removed an open cardboard box from the wood chair next to his desk. "Please. Sit with me."

"Father." Angie clasped her hands in her lap. "We have talked about George, and I'm so worried. You know this isn't like him. I think something has happened. Something bad."

Wung Hu dropped his smile. He reached over and laid his hand on Angie's arm. "Yes. I too am very worried for George. I just do not know what I can do."

"We must talk to Uncle Willie. We have no choice. We have to act quickly. George may need us."

Angie had not told her father about Su Wan and Curtis, or Sayonara for that matter. Keeping Sayonara's friendship a secret was of course, imperative, given the nature of their first encounter. And she sensed she should keep the latest developments with Su Wan and Curtis to herself for now. She didn't want to endanger anyone else, unless it appeared she would have to divulge that relationship to help find her brother.

Angie could see her father struggle with her request. She had asked him to speak to Uncle Willie, but he had been hesitant, saying he didn't want to involve Uncle Willie, to burden him with their family problems if he didn't have to. But her father had admitted he had no explanation for George's disappearance and knew no course of action to take to find his son. She and her father both knew George had been depressed. The family had been aware of George's troubled state, but they did not know the source of it. She knew her father was a proud man and thought it his responsibility to care for his family, but on his own, he had no means to help his son. She knew he felt powerless and frantic with worry.

"Please, Father, we must."

Angie could see the pain in her father's eyes. He squeezed her arm. "Yes, Angela. You are right. It is time. We must ask Uncle Willie for his help."

"Thank you, Father. Let's see him now."

Wung Hu nodded, and rose from his chair. He put his arm around Angie and gave her a squeeze as they headed for Uncle Willie's office. Arriving at his open door, Wung Hu poked his head in.

"Uncle Willie, may we speak with you?"

Uncle Willie looked up. Seeing Angie and her father in the doorway, he smiled, then stood up. "Of course. Please come in." He walked around his desk and took Angie's hands. "You become more beautiful with each new day. Far too lovely for those undesirables that hang around your neighborhood." He winked. "We must find you a fine man with whom your father will be proud. A smart one. Maybe a doctor, yes?"

Angie attempted a smile. "Yes, maybe a doctor. Maybe a veterinarian." She looked at her father, but the purpose of her meeting had taken the edge off her sense of humor.

"Yes, maybe," Uncle Willie grinned. "Please sit. Now, what is the pleasure of this visit from my dear Angela?"

Angie looked at her father then shifted her attention to Uncle Willie. "George is missing. He hasn't been seen for almost ten days now. We don't know where he is."

Uncle Willie's smile disappeared. "Missing? What do you mean?"

Angie explained that George had not been in his apartment nor had he contacted anybody as to his whereabouts.

Uncle Willie remained silent for a moment. "Hmmm. No. This is not like George." He looked at Wung Hu and then turned his eyes to Angie. "I saw him just about ten days ago. Talked to him on the phone later that night." Uncle Willie hesitated. He seemed reluctant to proceed. "George seemed very depressed. I think he is struggling to find himself. This is a process many young men go through, but his struggle seems to be greater than most. He is a bright young man, but the current within him runs very deep. I think he felt much pressure from the tough law curriculum at the University and from his studies at the Cultural Academy. I don't know for certain, but maybe this has something to do with his disappearance. Maybe he needed time alone. To clear his head."

Uncle Willie stood up and walked to the door, glanced out the hallway, pushed it shut, then returned to the chair behind his desk. He sat silent, leaving an opening for Angie to speak.

"We're very worried for George," she said. "I don't think he's disappeared of his own free will. I think something bad has happened to him. I think he's in danger."

Uncle Willie narrowed his eyes, glancing at Wung Hu and then back to Angie. "Danger? What makes you think he might be in danger?"

Angie hesitated, looking for the right words. "Something may have happened within the Program. I don't know. Maybe George heard something or he got involved with the wrong people. I just believe he would never disappear without reason, and so suddenly." She watched Uncle Willie's reaction, trying to see any sign that she may have aroused some knowledge. Some spark of recognition. But Uncle Willie revealed no emotion.

"I am not sure I know what you speak of, but I have friends in the community that I can talk to. I can ask if someone knows about George." He leaned forward and reached for Angie's hand. "Your family is my family. You know this. George is very dear to me. I pray no harm has come to him. I will pursue everything in my power to find him and keep him safe. Let me see what I can do."

Angie wiped at a tear, then looked up at her father. Wung Hu's eyes glistened as he stood up and took her arm. "Come, Angela. We must let Uncle Willie do what he can. I have faith he will help us find George."

As they reached the door Angie turned and glanced back at Uncle Willie. She studied his face and detected a hint of deep concern, an unsettling expression that had been masked over moments earlier. A pang of fear rushed in, delivered by a sudden chill. His face said it all. Uncle Willie knew something. Knew something about George.

CHAPTER THIRTY

I HAD BEEN lying across the bed daydreaming, thinking about the *Mockaritaville*. A few days ago I finally allowed myself to stop by the marina where her remains rested on the muddy bottom. All I saw was a vacant slip, an emptiness where she used to bob in peace, nudging her weather-worn beam against the dock. Now there was nothing. Any signs of the explosion had drifted with the current. It was as if she had never been. I had walked up the dock and stared at the scorched edge where a portion had been burned away in the fireball. Kneeling down, I had run my fingers along it releasing a burnt, charcoal smell that drifted upwards. Perhaps *this* was her last breath, I thought. The scorched edge crumbled and dropped into the dark pool below. My fingers had remained smudged with black ash. She was only a memory. I had to move on.

The hum of the television created a white noise in the background when a loud knock and rattle of the motel door startled me, brought me back to the present. This wasn't the day for the maid to clean. I hadn't expected company. I lifted myself off the bed and stepped over to the window, pulling the curtain back a few inches, peering outside. Thomas Hu stood on the walkway, his hands in his pockets, staring at the door. He was alone. What would Thomas be doing here? How would he know where I was staying?

I unlatched the lock and swung the door open. "Hi, Thomas."

He nodded as he shuffled one foot. "Can we talk?"

"Sure. Come in." I shut the door after him, set the lock, walked over and turned off the television, then flopped on the bed. "How'd you know where to find me?"

"I overheard Angie talking to you on the phone. Heard the name Pink Salmon Motel. The guy at the front desk couldn't find your name on the registration but when I described you he knew who you were and told me what room you were in." Thomas smirked, "I said I was your brother."

I made a mental note. *Don't* count on the desk clerk. "Ah, yeah. Okay. So, what's up?"

I was pretty curious why Thomas had come to see me. He hadn't been too forthcoming when we met at Angie's apartment, but now, here he is meeting me one-on-one. I hoped he would have something to add to my growing pool of information, even though I thought I already had most of what I was after.

Thomas settled himself on the only chair. When I thought about it, I'm surprised the room had a chair, but I suppose guests needed a place to pile their clothes for the one hour or so these rooms are normally in use.

"I wasn't straight with you the other day," he began. "There are things you don't know. About the Program I mean. I expect you already know most of what has happened within our family. The immigration part. And as George told you, there's more to it. But I can't go into that right now."

I nodded. "I know." I didn't want to let on I knew about the espionage connection. I had to protect Angie, my source. And, I needed to keep my options open.

"Within our family we don't talk much about the Program. I've been involved for so many years now, you know...my entire life. I guess I really don't think about it too much. But

I'm afraid George does. Way too much. It's really been eating at him the last few months."

Thomas removed his ball cap, leaned over and rested his elbows on his knees, twirling the cap in his hands. "George and I see it a little differently. I don't take the Program too seriously. It's my father and Uncle Willie's thing. Sure, I go along with it out of respect, but I try not to make a big deal of it. I see my family being manipulated by the Program directors, and for that and other reasons, I don't agree with it. They have too much control over my father's life. He admires Uncle Willie to a fault; leans on him and depends on him too much. It probably goes all the way back to his upbringing in China. You know. Unquestioned devotion. Following orders blindly. The Party first, the family and the individual second. I could probably spend an hour dictating Party dogma, but you don't want to hear it and I don't want to waste my time."

I turned and leaned back against the painted headboard bolted to the wall, stuffing two flat pillows behind my head as Thomas continued. I was getting a pretty clear picture of where he stood on the issue.

"Uncle Willie asked me to keep an eye on George. Keep him informed on how George was doing. I suppose I should have been in closer contact, but I got busy with my own life. We were in different curriculums, had a different circle of friends, so we didn't run into each other that much. He didn't always tell me everything, so maybe it wouldn't have mattered anyway."

Thomas sat up and placed his ball cap back on his head, adjusting it with both hands. "I do want you to know I'll support any efforts to find George. I love my brother, and I want no harm to come to him. I'm not even sure we see things that much differently, he just seems to have a harder time finding his own path. He worries too much about the consequences, instead of getting on with his life."

Having heard Thomas out, I had to ask. "What do *you* think happened to George?"

Thomas sighed, then spoke with deep concern in his voice. "I'm afraid to even say. There are some dangerous people in our community. They'd do almost anything for their cause. If they felt a threat, that is."

"And George may have been perceived as a threat?"

"Yes, after hearing what you had to say at Angie's the other night, I believe he might be."

"So you think the book might have had something to do with it?"

"Yes, most definitely. I wish you'd never written that damn book. And George should never have told you what he did, either, but he did. These guys take things pretty seriously. They don't fool around."

"Yeah. I'm beginning to believe."

Thomas's eyes twitched and he paused, but I could see he had a determined look on his face. "Curtis. I don't really know you, but I think you're an okay guy. I don't think you've pursued this story with any intent to harm my family. But, as you can see, it's created some serious problems. I'd like to ask you to abandon it. Forget the book and move on. It's only going to make things worse. Even though I don't agree with the Program, I don't want a story about it winding up in a novel. It would have negative repercussions for our family."

I was not all together surprised by this request. I was only surprised Angie hadn't asked the same thing earlier. And it wasn't like I hadn't thought along those same lines myself. "I understand Thomas. I don't blame you for thinking that way. At this point it's just a manuscript in my editor's hands, and a long way from becoming a published book. It may never happen. I believe we'll find George safe and get beyond this way before this book ends up on any bookshelf."

I shifted, feeling a bit uncomfortable, knowing my writing

had created serious angst for the Hu family and the young man who sat before me. "If you had a chance to read it, and maybe you will someday, you'll see the story line stays well clear of your family. There's no direct connection or resemblance at all. I understand there are hundreds if not thousands of immigrant families in the Program. This story could be about any one of them, or none of them. To readers of suspense novels, it will be just another paperback. One of thousands published each year. You and your family are more sensitive to the story line because of your involvement, but the general public will only think it's some writer's imagination, another work of fiction, which of course, it is."

Thomas nodded, stood up to go, and I lifted myself from the bed. I extended my hand, he accepted it. "I do understand your concerns," I said. "Right now, my priority is locating George, and assuring his wellbeing. Let's forget about the book for now and concentrate our efforts on finding him."

* * *

AFTER THOMAS LEFT I headed out to grab a sandwich, then drove over to the diner to call Jack Buick. I could have eaten there while making my call, but my stomach flipped over three times at the very notion of further abusing my digestive system.

My mind swirled with all that had happened and I began to believe the more I understood, the less I knew. Should I give up the book? I had dedicated a lot of effort and felt close to meeting with some success. Would it make any difference if I gave it up? Had the pursuit of my dream been the real cause of George's disappearance? What about my boat? Had she been destroyed because of this pursuit? As soon as I thought about her again, I became angry. With the passage of time, my grief had begun to fade, replaced by anger. I understand that's how it is with the death of a loved one. There's the denial stage followed by the anger stage. I couldn't remember what came next, but in my case it might be revenge. This was really beginning to piss me off.

I dialed Jack Buick's number and heard him pick up. "Mr. Buick. It's Curtis Beecham."

"Hey, Curtis, how's it going? No, never mind. I'm afraid to ask. Your calls haven't exactly been full of cheerful news."

"Yeah, you're right. And when you hear the latest, you'll see we're digging ourselves a deeper hole."

"How's that?" he asked.

"Well, to begin with, there's George Hu. He's the fellow who's given me everything I've used as background information for my manuscript. You know, the young man from the Chinese family. He's missing."

"What do you mean?" I could sense surprise in Jack's voice.

I continued to apprise Jack of the details of George's disappearance, then told him about my meeting with Angie at Fisherman's Terminal, her admission concerning the program's link to espionage and the bizarre story of Sayonara and the MSS agent who's looking for the author of the book, i.e., me.

"Jesus Christ, Curtis. You sure know how to dig up some shit, don't you? Now just the *rumor* of an unpublished manuscript is about to set off a cold war with China and whoever those guys are."

"MSS."

"What's that?"

"Ministry of State Security. China's espionage agency. Their CIA."

"Yeah, whatever. But Jesus, Curtis, I've never had a book stir up so much interest, and it hasn't even been published. Don't get me wrong, I love prepublication publicity, I'm just not sure this is the kind we want. I'd like to see it published, you know. But, I'm pretty fond of breathing."

Two fellows came in the front door of the diner and headed toward me. "Hold it a second, Mr. Buick." I paused and turned my back as they passed and entered the bathroom. The door swung shut and I continued. "I'm still not certain how everybody this side of Beijing seems to know I'm writing this book. My life is getting much more complicated because of it. And I'm getting really pissed off about my boat."

"Don't blame ya. What're you planning to do?"

"I don't know. But I'm not giving in to their threats just yet. There's still a chance Sayonara might provide us with some useful information. Something that'll help us find out where George is, and if he's okay. I feel somewhat responsible for him you know. And she may be a link."

"She may be more than that," Jack replied. "I've been thinking as you've been talking. This may well be an opportunity for us. A real opportunity. From what I'm hearing you say, you're peering over the edge of a goddamned pit of international intrigue. And like you've said, this Sayonara's the link. She's the pipeline to the world of Chinese espionage. Think of it. There could be some great material for your manuscript in there. Put some real teeth in it. Raise the bar. There's the making's of a fucking top-notch suspense thriller here. I knew there was something missing. This is just what you need. I see that now. A little real-life espionage to add suspense to your story."

Jack's thoughts caught me off guard. I had been worried about the appearance of this growing threat, but Jack is saying, "Hey, this is a good thing." I suppose sitting back in New York he has a different perspective. But it's my ass they're looking for. "Yeah, I suppose that's one way of looking at it, Mr. Buick, but I was hoping to receive a royalty check some day, and I prefer you not have to send it to the morgue."

"There's some risk, sure, but imagine the rewards," he said. "Just don't get yourself in so deep you can't dig yourself out. Let Sayonara and George and the rest of them take the fucking risk. In a way, they already have, so you can't blame yourself for their involvement. Just play along a bit more and see where it leads."

"Yeah, I'll think about it. I'll see what happens in the next few days then decide what to do."

As I drove back to the motel, I thought of my conversation with Jack Buick. He was right about this being an opportunity. There could be some interesting twists to the manuscript if I incorporated the espionage angle into it. I also realized the danger there would be. To me and to the Hu family. I would have to weigh that against any rewards it might bring. Like I told Jack, it's hard to cash a check when you're lying on a slab in the morgue.

CHAPTER THIRTY-ONE

UNCLE WILLIE KNEW to whom he should be talking. After hearing Angie's plea to help find George, he had no doubt Deng Qin was involved. Uncle Willie arranged to meet him once again at the cabin in the foothills of the Cascades. This time he made sure he arrived first.

A short while later Deng Qin pulled up. Bundled against the chill, his cold expression mirrored the weather. "What is so important that you have called me out here on a day like this? Do you have the name of the person who has been talking to the writer?"

Uncle Willie hesitated, but knew he could not be indecisive. He must project a convincing front so the agent would not detect his deception. "No, Deng Qin. I do not have a name for you. I wish to meet on another matter."

The master spy showed surprise. "You do not have a name? Are you certain? I would have thought by now you would have found this traitor." His eyes tightened and he stared, his gaze penetrating like rods of steel. "You are certain, Willie Wong? You have *no* name? You are *not* mistaken?"

Uncle Willie was unnerved by the intensity of his repeated questions. But Deng Qin had always been abrupt, overpowering. He often treated simple communication exchanges like interrogation sessions. There was no possible way Deng Qin could know George had earlier confided in him and discussed his breach of confidentiality with the writer.

"No, I have no name. But I hope to very soon. This other matter—"

"Yes," Deng Qin said, disdain in his voice. "Get on with it."

"I know of a young man from a good family, one of the Sons of the Red Dragon. An honorable man. A university student. He has been missing for over ten days now. His family is very concerned. I thought you might be able to help me locate him. His name is George Hu." Uncle Willie studied the man for any sign of recognition. Deng Qin had been well trained so he did not expect this professional to show any weakness, but Uncle Willie detected a slight flicker in his eyes.

"Why should *I* know of this George Hu?" Deng Qin mocked. "He is not *my* responsibility."

"Do not play games with me, Deng Qin." Uncle Willie did not use a respectful title. Under normal circumstances, it would be "Mr. Deng Qin." But he had had enough of the arrogance of MSS. "I believe you know of George Hu and you are not forthcoming."

"It is *you* who are playing games with me," Deng Qin sneered. "It is *you* who are not forthcoming. I know."

Uncle Willie stiffened. He tensed. *Does he know about George? Does he know that I know George is the loose goose? Is he baiting me?* "I do not know what you are talking about. You are paranoid. This paranoia is bred into the culture of MSS. You are distrustful of everyone. I believe you know of George Hu's whereabouts. It would not be good if something happens to him."

"Who are you to threaten me?" Deng Qin demanded. "You are a simple babysitter. You and your Sons of the Red Dragon." He spit on the ground. "You are not fit to hold my cock. MSS is superior in every way. Beijing depends on us, and us alone. They have no trust in your program. It is a laugh. *You* are a joke."

Uncle Willie felt his face flush, his body heat rise. He had to control his anger. Although he knew this man and MSS were very powerful, he would never admit to being in a position of subservience to such an ass. But knowing he had just lied to Deng Qin about George, he didn't want to antagonize him any further.

Deng Qin let his ego control his emotions. He continued talking with a display of bravado. "Soon you will see, Willie Wong. Beijing will present me with the highest award for service to our Mother China. I am onto something bigger than you can imagine. An event with no parallel in your safe little world." He grinned, enjoying himself. "Unmatched in my world as well. An achievement with no equal in the history of MSS. An American military contractor is about to give up his highly classified secrets. It will have monumental impact on the balance of military power. It will be a coup unlike you or your Sons will ever know. And *I* am the architect. Very soon, *I* alone will receive the rewards of Beijing."

Uncle Willie eyed him with disbelief. "What is this you speak of? You say much, but you do so little."

Deng Qin smiled and expanded his chest, full of himself, confident of his future. "You will see, Willie Wong. You will see."

* * *

DENG QIN HURRIED back to Seattle. He had an appointment to make. An important one. More important than this useless meeting with Willie Wong. Willie Wong was an old fool. He had made a fatal mistake. Deng Qin had baited Willie Wong. Tested him. But he had not given up George Hu. Deng Qin did not know why he would protect this George Hu. Why he did not admit his knowledge of George Hu's transgressions. That young man was a traitor and he would pay for his indiscretion. MSS would see to that. Willie Wong would pay as well. But not just yet. Deng Qin's attention was drawn toward more important issues that required immediate action. The major coup he had orchestrated was foremost in his mind. He had to review his plans in meticulous detail to assure everything had been set in place. There would be no second chances. But, first, he had to pay a visit to the mistress of gamesmanship. The woman who satisfied his dominance needs like none other had before. She understood him. She knew how to play the game.

Willie Wong had stirred Deng Qin's anger, and anger fueled his desire like liquor fuels an alcoholic. He squeezed the steering wheel until his knuckles whitened. His heart quickened in anticipation. She would be waiting...with her toys. He needed to feel the ecstasy of pure pain. He needed to see her curled up on the floor, naked, pleading, the agony unbearable once again.

CHAPTER THIRTY-TWO

I CHECKED MY watch and realized it was nearly 5:00 P.M. I had promised Shelly, my ex, I would get the kids back by five. I had also promised seven-year-old Teri Lynn, and five-year-old Michael, they could finish up the rides they still hadn't used in their ticket book. I'd get the kids back to their house late again, but Shelly was used to that. I'm sure she'd already put a one-hour buffer in her schedule to allow for the inevitable. Not that she approved of my tardiness, but she was resigned to my lack of structure in things I considered trivial, like schedules.

Although divorced nearly three years, we still had a pretty good relationship. The split was a mutual decision. Shelly couldn't put up with my lack of, what should I say, ambition, my laid-back lifestyle or my off-and-on career.

Her preferred lifestyle was a bit different. I didn't fit in with her perpetually organized, always on time, BMW, high fashion, career-oriented life. We disagreed on the *importance* of all those aspects as well.

The kids screamed and laughed as they zipped by on the rocket ride, stretched out their little arms and tried to touch my hand. They had given me a nice diversion from my anxieties, and I needed it. After catching a Disney movie at the Uptown in lower Queen Anne, I allowed myself to be talked into walking over to the Seattle Center. This large park-like area, originally developed for the '62 World's Fair, was surrounded by contemporary facilities for the ballet, live theatre and various performance arts. It also had a small arcade with carnival games and kiddie rides packed into an area beneath the Space Needle—my kids' destination of choice. Every time we got together, they convinced me this was the best way to end our day. Since I only saw them on the weekend, I wanted our time together to be special.

After hugs and kisses, I dropped them off at their house on top of Queen Anne hill, a little brick Tudor framed by two ornamental evergreens. I sat in the car for a few minutes watching as they scurried up the brick steps and Shelly opened the door. She glanced my way and acknowledged me with a slight wave of her hand, then closed the door, the warmth of their home extinguished in the dark. I watched through the picture window in the well-lit living room as they danced around their mom and discarded their coats. I could see them jabbering a mile a minute about their day: lunch at their favorite burger spot, a Disney movie and finally, rides at Seattle Center. I smiled. It *had* been a good day.

I pulled away from the curb and headed to the diner to call Angie. I wanted to maintain daily contact and keep up with any new developments. My phone conversation was brief. She told me she had heard from Sayonara, and that Sayonara needed to meet with both of us as soon as possible. We agreed to meet in two hours at Charlie's Pizza on Capital Hill.

* * *

I KNEW FROM experience parking around the retail core of Capital Hill would be difficult, so I'd have to leave the car in a nearby residential area. It was a unique district of Seattle, known for the concentration of alternative lifestyles that blossomed in and around it. An eclectic mix of gay, lesbian, rockers, punk, Goth and you name it. Pink hair, Mohawks, black leather jackets and chrome chains dangled from wallets and various body parts. Sayonara would blend in well. I wouldn't.

I found the neighborhood pizza joint, pulled open the solid wood entrance door and entered the dimly lit quasi-Italian eatery. Vinyl booths lined the walls and a few tables with checkered tablecloths filled the center. Music fit for an Italian funeral played softly in the background. I glanced around and noticed Angie's hand waving from the last booth in the back. I dodged my way between tables.

"Hi, sorry I'm late." I shrugged. "Parking, you know."

"No problem, we just got our drinks." Angie gave me a thin smile.

As I slid into the booth seat cross from the women I glanced at Sayonara and let out a gasp. "Oh, my God. What happened to you?"

She brought her hand up to her face and looked down. "It got a little rough. But I'm okay."

I grimaced, my teeth clenched, feeling her pain. Sayonara's face had been battered and even a heavy dose of make-up couldn't hide a black eye, a swollen and cut lip and a puffy right cheek. I suspected other bruises might be concealed beneath her high collar and the cloud of purple feathers surrounding it.

"Really," she tried to convince me, "I'm fine. I've been through worse than this, and *not* gotten paid." She attempted a smile.

"Did *he* do this to you?" I asked.

She didn't say anything.

I shook my head in disgust. "That bastard."

Angie sat silent. I suppose she had seen this before. I couldn't forget that Angie had been through hell herself at one time, so she probably understood.

"That son of a bitch should pay," I said. "Did you call the poli—" I stopped in midsentence. Of course she didn't. I suppose it was the risk associated with her job, but I still didn't like it.

Sayonara tried to grin as she flicked her wrist, a small team of thin gold bracelets jingled as she did. "Don't worry. He did pay. Big time. But I suppose our little session did get a bit out of control. More than normal. He was really agitated when he arrived. At first I didn't understand why. I sensed he was very upset over something, so I decided to start there. Dig right in to find out what was bothering him. To be good at this job, you have to sense these things. Know how and when to put the knife in. Metaphorically speaking, of course."

A waitress stepped up with a pad in her hand. She wore black. Everything black. Except a green streak of hair hanging down the side of her head, opposite the side that had been shaved clean. Her tank top had the letters D.O.A. stenciled across it. That seemed fitting. The hem was about four inches too short, exposing a white jiggling mass with a decorator jewel front and center. Ear, nose and lip rings set off the whole package. When she spoke a silver ball attached to her tongue bounced up and down.

"Something to drink?"

I played it safe. "Beer. How about Corona?"

She rolled her eyes. "Really! We got Bud. And Bud. Take your pick."

Mesmerized by the ball, I blurted, "Yeah."

She turned and disappeared.

Sayonara continued. "As I was saying, I decided to start by trying to find out what had agitated him. It turns out he had just had a meeting with someone, a Chinese fellow whom he has had some business relationship with, you know, MSS, and this guy really got to him. He told me he had to put him in his place. Now remember, my customer is a real piece of work. Has an ego *much* bigger than his cock." Sayonara paused. "Oh, sorry. I apologize. I get so used to being around these foul mouth jerks it sometimes carries over into my regular life."

Regular life? I thought. I glanced up as my attention was drawn to a jiggly white roll as it arrived bearing a frosty glass, then turned and left in silence.

Sayonara continued. "If I were Catholic, honey, I could keep three confessionals going at the same time. Teach those priests a thing or two about *adult* sex, too." She reached over and touched my hand. "You're not Catholic are you?"

I shook my head. "No. Agnostic."

"Good. Me too. Who else but the agnostics would take me into their fold?"

Angie and I exchanged a quick glance then turned our attention back to Sayonara.

"So my customer—"

"What's his name?" I interrupted.

"Deng Qin. So he gets his ego bruised by this guy. Had to put him in his place. So he tells this guy that he's in charge, he's the architect as he put it, of a grand plan that's in the works. Has something to do with American military secrets. Something really important. When he pulls this off, he'll return to China a hero and receive great rewards, as he put it."

"What's this plan?" I asked, fascinated she had extracted information from a master spy.

"He wouldn't say. I tried my best, as you can see." Sayonara pointed to her face. "And what you can't."

I swallowed, my mind not wanting to go there.

"No. He wouldn't tell me what it was. But remember. He's a self-centered egotist. He may be blowing this way out of proportion. But he did say something I think is most interesting."

I leaned forward, tipping the table and sloshing my drink.

"Think beauty queen, Curtis."

"Huh?" escaped my lips.

She stared at me, a sparkle in her eye. "His exact words, or

221

as close as I remember were, 'Miss Hong Kong is coming to Seattle and she will be picking up a box…or was it a container? Anyway, the contents within this box would comprise the greatest coup in MSS history. The balance of military superiority will soon shift.' That's what he said."

I sipped my beer as I listened. To anyone's ear, this sounded like a serious espionage threat. "He said that?"

"Not willingly. I had to beat it out of the little shit. A little whipping works wonders you know." She paused. "Or maybe you don't." She smiled, probably enjoying the memory. "But he loved every minute of it. He enjoyed showing me he had such knowledge, been trusted with such important information. Knowledge to him is power. He had to gloat."

I cringed as I reminded myself of the sessions Sayonara and this MSS agent shared, and she had described during our first meeting.

"Miss Hong Kong," I muttered. "What a perfect courier. Brilliant. A beauty queen. Who would suspect her? She'd probably be carrying so much luggage she could sneak a nuclear sub through airport security. Do you know when she's coming?"

"He clammed up after that came spilling out. But he said this operation would happen very soon."

I shook my head in amazement. "This is really serious. Like a major threat to America's security." I glanced from Angie to Sayonara. "What should we do with this information?"

Sayonara smiled. "Do as you like, honey. I'd like to see the bastard go down. Know what I mean?"

Looking back to Angie I remembered why we wanted to meet with Sayonara in the first place. "What about George? Did you find out where he is?"

Sayonara's face showed a sense of deep concern. She hesitated, seemed to be thinking. "As I told Angie before you got here, I tried my best. Deng Qin wouldn't admit to knowing anything about George's whereabouts. I don't know if he really didn't know or if he just wasn't sharing it. Maybe he's too involved in this big coup he's trying to pull off and George's situation wasn't important."

I looked at Angie. She hung her head, avoiding eye contact. I knew this news would be upsetting. After all, uncovering something to help us find George was our main objective. My excitement over the information Sayonara had provided had been dampened by this failure.

My mind went back to Miss Hong Kong, an intriguing tidbit. A self-anointed writer-in-waiting, I recognized intrigue. "Is there a beauty pageant anytime soon?"

Sayonara smiled, brushed her hair back with a quick flip of her hand and lifted her chest. A polished maneuver many *women* hadn't even mastered. "I haven't a clue, dearie. That's not *my* style."

I turned to Angie. "No. I mean, if Miss Hong Kong is coming here, wouldn't it be for some kind of beauty pageant? If we had a pageant date, then we'd know when she was coming."

Angie shook her head. "Could be some kind of promotional thing. Like a world tour or something."

"Yeah, I suppose." I paused and took a swig of beer. "What do you think Miss Hong Kong could be picking up? It would have to be small enough to fit into some kind of container. Something she could carry. Maybe a vase...or a jewelry box. Something small she could hide something in." My mind was running, grasping at ideas. "Maybe it's some kind of software disk with information on it. Detailed plans of some kind of military hardware. Or it could be a computer chip. Yeah. That's more likely. It would be small and hard to detect. And with chips today, it could have the entire archives of the Pentagon on it. Hell...it could be anything!"

Angie stared at me as I rambled on and Sayonara sipped on her drink.

I caught a flash of light out of the corner of my eye. I turned and gave a hand signal to the walking jewelry display as she gabbed with a few like-minded customers at another table. She rolled her eyes then headed our way. We ordered a large pizza to split between us and the jewelry queen disappeared.

I noticed Sayonara staring down, fiddling with her glass. She seemed deep in thought. She looked up at me for a moment, her lips pursed, a serious expression on her face, then she dropped her eyes again and turned her head toward Angie. "Angie. There's something else."

Angie's glass clinked as she dropped it against the tabletop, her face tensed. I braced myself. What next?

"Deng Qin said something else." She paused. "He said, 'That Willie Wong is a son-of-a-bitch liar. You can't trust him. He didn't give up that George guy. He didn't silence him like he should have.' " Sayonara reached for Angie's hand.

Angie's eyes glassed over and tears formed. "Oh, my God!"

I jumped in, "What do you think he meant?"

Sayonara looked at Angie with deep concern. "I don't know, honey. I just don't know."

CHAPTER THIRTY-THREE

I WALKED ANGIE to her car after leaving that jewel of a pizza palace so we could discuss the information we had gotten from Sayonara. Angie was upset to hear Uncle Willie's name brought into this and the implied threat to George, and I knew it.

"What if Uncle Willie's involved with Deng Qin in George's disappearance?" I asked.

Walking with her head down, she had folded her arms and wrapped them across her chest, fending off the chill. She sniffed. "From what Sayonara says, he must know Deng Qin pretty well. Father and I asked him to help us find George. I got a strange feeling that day, like he knew something. I...I just don't know."

I stared down at the sidewalk, watching for cracks in the uneven pavement. My heart went out to Angie. In addition to her brother being missing, now a dear family friend has been possibly linked to his disappearance.

I turned to her. "She said Deng Qin called Uncle Willie a liar. That he couldn't be trusted."

"And you think Deng Qin can be trusted?"

"No. I don't mean that," I said in defense. "But how well do you *really* know Uncle Willie? I know he's been like family to you, but he isn't really. After all, he does work for the

Chinese government, right? With the Program and all, I mean. You said yourself some of the Program members had a connection with MSS. Maybe he's more involved than you think. It's possible, you know."

Angie remained silent. I knew she was disturbed after hearing George's name mentioned. But what I picked up on told me he may still be alive. Was it Uncle Willie's *job* to "silence" him? And did silence to Deng Qin mean what I thought it meant? I tried to encourage Angie. "It sounded like George hasn't been harmed."

She looked up, eyes glistening, and leaned against me. I put my arm around her shoulders and held her as we walked to her car in silence.

After leaving Angie, I had mixed emotions. I couldn't suppress my excitement or my growing alarm. This was hard evidence of major espionage, and it could be a serious blow to national security. The kind of thing the FBI needed to be involved in, but I was hardly on speaking terms with them. Nothing we heard tonight would help us in our search for George, but it was vital information nonetheless. I know Angie said her family wasn't involved with MSS or any espionage activity, but I honestly didn't know where George fit in. Or Uncle Willie for that matter. What does he have to do with this? How's he involved? And if I did contact the FBI, how would Angie feel? I had already hurt her family once. I didn't want to do it again. On the other hand, this espionage situation appeared to be bigger than both of us. Stopping it may be more important than either my book or Angie's family honor.

* * *

THE NEXT DAY I called Angie. She told me she wanted to meet at the Pink Salmon right after work. She didn't explain anything, but made it sound urgent. At the appointed time, I heard a knock on the door. I peeked through the curtains, then let her in.

"Hi," I said.

She blew past me, taking a few steps before turning. "We've got to do something. I need to know if Uncle Willie's involved with Deng Qin in George's disappearance."

I stared at her. "How you gonna do that?"

"We have to check out his office."

I was taken back. "What do you mean, check out his office?"

"I found out he's going to Montana for a few days. Montana! What's in Montana? He's disappearing right when all this is going down? If he's involved, disappearing now would be pretty convenient. Don't you think?"

I shrugged. "What about Montana? Maybe it's business. Maybe it's a vacation."

"I checked. I talked to Father. First off, the Asian Antique Import Company doesn't do business in Montana. They have no customers there, and they sure as heck don't make Asian antiques there. And Uncle Willie doesn't export cowboy boots and ten-gallon hats to China! And second, Uncle Willie doesn't take vacations. If and when he travels, he goes to China."

She paused to take a breath. "Father said Uncle Willie was going to Hong Kong on a buying trip. But his secretary told me she purchased tickets for Uncle Willie to fly to Montana. Do you see a problem here? I do! Somebody's lying. And Hong Kong? Miss Hong Kong? Is that a coincidence or what?"

I tried to make sense of this. "Maybe somebody made a mistake."

"Yeah, and that somebody is Uncle Willie. He lied!"

"Hold on. It does seem that way, but you need to be sure. This is too important."

Angie took a deep breath and sat down on the edge of the bed.

"Look. Let's think about this for a minute," I said. "When's he leaving?"

"Tomorrow."

"Okay. Any way we can confirm this?"

"Yes. That's why I want to get into his office. Who knows, we might find something else. Something incriminating. Something to prove or disprove my fears." She looked at me. I could see the determination in her eyes.

I sat down next to her. "Okay, how do you propose we do that?"

"I got a key from Father. I told him I might have left my sweater there when I saw him a few days ago and I wanted to stop by after hours to pick it up. I used to hang around there all the time when I was a kid, so he didn't hesitate."

I took my baseball cap off and ran my fingers through my hair. "Thank God. I thought maybe you planned on breaking and entering. I can just see you tossing a brick through the window, or do you have a lock pick?" I smiled, trying a little levity to lighten her mood. It didn't work.

"When?" I asked.

"Tonight. But later."

"Good. We've got time to eat."

* * *

BEFORE HEADING TO dinner, I followed Angie to her house. She wanted to change out of her white uniform into something more appropriate for a late night break-in. She emerged in her black designer jeans, a long coat with gray faux fur and heels. "Where's your black hood and ski mask?"

She glared.

We drove to Anthony's Homeport, a seafood restaurant on the downtown waterfront where we were seated at a table for two. A wall of windows faced Elliot Bay and Puget Sound in the distance. In the darkness of the early evening, we could see the lights of West Seattle across the bay, and the distant flicker of Bainbridge Island. The occasional ferry glided past loaded with the last of the commuters. Rows of lighted windows reflected ripples that would eventually wash against the pylons beneath our feet.

We had a lot to talk about. But this time I made a conscious decision to take a break from the stress and tension surrounding George's disappearance, Uncle Willie's possible involvement and this whole spy thing. Keep our conversation more personal. I wanted to get to know Angie. The waiter approached, took drink orders and recited the list of daily specials.

"You mentioned earlier, you work at a veterinary clinic."

She smiled. "Yes. Not far from here actually."

"You must love animals?"

"Yes. I could spend all day with them, and I do. They love people unconditionally. All they need is a little food and water. Shelter's nice, but they can survive fine without it. Unlike us. And they want to be loved. Even more than us."

I could see the glow on her face as she talked about the animals. "How about snakes and turtles? The cold blooded ones?"

"Even they need love. You'd be surprised how they respond to tender care and affection. But of course, most of what we care for are the warm-blooded, soft, fuzzy ones. They're very affectionate."

"Like you?"

Angie blushed, broke eye contact as she picked up her napkin and set it in her lap, laying her flatware on the table. "Like the animal world, the people world can harbor cold blooded creatures too," she said.

I reached for my napkin. "Yes, they can. Snakes. Unfortunately, we know that all too well."

I quickly let that train of thought fade. "So you enjoy your work?"

"Yes. I really do. It's my life. Father wants me to go back to school. Veterinary school. But I'm not sure."

For the first time since I met Angie she seemed relaxed. She opened up, and I could see inner warmth that would take the chill off any man.

"So, how about you?" she asked. "Your family."

"I have a dad. He lives in Ballard. Lost my mom to cancer a few years back. I see my dad some, but we're not real close. Not like some people. He's a tough old guy..." My thoughts drifted and Angie picked up on it.

"I'm sorry to hear that. I'm very close to my family."

"Yeah. I envy you. But, my family was different. I know my dad loves me. He just can't show it. It's a man thing. He hides his feelings. Afraid if he shows them it's a weakness. I'm more like my mom. She was a lot more loving and not afraid to show it. It's been hard to live up to my dad's expectations. Not that they're high. They're just different than mine. It's kind of hard to explain."

We continued to talk of life, our world and our place within it, but I made an effort to avoid discussing her family's past, or the emigration program. I wanted this to be a pleasant respite from the troubled world we would face after we shared a warm dish of chocolate lava cake.

* * *

AFTER DINNER WE drove to the International District and the warehouse that housed the Asian Antique Import Company on King Street. We passed the building doing a quick reconnaissance. It was dark, appeared vacant. I pulled into an alley and parked. The streets were empty, quiet. We walked with a determined step, our presence the only movement, the clicking of Angie's heals the only sound.

As we passed a chain-link fence that surrounded a

boarded-up brick building, a sudden blur flashed out of the darkness. A Doberman crashed against the fence, growling, snarling, paws rattling the wire mesh, teeth bared. The sharp clatter of the metal links and the suddenness of the lunge startled me. I grabbed Angie and pulled her back. She gasped as we both caught our breath. I stared at the canine, then met Angie's wide eyes. I swallowed. "Come on." The growling subsided as we continued toward the front door.

"No lights," she whispered. "We'll use this." She held up a flashlight she had pulled from her coat pocket. "Stay close."

As the door opened a high-pitched shriek cut through the silence. Rhythmic. Incessant. I stiffened. Angie hadn't warned me. She didn't flinch.

I followed her to the back wall behind what appeared to be the reception desk. She flashed the light against an alarm panel. Her fingertips danced along a grid of alphabetized keys as she inserted a six-digit code. The screeching ceased. Then she reentered the code followed by a single beep, resetting the alarm. The flashlight beam bounced around the neat and tidy desktop.

"Hold this." She handed the light to me, then pulled out a few drawers and shuffled through them. She turned on the computer. After a few moments the screen opened throwing a warm glow against her face, providing light to see about the room.

I glanced at the front door. I felt my body warming up beneath my jacket. I looked down to the computer monitor. "You have a password?"

"Damn. No." She sat back, staring at the computer. "Wait," she said. "This is a business account. For the company. It's not like a personal account. When Regina's not here, other people use this computer and the email account. Maybe it's something simple. Something everybody uses and would know."

Angie tried various combinations.

I took the flashlight and started to search through file folders in the sliding drawers on the bottom of the desk. There must have been fifty in the first drawer, in alphabetical order. I started with E for email. Nothing.

I glanced up to look at the monitor. "What software does she use?"

"Outlook."

I flipped through the files, my fingers moving with a sense of urgency. I went straight to O. "*Voilà,*" I murmured. "Outlook." I pulled the file and flipped it open on the desk. I thumbed through loose sheets, emails and other papers. I picked up a thin manual, and flipped the pages, concentrating on the first few. "Yes!" I almost screamed. "Here it is. Has to be." I lifted the manual and held the page open. On the top left corner of the second page scrawled in pencil was written, AAIC-R. ASIAN ANTIQUE IMPORT COMPANY- REGINA.

I read it to Angie. Within a few clicks the email popped open. "Yes! Yes! Yes!" She scrolled down a few lines at a time. "There!" she whispered, her finger pointing halfway down the column. I leaned down.

"Look." She clicked on a line identified as Horizon Airlines. The email opened up and we read to ourselves, our lips moving in silence.

It was a flight confirmation. My eyes scanned the page.

DEPART: 12:00 PM SUNDAY, DECEMBER 20,
SEATTLE, WA, FLIGHT # 2460
ARRIVE: 2:45 PM SUNDAY, DECEMBER 20,
BOZEMAN, MT

I skipped down a few lines.

PASSENGER FIRST NAME: WU
PASSENGER LAST NAME: WONG

"It says Wu Wong? Is that Uncle Willie?"

"Yes, that's his given name."

"Well then, there you have it," I whispered as she stared at the screen. "He's going to Montana."

"Just because he has a ticket doesn't mean he's going. Remember Hong Kong?"

"See if you can find any tickets purchased for Hong Kong," I suggested.

Angie zipped through page after page, all emails for the past three months. I glanced back to the front door, watching the doorknob, fearing at any moment there might be movement.

"Nothing." She sat back and sighed.

"So what do we make of this?" I asked.

"I don't know."

She closed the email account and shut down the computer. "I'm going to check out his office."

"Are you kidding me? Haven't you found what you wanted?"

She grabbed the flashlight. "Come on."

We passed through the door behind the reception desk. I eased it closed and followed her down a short hallway. Any light had been sucked out of the darkened corridor, leaving it pitch black beyond the illumination from the beam. Angie waved it back and forth as she cleared a path. She stopped at a closed door on the right and turned the handle. It opened. We slipped inside. She zeroed in on the desk.

"Hold the light," she whispered. I directed the beam as I traced her hand movements. She opened the top middle desk drawer, searched with nimble fingers, replaced everything as she found it with a thoroughness that could be construed as experience, a sobering thought.

"What are you looking for?"

"I...I don't know." She looked at me. In the dim light I could see her lower lip quiver. "I just feel I have to do this.

Maybe there's something here. I don't know."

She closed the middle drawer and turned her attention to the top drawer on the left, leafed through a stack of loose sheets and notes. Nothing. Then the one below. I could see frustration setting in. Minutes were ticking off. I glanced in the direction of the door, saw nothing but blackness. I shifted the flashlight to the other hand, holding it up, directing the beam.

She let out a deep breath. "Just these two drawers then we're done."

I moved the flashlight to the right. As the beam passed, I caught a glimpse of something beneath the desk. A flash of light. A brass plate. "Look!"

Angie reached down and lifted a case, examining it in the narrow beam. "His briefcase." She laid it flat on the desk and flipped the locks. They snapped open with a sharp click. I peered over her shoulder to see stacks of papers, folders and a leather notebook crammed inside. Using her fingers she sifted through pages attached with paper clips, picking up and flipping one stack with her thumb. A smaller sheet slid out and drifted to the floor. She bent down and picked it up. I lowered the beam.

"Wow! Look at this," she said. We both stared. "It's a bank withdrawal for one hundred thousand dollars. What the heck do you think this is all about? It's dated yesterday."

"That's a lot of—" I jerked my head up and froze. I listened a moment as I placed my index finger across my lips. Angie stiffened. The sound of a key in a lock. A high-pitched shriek, the rapid pulse of the security system. Her eyes were wide, her face tense. I motioned for her to close the briefcase, slip it under the desk. She fumbled with the latches but succeeded in replacing it without a sound.

We tiptoed out of the office and Angie closed the door. She leaned over, slipped off her heels and handed them to me. Taking the flashlight, she grabbed my free hand. She jerked her head to the side, pointing down the short hallway to our right. I didn't hesitate. My heart pounded. We slipped down the hall, opened a door and entered a cavernous area lit only by the thin beam of the light. She had mentioned she often played here as a youngster. We passed through a narrow space of tall dark shapes that appeared to be boxes and crates. She led me to a wall. We felt our way along, found a corner behind other large shapes and stopped. She motioned for me to crouch down as she flicked off the light, leaving us in complete darkness.

In the silence I heard the muffled sound of a door open from the direction we had just come. A light went on and a faint glow found its way through the maze of boxes. I detected Angie's dark shape surrounded by tall towers. I didn't move or make a sound. My heart pounded against my chest. Angie grasped my hand. Her palm was warm, moist.

We sat motionless in near darkness. Minutes passed. I heard footsteps approach in the distance, muffled by the boxes. A switch clicked. We were bathed in light. I stared at Angie. The suddenness of the bright light made me blink. I stiffened. She squeezed my hand. We sat like two ducks on a pond that had just noticed a pair of double-barrels poking out between the reeds. It seemed an eternity. Then another click. Angie disappeared.

I could hear my breath as I exhaled. I hadn't realized I had stopped breathing when the light went on. The door closed. The footsteps faded. In the dead silence we heard another door close seconds later. The door to the reception area. Are we locked in? It had to have been Uncle Willie. I didn't want to imagine what he would have done if he had caught us. We did not have a good explanation for being in the warehouse. Not one we could share.

The cold hard concrete floor had become uncomfortable, but I was afraid to shift. Thoughts filled my mind. The danger we had put ourselves in. We had been sitting paralyzed for at least half an hour when I felt Angie move. She nudged me, turned on the flashlight, held her hand over the lens and diffused the light.

She slipped by me, took my hand to lead me back through the maze, checking around the corner of each stack of boxes, until we stood near the door. I saw no light-leak from underneath. I tensed. She stopped, listened, then opened the door leading to the hallway with the offices. We continued down the hall to the door leading to the reception desk. For all I knew there could be a team of assassins waiting on the other side.

She put her head to the door and listened, then twisted the knob, cracked open the door and peered out. Turning to me, she nodded, then opened the door and we tiptoed past the reception desk and headed for the front door. She paused, hesitated a minute. In the beam of the light I could see her motion to me.

She whispered, "Wait here." She crossed over to the Venetian blinds that covered the front window, lifted one thin louver and peered out, looking both directions, then turned and headed back toward the reception desk.

I mouthed, "What are you doing?" She pushed through the door and disappeared down the hall.

Shit, now what is she doing? I heard an office door open and a few seconds later, the sound of it click shut. She appeared back at the doorway, reached for the keypad on the alarm system, turned it off, then reentered the code, giving us a few minutes to exit the front door. Retrieving her shoes from my sweaty grip, she placed them on the floor, and slipped her feet in.

She grabbed the doorknob to the front door, cracked it open and poked her head out. Seeing no one, we stumbled out onto the sidewalk. She locked the door, slipped the flashlight into her pocket, grabbed my arm and we walked with a brisk pace back to the car. This time we ignored the aggressive Doberman, though he made his presence known.

After seating myself and locking the door, I took a deep breath, feeling relief, then glanced at Angie. She stared straight ahead, motionless. I turned the key and pulled out of the alley onto King Street, anxious to leave the Asian Antique Import Company in my rear view mirror.

"What were you doing back there?" I asked. "Why'd you go back?"

"The briefcase. I wanted to see if the briefcase was still there."

"Was it?"

She turned to me. "No."

CHAPTER THIRTY-FOUR

I SLEPT IN the next morning, awakened by a strange fragmented dream about the death of the *Mockaritaville*. It floated around in my unconsciousness until I realized I had awakened and left the dream behind, fading in the distance like a mirage. My eyes opened and focused on the ceiling, as I collected my thoughts.

I stumbled into the bathroom, stared in the mirror, wondered if I could talk myself out of continuing down this path of uncertainty. A path that in all likelihood would be dangerous. My life until now had been pretty normal, having never experienced anything more perilous than running a yellow light through a busy intersection. After showering, I dressed and took a firm hold of my computer case, then took one last look in the mirror. My face had become one of determination. I knew what needed to be done.

I wasn't going to take the easy way out like I might have in the past. This was the first time I had ever been faced with a situation that seriously and adversely affected other people, and I had an opportunity to do something about it. Maybe even a responsibility. I owed it to myself. I had started something. Now, for once, I knew I had to finish it. There was too much at stake.

I had a great amount of guilt over George's disappearance,

and the loss of my boat still pissed me off. They had information that the Chinese were stealing sensitive American military secrets and I had my first manuscript in the process of being published. I tried not to weigh those insignificant issues against the value of life. In particular, my life. Because if I did, I'd quit. Catch the first flight to some tropical island and open up a beachside stand selling umbrella drinks in coconut shells.

I headed to a coffee shop with Wi-Fi to research beauty pageants, Miss Hong Kong and anything else that seemed relevant, hoping to find some dates or schedules that would be meaningful.

My Google search told me there were nearly seven million web sites for Miss Hong Kong. A daunting task that most likely would take longer than my lifetime, even if I fled to the safety of some island to sell coconut drinks. Starting with those on the first page I browsed each site searching for something of value. Most of the information seemed insignificant. I took note of her name and scribbled it down on a piece of notepaper for future reference. A delicate Asian beauty, her photos showed poise and charm. I had assumed spies had rough, tough faces with bent noses and more often than not, a shaved head. Studying her picture I tried to detect any of these conclusive qualities, but couldn't.

From my research it appeared she could be involved. But so could a billion other Chinese. I had no way of knowing her personal schedule or even if she would be in Seattle. This was information I had no access too. Realizing I had gone as far as I could on this lead, I had to pass on what I knew to the FBI. They had the resources.

* * *

THE PRUDENT COURSE would be to make this particular phone call from another phone, someplace other than the honky-tonk diner. A location far from where I lay my head at night. Crossing the I-90 bridge to the East side I searched for a phone with privacy and relative quiet, finding a small café in the suburb of Redmond with a public phone attached to the back wall. Placing my computer on a table, I unzipped the case and searched through the pockets for the business card I had placed there after the two FBI agents dropped in on me and the *Mockaritaville* for that little love chat a couple weeks back.

Is this the right thing to do? I wasn't convinced, but I needed to do something. I wouldn't talk long. Could they trace the call? I didn't know, but it would be okay if they did. I'd be gone. My fingerprints? So what. They knew who I was, just not where I was.

After dialing, I spoke up with a strong, confident voice. "Supervisory Special Agent Lou Jengwi, please."

"Speaking."

"Mr. Jengwi. This is Curtis Beecham."

Silence met me for a second. I had to assume he was signaling someone to run a trace.

"Mr. Beecham. I hope you're well?"

Of course *my* health would be foremost on his mind. I ignored him. "You gave me your card. Said to call if I wanted to talk."

"Yes, of course. Feel free, but we need to meet face to face."

"No. What I have to tell you I can say on the phone."

"Somewhere private? Just you and me?"

"Just listen. I have information concerning the operations of MSS." I knew this would catch his attention. Get him focused on the intelligence I was providing rather than concerning himself with my whereabouts. "I can't tell you how I obtained this information, but the source is reliable. There are plans in place by MSS to steal some very important military secrets. Something highly sensitive. And I'm told Miss Hong Kong, the beauty queen with obvious Chinese connections, has something to do with it. She's apparently going to be the courier, sneaking it out of the country and back to China in some kind of container."

The phone remained silent for a second. I waited for him to take his cue. "Mr. Beecham. We receive unsolicited, unverified tips every day. People pop out of the woodwork claiming to have heard secret conversations by shady looking characters in bars, bathroom stalls…even the ferry. You're telling me the Chinese are going to steal some important military secret. Unfortunately, that happens quite often. That's what they do. So, for my benefit, could you be more specific?"

"I wish I could. But I'm convinced this information is reliable. It's something big. Bigger than your everyday military heist. And Miss Hong Kong has something to do with it. That's the best I can give you."

"Who's your source?"

"I can't reveal that. I'm sure you understand." I smiled, remembering the uncomfortable conversation we had had on my boat.

"Why are you telling me this? Has it something to do with your book?"

I hesitated before answering. "I've been doing some research. A contact passed this on to me. This contact has gotten very close to MSS."

"How close?"

"Can't tell you that."

I could hear frustration in his voice. "Then what the hell can you tell me? You're not giving me much. An unsubstantiated story about a theft of military secrets by a beauty queen. That's thin, Mr. Beecham. Sounds like your writer's imagination at work."

"Look. You wanted my help. I just gave it to you. Now, do your job and follow up on Miss Hong Kong."

"Listen. Like I told you before, you're in over your head.

There are dangerous people out there. Dangerous like you can't imagine. I understand you recently lost your houseboat in a suspicious fire. Terrible thing. Lucky you weren't on it. I told you some people would go to any length. You need to trust us. We can help you. Keep you safe."

I held my tongue. As he continued, my impatience and irritation grew, and I couldn't help but remember, the FBI was still on my short list of suspects. "If I find out anything else I'd like to share, I'll call you. In the meantime, check on the whereabouts of Miss Hong Kong. She's the key. Oh, and, I'm told it'll be happening very soon. Got that?"

"Of course, we'll do that, but I'd like you to—"

I hung up and took a deep breath. I had just talked to the FBI. The Federal Bureau of Investigation. Maybe the most thorough and sophisticated investigative organization in the world. In helping their cause, I might have hurt mine. They're looking for me and I just passed on valuable information, which might make them more determined then ever to find me. I had to collect my thoughts and figure out what steps, in my own best interests, to take next.

* * *

LOU JENGWI PICKED up the phone and punched in Skip Chouw's number. "Get in here."

Within a minute Chouw knocked on the door, walking in at the same time.

Jengwi stared with a scowl. "Guess who I just talked to?"

Chouw shrugged.

"That son of a bitch writer. Curtis Beecham."

Chouw sat down. "Really? What'd he say?"

"Said there's a major theft of military secrets breaking soon. Said Miss Hong Kong, the beauty queen, is involved. She's the courier. Returning to China with it."

Chouw stared at Jengwi. "He told you that?"

Jengwi leaned up and slapped his desktop. "Yes, dammit. That's what I just said."

"You believe him?"

Jengwi sat back thinking of the brief conversation. Curtis's voice. The tone. The lack of concrete evidence. "Not sure. But I wouldn't put it past him to know something. I've suspected all along he's involved somehow. In deeper than he'd ever admit."

"Who's his source?"

"In the tradition of the Bureau, he said he couldn't reveal it." Jengwi sneered and pointed at Chouw. "But when we find him, we'll make damn sure he does his civic duty."

"So we haven't a clue what it is. How about where, or when?"

"Don't know the where. But she's gotta be passing through us. The when, he says, is very soon."

"Not much to go on, Chief."

Jengwi stood up and leaned on his desk. "Get me everything you can on the current Miss Hong Kong. I want her schedule. I want to know where she is right now and where she's gonna be every last minute until the day her title expires."

Chouw got up to leave. "I'll check with State. See if she's been issued a Visa. If she's here, we'll find her."

"Good. When you do, put a tail on so tight she'll think we're part of her corset. She's not leaving this country without us ripping through every bag, tearing out every seam of every gown and searching every lump, bump and cavity on her beauty queen body. *Including* implants."

CHAPTER THIRTY-FIVE

AS HE SAT at his desk, Special Agent Skip Chouw polished off a lunch special from Ivars Fish Bar: two orders of take-out fish 'n chips, three containers of creamy tartar sauce. It was Thursday, but he was already looking forward to the weekend and a few hours of leisure, lying on the couch, watching his big screen as twenty-two guys in pads battled over a ball of pigskin that defied any known shape.

Having been an offensive guard on his high school football team, he loved analyzing the techniques used by the pros. A knowledgeable fan, he knew the success of a team starts with the offensive line. Without a good line the quarterback finds himself eating dirt all afternoon, although it's the QB who receives most of the credit for the team's success. A parallel Chouw found in the real world, including the Bureau. After twelve years Chouw was still on the offensive line, skirmishing in the trenches as the credit settled further up the food chain.

Special Agent Chouw had been following up on reports from their ongoing investigation, browsing through the thick file that had accumulated on the Boudie case. Boudie Aerospace occupied a three-building complex on the east side high-tech corridor. They had secured numerous government contracts to manufacture parts for military aircraft.

A suspect had been brought to the FBI's attention in the Boudie case, just as it had with WUZ-Tech International and Microturnkey earlier. In this case however, a Chinese American female engineer had been working on the development of sensitive equipment. She had been reported as having suspicious and excessive activity downloading company files. Without her knowledge, her computer had been given a thorough once-over by FBI techies and they confirmed management's suspicions. The suspect's actions had indicated she had been involved in activities beyond her normal duty assignments. And, as in the case of WUZ-Tech, they had no lead on her outside contact. This one seemed too similar in nature to WUZ-Tech and Microturnkey. There appeared to be a common thread. Chouw needed to find the spool these threads wound around. They would lead him to the source. He was sure of it.

As he flipped through a few pages, the phone rang.

"Special Agent Chouw here."

"OPUS. China Five-Zero."

Agent Chouw took a deep breath upon hearing the voice and code name of the asset who had been providing confidential tips on Chinese espionage. He grabbed for a pencil. His arm knocked the take-out bag over and a container half-filled with tartar sauce flipped upside down on the Boudie file. He gritted his teeth and grabbed for a napkin, holding the phone against his ear with his shoulder as he wiped. "Yes, OPUS. Always nice to hear from you. Hope all is well?"

OPUS got right to the point. "I hear a major theft is imminent. It is of a highly classified nature and will be stolen from an American military contractor."

Chouw scribbled down a few quick notes. "Can you give me any specifics on this theft?"

"No. I can only tell you it will occur soon, in Seattle."

"A date. Do you have a date? A location?"

"No. But I will give you something else of great value."

Chouw sat up, his attention piqued.

"A name. Deng Qin. Watch him. He will lead you like a rat to cheese."

Chouw continued to scribble. Deng Qin. Rat. Cheese. "Who is this Deng Qin?"

The phone clicked, then went silent. *Damn. I got a name. A Chinese name, Deng Qin. What does he have to do with this?* But more important, in five seconds OPUS had just collaborated Curtis Beecham's story. A major theft of something highly classified from the military. It will occur soon, just as Curtis Beecham had told them. But OPUS never mentioned Miss Hong Kong. Chouw looked at his scribbles, WATCH *HIM* AND *HE* WILL LEAD... Well, Deng Qin is certainly no *Miss* Hong Kong. So, who is he?

Chouw took a few minutes to flush out his notes on the brief conversation with OPUS. He would file a contact report and update his boss after he had information better organized. But first, he needed to begin a preliminary search of the name Deng Qin. He went onto the computer and accessed the Bureau's files. He contacted the State Department, Immigration and the CIA, requesting information on Deng Qin in order to develop a complete up-to-date dossier. After setting that process in motion, he would finalize the contact report on OPUS, then continue looking through the files on the Boudie case. He had a hunch a connection existed between the three aerospace companies on suspected espionage activity and wanted to pursue it. He needed to search phone records and listen to wiretap recordings of all three suspects. A process certain to be labor intensive.

* * *

THE FOLLOWING AFTERNOON as Chouw concluded his research, he stared at the three phone numbers. A perfect match. All three suspects had called the same Lotus Blossom Restaurant and transcripts indicated they had all ordered fish soup to go. One with squid only. One with white fish only. One with oyster only. He studied these three conversations. An odd but obvious pattern. Could it be a code? His gut told him there was something to this. He picked up the phone and dialed the local number.

"Good afternoon, the Lotus Blossom Restaurant."

* * *

AFTER CALLING THE restaurant and speaking to the person on the phone, Agent Chouw set the Boudie file aside to organize the information he had received from local and federal agencies regarding Deng Qin.

Over the next few hours a preliminary composite began to develop. According to records of U.S. Citizenship and Immigration Services one Deng Qin resided in the Seattle area. Chouw had an address and an employer for this person of interest. It remained to be seen if any of this information was valid or current. Was he now using an alias? Had he moved? Had he disappeared, gone underground?

Chouw was deep into his research when his boss, SSA Lou Jengwi, appeared at the opening to his cubicle. "I'm heading to Warner Programming. East side. Their IT manager has something. Get your coat."

"Sure, Chief. Let me shut down." Chouw reached for his overcoat and quick-stepped to the front lobby. As he approached, Jengwi turned, pushed through the double glass doors and headed for the elevator. Neither man spoke. They never talked until they were in the car and had pulled into traffic.

* * *

"WHAT'S UP, CHIEF?" Chouw asked as he waited for

the light to turn green.

"Another case similar to Boudie. Excessive downloading. Guys at IT want to show us what they have. Shit. Can't we keep even one damn secret out of Beijing's hands?"

Jengwi lit a cigarette and cracked the window. "Hell, in the ole' days the Russians would send their operative over in a submarine. Land him on the beach in the middle of the night. One agent fully equipped. His mission. Kidnap the President's Chief of Staff and blow up the Pentagon. Hell, that was a real war. Real spies. They were tough. And good. We could do our job. No Congressional Oversight Committees watched our every fucking move."

Jengwi turned to Chouw and smiled. "Maybe that's a little exaggeration. But now we're facing an invisible army of a thousand so-called contacts spread throughout a hundred different companies and at the end of the day each one walks away from the office with a small disk tucked in his briefcase. Hell. There's little risk. Little glory. But in the long run, it's just as damaging to America's security. Somehow, someway, I've gotta shut those bastards down."

Chouw kept his eyes focused on the road as he swerved onto the I-90 bridge ramp. "That's the plan, Chief."

Jengwi took a puff, turned and exhaled out the cracked window. "What have you got?"

"OPUS called. We've got a name."

Brake lights flashed ahead and Chouw glanced in the rear view mirror, hoping no one would be running up his tail. "OPUS confirmed Curtis Beecham's story. Said the word is, a major theft of something highly classified is imminent. Something of a military nature. Wouldn't or couldn't tell me what. Said it was big and would be going down soon, in Seattle. No mention of Miss Hong Kong, though. Didn't talk long. The name he gave me is Deng Qin. He said, 'Watch him and he'll lead you like a rat to cheese.' " Chouw smiled. He liked metaphors of a culinary nature.

Jengwi frowned. "Sounds like someone we need to look at real close. That's good. I like names. Makes the job easier. This cheese. Think he might be referring to a boss? You know, a 'big cheese'?"

"He didn't elaborate. Like I said, he only talked a minute."

"What have you got on this name?"

"Working it now. Database search. Contacted Immigration, the Agency. Found nothing unusual. Got an address and an employer. Manages an import company, The Longzee Import and Export Company. I was checking it out when you corralled me."

"Good. Get all you can on him. Let's find out who the hell this Deng Qin is." Jengwi paused. "How's Boudie?"

"Think I'm on to something there. I checked phone records and found something real interesting. Those three guys from Boudie, Microturnkey and WUZ-Tech. All three have called the same phone number on numerous occasions. At first glance I thought that's unusual. Maybe it meant something. Then when I saw the phone number is a restaurant, the Lotus Blossom in the District, I thought, well, maybe that's not so unusual. Chinese Americans eat at Chinese restaurants all the time. I do. But these three all ordered take-out. The same thing, with one slight difference."

Jengwi turned to Chouw, his face showed he had him fully engaged.

"They all ordered fish soup. One with squid only, one with white fish only and one with oyster only. I saw a pattern here. Anyway, I sensed something. Too coincidental. Why such similar orders with one slight difference? So I called the Lotus Blossom. I ordered fish soup to go."

Chouw turned to Jengwi. "They told me they don't have fish soup. It's not on the menu, they've never served it."

CHAPTER THIRTY-SIX

New York City

ROGER LEE LEFT China Gate Publishing and headed across town to Jack Buick's office in the Bradford Building, although he had no intention of meeting up with his old friend. For twenty minutes he waited on the opposite side of the busy street, his back against a granite wall. An open newspaper shielded his face. At 11:54 A.M., he spotted Jack passing through the entrance doors, a black winter coat wrapped around his wide girth as he joined the noon-hour throng of bobbing heads winding down the broad sidewalk. He stared after him until he disappeared among the crowd.

Roger Lee folded the newspaper under his arm, crossed the street and headed toward the entrance where he entered Jack's building. He wore a dark suit under a heavy trench coat, carried a briefcase, albeit an empty one, and, appeared to be just another businessman, giving no reason to arouse suspicion from the security guard.

He discarded the newspaper into the round trash container as the elevator dinged and the green arrow lit up in response. Stepping in, he pushed the chrome button for the forty-ninth floor; a floor composed of editorial offices of Kaleidoscope Book Publishing. Three other persons shared the tight confines of the elevator, the awkward silence broken by the deep sexy voice announcing each floor. No one moved to exit as he stepped out into the empty corridor and glanced both ways. He turned to his right, then strode down to the third door on the left. The attached brass plate stated, JACK BUICK.

Roger paused and glanced around. Seeing no one, he reached into his pocket and withdrew a copy of the master key he had obtained from a Chinese American employee of the cleaning crew that serviced the building. He inserted the key and turned the knob. The door eased open and Roger slipped in. He closed the door behind him and took a step toward the desk, then paused, turned back and engaged the lock.

Surveying the area, he scanned the desktop and the piles of paper strewn across it. His eyes swept to the left, captured by a large ornately framed painting of two large, crusty looking bulldogs playing poker. He smiled. *Jack, you old fool. They're gonna kill you...if we don't.* He lowered his gaze to the floor and the stacks of file folders and manuscripts piled against the wall.

He stepped over and knelt down at one end, lifted and examined each file, then restacked them in precise order. The temperature within the office was cool but his body warmed beneath his heavy coat. Sweat beaded on his forehead as his fingers flipped through one stack after another. The room remained quiet except for the sound of shuffling papers, as he went about his methodical search. He had time, but the clock in his head told him to move faster.

He plopped one stack of papers down then reached for another, but stopped in mid motion. Jerked his head up. Froze. Voices from the hallway filtered through the closed door, breaking the silence. At first muffled, the conversation grew louder as they neared Jack's office. They paused in front of the door but their discussion continued. Roger Lee listened, concentrated, his eyes on the doorknob. He strained to detect the familiar gruff pitch of Jack's voice, but could not. After a few moments, the voices appeared to separate. One set of footsteps continued down the hall, the other turned and headed back in the direction they had come.

Roger Lee waited a few seconds as the hallway fell silent once again. He breathed out a long heavy breath, then continued to flip through the stacks at a rapid pace. He lifted a heavy file and the rubber band holding it secure burst and hundreds of pages cascaded out. *Shit!* He jerked his hand down to stop the flow as they fanned out across the floor. Despite spreading out over the carpet, they remained in perfect sequence. He cursed under his breath, gathered the papers together, found another rubber band in the desk drawer and slipped it over them.

Seconds passed. The near disaster left his hands trembling. He moved at a more frantic pace, flipping files with urgency. He wiped his sleeve on his brow as a drop of sweat hit the soft manila surface of a file, leaving a dark wet spot. He rubbed the splotch to no avail, then gave up and buried the file beneath others.

He continued to shuffle from one pile to the next. There were only two stacks remaining. *It must be here.* He turned over one manuscript, then another and another. *No. Wait.* He flipped back to the first page again and read a handwritten note attached with a paper clip. NEW INFORMATION TO COME. CHINESE SPY ACTIVITY. He scanned the page. *This has to be it.* He hadn't known the title or the author's name, but this had to be the manuscript. He glanced through a few more pages. *Yes. This is it.*

He reached for his briefcase and clicked it open as the latches made thunderous claps in the quiet room. He slipped the file in and snapped the locks, taking a mental note of the exact stack and position where he had found the file, then arranged all the folders just as they had been when he entered.

He stood up, a tight grip on his briefcase, looked around Jack's office to be certain everything appeared to be the same as when he arrived, then stepped to the door. He put his ear against it, but heard no sound. Listening for a second, he took a deep breath, then opened the door.

A man stared back, his face not twenty-four inches away.

Roger jerked. His heart took a quick leap.

"Mr. Jack Buick?" the man asked. The courier, wearing the familiar brown uniform of UPS, looked up from his hand-held electronic device to Roger's shocked face.

"Sign here, please." The man shoved the unit at Roger.

Startled, Roger stared, his mind frozen for a moment, before he realized the courier had mistaken him for Jack Buick.

The man waited with an impatient look.

Roger reached out for the stylus and in an unsteady hand, scribbled a name. Jack's name. But not Jack's signature.

The courier grabbed the electronic pad and the stylus, handed Roger a sealed letter packet, then turned and headed down the hall, shaking his head.

Roger Lee stood in the doorway, his breath caught in his chest. He looked down at the letter packet in his hand, addressed to Jack Buick, glanced up and down the hall, then pulled the door to, bent down and placed the package against the door. He had signed for it and didn't want UPS investigating its disappearance. Leave it by the door. Jack would pick it up when he returned from lunch. He wouldn't think anything of it.

Roger Lee hurried toward the elevator. Despite his rattled nerves, he forced a smile. Lin Fongyeh would be very pleased with him. But first, he had to disappear before Jack showed up. And tomorrow, after copying the entire manuscript, he would have to reverse the process, returning the file to its proper place. He only hoped Jack wouldn't be looking for it between now and then.

* * *

"HEY JACK, DON'T forget. Friday. The Blue Room, right after work."

Jack Buick waved his hand in acknowledgement as he stepped off the elevator. "I'll be there."

He walked down the corridor toward his office, leaning down when he came face to face with his nameplate to pick up a UPS envelope leaning against his door. After examining it, he looked up and down the hall, shrugged and unlocked the door while scanning the address line. He walked in, tossed the envelope on his desk and removed his coat. Bending over at the waist he stretched out a kink in his back, a nagging reminder of an uncomfortable night's sleep. As he did, something caught his eye. He stepped over to the chair in front of his desk, leaned down and picked up the object. *Hmmm. A large busted rubber band.* He glanced around. *Where'd this come from?* He shrugged again, walked around his desk and tossed it in the trash.

CHAPTER THIRTY-SEVEN

Seattle, Washington

I PICKED UP a disposable phone at one of those big-box electronic retailers on Aurora Avenue. Now I could avoid having to use the pay phone at the diner. The stale smell of fried everything from that greasy kitchen had started to get to me. And besides, I'd been told disposable phones were nearly impossible to trace. I intended to ditch this one after a few days anyway, to be on the safe side. I called Angie to tell her about my failed attempt to find out anything of significance on Miss Hong Kong.

"Curtis, I'm glad you called. Are you at the diner?"

"No. I picked up a disposable phone. Thought I'd try to avoid the diner for a while. This thing only allows outgoing calls, so I can call you, but you can't call me. No bells or whistles. But it's cheap."

"That's okay. I wanted to tell you Sayonara called. Said she has some new information to share. *Very* important information as she put it. She said it changes everything, it's not what we think, but she couldn't say anything more on the phone. She sounded nervous. Her voice wasn't more than a whisper, like she didn't want anyone to hear. There was a sound in the background, like running water. It made it hard to hear her, so she didn't come across real clear."

"Was she in danger?" I asked with growing concern.

"She didn't say. She was real brief. Said to meet her tonight at the club. After the show."

I flipped my turn signal on and pulled off Aurora Avenue into a parking lot and stopped the car so I could concentrate on Angie's call. "She didn't say anything else?"

"No. She sounded scared, and I'm worried."

"Yeah. Me too." I paused to think. "So, tonight?"

"Yes. After the show."

"I'll pick you up. About ten-thirty?"

"That's fine."

I tried to sound positive. "Don't worry. I'm sure she's okay."

I hung up, but didn't like the fact Sayonara sounded nervous. Scared. And what did Angie mean by it changes everything? It's not what we think? Again, I had more questions than answers. It was 3:00 P.M. I wouldn't have long to wait.

* * *

I PICKED UP Angie at 10:30 as planned and we headed for The Bamblue Club. I parked on a side street and we walked down the alley to the inconspicuous door. Angie knocked. A few moments passed, then the peephole opened and a yellow eye appeared.

"We're friends of Sayonara," she announced.

"She no here tonight," the eye stated.

"What do you mean?" Angie asked, startled. "She's working tonight, isn't she?"

"Schedule to. Not show up. No fuckie show tonight."

I looked at Angie and saw a worried look cross her face. "Oh, my God. Something's happened!" She raised her hand and covered her mouth.

I hugged her. "We don't know that." I brushed her hair

back from her face and tipped her chin up as she dropped her hands. "She might have gotten delayed...or maybe she's just sick." I thought for a moment about her customer, Deng Qin, and the condition he had left her in when I last saw her at the pizza restaurant. I tried to reassure Angie. "You said she was nervous about something. Maybe she's just being cautious, thought it too risky to show up tonight. There could be a lot of explanations. Okay?"

Angie sniffed and nodded her head.

"Hey. Call her. You have her number."

She nodded again and began to dig into her purse. She located her cell phone and dialed Sayonara's number as I stuffed my hands in my pockets, backed up to the brick wall and leaned against it.

The phone rolled over into voice message. "Look," I said, "there's probably a good explanation. Maybe she's involved with a client."

Angie glared.

"I mean, a good client. Not that bastard. I'm sure she's as far away from him as she can get." I put my arm around Angie's shoulders. "Come on. Let's get some coffee. We'll try again later."

She stuffed her phone back in her purse and looked up at me with concern in her dark eyes. I gave her a forced smile as we started back up the alley.

The sudden roar of a fast approaching vehicle broke the silence. The high-pitch whine of the engine reverberated off the brick walls of the alleyway. I spun around to see the front end of a white van as it raced toward us. I pushed Angie up against the wall, spun her around to face the bricks and shielded her body with my own. The van raced past, bounced through potholes, and threw a shower of water in our direction. The brackish water slapped against our jeans and splattered the brick wall. As the splash pelted my body, I pressed into Angie, held her tight, closed my eyes and stiffened.

I turned as the vehicle passed. "Bastard!" I raised my arm up in an obscene salute; an angry impulse, and a not so smart move considering I had no idea who was in the van.

The van slowed to a stop at the end of the alley and idled, chugging exhaust fumes into the cool evening air. A streetlight at the end of the alley lit the backend. I could see it was a delivery van for the Asia-Pacific Fruit & Vegetable Company. I held Angie. A minute went by before the van turned onto Jackson Street. I noticed the driver had on a black hoodie but I couldn't see his face.

I squeezed Angie. "Let's get out of here."

* * *

THE NEXT DAY I called Angie twice, but she still had not been able to contact Sayonara. The clock was working against us. I knew the more time that passed without hearing from Sayonara, the greater the chance something bad had happened. Angie wanted to stop by Sayonara's apartment after she got off work. I told her it wasn't a good idea. Someone may be watching to see who shows up at her apartment. I was also afraid of what Angie might find, though I never mentioned this.

I stopped by the Seattle Police Department that afternoon and talked with Lieutenant Sam Watkins. He had no information to offer with respect to George Hu. Unless Angie wanted to report him as a missing person, there was nothing more he could do. Angie still hadn't had any contact from George, and we had no new clues as to his whereabouts.

I returned to the Pink Salmon Motel and flopped down on the frayed chenille bedspread. Picking up the TV remote, I flipped on the local news, then reached for the James Michener novel, *Caribbean*, I had been reading off and on for months in an attempt to retreat for a few moments to a more comforting place. The idyllic Caribbean as seen through the generations of those that passed through, conquered, lived and died there. An escape.

My escape didn't last long.

I dropped the book against my chest and jerked my head up, staring at the TV. What'd he say? Damn. Without a DVR, I couldn't rewind. I strained, trying to follow and reconstruct the news story. A murder. A body found in an alley. A woman reportedly. But no identification. Asian ethnicity. A white sheet draped over a body. Police are investigating.

I choked. No! Please, No!

I remembered there being a newspaper box just outside the entrance to the front office. I jumped up and grabbed my keys, then slammed the door behind me. My heart pounded. My feet slapped against the pavement as I rounded the corner, making a quick dodge to my right to avoid a lady dragging an overstuffed bag. She turned and hollered a few deserving insults in my direction. I kept going. The box was next to the door.

It was early afternoon and a large stack of newspapers could be seen in the little window. I fumbled around in my pants pocket before dragging out two quarters and a dime, then inserted the two quarters into the slot and yanked the glass door down. Grabbing a paper I stared at the headlines. Nothing. Then flipped the paper over and scanned the articles near the bottom. Lower right corner.

WOMAN'S? BODY FOUND DUMPED IN
ALLEY.

My heart raced. Read on. Read on. Slow down. Read faster. I paused. I can't do this. Folding the paper, I tucked it under my arm and crossed them in front of me. A chill set in. I looked at my bare feet, turned and walked back to my room, fearing the worst.

I locked myself in my room, then sat on the bed, my legs

crossed under me. I unfolded the paper and laid it out, smoothing it flat with my hand. My eyes drifted down to the bottom right corner once again. I began to read.

> EARLY THIS MORNING THE POLICE WERE CALLED IN TO INVESTIGATE THE DISCOVERY OF A NUDE BODY IN AN ALLEY OFF BOREN AVENUE. A CLEANING SERVICE EMPLOYEE FOUND THE BODY LYING AMONG CARDBOARD BOXES BEHIND A TRASH DUMPSTER. THE POLICE INDICATED THEY HAVE NOT IDENTIFIED THE VICTIM BUT THE BODY HAS BEEN REPORTED TO BE OF ASIAN ETHNICITY, APPROXIMATELY THIRTY YEARS OLD. THE CLEANING SERVICE PERSONNEL TOLD *THE SEATTLE TIMES* HE WAS DISTURBED BY THE DISCOVERY. THE MAN, WHO WISHED TO REMAIN ANONYMOUS, WAS QUOTED AS SAYING, "I WAS SHOCKED TO STUMBLE UPON A DEAD BODY. BUT THIS BODY, WELL, IT LOOKED LIKE A WOMAN BUT HAD MALE, YOU KNOW, PARTS."
>
> THE POLICE ISSUED A "NO COMMENT" WHEN ASKED TO CONFIRM OR DENY THE EYEWITNESS'S ASSERTION.

I stopped reading at this point and folded the paper. I tossed it on the floor and turned over on the bed, laying my head on my arms. My throat tightened. Sayonara. It has to be. First George. Now Sayonara. What's going on? This is serious and dangerous beyond anything I had imagined. And that bastard Deng Qin is behind it. I know it. I just know it.

I lay there as thoughts rushed through my mind, jumped from one image to another, creating pictures that flipped past like an old silent movie. I remembered my first meeting with

Sayonara. Wow. Was she ever out there. Lived life on the edge. Maybe a little too close to the edge. Was it her association with me that landed her in that alley? Or was it her lifestyle? Either way, I knew Deng Qin had something to do with her murder, and that puts me right in the middle. I'll make sure that bastard pays.

My mind continued to race from here to there and back again. Always back to Sayonara. I thought about a lot over the next hour. My life. My kids. My future. Angie. Would there be a future? Who would be in my future? Then I thought again of Angie. Fragile Angie. Will she be able to hold it together? I can hardly imagine what she'll go through when she finds out. Or does she already know?

I rolled over and covered my face with my arms, shutting out the light, shutting out the world.

* * *

FOR THE SECOND time today I found myself driving to the police station to see Lieutenant Sam Watkins. The workday was over for most folks, but not the Lieutenant. To my discomfort, I was becoming a familiar face to the desk sergeant. He didn't even ask my name.

I told the Lieutenant I thought I might know the victim.

He eyed me. "Mr. Beecham. Mind if I call you Curtis?"

I nodded. "That's fine."

"So, Curtis, what makes you think you know this victim?"

"I believe she's a friend of Angie Hu. You know, George Hu's sister. And I've met her a couple of times. Her name's Sayonara."

Watkins picked up a large manila envelope and slipped out a number of color photographs. They slid across the top of his desk. He shuffled through them and then handed one to me. "Is this Sayonara?"

I held the photo up and tipped it to reduce the glare

reflecting off the glossy surface. My hand trembled as I stared at a facial close-up. Sayonara's face. It was her, but she looked waxy, lifeless. My throat tightened and I swallowed hard. I nodded, then handed the photo back.

The Lieutenant looked down at his notes. "We ran her fingerprints. The victim's birth name is Kenji Ito. Changed it in nineteen ninety-six to Midori Ito. Has a record. A few minor offenses. One prostitution conviction." He squinted at me. "You know she lives her life as a female, but she, or he I should clarify, is a male."

I glanced down and fidgeted with my hands. "Yes. I knew that."

Watkins kept his stare. "How familiar *were* you with this Sayonara?"

I looked up. "Not like that. I knew her through Angie. Angie told me about her. Sayonara had saved Angie from an attempted rape a few years ago and Angie had befriended her. She wasn't what you think." I didn't want to tell the Lieutenant about Sayonara's exotic dancing career.

"She wasn't, huh? A poor misguided angel? Just happened to fall in with the wrong crowd? Yeah, Curtis. I've heard it a thousand times. Nobody's ever a bad person, just misunderstood." He inserted the photo back into the manila envelope and slipped it into the file. "I'm not a social worker. I don't care who she, or he, was. Or what she did in her bedroom. I'm a cop. My job is to put the bad guys behind bars. So, now I've gotta find the guy that did this to your friend."

He scratched his ear with the end of his pencil. "And here you are again. Every time something happens, you show up. Coincidence? I don't think so. I don't take you for an arsonist. I don't take you for a killer either. But my intuition tells me you're in deep—not just some crackpot chasing headlines. You're involved somehow. I know it."

I felt like I was back in high school, being admonished by

the principal. This is much more serious, though. It's not a schoolyard game anymore.

The Lieutenant continued. "You said you couldn't help me when your boat blew up. You were at a loss when George Hu disappeared. Why do I sense you're gonna tell me now you can't help me with this murder? If she's a friend, I'd think you'd want to help me find her killer. Am I right?"

I could feel his intensity ratchet up a notch. And I could see from his perspective he had good reason to wonder why I'm in the middle of everything bad that's happened lately. I'm asking myself too. It's like this swirling tornado is heading directly for me, destroying everything in its path.

"Yes. I do want to see the person responsible caught." I wasn't sure how much I should say. I had reason to hold back particular information, so I hesitated. "I believe it might have something to do with her lifestyle."

"How's that?" he asked.

"I believe she was seeing guys. For prostitution. Maybe one of them got carried away. Or a jealous boyfriend. Something like that."

"Great. You've just solved my case. Prostitution. A jealous boyfriend. *Any* couch detective could make that assumption. It's meaningless. Give me something concrete."

I didn't want to mention Deng Qin's name just yet. If he did kill Sayonara, he would pay. But I wanted to buy a little time. I could sense the military theft he had gloated about was imminent. It was coming together. I felt I was one vital piece away from figuring it out. Sayonara had given me information that would help derail Deng Qin's big coup and I was determined, now more than ever, to ruin his day. He would go down for the murder of Sayonara *and* the theft of military secrets. I just needed a little more time.

"Look, Lieutenant. I don't have anything more to tell you. I was afraid this victim was Angie's friend. I wanted to confirm it before I spoke with her. She'll be upset. I wanted to be certain it was Sayonara before I had to tell her."

Watkins sat back in his chair and laced his hands behind his head. "Okay, Curtis. But I know you know more than you're saying. Your boat is gone. George Hu is missing. Now your friend is dead. The seriousness of the events in this case is escalating. All these things are related in some way. You're in the middle of this. And tomorrow I don't want to have to contact *your* next of kin."

CHAPTER THIRTY-EIGHT

NIGHT CAST A cloak over the Emerald City. A darkness filled with evil, not romance. The lights of the living flicked on in the homes of the surrounding neighborhood, unaware, maybe even indifferent that a hand without mercy or remorse had switched off the light within Sayonara. Another stranger. Another death. Heavy low clouds hovered as they affronted the urban core. Tall office-towers proved worthy skyscrapers as they punched holes and disappeared into the thick gray mass.

Nature had yet to shed a tear.

For the moment, the city was spared a wet hand.

I sat in my car, my arms crossed on the steering wheel, my head resting against it. I had turned off the ignition and sat in silence. I lifted my eyes and stared up toward the glow emanating from Angie's apartment. A dark blur flashed against her window and a fuzzy cat appeared on the windowsill. It stretched, front paws out, head down, haunches up, tail swishing.

A hand reached out and the blinds cascaded down with a quick drop. A twist of the wrist and they closed for the night. The feline disappeared in one quick motion.

I opened the car door and headed for the stairs. I thought about what I should say. The words I formed seemed trite. When I lost my mother, I had my father to share my pain. I

265

hadn't known Sayonara as well as Angie had. But I wanted to share Angie's sorrow. I wanted to provide what support I could. But I knew my best would still be inadequate. Added to the worry of her brother, Sayonara's murder might be more than she could handle.

I knocked.

A minute later I heard her voice, it was weak, scratchy. "Who is it?"

"It's me. Curtis."

The door opened and Angie stood there in silhouette. Her eyes glistened and appeared puffy. Tears rushed to the surface. She stepped forward, threw her arms around me and buried her head in my chest. Her sobs muffled against my jacket. She squeezed. I wrapped my arms around her and held tight. No words were necessary.

CHAPTER THIRTY-NINE

I DIDN'T STAY long at Angie's place. She told me she had thought about Sayonara all day and had to stop off at her apartment after work. There she found a notice attached to the door from the Seattle Police Department. She knew what that meant.

I still had a lot of questions but I didn't want to discuss anything with her that night. I provided what comfort I could, then left after she had cried herself out. She was exhausted and needed sleep so I told her to take something, go to bed, call in sick tomorrow and rest.

* * *

I CONTACTED LIEUTENANT Watkins again, this time on my disposable phone, and asked about Sayonara.

"I have the autopsy report right here," he began. "She died from a single gunshot to the back of the head. Point blank. Death was instantaneous. Probably never saw it coming."

He might have said that as an act of kindness. It would ease the pain if Angie knew she hadn't suffered. He said her family had claimed her body. I thanked him and hung up.

* * *

IT HAD BEEN two days since I saw Angie. I called to see how she was holding up. She wanted to meet after work. Dinner would be nice, she said. I thought she probably saw this as an opportunity for us to say our own goodbyes to a friend.

I arrived at her apartment by seven. She had a determined look on her face as she pushed past me, slipping her arms through the sleeves of her coat. "Come on. Dinner can wait."

"What? Where're we going?"

"The Bamblue Club."

"Are you crazy? What're we going there for?"

She stopped on the step and turned to me. "Sayonara had information for us. I don't know what it was. But we're going to find out. We at least owe her that."

She turned and stomped down the remaining steps. I followed.

I drove in silence for a few minutes, not sure what to make of Angie's ramped-up attitude. "What do you think we'll find? How are we getting in?"

"I don't know. Just leave it to me."

Within fifteen minutes we were at the door to the Bamblue Club once again. Angie took off her coat and tossed it to me. I watched her, puzzled. She undid three of the top buttons on her blouse. I stared, more puzzled yet. She knocked. We waited. She knocked again. A few minutes passed then the yellow eye appeared at the window just as before.

"Sorry closed. No fuckie show."

"Listen." She moved close to the door. "I need to get something from Sayonara's dressing room. I left something there and I need it back. She was my friend." Her hand dug into her pocket and she pulled out a wad of green bills. She peeled three off the top and held them up to the window. The yellow eye blinked and followed her hand, then scanned down to her busting bosom. A few seconds passed then the eye disappeared as the small window slid shut. I heard the sound of a locking mechanism, the clicking of metal, a sliding sound, then the door opened.

A faint light flooded the alley as Angie stepped in. I followed.

The old Asian fellow grinned and held out his hand. Angie handed him the bills. He nodded and pointed down the hall.

"Yes, I know," she said. "We'll only be a few minutes."

"Think he even knows…?" I whispered.

Angie shrugged, but kept moving through the corridor. We reached Sayonara's dressing room door and Angie pushed it open. Feeling around for the light switch, she flicked it on. The room became bathed in a cool light. Everything looked as it did the one time I was there.

"Check around, look in the closet," she ordered. "I'll check her vanity."

"What're we looking for?"

"I don't know. Anything. Something. Whatever."

I shrugged and began my search. It felt strange sifting through a woman's things, but I knew under the circumstances she wouldn't mind. I encountered sexy dresses, red feather boas and shoes with heels so steep they looked like miniature pool slides. Even hats. Feathers fluttered and sequins sparkled. As I pushed and pulled, groped and fondled, a musty odor of sweat and dampness filled my nostrils. I sneezed.

I wiped my nose and turned to Angie. "It doesn't appear the cops have clued into this place yet. When I talked to Lieutenant Watkins I never mentioned this club."

Angie ignored me. She had gone through every bottle, container, box and tube sitting on the top of the vanity and was now sliding her hand along the edges, underneath and around the back.

She stood on her tiptoes, leaned over and stretched.

"There's something here!" Her eyes flicked and her facial expression showed deep concentration as she began fiddling on the backside of the mirror.

"What is it?" I asked.

"Don't know." A second later she retrieved her hand, gripping a small envelope between her fingers. "Something's in it."

She held it up to the light. "A key." She tore open the envelope and pulled out a piece of paper with a number written on it. Taped to the paper was a key with a small round ID tag. She turned the tag over and read, "Seven four three two South Hampton. Where's that?" she asked.

"I think that's in the industrial district south of town. What about the piece of paper?"

"Numbers. Just numbers." She shrugged. "Eight, eight, two, four."

"It could have been attached to the back of that mirror for years. Think it was hers?"

"Don't know. But it might be." Angie continued searching. "I know Sayonara had a secret location where she met clients. She didn't trust hotels, considering the activity she was involved in. She told me that. But she never took me there. This might be the place." Angie looked up. "Find anything?"

"Nothing. Unless you're looking for a new wardrobe." I held up a sequined outfit that employed less fabric than a dinner napkin. I grinned. "This would look nice on you."

"Yeah. I need a new outfit for our next family dinner. Father would be *real* happy to see me in that."

I chuckled then did a three-sixty, scanning the walls and corners. I glanced at the vanity, then reached over and picked up a fancy perfume bottle with a glass rose topper. "Here. I'm sure Sayonara would like you to have this."

Angie looked at the bottle, then up to me. Her eyes glistened. She removed the stopper and waved it under her nose, closed her eyes, took a deep breath, then held the bottle out. A jasmine scent sweetened the air. "Yes. She would."

* * *

THE NEXT DAY I picked up Angie during her lunch hour and we went in search of the address on the key tag. We drove through the industrial area south of town. I had searched Goggle maps so I had the location pinpointed.

"There it is. Seven four three two South Hampton," I said. The street was only six blocks long and backed up against the railroad tracks that passed through town. I slowed then came to a stop in front of a nondescript gray concrete block structure, idling the engine as we rested on an area of loose gravel. It appeared to be a warehouse with an industrial steel door. The windows were metal frame with glass panels that had been painted over in the same gray. There was no signage other than the address. It didn't look like a den of kinky sex, but I had never been to one so I wouldn't know what to look for. I suppose if it had been painted red with flashing lights and a neon marquee out front it might have attracted a little too much attention in this neighborhood.

I looked around then moved on and parked around the corner so the vehicle wouldn't be seen out front, then we walked back to the front door and Angie inserted the key in the lock. She turned it. It clicked. She pushed the door open and instantly a loud *beep, beep, beep*, affronted us.

"Inside, quick. Close the door," she whispered.

As I did, we were thrown into total darkness.

I opened the door again allowing daylight to stream in then turned to the wall next to the door and located a series of light switches as the beeping continued it's countdown before setting off a full-out alarm. I flicked the first one on, providing light to see by, then quickly closed and locked the door, sliding a security bolt into place to assure we wouldn't be surprised by unexpected visitors.

"Where's that paper with the numbers?" I asked.

"Here." She pulled it from her pocket. The beeping continued unabated as we glanced around searching for the source. It seemed louder now.

"There." We said in unison as we stared at the wall to the right.

"What are the numbers?" I asked. We had made an assumption the four numbers would be the code needed to disarm the alarm system. It was all we had. If it didn't work, we might soon be staring down the barrel of a gun held by a security officer.

She lifted the paper. "Eight, eight, two, four."

I punched in the four-digit code, then held my breath. An agonizing moment passed then the rapid beeping stopped and a high-pitched whine continued for three seconds. There was silence. I looked at Angie. We both exhaled then took a fresh breath. My heartbeat settled down and my breathing returned to normal. I had my first chance to glance around.

We were in an entrance area separated from the rest of the warehouse by Japanese Shoji screens, natural-wood frames with white rice-paper panels. Thirty feet above us a grid of steel beams stuffed with rolls of gray insulation served as the ceiling. The surrounding block walls were painted black. The concrete floor had been stained with a deep-red sponge-like texture. On the left a red leather couch with a black lacquered Chinese end table holding a bronze Erté nude lamp sat in a small grouping on an Oriental rug. The décor, though a bit garish, hardly resembled the abused furnishings of Sayonara's dressing room at the Bamblue Club. I detected a faint but distinct sweet but woody smell that probably came from the burning of incense or candles, and had been absorbed into the furniture. To my right, a closed door painted black blended in with the wall.

My eyes scanned the room, then they met Angie's. She

gave me a thin smile.

The Shoji screens were placed in two long overlapping arcs, one on the left, one on the right. The arc on the right was set farther back, about five feet, leaving a gap between them to serve as a passageway into the warehouse. Because they were offset, we couldn't see the rest of the warehouse from the entrance.

I turned back to the panel of light switches and tested a few, setting off various lighting patterns in the darkness beyond the Shoji screens. As the interior was illuminated, I could see the tops of green foliage reaching upwards. I left all light switches on. Since the windows were painted over, nobody could see in.

Angie turned and passed between the two screens. "Wow! Take a look at this!"

I caught up and stopped in my tracks, my focus drawn to the center of the room. I stared as my eyes swept the entire area from left to right. "Holy shit!" I mumbled under my breath.

Before us materialized a Japanese garden complete with a rippling stream and stone walking paths that wound their way through a pebble landscape. Groupings of bamboo, azalea, and rhododendron plants in oversize woven baskets were placed about. In the middle, a large shallow pond edged with natural rock formed a pool that surrounded an elevated circular bed, rising center stage like a throne for a queen. A drag queen. The platform seemed to float on the water's surface. Pillows covered in red velvet were piled atop a matching bedspread. Above the bed a configuration of leather straps and a contraption of some sort hung from the ceiling.

To the left another series of Shoji screens placed in the shape of a three-sided box stood among pots of bamboo. On the right among potted plants a metal contraption resembling a swing set had straps and harnesses hanging from it.

I stepped onto the stone path and walked toward the pond. Reaching it, I placed a foot carefully on one of the "floating" steps to check for stability, then, finding it provided a firm foothold, crossed to the floating bed, circled it and pressed my hand down on the bedspread. I turned to Angie. "Waterbed." I looked up above the bed and pointed. "What do you make of this?" I allowed my imagination to relax my guard for a moment, winked, then turned my attention to the swing set.

Angie crossed her arms in front of her, planted her foot and glared.

"Come on," I said. "This is some neat stuff."

"For who? You guys are all alike. Whatever happened to romance?" She walked over to the area behind the Shoji screens, stood there and stared. As I walked up behind her I took my fingers and rubbed them along a length of bamboo. "Plastic." I stared at a rack I hadn't noticed, tucked out of sight. Hanging from it I found a collection of leather whips, masks, bras—some with the nipples cut out—straps, belts and buckles the likes of which, for the most part, I could only guess what purpose they served. A shoulder-high wall attached with wrist and ankle straps stood next to it.

"Tools of the trade?"

Angie shrugged then turned and walked behind the Shoji screens. I lingered to study the assortment of "leather for pleasure."

"Hey," Angie called out. "Back here."

I turned and followed her voice, finding her standing in front of a free-standing closet flipping through a collection of ladies lingerie. Lacy. Silky. All of it on the sexy, skimpy side.

I leaned over Angie's shoulder and took a quick inventory of Sayonara's assets. She closed the door and opened the other side. A variety of uniforms and outfits hung side by side, from samurai warrior gear to plaid schoolgirl attire.

"Jesus. Looks like a costume rental store."

She shut the door and we surveyed the garden of Eve and evil. "What did you really expect to find?" I asked.

"I don't know. I just hoped we'd find *something*."

I looked over at Angie. "We still don't have a clue what she meant by 'everything's changed. It's not what we think.' "

"No, we don't. I know it must be important. She sounded urgent."

"But we've found nothing to help us." I glanced at my watch. "Let's get going. I don't want to be caught here if someone shows up."

Angie seemed hesitant to leave. It was as if she knew something was here, somewhere, and she hadn't found it. She glanced around, searching the area with a determined expression. "Hey! What's missing?"

I looked at her, puzzled. "I don't know, what?"

"A bathroom. Where's the bathroom? No woman would have a bed without a bathroom nearby."

"You're right." I scanned the wide-open warehouse, my eyes settling on the screens at the entrance. "That door up front."

"Right. That's what I'm thinking."

We headed for the black door against the wall. I turned the knob and pushed. It opened into a small bathroom containing a toilet, sink, and a corner shower enclosed with frosted glass. A Formica top supporting a hairbrush and a collection of ladies cosmetics and toiletries surrounded the sink. A mirror covered the wall above the vanity. I looked through the cabinet underneath then picked up the lid to the toilet tank. Nothing. Poking my head around the vanity I noticed a small garbage can on the far side. I peered in and saw something like shiny plastic in the bottom among paper debris. I picked up the can, hesitant to reach in. I shook it. It rewarded my abrupt shaking with a clunk. Forced to stick my hand in, I gripped the item with two fingers and pulled it out. A cell phone.

"Look at this!"

Angie moved closer and stared. "In the garbage?"

"Yeah. What do you think it was doing there?"

Angie reached out. "Let me see."

She flipped the phone open and turned it on. A phone number lit up the digital display. "That's her number. This is her phone." She began working her way through various functions.

"Why would her phone be in the trash?" I asked, more to myself than to Angie. I emptied the can onto the floor of the bathroom, then sifted through the few items of paper and trash. I picked up and examined each piece, wishing I had a pair of surgical gloves. I unwrapped one piece that was folded in a tight package. I lifted it up to the light and read the handwritten note, RCQU3054383. It appeared to be some kind of code or serial number in a sequence of four letters and seven numbers. I turned the numbers toward Angie. "What do you make of this?"

Angie, deeply involved in her phone research, glanced and shrugged. I folded it again and stuffed it in my pocket.

"Look," she said. "Her last call was to me. Three days ago. That's my number."

I looked around the bathroom, my eyes stopped on the sink. "The water you heard in the background. This is it. The sink. When she called you, she was here in the bathroom."

"She was scared. Someone must have been in the building with her. She wanted to talk to us without them knowing."

"Who called her just before you?" I asked.

"I don't know." Angie hit a few keys. Her face froze, her eyes widened. "Look!" She held the display out. I stared in disbelief. Staring back was the name, DENG QIN.

CHAPTER FORTY

New London, Connecticut

BY 4:17 P.M. the shipping and distribution crew of the Propulsion and Power Division at United Electric Aircraft Engine had loaded the heavy crate onto the waiting railroad car. They checked and confirmed that the serial numbers matched the manifest. Earlier, the jet aircraft engine inside the massive box had been secured to a custom-built steel rack with heavy-duty industrial tires for ease of movement. The rack was bolted to the floor of the wood crate, strapped down and covered with heavy tarps. The package would be rolling the rails to Chicago by early the next morning.

United Electric had a long history in the research, development and production of engines for industrial and military applications. One of their current contracts with the Department of Defense called for them to provide the power plant for America's Joint Strike Fighter (JSF), the latest generation of America's fighter jet. America's allies, who maintained their own air force and flew this same plane, often purchased replacement engines. Taiwan, an ally of the United States, was a routine buyer of the most sophisticated weaponry from America's military contractors. Their purchases often included aircraft engines.

The sales and purchase contract listed Jong Kim, a Korean-born arms dealer working as a liaison to the government of Taiwan, as the purchaser of record. He had ten years experience as an international sales consultant for American military manufacturers and previously passed a rigorous vetting procedure dictated by the U.S. government.

This jet engine was on the U.S. Munitions List—a catalog of restricted arms and technology administered by the State Department's Bureau of Political-Military Affairs—and illegal to export without a special government license. Jong Kim had gone through the proper formalities and was permitted to make the purchase.

Hours before the engine was loaded, a team of highly-trained computer experts located in a top secret government facility in Beijing, China, had broken through the firewall of the main frame computer at United Electric Aircraft Engine. Earlier tests over the past weeks had proven they could hack the main frame, but they waited until this particular day before they entered and made changes to the distribution manifest and the purchase request.

With clandestine help from a Chinese nationalist working in the engineering department of United Electric, the Chinese hackers switched model numbers and contract codes of the engine that had been approved by the government for sale to Jong Kim with those of a highly classified and top-secret prototype. Thus, unknown to the shipping crew, the engine being strapped down to the railroad car was not the engine currently deployed on the Joint Strike Fighter that had been previously approved for sale, but a highly secret prototype known as the Trapped Vortex Combustor, or TVC. This prototype exhibited cutting edge technology and was one of the most promising breakthroughs under development by the Department of Defense to meet future military needs.

This minor switch of numbers and codes would be a major breach of security and put America's most highly sensitive technology for future production of aircraft engines into the hands of Communist China. Within hours of the prototype being removed from the Propulsion and Power Division facilities, the hackers once again entered the main frame and reversed the previous procedure, restoring the files to their original state and eliminating evidence. By the time the switch could be traced, the prototype would have disappeared, having been placed into the hands of the Chinese. It would be a major embarrassment to the Department of Defense and a breach the American public would never be aware of.

On arrival in Chicago's Corwith Intermodal Facility the freight car from New London, Connecticut was uncoupled and sent to the classification yard. There the crate carrying the aircraft engine was transferred into a steel shipping container owned by China Shipping Container Lines and loaded onto a railroad car chassis. This railroad car was then hitched to a series of powerful locomotives of the Burlington Northern Santa Fe Railroad to be transported to its final destination, Seattle, Washington. Protocol would be strictly enforced, documents checked and procedures followed to assure accurate delivery of each and every railcar.

The router studied the manifest and confirmed that the locked container with the identification number RCQU3054383 had been loaded on the outgoing Burlington Northern special, departing for Seattle the following day. Unbeknownst to him, the manifest he had been provided had been altered by those same Chinese computer hackers. What was identified as a replacement engine for the Joint Strike Fighter destined for Taiwan, and was in fact the top-secret prototype, was now identified as a hydraulic turbine engine destined for Shanghai, an industrial port in the People's Republic of China. A purchase that was not so unusual, as industrial turbine engines had been purchased by Communist China on previous occasions for use in hydroelectric dams.

An electronic copy of the altered manifest had also been forwarded to China Lines, the Port of Seattle and the new purchaser and exporter of record, the Longzee Import and Export Company and its principal, Mr. Deng Qin.

CHAPTER FORTY-ONE

New York City

JACK BUICK RETURNED from an editorial meeting and stopped by the front desk to pick up messages from Loraine. He spent a moment flirting with the attractive, silver-haired widow of about sixty before glancing at his messages. He flipped through the note-size sheets as she looked up from her computer.

"Oh, Jack. I almost forgot. A Mister Vincent called. Said he was an old friend of yours and wanted to remind you of your fishing trip. He said to tell you he planned on taking you fishing in the East River. He didn't leave a number."

Jack froze. His hands holding the messages began to twitch. One fell to the floor. He didn't notice. He stared at Loraine, his face feeling flushed. "When did he call?"

"Oh, maybe twenty minutes ago."

Jack turned and glanced at the glass entrance doors. He fumbled with the messages then pulled a handkerchief from his back pocket and wiped his forehead. He closed his eyes, leaned over and propped his hand on the desktop.

"Jack, are you okay?" Loraine asked.

"Ah, yeah. Yeah. I'm okay. Did he say anything else?"

"No. Not really. But I thought that was an odd call." She hesitated and studied Jack. "I didn't know there were still fish in the East River."

Jack ignored her, his mind racing. *Shit! Has it been ten days?* He knew he had to pay The Boys. Clear up his debt. But he hadn't had much luck of late. He hadn't won that big pot he had counted on. His luck had always come through in the past. But he'd been on such an unlucky streak. He had to figure something out. Some way of coming up with the money, or he *would* be going fishing, from the inside of a fifty-five gallon drum.

He hurried down the hall, took the elevator up and rushed toward his office, glancing over his shoulder at each turn. He pushed himself through his door and locked it. *Damn! Now what do I do? Where am I going to get that kind of money?* He collapsed into his leather chair and swiveled back and forth.

First it was those guys from the Chinese whatever threatening me, then the damn FBI came calling, and now this. Shit. How do I get myself into these damn situations? He kept running various scenarios through his head, but each one ended up with a fishing trip. *I should call Roger Lee. He might have some advice. It's not like he hasn't been there himself. He knows how this game is played. Yeah, that's it. I'll call Roger.*

Jack reached for the phone and searched his quick dial for the number of China Gate Publishing. After a few moments he heard Roger's voice.

"This is Roger Lee."

"Roger. Jack Buick."

"Hey, pal. How's it going?"

"Not good. Listen. I'm in deep shit. I owe The Boys. Big. Real big. Know what I mean? They want it now. And I ain't got it."

"Jesus, Jack. I told you not to push those guys." There was a pause. "How much?"

"Hundred and sixty-five grand."

"Jesus, Jack. Don't you know when to fold? What're you gonna do?"

"Don't know. Thought I could get some of it back, maybe a little here, a little there, but I've crapped out. It's been a really bad streak, Roger. Ain't seen nothin' like it. Maybe I'm losing my touch. I don't know what to do."

"How serious are they?"

"Damn fucking serious. They're talking fishing the East River."

"Okay. Let's think for a minute. Is there anyplace you can get it?"

Jack pulled out his handkerchief and wiped his head. "Hell no. I'm flat tapped out. I ain't got no place to go. I'm desperate."

"Jeeze. I don't know what to say."

"Come on, Roger. I really need help. You've been there. What'd you do?"

The phone was silent for a minute. Then Roger spoke up. "Listen, Jack. I got friends. Friends that could help you. But I'm hesitant—"

"Hesitant, shit!" Jack interrupted. "Listen, The Boys are probably on their way here right now. I don't have time to be hesitant. What are you saying?"

"I got friends that could help you," Roger continued. "But I'm not sure you'd accept their help."

"And why's that? Don't you understand? I'm not in a position to negotiate right now. I need to make a deal." Jack hesitated. "So what're you saying? You know someone who can help me or what?"

"Yes, Jack. I do."

"So who are they? What do they want?"

After concluding his conversation with Roger Lee, Jack was pissed. He was pissed at Roger for betraying him. Having heard Roger had passed on information to the Chinese Cultural whatever about Curtis Beecham's manuscript, he could have gone through the phone and strangled him. He was pissed at the FBI. He was pissed at the mob and he was pissed at himself for allowing his dumb ass to get into this situation. Now he was being forced, blackmailed to compromise his ethics. Sell his soul. And betray a promising writer that had placed his trust in him. Damn them. Damn me.

Jack had no choice. He had run out of options. If he wanted to look into the mirror and see his living breathing face staring back, he had to do something. After all, the reflection of a double-crossing scumbag in a steamy bathroom mirror was better than having no reflection at all.

But first, he knew he had to get away. Get away quick. Disappear before The Boys showed up. He knew they would. He needed time. Time to think about Roger Lee's proposal. He hated to think he might just have to accept this unsavory proposition, but it might be his only option. He could call his boss later and explain there was a death in the family. It wasn't much of a stretch. The holidays were coming up and most of the staff had taken the week off. He had some vacation time coming. He could use that if he had to. He'd be back in a week or so. By then, the plan would have been carried out, and he could straighten everything out with The Boys. But for now, ol' Jack had to disappear before he found himself sucking in city sewage.

He opened his computer and searched his files until he found Curtis Beecham's manuscript. He clicked on it and dragged it to the trash, clicked EMPTY. He opened his desk drawer and searched through a pile of disks for the one Curtis Beecham had provided, sliding it out, putting it in his briefcase. Then he knelt down in front of the stacks of files on the floor and flipped through them until he came to the folder holding Curtis's manuscript and placed it in his briefcase. He stood up, slipped on his coat and scanned the room one more time. After a brief glance at the lithograph of the bulldogs, he walked out and locked the door.

* * *

THE HORIZON AIRLINES flight landed in Seattle as the city began to wake, greeted by the dreariness of winter. The weather matched Jack Buick's mood. He had exchanged New York's snow flurries for Seattle's light drizzle.

Over the past two days Jack had been traveling nonstop. He had called a poker buddy who had a pilot's license and his own private plane. He flew Jack to St. Louis, erasing a small debt acquired over a hand of Texas Hold'em. From there Jack took a series of short hops by bus and two commercial flights connecting four different cities before ending up in Boise, Idaho. In Boise, he had picked up the Horizon Airlines flight to Seattle. He didn't want to leave a clear trail The Boys would find easy to follow.

His circuitous route should provide a margin of safety and give him the time he needed. He had to find a hotel and get some rest before figuring out how he would handle Curtis. But he knew Curtis trusted him. It shouldn't be difficult.

He had two options. One had been arranged through Roger Lee and his contacts with the Chinese Ministry of State Security and their operatives in Seattle. The other he would pursue on his own without Roger Lee's knowledge.

Safe from The Boys reach, he would bide his time. Place a couple of phone calls to get the ball rolling. Then he'd sit back and wait. Maybe visit one of those Indian casinos and try his luck. After playing with the sharks in Atlantic City, the salmon packers of the Pacific Northwest should be easy pickin's.

CHAPTER FORTY-TWO

Seattle, Washington

I SPENT A nice afternoon and evening with my kids, Teri Lynn and Michael. Shelly had invited me to share Christmas with our two children. I was pleased to be able to spend time with them on what they considered the most important day of the year. I watched them open the gifts I'd brought. Too many by most standards. I guess I tried to make up for not being a full-time father. I loved my kids and took any opportunity to spend time with them. Shelly knew that and was quite accommodating.

It was dark but still early evening when I left the brick Tudor on Queen Anne. I was going to drop down the hill to Ballard and stop by Dad's place. I had picked up some undershirts, briefs and a box of his favorite candies, Frango mints, and had them gift wrapped for Christmas. He was impossible to buy for. But I knew he would eventually need the underwear, and the candy would be a nice treat.

The streets were slick from a constant drizzle. My Jeep coughed and sputtered in defiance of the cold damp air. I urged her on with a little tap on the dash as my mind wandered back over the last few enjoyable hours.

The sound of an accelerating vehicle startled me, bringing

me back to the moment, although I hadn't noticed any headlights in my rearview mirror.

"What the...?" Some idiot had raced up from behind with the intent to pass. I glanced to my left as a white van pulled beside me. I caught a quick glimpse. A hooded face in the passenger seat. The road was dimly lit, the street narrow, so my eyes darted back to the glistening pavement. My mind retrieved an unpleasant memory and flashed it before my face. The Van!

Pop! Glass shattered. My driver-side window exploded. Auto glass peppered me. A stinging sensation riddled my arms and the side of my face. I ducked, jerked the wheel. A second *pop!* My windshield shattered with a crack, spraying more glass. My foot pressed down on the accelerator. The tires squealed. The Jeep hit the curb and bounced over the sidewalk. The right side crashed against a rock retaining wall, the fender crushed inward with the wrenching sound of crumpled steel. The vehicle careened along the wall, grinding against the rock surface, ripping metal and shredding debris on the passenger side like a cheese grater.

My airbag inflated with a *whoosh*. It slapped against my chest, pressed pieces of broken glass into my face. Even as the seatbelt pulled across my chest I bounced uncontrollably. My head, jerked to the side, smacked the doorframe. Jostled free of the gas pedal, my foot chased after the brake.

The car spun sideways as the back end whipped away from the wall and skidded into a curbside telephone pole crushing the driver-side door against me. The vehicle stopped cold with a sudden jerk, pinning it between the proverbial rock wall and a hard place.

The radiator exploded. Steam poured out of the crushed hood with a *hiss*. The smell of burnt rubber, fused metal, antifreeze and gasoline fumes stung my nostrils.

Everything had happened in seconds. I tried to move. Tried to focus. I could see blurry brake lights farther up the street, reflecting on the wet surface. I strained to keep my eyes open, stay alert. The van had stopped. Doors opened. Two dark figures hopped out and ran toward me, their faces obscured by hoods.

A white glimmer of light appeared, dancing across the pavement. Vehicle headlights from behind me. The figures slowed, hesitated, turned and jumped back into the van. The red taillights moved on, grew smaller.

I began to fade as a voice broke through the thick fog attempting to consume my consciousness.

"Hey! You okay? Oh, shit. Charley, call nine-one-one! This guy's…"

* * *

I WOKE UP and blinked, my vision bleary as if a thin veil covered my face. I was held down beneath a tight sheet. The room was cold. I felt a chill. The strong scent of antiseptics permeated the cool air. A mild hum and a steady, slow *beep, beep, beep* cut through the eerie silence. I reached up and rubbed my eyes. I felt a twinge near the elbow and looked at my right arm. An IV. A hospital room. But where? My left arm was wrapped in gauze but I could move it. I slid it across my legs. They were sore, but I could feel the light touch of my fingers. Soft cotton fabric moved against my skin. A hospital gown. I felt my forehead. A bandage. I winced against a throbbing pain.

My mind jumped from the cold sterile room to my car. An accident. When? Where? Voices. There was a shot. Yes, someone shot at me. A white van. A hooded guy. He shot at me. Jesus Christ! He shot at me! He tried to kill me!

I went over the events in my mind. Tried to reconstruct the incident, recall details. It happened so fast, I couldn't remember anything more. I couldn't remember a face. Just a hood.

My computer! It was in the car. I always carried it. I didn't trust the flimsy locks at the Pink Salmon. But where is it? I slipped out of bed, pulled the rolling IV tower behind me and opened the closet door. The jeans, shirt and jacket I wore were draped on hangers, wrinkled, covered with spatters of dried blood. I glanced down. My sneakers. Beneath them, my computer case. I knelt down and unzipped it. I smiled with relief, stood up, then grimaced. Every part of my body ached.

Exhausted by this effort, I climbed back into the narrow bed, closed my eyes and breathed out with long slow breaths. I thought back to the events that brought me here. They tried to kill me. A chill racked my body. I stared at the ceiling. The room remained quiet except for the incessant hum and a constant *beep, beep, beep.*

* * *

I DECIDED NOT to call Shelly and upset her and the kids. I didn't want to expose them to the danger I had gotten myself into. From the lobby of Harborview Medical Center, I called Angie. I had been discharged with cuts, scrapes and a minor concussion. I was fortunate. The police were investigating the "accident" but had no leads on the van or the gunmen. I mentioned the Asia-Pacific Fruit & Vegetable Company van I had seen days earlier in the alley. They checked the name out. The company didn't exist.

Angie picked me up to take me to a rental car agency she was familiar with, a local one with older cars and lower prices. She stared straight ahead and remained quiet as I slipped into her car.

"Hey," I said. She remained stone silent. Her face tightened. "You okay?" I asked.

She turned to me. "Yes. *I'm* fine. But look at you."

"I'm okay." I glanced down at my blood-stained jacket and swallowed.

"Yes, but you could have been killed. And who knows when they'll try again. Or where."

"I know. Believe me, I know. It was that white van again.

Remember the one from the alley? Somehow they're involved. And I bet they're connected to Deng Qin."

She glanced at me. I could tell she was tense. "So what now? The stakes are higher. And we're no closer to finding George or figuring out this Miss Hong Kong thing."

"I know. I know. But we do have those clues from Sayonara."

"They're worthless," Angie said. "Deng Qin's phone number. What are you going to do, call and threaten him? Some letters and numbers on a piece of paper. Who knows if it means anything? Sayonara said it's not what we thought. So what the hell does that mean? We have nothing more to go on. We're at a dead end."

I slumped back into the seat. This was the first time I'd heard her curse. "Maybe. But I'm sure something will break soon. I just feel it. I'm not ready to quit. Not just yet."

She looked at me. "I've buried one friend. I don't want to go through that again."

* * *

AFTER I PICKED up the rental car—an eighty-seven Mercury Topaz four-door with tires that looked like the originals, though only three were whitewalls—I drove to the tow-car lot to retrieve the gift I'd had in the car for my dad and delivered it to him. I told him I'd had an accident, wrecked the Jeep—though I gave him no details—so I hadn't been able to get by on Christmas day. I tried to make it up to him the best I could. He liked the box of candy.

After leaving Dad's I headed to the diner to call Jack Buick. I didn't want to use up the minutes I had left on my disposable phone.

"Mr. Buick's office," a woman's voice said.

"Mr. Jack Buick, please."

"I'm sorry. Mr. Buick had a family emergency. He's out of the office."

"When do you expect him?"

"I don't have that information. Would you like to leave your name and a contact number?"

"Yes. Yes, I would. This is Curtis Beecham."

"Oh, Mr. Beecham. Mr. Buick left instructions for you to call him on his cell. He said he specifically wanted to speak with you."

This relieved an anxiety that was fast building. I grabbed a pencil from the bar and jotted the number down on a piece of scrap paper, then hung up and called Jack's cell. It rang three times.

"Yeah, Jack here."

"Mr. Buick. It's Curtis."

"Curtis. Glad you called."

Jack sounded upbeat. More cheerful than I thought he'd be. "I hope the family emergency isn't too serious," I probed.

"Nah. My grandmother. She's in a home."

Grandmother? "Well...glad everything's okay."

"Curtis," Jack jumped right in. "Where are you?"

"Right now, I'm at the diner."

"Okay. Good. Hey, listen Curtis. I was thinking about coming out to Seattle and spending a few days. Relieve some of the stress of looking after my grandmother. The office is slow around the holidays anyway. I'd like to see the great Northwest. Maybe I can be of some help. You've been doing research into that spy angle, haven't you?"

"Ah, yeah. I have. You're coming here? This time of year?"

"Sure. It'd be a nice break. Can't be any more miserable than New York."

"Okay," I said, still a little surprised. "That'd be great. When?"

"In a few days. I'll let you know. By the way, where you staying?"

"The Pink Salmon Motel. On Aurora Avenue. Easy to find. Third dump north of the Aurora Bridge."

Jack chuckled. "Okay. I'll call and leave a message at the motel when I arrive. If you want to talk, you have my cell."

I hung up then realized I hadn't told Jack about the shooting. But he'd be here soon, I'd fill him in then. A lot had happened. Then again, a lot hadn't. Jack had a vested interest in the book. Another mind working this spy angle would be helpful. His experience and all. Yeah, sure. Having Jack here would be a real benefit.

CHAPTER FORTY-THREE

AFTER ARRIVING IN Seattle, Jack Buick had spent the past two days relaxing while losing a few bucks at the Indian casino. He felt the stress of New York fading as his own plan began to develop. When he fulfilled his end of the agreement, he would receive payment for doing a small favor. He could then clear his debt. It seemed so simple. Too easy.

After Curtis called, he dialed the first of two phone numbers that would set his plan in motion.

A voice answered. "Supervisory Special Agent Lou Jengwi, here."

"This is Jack Buick. From Kaleidoscope Book Publishing in New York."

There was silence for a few seconds. "Yes, Mr. Buick. I know who you are. What can I do for you?"

"Well, this isn't a social call as you might have guessed. You paid a visit to Curtis Beecham and your goons called on me in New York. Unpleasant to say the least. I wasn't happy about it. I understand you boys are just doing your job, but things have changed. I might be able to help you after all. I could provide information you might be interested in."

Jack paused so Jengwi urged, "Go on."

"I can give you Curtis Beecham and I can see that his book doesn't go anywhere. I can even fill in some of the gaps in your Chinese espionage investigation."

From the silence on the other end of the line, Jack knew he had the FBI agent's attention. And he knew if Jengwi were at all like him, he'd be willing to deal.

"Sounds interesting. Any information a law-abiding citizen wants to share with his government would be appreciated. Probably get you an *unsigned* commendation from the President. Do I understand you intend to share this information?"

"For a price. After all, one has to take care of one's self. And I'm taking the risk. So, yeah, I intend to share this for a modest fee. To cover expenses."

"Well, of course, Mr. Buick. I expect that. We have on occasion paid informants a small retainer. Modest, as you say. After all, we're just a small line item in the federal budget. We don't have a direct conduit to the Treasury, you understand. What have you got in mind?"

"Six figures. No less."

There was a pause. "With all due respect, Mr. Buick. I couldn't accommodate such a request if I wanted to. Payments are based on value. This information is not that valuable. A writer? A book? This is certainly something we can handle ourselves. We do have *some* experience in investigations of this type."

Jack kept it brief. "I'll call back in two days. Remember. Curtis Beecham. His book. And serious evidence regarding espionage activity in Seattle and New York with names. Six figures. No less."

Jack hung up, smiling. He knew he had the FBI on his hook. Now, it was time to make the second call. A number provided by Roger Lee.

He dialed, it rang and from the connecting line he heard,

"Good afternoon. Lotus Blossom Restaurant."

Jack responded. "Yes. I would like to order fish soup to go, with American cheese."

* * *

JACK BUICK HAD left the proper code with the Lotus Blossom's headwaiter, Yung, who passed it on to Deng Qin. Deng Qin then contacted Jack as prearranged by Roger Lee, and now the two had set a time to meet. Jack followed the directions he had been given and met Deng Qin at the China Tea House in Seattle's International District. He entered a dimly lit dining room with dark-wood booths softened by red and gold embroidered cushions. The back wall had a long counter and a door with a small window that most likely led to the kitchen. One man sat alone at the last booth on the right. As Jack entered, a young Asian woman in traditional silk garments pointed toward the lone customer, bowed to Jack, then disappeared into the back room. Jack walked toward the Asian man, stood for a second by the table, looked around, then slid into the opposite seat, facing him.

"Mr. Deng Qin?"

The man did not rise but he did bow his head. "Yes. You must be Mr. Jack Buick."

Jack nodded. The cold eyes of the Asian pierced into him. The seriousness of the situation became apparent. He had thought this would be easy, but now Jack was having second thoughts. He was sitting across the table from a master spy of Communist China. A real pro. Dealing with the mob was one thing—Jack knew how they worked. Dealing with secret agents was a whole 'nother ball game, and maybe Jack was way out of his league. Everything he knew about the Chinese came from Hollywood movies and his perception was that the Chinese were better and more creative than the Sicilians when it came to killing people.

"Mr. Roger Lee has informed me of you," Deng Qin

began. "He indicated you might be able to help us."

"Yes, I can."

"And why would you do this? Why would you help the People's Republic?"

Jack was smart enough to know he shouldn't use political or moral justifications in his response. He had no reason to help them, and he knew they knew it.

"Money," Jack said without flinching. He paused while studying Deng Qin's face. A longtime poker player, Jack wondered if his poker techniques would work on a pro? The stakes here were bigger than any poker table he'd ever sat at. "I have some debt I need to clear up."

"Yes. I am aware." Deng Qin did not rush the conversation. He took his time between responses. He appeared to be studying Jack. Feeling him out. Maybe, Jack thought, he's a poker player too. Jack figured Deng Qin didn't get where he was by showing his hand too soon. This man would be cautious.

Jack took the initiative. "I understand you're unhappy about a certain book. And a certain writer." He paused a moment. "I can make them go away. The FBI is also interested in what this book has to say. I can be sure they never find out. I'm not interested in what you do. I'll disappear along with the writer and the book."

"I would be pleased if you took this problem off my hands. I understand you will be taking a risk, so we will pay you handsomely. In your American dollars of course."

Jack liked the direction the conversation was going. "Yes. I'm putting myself at great risk," Jack emphasized. "And, as you said, my efforts should be rewarded handsomely. Where I come from 'handsomely' falls in the six-figure category."

Deng Qin didn't flinch. He had yet to show any emotion since they had begun their discussion.

"We will talk again," Deng Qin said. "I must see results,

you understand. But I believe we can come to some sort of agreement. Leave a message with Jong at the Lotus Blossom when you have your plan finalized. I want this to move quickly."

Deng Qin rose and stepped away from the table. Jack stood up and slipped out of the booth but hesitated to offer his hand. He nodded and crossed the still-empty restaurant, stepping out into the bright light of midday.

Jack walked with a quick pace toward his car. He smiled to himself, confident now that he could pull this off. If he worked it right, he'd get both the Chinese and the FBI to hand over a suitcase full of hundred dollar bills. Pay off his debt. Hell, maybe he wouldn't do that either. Maybe he'd just keep the money for himself. He could find better use for it than the mob. That kind of cash would be serious front money for the tables. He could turn it into a fortune.

He passed a few pedestrians and a man leaning against a storefront reading a Chinese language newspaper. The man glanced at him as he approached, then looked down, the newspaper covering his face. A quick shiver shot through Jack. He stiffened. Something odd. What was it? He reached his car and glanced back. The man had disappeared. Jack slipped in and pulled out into traffic. He glanced into his rearview mirror. A dark sedan pulled out and fell in line two cars behind him.

Arriving at his hotel, he pulled into the driveway, stopped, turned his head and looked over his shoulder. The black sedan appeared at the entrance, slowed, then accelerated and continued down the block.

After the vehicle disappeared, Jack pulled into a parking spot, stepped out of his car, glanced around and headed for the lobby entrance. *Okay. If they're going to play that game, I'm on to them. They won't outsmart me.* He walked past a white panel van that had apparently pulled in to make a delivery. On the side he noticed the name ASIA-PACIFIC FRUIT & VEGETABLE

COMPANY. He smiled and nodded at the young Asian fellow who glanced at him from the open window, then Jack proceeded to his hotel room. *Yeah, they can't outsmart me.*

CHAPTER FORTY-FOUR

I HAD JUST finished off a couple of dinner tacos from a drive-up window as I neared the Pink Salmon Motel. Since the shooting incident, I'd been paying close attention to everyone and everything around me. A little justified caution and prudence on my part. As the rented Mercury bumped over the lip into the asphalt parking lot, my stomach knotted.

At the far end sat a lone white van. Two dark figures could be seen through the windshield. The name on the side of the vehicle read, ASIA PACIFIC FRUIT & VEGETABLE COMPANY. The van! A stab of fear slashed through my tensed body. My God! How'd they find me? I slumped down in the seat, jerked the wheel and turned, keeping a row of parked cars between us, aiming for the exit that would put me right back on Aurora Avenue. Would they recognize the rental car? I glanced over my shoulder then merged into the heavy afternoon traffic, heading downtown.

A moment later I checked again. Damn! They had picked me up and were following a few cars back. Blocked in traffic, I couldn't accelerate. I crossed over the Aurora Bridge. The air inside the car became stuffy, my sweatshirt felt heavy, constricting my movement, raising my body thermostat. My back and neck tensed as I squeezed the steering wheel, eyes bouncing back and forth between the mirror and the road. The van hung back. In traffic with lots of witnesses, they wouldn't try anything. Or would they? I needed to shake them, return to the Pink Salmon and collect my meager belongings. Or ditch my stuff. Nothing I had would be of any great loss.

How'd they know I was staying at the Pink Salmon? Still more questions. I needed to get smarter than they were, and quick.

I stayed on the busy thoroughfare, heading downtown hoping to lose them. Keeping a firm grip with both hands I continued my vigilant watch in the mirror as traffic entered the Battery Street Tunnel. Once we passed through it, Aurora Avenue became the Alaskan Way Viaduct. With no exits, it'd take me past downtown where I'd be more vulnerable.

I made a quick decision, cut across one lane of traffic and took the Battery Street off-ramp, the last one before the viaduct. I sped down the exit. Reaching the light at the intersection, I made a right turn onto Western Avenue. I could see the van, still following, six cars behind. I hit the accelerator and raced down Western, a two-lane one-way street. I flipped from one lane to the next through narrow gaps between vehicles, nearly scraping bumpers in a reckless manner. The van kept pace.

After four blocks I cut off a pickup truck as I made a sudden left turn in front of him. A blast of his horn and a one-finger salute signaled his displeasure. I knew this one-way street came to an end after two blocks where it ran into Alaskan Way—the four-lane boulevard that meandered along the downtown waterfront. It would be crowded with traffic and pedestrians. I hoped the congestion would allow me to lose these guys. I gunned it, passed through the first green light, then stared in horror at the sight of flashing lights ahead, and the railroad-crossing arm being lowered as I sped down the last block. I glanced in the mirror. The van made the light. They were four or five cars back.

Brake lights signaled the inevitable slowdown. With a train approaching, I knew there would be a dead stop in traffic. I couldn't move left. Cars were quickly stacking up. The horn of a freight train blasted above the noise of traffic and braking vehicles. On my right, a possible escape route paralleled the railroad tracks; a dirt service road behind a row of industrial buildings. Cars were parked at an angle on one side. Pulling onto the dirt shoulder, I cut around the right side of the car in front of me. I passed the vehicles waiting in line and took a sharp right turn behind the warehouse on the corner. The old Mercury fishtailed, throwing up a cloud of dust.

As I cleared the corner my heart jumped. I hit the brakes, slid to a halt. A row of barricades with flashing yellow lights cut off access to the street. Behind them utility crews had dug a ditch. I looked behind me. There was nowhere to go.

I hesitated a moment, then nosed into the one remaining parking spot, reached over, grabbed my computer case, threw open the door and jumped out. A loud, long, horn blast made me stare at the freight train closing on my right, nearly even with me. The powerful diesels pushed it at the steady pace required within city limits.

I leaped over the low barrier separating the row of cars from the railroad right-of-way and bolted toward the tracks, picking an angle I hoped would put me in front of the oncoming train. Committed, I couldn't glance for even a second to check its speed. Hesitation would be fatal. I closed the gap, my pulse racing, adrenaline pumping.

Movement appeared out of the corner of my eye. A black steel force towered over me, driving forward, an unyielding presence without regard for any lesser thing in its path. I kept running. Could feel its breath as it sucked in air. The locomotive continued its incessant shriek with a sense of urgency. The rattling rail cars and the grinding screech of steel wheels overpowered the thumping of my own heart. With

301

blind faith, I jumped the first rail, took two stutter steps on the ragged wood railroad tie and hurdled the second rail. The horn raged, louder, closer. My eardrums cried out. Fear kept me focused.

I repeated the delicate footwork on the second set of tracks while blasted by a wall of hot air and the unrelenting train horn that screamed in outrage. I picked up my pace when I hit the pavement of Alaskan Way, ran through a row of idling cars that had stopped for the oncoming train and dodged my way among wide-eyed stares of pedestrians. I glanced behind. The train had passed the intersection. The van remained hidden behind it.

Two blocks away the Waterfront Trolley had stopped at the Vine Street station. The shriek of the train began to fade among the traffic noise. I ran with desperation. The trolley only paused for brief moments at the few stations along the waterfront if someone were waiting. I ran faster. Pushed myself. One more block. My computer bag swung out from my grip, slapped against my leg. I dashed up the concrete ramp and jumped through the open doorway, my breath coming hard and fast in a hyper rhythm that matched my heartbeat. The trolley conductor turned with a look of surprise. I exhaled, held my hand against my heaving chest, walked to the back, leaned down and stared out the back window. No one followed. I collapsed onto an empty bench seat, my computer resting on my lap. The trolley blew its shrill whistle and moved on with a rattle and a slight jerk.

I rode the trolley down Alaskan Way until it reached the Yesler Way station where I exited. Hurrying across the street I mingled with the crowd of tourists and ferry commuters who filled the wide pedestrian walkway fronting the waterfront shops and restaurants.

A tattered homeless fellow pushing a grocery cart loaded with a lifetime collection of ragged fashions and home furnishings passed. A skinny dog with a checkered scarf tied around his neck followed closely behind. I walked on with my usual indifference but after two paces I stopped and spun around.

"Hey, you," I yelled. He ignored me.

I hurried back and placed myself in his path, my hand on his cart to halt his progress. "Hey. I got a deal for you."

His wiry natty beard, sunken cheeks and blurry red eyes looked at me dumbfounded. "Look, I got a deal for you," I repeated. "It's your lucky day. How 'bout we trade coats. And hats." I cringed. Sucked in a little air. "Yeah," I repeated. "My coat and hat for yours."

He stared. Then reached over and felt my jacket. My finest Eddie Bauer.

"Come on. I don't have all day. Wanna trade or not?"

He smiled, then peeled off his ragged black trench coat. I handed him my warm cozy jacket, plucked his wide-brim hat off his head and replaced it with my baseball cap. He slipped into my coat and brushed his thin hands and long filthy nails across the chest. He grinned a toothless grin. I slapped his hat against my knee. A light puff of dust filled the breeze as heavier particles fell to the pavement. I placed his hat on my head, swallowed, held my breath and wrapped myself in his old coat, a cocoon of street smells that reeked of stale body odor tinged with urine, forcing me to suppress a gagging reflex.

Hunched over with my computer out of sight under the coat, hidden among the crowd, I kept a watchful eye on the street as I continued down the walk. Then it appeared. The white van. Moving my way in the heavy traffic. I was pretty well concealed within the crowd of pedestrians. And with my newly acquired disguise they surely wouldn't recognize me.

My head down, I followed them with my eyes as they passed. I kept walking but picked up the pace. A minute later horns honked and I heard shouting behind me. I turned. The white van had stopped in the middle of the street. The door, open. I scanned right to see a hooded person talking to the homeless guy. The homeless guy pointed in my direction.

I ducked and moved through the pack. Business professionals and office workers migrating from downtown high-rises carrying briefcases and backpacks streamed into the ferry terminal. I followed them as they entered the terminal and moved toward the ticket booths. Most had monthly passes. They continued on.

"One please," I said.

"Bainbridge or Bremerton," she said, not looking up.

"Bainbridge." I handed her a twenty.

She slipped me a ticket and change. I joined the throng. Taking the stairs to the passenger boarding level, I glanced back. In the entryway I could see the Hood searching the crowd that passed around him like a rock in the middle of a stream. I turned and ducked as I ascended the steps.

Once onboard, I joined other passengers in the enclosed salon and snack bar area, certain everyone was staring at me. A homeless man on the Bainbridge ferry? Maybe not the best disguise. But I didn't think I'd find anybody willing to trade.

I walked toward the front, passed through the double doors that led to the outside deck searching for a place to hide. I didn't know if the "Hoods" were on the ferry, but I had to assume they were, and play it safe. I skirted the steel deck and found an area near the lifeboats that offered protection, figuring I could duck under one and not be seen.

A few people milled about, but most passengers seemed to be regular commuters, interested only in relaxing in the comfort afforded inside, reading a newspaper or a paperback and sipping a latte. Wrapping my arms around my waist, I squatted down and leaned my back against the steel bulwark.

The breeze blew cool off the waters of Elliott Bay. I stared out at the vast port, nestled within the green hills that surrounded the city. Ferries crisscrossed the bay while container ships succumbed to the invasive fingers of nimble cranes in the never-ending process of loading and offloading. At the far end, shipyards offered maintenance and repair to the maritime industry. In summer, cruise ships destined for Alaska added glamour and an economic boost. Having once lived on the water myself, I allowed my mind to wander. Would I ever again have another boat of my own? Or is this homeless coat an ominous sign of things to come? I shuddered.

Three short blasts sounded from the ship's horn and the ferry began to slide from the dock leaving a trail of churned white seawater, but with such a smooth motion you sensed the departure only by the passing of the surrounding pier shops. I allowed my body to relax for a moment as I watched the skyline grow smaller. But my mind wouldn't let me forget the Hoods. Were they on board searching even now?

A few passengers strolled by. A man and a young boy stopped and stared across the bay. They didn't notice me as I remained hidden from view. The boy was about the age of my own son. Maybe six or seven. The man spoke to the boy and pointed with his arm as I eavesdropped. "Those are container ships. See the big cranes?"

The boy gripped the handrail, stood up on his tiptoes and nodded. "What's in the big boxes, Daddy?"

"Those are containers. All sorts of things are shipped in them, back and forth across the Pacific Ocean between countries like Japan and China, and America. That's how most of your toys and video games get here."

The boy looked up. "Like my Game Boy?"

"Sure. And see over there." The father leaned down and pointed again. "That ship's name is *Miss Shanghai*. It's named after the city of Shanghai in China. See the big letters on the back of the ship?"

"Why do they call it Miss?" the boy inquired.

I jerked up. My mind searched for a rewind button. *What'd he say?*

The father continued. "Oh, it's an old tradition. They often name ships after important cities and add the affectionate title of Miss in—"

"Excuse me," I blurted as I crawled out. "Did you say '*Miss Shanghai?*'"

The man turned to the sound of my voice. My appearance startled him, he pulled the boy close to him. I snatched off my hat and held it behind my back. "I'm sorry to interrupt, but did you say '*Miss Shanghai?*'"

He eyed me, hesitated, then turned back and pointed out across the bay to the container port. "Yes. Over there. That's the container ship *Miss Shanghai*. She's just one of…"

I didn't hear him finish. I stared out across the water at a massive steel vessel with CHINA SHIPPING LINE in large letters displayed along the side. "*Miss Shanghai*," I mumbled to myself. I'll be damned. That must be it. Sayonara had said, it's not what we thought.

I watched the *Miss Shanghai* fall astern. "No, Sayonara. I bet it isn't." I smiled, a tinge of excitement building as I began to realize, despite what we were led to believe, "Miss Hong Kong" may not be a beauty queen after all.

CHAPTER FORTY-FIVE

Bainbridge Island, Washington

AFTER THIRTY MINUTES of deep thought on my part during an otherwise uneventful crossing of Puget Sound, the ferry approached the Eagledale dock on the eastern shore of Bainbridge Island. I hadn't seen the Hoods since we left the Seattle waterfront. I had remained concealed behind the lifeboat but knew I'd be vulnerable when we disembarked. A stream of off-loading vehicles would form two lanes as they rolled out the front end of the ferry and a horde of walk-on passengers would disembark through the pedestrian walkway. If the Hoods were on board, it would be easy for them to station themselves at the exit and scan the crowd. My homeless disguise would not be sufficient to slip past them.

I left the safety of my hiding place and found a stairwell that led down to the vehicle deck. Pushing open the steel door placed me in the rear of the ferry where the last cars had crammed into the final spaces. Daylight flooded in and cool salt air swirled through the open ends. I scanned the assorted cars, pickups, vans, campers and delivery trucks packed bumper-to-bumper within this cavernous steel assembly area. There were a few white vans scattered among them but I didn't see my pursuers.

Along the length of the ferry hidden from view on both sides were single lanes of waiting vehicles behind steel bulwarks. I moved toward the middle of the vehicle bay where there were more shadows, and ducked down behind a silver import. Passengers with keys in their hands had begun to emerge from the snack bar and lounge areas and return to their locked cars. Others had remained in their vehicles during the short trip reading or sleeping. I studied the passengers as they snaked their way through the tight rows searching for their own wheels.

My eyes fell upon a man with a frenzy of wild hair sprouting from beneath a stained yellow baseball cap emblazoned with a farm equipment logo, his face hidden behind a full red beard. He wore faded jeans and a denim jacket open to a plaid shirt, carried a large frame and sported a beer belly. He seemed like the kind of guy who wouldn't mind helping someone out in a pinch and wouldn't be overly concerned with someone in a homeless guise. If I worked it right, he'd be my ride. I watched to see which vehicle he headed for, thankful when he stepped up into the cab of a delivery truck four rows away.

I bent over and scurried between cars to the driver's side window. He was fastening his seat belt as I tapped on the glass. He looked down with an inquisitive look, just as I removed my frayed hat and motioned for him to roll down the window.

"Excuse me," I said. "I have a serious problem and I'd like to ask for your help."

"Car dead?" he asked.

"No. Nothing like that." I glanced around, figured I take the direct approach. "Look, I'm in danger. I need to ask for a ride. Just till we get off the ferry. Even one block would be helpful."

He looked at me, squinting with one eye. "You a criminal or somepin'?"

"No. Really. I'm harmless." I opened my ratty coat to show him I had nothing hidden beneath it but a computer. Though that seemed pointless. "Look. There are members of a Chinese gang after me. I'm trying to lose them. They're really bad dudes and I'm afraid of what they'll do if they catch me."

"Chinese gang? Here?"

"Yeah. And I need to hide in your truck, just until we get off the ferry. Can you help me?"

He looked around the vehicle deck through the windshield. "Where? You see em?"

"I think I've lost them for now. But they could be anywhere."

He turned his head back and stared. "They're dangerous, huh?"

"Yes, really dangerous. I need your help."

He studied me.

"Please," I begged. "I can pay."

"Naw. Don' need to pay. Hop in."

My heart leaped in gratitude. "Thank you. Thank you so much."

I rushed around to the other side of the truck, stepped up and slipped into the high seat. "Hey, I really appreciate this."

"No problem. Name's Willard. But most people call me Will." He held out his hand.

I grabbed it tight. "Curtis Beecham. And thanks again."

"Don't think nuttin' of it. You said these are some real bad-asses?"

"Yeah. Killers."

He looked at me, his eyes wide. "Sum bitch. Real killers, huh. Never shoulda let them yellow bastards in the country in the first place. All troublemakers if ya ask me. Those that aren't, well they're too smart for their fuckin' britches. Taking all the good jobs. Doctors. Scientists. The countries overrun wit 'em." He gripped the steering wheel and stared out the windshield, his eyes darting back and forth. "America'd be better off if we put 'em all on a leaky boat and sent 'em back to where dey come from."

I looked at Will and gaped although I suppose I shouldn't have been too surprised at his fervent diatribe. I didn't agree with him, but I knew he was the one person I wanted sitting next to me when we rolled off this boat. Hopefully, I'd only have to listen to a few moments of insensitive racial slander. Anything to get to safety.

The ferry pulled up to the terminal with a shudder, then a thump, rocking the vehicles. Car engines clicked over and revved, sending the sound of many a piston reverberating off the high steel walls. The scent of exhaust began to creep through the air vents. Vehicles began to exit, following the directions and signals from the orange-vested ferry workers. Cars on the outside lanes were waved forward, then cars from the hidden lanes on either side emerged from behind the steel bulwark. I watched, swallowed hard and took a deep breath. The white van appeared from behind the wall. The Hoods had been on board. Following the lead vehicles, the white van rolled across the ramp and disappeared among the traffic beyond the terminal.

I clenched my teeth. Should I tell Will I saw them? Just the mention might start World War III. I decided to keep it to myself.

"Hey, Will. How far you going?"

"Got a couple stops near here, then I gotta get over ta Fletcher Bay. Got one stop there. Regular customer."

My eyes lit up. "Fletcher Bay?"

"Yep."

"Hey, I hate to impose on you, but can I ride to Fletcher Bay with you? That's where I'm heading. I'd be glad to help you with your deliveries if there's something I can do." A long-time friend of mine lived near Fletcher Bay with her husband. I knew I'd be welcome there and they'd put me up for the night, even if I showed up unexpectedly.

Will started his engine and our line began to move. "Sure. Could use the comp'nee."

I breathed out and sat back in the seat, feeling safe, for now. The Hoods would never suspect I was slumped down in the cab of a Porta-Potty delivery truck. I only hoped I wouldn't have to hide in one.

I kept my head down as we rattled across the metal grate and the tires hit the pavement. I guessed the white van would have pulled over in close proximity to the terminal somewhere, watching everything that passed. I hoped I had seen the last of them.

* * *

AFTER MAKING HIS initial stops, Will drove me to his last delivery in Fletcher Bay. I left him there with a grateful handshake and walked down the street to a coffee shop promoting Wi-Fi that was tucked in a strip mall.

As I entered, I removed my hat and coat so I didn't stand out or offend anyone, sat down at a table with a cup of coffee, then pulled out my computer and went to Google, typing in MISS HONG KONG CONTAINER SHIP. Google identified over three thousand sites referencing a container ship by that name. It was owned by China Shipping Lines. I sipped my coffee and smiled. Yes. This is it.

I returned to Google, typed in PORT OF SEATTLE CONTAINER SHIP SCHEDULE and hit search. The first site listed was PORT OF SEATTLE: CARGO FAQ. I clicked and found a side bar for SHIP SCHEDULES. I clicked and a schedule grid popped up. I scanned down the column. Under NAME, six items down I found:

MISS HONG KONG
LINE/AGENT: CHINA SHIPPING LINE
BERTH: T5N

ETA: DECEMBER, 30, 2009

I stared in disbelief. In seconds I had verified the existence of the container ship *Miss Hong Kong*. I knew when she would arrive in Seattle, and what terminal she would berth at. Pieces were coming together. I had a solid lead. Though not absolutely confirmed, this was too coincidental to ignore. I had to believe Deng Qin would be using this container ship to transport the merchandise from his military heist. And though the *Miss Hong Kong* might be a fine looking ship, she was no beauty queen.

I packed up my computer and headed down Fletcher Bay Road, sticking to the edge of the tree line while keeping a constant watch over my shoulder. Dusk had fallen as the sun dropped below the Olympic Mountains and long shadows merged to form a sheet of darkness.

I pulled out my disposable phone and dialed Angie's cell. I couldn't wait to share the information I had pieced together. And I suppose I would have to explain why I was on Bainbridge in the first place and the run-in I'd had with the Hoods.

"Hello, Angie."

"Curtis? Where are you?"

"Bainbridge Island."

"What? Why are you on Bainbridge?"

"Ah, well, it's a long story. I'll fill you in when I see you. Probably tomorrow."

"Are you okay?" she asked.

"Yes. I'm fine. But I have something to tell you. I found out what Sayonara was referring to. Remember when she said, 'it's not what we thought.' "

"Well, yes."

"On the ferry crossing we passed the container ship facility. There's a ship off-loading containers there. The ship is owned by China Shipping. The name of the ship is *Miss*

Shanghai."

"I don't understand. What's that—"

"*Miss Shanghai*," I repeated. "It's a ship named after a port city in China. So I got to thinking. Could there be a container ship named after the port city of Hong Kong? And guess what. There is. A ship named *Miss Hong Kong*. And, she'll be berthing in Seattle in two days."

I could hear Angie gasp. "*Miss Hong Kong?*"

"Yes. *Miss Hong Kong* is a container ship. Whatever Deng Qin is about to steal must be in a container and will be shipped aboard *Miss Hong Kong*. Can you believe it? She's a ship, not a beauty queen. And the container? We were thinking small. This is big. It has to be something really big, or a lot of whatever it is to fill a shipping container."

"Oh, my God," Angie said. "We just assumed Miss Hong Kong was a beauty queen. Were we misled?"

"I don't know," I replied. "But it doesn't matter."

"Those ships carry a lot of containers. How will we know which one it is? And what do we do now? Contact the FBI?"

"I don't know just yet. I need to think this through." I paused. "Any word on George?"

Her voice dropped. "No, nothing."

I could sense her pain. I gave her a minute as I bit down on my lip.

"There's something I need to tell you," Angie continued. "I was going through Sayonara's cell phone and I found a phone number listed under Miss Hong Kong. Of course at that time I still thought we were looking for a beauty queen. But this was her phone number. So I dialed it."

"You did what?"

"I dialed it. I wanted to see who would answer. I figured as soon as I got a voice I'd hang up. I wanted to know if it really was her phone number."

Vehicle headlights behind me began to close in so I

scooted off the road and ducked into some shrubs. "And…" I prompted.

"It was an invalid number. It had eleven digits. A phone number with an area code only has ten."

"Really? That's odd."

"Yeah, it is. I wonder why Sayonara saved it in her phone book."

"Maybe she entered it wrong," I suggested. "Hit too many keys."

"Maybe."

"We'll talk more tomorrow."

"Sure," she said.

We hung up and I dialed my friend Sarah, told her I was on the island and wanted to stop by. She said she was home, had no plans and was always up for company.

I picked up my pace. Darkness had fallen, so had the temperatures, and my homeless coat provided little protection from the elements.

Sarah Hartman had been a friend of mine for a number of years. In our initial relationship, she was a client. She had been the editor of a corporate publication and had hired me as a freelance writer. We worked well together, as we had great respect for each other's talents, but we had little in common in our personal lives.

Sarah's idea of fun was a six-week trip to India to meditate and work with patients in a leprosy clinic. My idea of fun was any length of time spent on any warm beach with a margarita in my hand. We had more differences than similarities, but we had an unusual bond between us. A bond of respect, or was it a bond of incredulous fascination with the other's lifestyle which we each considered to be unusual and bizarre?

As I continued toward Sarah's house, I once again had to duck within a stand of trees as headlights approached, although no white vans passed. About twenty minutes later I arrived at her front door. I removed my hat and knocked twice. The door opened and I was greeted by a naturally attractive woman about thirty years old with soft features and smooth pale skin.

Sarah's smile of welcome all but vanished as she scanned me up and down. Normally she'd give a warm, light hug. Not this time. "Hi, ah, Curtis. Come in."

"Thanks." I glanced down and held the coat open. "Sorry about the coat. I have a good explanation."

She rolled her eyes. "I hope so."

She had a good blaze going in the fireplace and the house radiated cozy warmth. I removed the tattered garment. "I'll leave it out on the front porch." I held up the hat. "This too."

She grimaced.

I opened the front door, leaned out and tossed them on a wood bench that graced the entrance beneath the covered porch. She stared, her hands on her hips.

"Okay," I said. "To begin with, it's not *my* coat. Or *my* hat." I looked beyond her to the living room. "Maybe we should sit down. I've got a story to share and it might take awhile."

CHAPTER FORTY-SIX

SARAH HARTMAN AND I had a long talk as I explained everything that had occurred over the past few weeks.

"Curtis, this is hard to believe. It all sounds so dangerous."

"Yeah. I had no idea the hornet's nest I was going to stir up. Espionage? I didn't count on that. It's gotten very serious. Sayonara murdered. Attempts on my life. And George? I feel terrible about his disappearance. Responsible, you know. It's a bit overwhelming, but I'm getting a better idea of what I'm facing. I just need to sort a few things out." I frowned, contemplating the difficult challenge facing me. "Make sure I stay one step ahead of those bastards."

Our conversation helped me recap the events and take a more objective look. I could see that pieces were falling into place, but I still had questions. A major incident of Chinese espionage was about to take place. I had to develop a plan of my own if I wanted to remain close to this case, bring closure for Sayonara, do what I could for George and if lucky, maybe even uncover that scintillating material for the rewrite my editor was looking for.

Sarah's husband wouldn't be home until very late, so we continued to chat as she fixed us a light supper of peanut butter sandwiches. She was a vegetarian and her idea of a good meal was, well, a peanut butter sandwich. If you asked me, my idea of a good meal would be a big juicy steak. She didn't ask.

After finishing off two sandwiches, I picked up my plate and empty teacup and followed her into the kitchen. "I'd like to get back to Seattle as soon as possible. But I know there's a bit of risk in taking the ferry."

She took my plate, held it under the faucet as she rinsed it in the sink. "There aren't many passengers on the late night ferries, it'd be hard to hide." She turned back to me. "If those guys are waiting for you, well…"

"I know. I'm not sure what I should do."

"Stay here tonight," she suggested. "I have a guest room. You can leave tomorrow when it's safer."

I thought for a moment. I wanted to get back to the mainland, but I knew it wouldn't be smart to try to return by ferry tonight. If the price of safety was a dinner of peanut butter sandwiches I was willing to accept. "You sure it's no bother?"

"Not at all." She eyed me. "I'll give you a clean pair of Robert's underwear, I'm sure he won't mind. And a toothbrush."

I grinned. "Thanks. I suppose I could use both."

* * *

THE NEXT DAY I slept in late because that night I laid awake for hours tossing this entire mess around in my head as an idea began to formulate in my mind.

For my plan to succeed I needed one critical piece of information. The identification number of Deng Qin's shipping container. Though this seemed to be an insur-mountable task, I thought I just might have an idea that will lead me to it. I reached for Sarah's telephone as I sat at her kitchen counter sipping hot tea. Sarah was a hot tea kind of gal. I was a double-tall latte kind of guy. I dialed Angie at work.

"Angie. It's Curtis."

"Curtis?"

"Yeah, sorry about calling you at work, but it is important. I need to know the phone number for *Miss Hong Kong*. You know, the number you found on Sayonara's cell phone."

"It's not a valid number, remember."

"That's the point. Sayonara knew *Miss Hong Kong* was not a person, but a ship. So why would she put an invalid phone number in her phone index under a ship's name? Ships don't have phone numbers. But I have a theory. I think that number may be an important key. You have it with you?"

"Yes," Angie replied. "It's in my purse. Hold on."

There was silence for a few moments.

"Got something to write with?"

"Yeah, go ahead." I scribbled down 727-830-54383. "Thanks. I'll call you later."

I pulled out my computer, went to Google and searched under shipping containers. As I read, I learned that each container has its own unique identification—a series of letters and numbers the industry assigns each container to identify it. Each identification number begins with an ownership code consisting of four letters, the last letter being U, followed by seven numbers. Thus, every shipping container had an identification code that consisted of a total of eleven letters and numbers.

I glanced over and picked up the piece of paper I had written the invalid phone number on. The number Sayonara may have given her life up for. It had eleven digits as Angie discovered earlier. Eleven digits. The same number of digits in a container identification code. Was this a coincidence? Could this be the code for Deng Qin's container? I looked at the keypad on the kitchen phone to match up numbers with letters to see what letters the first four numbers represented. But each number corresponded to three different letters. There were too many possible combinations of letters that were represented by those four numbers. Too many to identify the correct code with any accuracy.

I sat back, clasped my hands behind my head and closed my eyes. That combination of four letters and seven numerals seemed familiar. It stirred something deep in my memory. Four letters followed by seven numbers. Hmmm. I rolled this around in my mind and dug deep. Four letters, seven numbers I repeated to myself. Where have I seen this? Where? Where? Where? I rocked back and forth. Thinking.

I hummed to myself, deep in thought, until it hit me. Wait! That piece of paper from Sayonara's trash can! I jumped up and dug into my pockets. Were these the jeans? I pulled out a few folded bills. Then a key. Then a piece of paper, crushed and tattered. My hopes soared. I gently opened it and stared. RCQU3054383. Four letters. Seven numbers. Yes! This is it. Has to be. I kissed the paper and looked up at the ceiling. "Thank you, Sayonara. You little hell raising angel. Bless you."

I held the two sheets of paper up. The one on which I had scribbled down the invalid phone number from Sayonara and the one with the ID code I had previously retrieved from the trash. I compared them. The last seven numbers of the phone number were identical to the last seven numbers of the code. "Yes!" I then compared the first four digits of the phone number from Sayonara's phone to the letters of the alphabet they represented on the phone keypad to the first four letters of the code on the paper. They matched. Sayonara had put the identification code into her phone as if it were a phone number, albeit with eleven digits, when in truth, it was the ID code. Finding the piece of paper in the trash confirmed it. I knew for certain, this was the ID for Deng Qin's container.

This information would be the key component of my plan. This venture would be risky but I just might be able to get George back *and* stop Deng Qin. Timing was critical. *Miss Hong Kong* was due in port in a couple of days. But I believed, with a little luck, I could pull it off.

* * *

SARAH AND I discussed the danger of my leaving the island by ferry. She was concerned, so she asked her brother Barry if he would return me to Seattle on his fishing boat. We all agreed it would be safer to leave at a late hour to improve my chances of not being seen. He'd pick me up around 10:00 P.M. at a nearby boat launch.

I called Angie once more and explained the plan. Barry would deliver me to the Elliott Bay Marina on Magnolia around 11:00 P.M. She agreed to pick me up.

"Angie, I need one more thing. A shipping manifest. One they would use for a container. You said your Uncle Willie receives containers of merchandise for his import business all the time. He would have some old manifests filed away someplace. Can you get a copy of one for me?"

"Sure. Shouldn't be a problem. Why do you need it?"

"I'll explain later."

"I'll have it for you tonight."

I then gave my editor, Jack Buick, a call on his cell. I wanted to know when he would be in Seattle.

"Yeah, Jack here."

"Mr. Buick, it's Curtis Beecham."

"What? Curtis? Are you, ah, hey, what's up?"

"A lot. I've been running from two Chinese thugs for the past two days. Remember that white van I told you about? It's those same guys. Somehow they found out where I was staying and they've been on my tail ever since."

"Ah, really? What do you think they want?"

"They wanna kill me, for Christ's sake. I believe they're working with Deng Qin. He's the guy I suspect killed Sayonara."

"Hmmm. Sounds like a dangerous guy."

"Hell yeah he's dangerous. But if I survive this, I can add significantly to the manuscript. A stronger espionage angle. Real stuff. First hand. But it comes with a lot of risk, and believe me, I've been thinking seriously about that these past two days."

"Hey, that's good, Curtis. I mean about the manuscript." There was silence for a minute. "Say, where are you now?"

"Bainbridge Island. It's a small community thirty minutes from downtown Seattle. I ended up here while trying to avoid those bastards."

"Bainbridge Island, huh. In a motel?"

"No. Why do you ask?"

"Hey, Curtis. I'm worried about you. We're in the middle of a book. I gotta be able to contact you."

"Oh, yeah, sure. I'm at a friend's house. But I'm leaving later tonight in a small boat heading back to Seattle."

"Where to? The ferry docks downtown?"

"No. Elliott Bay Marina on Magnolia. My friend, Angie, is picking me up around eleven. It's late to be crossing in a small boat, but considering the circumstances, I believe it's much safer this way."

"Yeah," Jack said. "I'm sure it is."

"Did you decide when you're coming to Seattle?"

"No, I haven't. Still thinking about it."

"Mr. Buick. You mentioned the ferry docks downtown. How'd you know about the ferry docks?"

"Ah, well, I guess I saw a picture. Maybe a movie. Yeah, maybe that *Sleepless in Seattle* one."

"Oh, okay." I paused. "I'll let you know how things progress. I think something will break pretty soon."

"Okay, Curtis. And say hi to your friend. What'd you say his name was?"

"I didn't. But he's a she. Sarah. Sarah Hartman."

"Hartman, huh? Okay. Say hi to Sarah for me. And be

safe."

"Yeah, that's my intention."

After hanging up with Jack I sat staring out the kitchen window, sipping my hot tea, thinking about our conversation. Jack seemed different. He didn't ask about the manuscript or any details on the espionage angle. Whereas he seemed quite excited about it before. Is he losing interest? First he was coming to Seattle, now maybe he isn't. The conversation seemed odd. He didn't ask about anything important, yet he asked a lot of questions. I couldn't put my finger on it, but for some reason, something seemed off. He wasn't the same ole' Jack.

CHAPTER FORTY-SEVEN

Seattle, Washington

DURING HER LUNCH hour, Angie drove to her father's office to obtain a copy of a shipping manifest for Curtis, as he had instructed. She remained apprehensive, concerned she might run into Uncle Willie. She hadn't seen him since the night she and Curtis sneaked into the warehouse. Although she hadn't actually come face to face with him that night, she was in his presence. It had not been a fond remembrance.

Regina, the receptionist, sat staring at her computer, the phone pressed against her ear. She looked up and waved as Angie entered, and with a flip of her hand motioned for Angie to head back to her father's office.

Poking her head in the doorway she announced herself. "Hello, Father."

Wung Hu looked up. "My dear, Angela. What a pleasant surprise. What brings you here during the middle of the day?"

"I'm on my lunch break. I wanted to see you."

Wung Hu studied her a moment, then broke out into a wide grin. "Yes. I am sure. Now, do not tease an old man. What mischief are you up to?"

"Father," she batted her eyes with great exaggeration.

"There's no mischief on my part." She sat down on the edge of his desk and crossed her arms. "But I do need something."

"Ah, ha!" Wung Hu teased. "I knew my princess was needy. What do you want of me? My knowledge? My money?" He crossed his arms mimicking her and winked.

"You know me too well."

"I should. After all, I *am* your father."

Angie smiled. "And there isn't a better one." She placed her palms on the edge of the desk and crossed her legs. "I need something for a friend. He's doing research for some project he's involved in. He needs a sample of a manifest for a shipping container. Like the ones you would use here. Just a copy." Angie did her best not to lie, but at the same time, she avoided the facts.

Wung Hu leaned back. "Is that it?"

"Yes, Father."

"Well it just so happens I have one right here." He reached over and lifted a sheet of paper from a basket. "I received it a few days ago." He gave the form a quick glance. "Yes. This is it. The container from Shanghai that is arriving on China Shipping's *Miss Hong Kong*. It should be delivered to our warehouse by the end of the week. Just as soon as she clears customs."

Angie stared, a lump quickly formed in her throat nearly causing her to choke. "You have a container arriving on the *Miss Hong Kong*?"

"Yes. This is not unusual. As you know, we receive shipments from China on a regular basis."

Angie's mind raced, her thoughts elsewhere, her eyes dancing back and forth. "Yes. Yes, I know."

"What is it, Angela. Are you all right?"

"Ah, yes, Father. I'm fine. I was just thinking about something." Angie looked at her father. "Really. I'm fine." She paused, her course becoming clear. "Could I have a copy of *that* manifest?"

"Sure, princess. Let me make a copy."

Wung Hu stood up and patted his palm against her knee. "I'll just be a minute. Regina will have to help me with that fancy new copier." He disappeared through the door.

Angie dropped her head, stared at the floor, lost in thought. Her feet swung back and forth. A light tapping echoed against the side of the desk.

A deep voice startled her, breaking her concentration. "Why hello, Angela."

She looked up. Uncle Willie stood in the doorway. "Oh... ah, hi, Uncle Willie."

He approached. "What is it? Did I surprise you?"

"Ah, yes. I wasn't expecting you." She paused. "I thought you were on a business trip...was it Hong Kong?"

Wung Hu returned and the two men locked eyes. Angie caught Uncle Willie wink, then he glanced up and down the hallway before stepping in and closing the door. Wung Hu slipped behind his desk, sat back and folded his arms across his chest. Angie studied him, then stared up at Uncle Willie as he leaned against the oak doorframe.

"Angela, your father and I have a secret to share."

Angie's heart raced as anxiety spread through her body. *Oh, my God,* she thought. *Is this what I had been expecting all along?* She braced herself.

"We will soon be announcing this to the whole family, but I would like you to know it now. It is a secret. You can not tell anyone." He allowed a slight grin. "Can you be trusted?"

At this point, Angie didn't know what to think. Uncle Willie seemed pleased with his news, so it might not be related to the wild accusations that had been running through her head. But considering everything that had happened lately, she prepared herself to expect the worst. "Yes...I, I think so."

"You think so?" Uncle Willie teased. "Is that the best you

can do?"

"No. I'm sorry. I guess I just wasn't prepared for this. But, yes, I can keep a secret."

"No crossed fingers? No crossed toes?"

Angie gave an uneasy smile. "No. No crossed fingers. No crossed toes."

"Good." Uncle Willie said. "Let me begin by announcing to you first of all, that I am retiring as the owner of the Asian Antique Import Company effective January thirty-first. Your father will be taking over the business as principal owner." He spread his arms wide. "This will all be his, while I take up the quiet life of a gentleman rancher." He broke out in a big smile, leaned down closer to Angie and whispered. "A real cowboy."

Angie gasped. "You're retiring?" She looked at her father. "Father. This will be *your* business?"

Wung Hu grinned with pride.

"That's wonderful news," Angie said.

Angie turned back to Uncle Willie, puzzled. "A cowboy?"

"Yes. Imagine that. It's been my dream for a very long time. You know I've always loved the story of the American West." The corners of his mouth curled up to flash a perfect set of porcelain. His dark eyes sparkled. "As of yesterday, I am the proud new owner of a horse ranch in Montana. That's where I've been for the past week. I tried to keep it a secret, so we told everyone I was on a business trip to Hong Kong." He raised his hand and brought his thumb and forefinger together until they almost touched. "Just a little white lie. Please forgive me. I've made a down payment of one hundred thousand to seal the deal. Now, I just need to purchase a big white cowboy hat and a pair of snake boots so I look the part."

Angie released a long, slow breath as a wave of relief washed through her body. She shook her head while breaking out in a chuckle.

"What are you laughing at?" Uncle Willie asked.

Angie's eyes moistened and she grinned as elation swept in to replace her anxiety. "I'm so thrilled for you. And Father. You don't know how happy I am to hear this." She reflected on the devious thoughts she had had of Uncle Willie. He wasn't mixed up with the murderous Deng Qin after all. Uncle Willie would not be a spy for China, but a hard-riding, bronco roping cowboy.

Her mind flashed back to an ornate framed painting she had seen on numerous occasions displayed among Uncle Willie's art collection. With Uncle Willie's full head of white hair and matching goatee and mustache, all she could envision in her mind was a very senior Chinese version of the Wild West showman, Buffalo Bill Cody.

CHAPTER FORTY-EIGHT

Bainbridge Island, Washington

SARAH AND I spent the late afternoon relaxing on her front porch enjoying the comfort of two wood rockers, talking, watching neighbors pass as they involved themselves in various levels of personal fitness, when I noticed a car at the end of the street. A black Chrysler Town Car. It sat off the side of the road, idling at the far corner by the stop sign. A steady puff of exhaust escaping from the tailpipe into the cool evening air caught my attention.

I suggested to Sarah we move inside, giving her an exaggerated body shiver to indicate a chill from the dropping temperatures. I didn't want to alarm her, as my elevated concern may just be my own paranoia. As she wandered into the kitchen, I continued to watch the vehicle through the front window. After a few moments it moved on. I was satisfied it meant nothing.

With last night's dining experience fresh in my mind, I talked Sarah into taking our appetites on the road. I told her if she'd drive, I'd pay. Someplace simple and quick that didn't have a dress code. She suggested Mac's Diner where she assured me they had meat. That sounded great. Before walking out the door she opened the coat closet and pulled out two parkas.

"Pick one," she said. I glanced from the yellow one to the green one.

"Green."

As we rounded the corner I noticed that same black Town Car parked on a side street a short distance ahead. There wasn't a lot of traffic or big luxury vehicles in this area, so one would notice something like that. As we passed, I glanced over. The windows were deeply tinted. My radar went up. I turned and watched through the back window as Sarah drove.

She headed straight to the diner and we had a quiet meal. I had a burger loaded with everything but onions. Sarah had a burger loaded with everything but meat. After paying the tab, we left and headed for the car. The parking lot was lit by the glow of the diner and the flashing neon sign on the cedar-shingle roof. Other cars were scattered throughout the gravel lot.

Located on an isolated stretch of the highway, the diner's only neighbor was a rural two-pump gas station some distance across the street. The only source of light in the area, besides that emanating from the diner, came from the signs and windows of that lonely station. Parked next to the fuel pump was the black Town Car. A dark figure leaned against the side, a man in a black trench coat. I stopped and stared. A chill ran up my spine. I could see the flicker of a light in front of his face. He was smoking. Looking my way.

I threw my arm out, stopping Sarah's progress. "Sarah. I think we're being followed."

She blinked, appeared confused. "What?"

"Don't look. But I have this weird feeling." I grabbed her arms with both my hands, turning her so her back was to the gas station and I could observe the station over her shoulder.

"Curtis. What are you doing?"

"Pretend we're talking. Keep your eyes on me."

"Curtis, you're frightening me. Does this have anything to do with those guys chasing you?"

"I think so. But these are different guys. Different car."

"My God. What should we do?"

"They're over there. At the gas station." I didn't want to further alarm her. "Maybe they're just trying to scare me."

She jerked her head around and stared in their direction. "*You're* doing a good job of scaring me."

"I'm sorry. I didn't mean to get you involved."

"I'm involved?"

"Well, not yet. But let's get out of here. When we get back to your place I'll get my computer and leave right away."

I pulled on her arm. "Come on." We took a few steps toward her car. "Maybe I should drive," I said as I glanced back toward the station. The man opened the door of the Town Car and jumped in. "In case they—"

An explosion erupted in front of us with a resounding boom. A giant fireball shot skyward scattering sharp metal and particles of glass through the air, striking anything standing. The body of Sarah's car leapt three feet off the ground, surrounded in a cloud of dust, wrapped in a blanket of black smoke. Flames shot out like forked tongues of a fiery beast. The force of the blast knocked us back, slammed us against the loose gravel.

Heat radiated against my face. I leaned up on my elbows, stunned. In moments the fireball had engulfed her vehicle, reduced it to a charred wreck then subsided to a fire contained within the interior. I looked over at Sarah, crawled to her on my knees. "Are you okay?" She was lying still, staring up, her eyes wide. She blinked and tears flooded down her cheeks. I reached over and placed my hand on her face. She began to shake.

I glanced back to the gas station. The Town Car had disappeared. I looked at Sarah. Her lip trembled.

Turning back to the burning car, I watched black smoke continue to pour out gaps where a hood and windows used to be. Flames consumed the seats and danced across the hood and trunk.

I heard the crunch of running footsteps. People poured out of the diner and hurried to us. Some stared at the car, stunned looks on their faces. Others circled us, stared down.

"You guys okay?" someone asked.

"Someone call nine-one-one," a voice yelled. "Quick. We got some people hurt here."

Someone repeated. "Mister, you okay?"

My ears were ringing. I nodded. "Yes. I think so."

I leaned over Sarah. "Can you stand up?"

With wide, terrified eyes, she nodded.

"Someone get her other arm," I said, looking over my shoulder.

Two guys jumped in and we lifted her to her feet. I brushed the dirt off her coat then took my thumbs and wiped her cheeks. With my arms around her, I held her tight. "Thanks. I think we're okay."

"Here," one man suggested. "Let's get her inside. She needs to sit down." He looked at me. "You too."

We walked back to the diner and sat down on two chairs stationed in the entrance foyer.

"Get 'em some water," someone hollered.

I took Sarah's hand. "I'm so sorry. I shouldn't have gotten you involved."

The crowd dissipated, returned to their tables. I held her hands and we sat without saying anything until we heard the sound of sirens in the distance. Within moments two fire trucks, an emergency medical vehicle and three police cars surrounded the parking lot.

Sarah and I were not hurt, though quite shaken up. Of course, we had to answer to the police. I didn't have much to give them other than the actions of the suspicious Town Car. They put out an APB.

After a visit to the police station to file a report, we rode in a squad car back to Sarah's house. I grabbed my computer and gave her a warm hug. "I'm truly sorry about your car. Involving you. I would never have come if I thought you'd be in danger."

"I know. It's just a car. Don't worry. That's what insurance is for. But these guys. They must have been following you."

"I don't know how. Seems if they had been following me, they'd have done something yesterday as I walked the highway to your place. I was vulnerable then. I just don't know how they found out I was staying with you."

She brushed some dust off my shoulder. "Be careful. And hurry. Barry will be there. You can count on him."

"Thanks. Keep your doors locked. Call nine-one-one if you even think someone's snooping around."

I headed out into the dark night on foot, making my way to the boat ramp where I had arranged to meet her brother Barry. He'd take me to Magnolia where Angie would be waiting.

* * *

MY FOOTSTEPS THUMPED the wet pavement as I glanced over my shoulder and searched through the darkness that swept the rural road. No headlights. No sign I'd been followed. Faded yellow centerlines became a blur. My mind fought to maintain focus as I struggled against fatigue. I blinked once, twice, raised an arm, swiped my eyes with the back of my hand to remove the sting of sweat. My breath came heavy. A muscle spasm developed in my calf as pain and fear compelled me to keep running, knowing if they caught me they'd kill me.

A black mass of clouds had settled over the area, a storm spinning in from the Pacific. The front promised discomfort, but adverse conditions would provide a measure of cover.

Subtle whiffs of saline, the scent of ocean air, alerted me to the nearness of the shoreline. As I rounded a curve, the undergrowth disappeared and my sprint to safety ended against the sharp edge of Puget Sound.

Stopping beneath an evergreen rising from the perimeter of the concrete boat ramp, I bent over, pressed my palms against my knees and hung my head. Sucking deep breaths, the warm air from my lungs released white puffs into the cold air.

I kept an anxious watch on the road where it emerged from a thin curtain of young spruce. This narrow entrance wound its way into the vacant parking lot, bathed in the soft illumination of a single streetlight. Droplets breaking out of the night sky glistened, a shower of slivers in the glow of the lamp as they splashed against the pavement and reflected in puddles on the uneven surface.

Sweat combined with the cool mist created a chill that penetrated to the bone. I tugged on the forest green parka Sarah insisted I take, pulled it tight, hunched over and jammed my hands into my pockets. My jeans clung heavy, damp. Sneakers, speckled with droplets of mud, squished, oozing wetness as I shifted from foot to foot.

Where was Barry?

I checked my watch. I'd only been waiting fifteen minutes. Seemed longer. The strap on the satchel holding my laptop dug into my shoulder as if I had dragged a mainframe. It slid down my arm and rested at my feet, balanced atop a fallen limb.

The rain continued. Accumulating in the canopy above my head, the heavy droplets created a staccato rhythm against my parka as I listened for the distant whine of a small marine motor.

It began as a faint hum, barely audible over the patter of rain, but grew louder as the outboard rounded the bend. I could see a small light on the bow and then a dark figure highlighted against the ripples of the bay.

I glanced around once more, then ran to the concrete ramp and walked down the wall along the water's edge to a depth that allowed the boat to approach. I waited as the lone figure maneuvered the craft toward me.

"Barry?" I called out.

"Curtis?" came a response.

I exhaled a sigh of relief.

The boat nudged the wall. I sat down and used my sneakers as fenders to keep the aluminum sides from scrapping the concrete as the boat bobbed up and down with a slosh.

I held out my computer bag. "Can you take this?"

Barry set my satchel on the bench seat then stepped back, leaned over and gripped the wall. I slipped in and sat down, setting my computer on my lap. Barry took a seat behind me and grabbed the throttle.

"Thanks so much, Barry. I really appreciate this. Especially dragging you out so late."

"Hey, no problem. Glad I can help. Sarah explained everything." The small boat turned and headed back in the direction Barry had come. "Boy, you sure got yourself in a mess."

"Yeah, don't I know it."

We rounded the bend and Barry angled the boat in a direct line toward the lighted shore a few miles away.

I looked across the bay. It had been a tough night. And it wasn't over yet. With the danger mounting, I was more determined than ever to see Deng Qin pay.

My list of grievances was growing. So was my resolve.

The engine whined and the bow made a rhythmic thump as it bounced against the rough chop, sending small white splashes to either side with each thrust. The northwest rain cleansed the salt air as I hunched down against the stiff breeze. The distinctive pattern of light from a passenger ferry leaving

Seattle emerged to our right, growing larger as it glided by in the distance. Bainbridge dimmed behind us and Elliott Bay Marina twinkled ahead from lights mounted atop hundreds of masts. The outline of the towering rock face of Magnolia bluff rose skyward, silhouetted against the glow of the city.

A few more minutes and I would be at the marina, and once again safe.

CHAPTER FORTY-NINE

Seattle, Washington

BARRY BROUGHT THE boat into the calm water just inside the marina and nosed it along the edge of the breakwater. He cut the engine, then leaned over and grabbed hold of a large rock, holding the boat steady.

I stood up, balanced myself and turned to him. "I can't tell you how much I appreciate this."

"Hey, glad I could help." He smiled. "Save me an autographed copy of your book."

I grinned. "You bet."

I slung my computer bag over my back and stepped off onto a boulder that looked like it would provide a good foothold, then scrambled up rocks the size of coffee tables. I reached the top and turned around just as Barry pushed off and the engine revved to a high-pitched whine. I waved but he had already turned away.

I glanced around to get my bearings, then walked along the barrier toward shore and the parking lot that fronted the marina. To my right were buildings that housed restaurants, shops and marina offices. Because of our slow pace against the choppy seas, it had taken us longer than I expected to cross the bay from Bainbridge. With the late hour and the inhospitable weather, I wasn't met with the normal presence of dog walkers and couples strolling the path that edged the marina. The entire area remained quiet. Because of the rain, I figured Angie would be waiting in her car in the parking lot. Maybe dozing. As usual, the lot was full of vehicles belonging to live-aboard boaters.

I scanned the area but saw no sign of Angie or her car. I ambled further down the walkway, to a building with a display of leaflets advertising boats for sale. I was tempted to browse but knew I had to keep moving. I rounded the corner leading to the street, then froze, as an unexpected rush of terror blindsided me.

A white van, with the large red and gold lettering of the Asia Pacific Fruit & Vegetable Company blocked my path. The door flew open and a figure emerged, two glowing eyes staring out from within the black recess of a hood. The dark silhouette rushed at me.

My heart raced and my mind went into a panic mode. I turned to run. A hard crush slammed against the back of my head. My vision blurred. My knees crumbled. My body dropped. Everything went black.

* * *

ANGIE LEANED AGAINST her car as she stared in the direction of the marina, a quarter mile away. Sitting in the middle of the street, the car had been positioned in such a way as to block both lanes. The hood was raised, exposing the engine. The rain continued in a steady, uncomfortable assault. It soaked her clothes, plastered her long black hair flat against her face like a finely spun wet mop. Raindrops traveled down her bangs onto her forehead and dripped off her nose. She reached up and wiped her wet sleeve across her face. She appeared desperate, defenseless, a woman alone with a broken down vehicle that had skidded out of control on the wet pavement.

She stared with intense concentration, waiting and watching for the signal. Her brother, Thomas, had stationed himself farther up the road, closer to the marina on a slight rise, positioned to observe anyone approaching. His arms shot up above his head, raised in a waving motion before he dropped and disappeared behind a clump of brush.

A moment later a white van appeared over the rise, moving fast. Angie turned back to her car, leaned over her open hood and stared at the silent engine, thinking about what she would have to do. She closed her eyes and summoned up her inner strength, slowing her heartbeat, calming her nerves. They would be here in a minute. Maybe less. She listened to the racing engine grow louder as it barreled down the road toward her. As the vehicle approached, she heard it decelerate. There wasn't room for the van to maneuver past her. They would have to stop. For two thugs, the sight of a young woman alone, helpless, should be enough to pique their curiosity.

She turned to face them and waved both arms in a signal of distress as they slowed to a stop. The two figures sat motionless. She flipped her head so her hair, though wet, would draw their attention and interest.

They watched a few moments, then both doors opened. Two Asian men stepped out. Dressed in black hooded sweatshirts, jeans and high-top sneakers, hands stuffed in their pockets, they closed the distance to Angie with a slow purposeful walk. They stared like a hunter stalking prey, their eyes moving up and down the clothes that clung to the subtle curves of her body.

"Please, I need help," Angie called out. "I skidded on the wet pavement and the car died."

They didn't respond, just kept moving toward her, their eyes burning holes through her.

She walked around the car to the other side to put the

vehicle between her and the two men, careful not to kick over the two jars she had placed on the ground earlier. The lids had been removed and a medicinal odor drifted in the heavy night air. She pointed down at the engine as they stepped up.

"I think this hose came off. I can't get it back on."

They leaned over and looked to where she pointed, their hands remaining in their pockets, showing little interest in her predicament. Their attention diverted for one quick moment.

The moment she needed.

She bent down, grabbed the two containers by her feet and straightened up. "Hey!" she shouted. They looked up. Angie's arms flew forward. Each hand gripped an open jar filled with Isoflurane, a pungent smelling liquid. The fluid shot out of the containers and splashed against the two shocked faces, soaking the hood and chest of both sweatshirts.

The men cried out, coughed and spit, spewing frothy saliva and spittle. Hands flew from their pockets, slapped at their faces. They grabbed their sweatshirts and wiped their faces with their sleeves. They spun, screamed and cursed, blindly swinging their arms in desperation. A final gasp of bitter defiance. Movements slowed. They calmed. One man dropped to his knees, the other groaned then followed, before they both collapsed face down on the pavement.

Angie remained behind her car, shaking with fear in the aftermath of the confrontation with the two dangerous men. She watched as they lay motionless. Thomas arrived, breathing hard from his quick dash down the street. In his hands, a baseball bat.

He stopped and stared at the two men lying in the middle of the road. Then his wide eyes shot up at Angie, who hadn't budged. "You okay?"

She nodded.

"The van!" he shouted. He ran to the rear of the vehicle. Angie followed. He opened the back door and they stared down at a lump of clothing. Curtis Beecham lay stretched out on his back, his hands and legs bound with ropes, eyes closed, chest moving up and down with a slight pulse.

They crawled inside. Angie put her hands around Curtis's face and rubbed.

"Curtis. Curtis. Wake up" She tried to arouse him with a gentle shake.

Thomas went to work on the ropes, untying them as Angie worked on Curtis.

Curtis groaned.

She ran her hand around the back of his head. She felt a lump and a wet sticky substance. She examined her fingers. Blood. "Curtis. Wake up."

He groaned and rocked his head back and forth. He squinted, peered up at Angie, then smiled. Closing them again, he grimaced.

"We have to move quickly," she said. "We don't have much time. Can you get up?"

She slid her arm under his head and Thomas reached under his shoulders.

"Come on, Curtis," Thomas said. "We have to get going."

Curtis raised himself up on his elbows. He hung his head and closed his eyes. Angie allowed him a second to clear the cobwebs.

Thomas looked at Angie. "Let's go."

They lifted Curtis into a seated position, then scrambled out of the van, pulling him with both arms. Another minute and Curtis was lying down in the back seat of Angie's car, his arms folded across his face. Thomas went to check on the two Hoods. Angie turned her back, removed her soaked blouse, twisted water out of it then tossed it on the front seat as she reached for her dry jacket and slipped it on. She leaned over the seat. "How you doing?"

"I'll live. I think."

She wrung her blouse out again, folded it up and handed it over the seat to Curtis. "Here. Put this under your head."

Curtis reached for it, lifted up and opened his eyes. "My computer!"

"Where is it?" Angie asked.

"I had it—"

"Thomas," Angie yelled. "Check the van for Curtis's computer."

Thomas ran to the van, stuck his head in the door and returned with a black case. He jumped into the driver's seat and handed the computer to Curtis. Thomas turned the key, the ignition cranked over and they sped away, leaving a white van idling and two Hoods splayed motionless on the blacktop.

* * *

BY THE TIME we arrived at Angie's apartment, I had cleared my head and had all my senses, although I sported a throbbing headache. I sat down at Angie's dining table while she examined me. She often had to apply stitches to dogs and cats, so I figured she was qualified to work on me. She said I'd be okay, no stitches were necessary, then she cleaned the wound.

"So what happened?" I asked. "Last thing I remember I was at the marina, and I saw one of the hoods jump out of the van. Where were you?" I asked. Then I remembered Angie and Thomas had pulled me from the van. "Wait a minute. *I* was in the van. *You* got me out. Where were the Hoods?"

Angie walked over and slumped down on the couch, next to Thomas. She smiled. "We kicked their booty."

I looked from her to Thomas. "Come on. What's up?"

"Angie did everything," Thomas said. "When we drove to the marina to pick you up Angie spotted the white van parked along the curb. She was sure it was the same one that nearly ran you two over in the alley, and the same one those two guys

341

were in when they shot at you a few days ago. So we just kept going. They didn't notice us. They probably didn't recognize Angie's car. We figured somehow they found out you were returning to the marina so they were waiting."

My mind started racing. How *did* these guys find out about that? No one knew except Angie, and Sarah, of course.

Thomas continued. "We knew they were going to snatch you. We figured they'd take you somewhere and dump you, the victim of a hit and run or something. Angie got the idea to set a trap. Me, I just wanted to use their heads for a little batting practice. But Angie said they had the advantage, being two of them. Personally, I thought they were at a disadvantage, being just one of me." Thomas grinned.

"She said we had to catch them with surprise so they wouldn't be able to react violently. She was right. I checked them for weapons. They each packed a handgun stuffed in their waistbands. She figured out the whole plan, from the stalled car scenario with the young helpless woman alone on an empty street to the Isoflurane."

"The what?" I asked.

"Isoflurane," Angie spoke up. "It's an anesthetic. We use it to put animals to sleep when we operate. It's the same stuff we use when we have to put one down, only then we use a much larger dose. The clinics only a few blocks away, so I raced back there and grabbed two jars of it. When the thugs approached me, 'the poor young girl with the stalled vehicle,' I threw it in their faces. They didn't like that too much, but they passed out before they could do anything about it." She looked at her watch and smiled. "Probably waking up right about now wondering what happened."

I grinned. But my grin turned into a frown as I thought again about the Hoods. *How'd they know about my arrival at the marina,* I asked myself. I stared at the floor.

"What's the matter?" Angie asked.

I looked up at her. "How'd those guys know I'd be there?"

"Did you tell somebody?"

"Just you."

"Did you call anybody else? Maybe just happened to mention it to someone?"

"No, just you." I thought back. "And, Jack. I called Jack Buick." I paused as a bad feeling passed over me. "He asked all about my plans. Even asked about Sarah. Wanted her name. I told him everything. He knew every move I was going to make. Of course *he* wouldn't tell anybody. Why would he do that? He's my editor. He's in New York. That doesn't make any sense."

"So how'd they find out?" Thomas asked. "If only Angie and Jack knew then…"

"I know. It doesn't add up. I'm gonna call Jack right now." Angie looked at me with wide eyes. I understood her reservation. "I won't say anything. I'm just going to talk about the weather or something, I don't know."

I pulled out my disposable phone and dialed Jack's cell. I let it ring a dozen times, then I hung up. "He's not answering. Probably asleep and didn't hear it. I'll call again tomorrow."

Angie's fluffy fur ball jumped up into her lap and began nosing around her hands, sniffing, then quickly jerked back and leaped off, darting down the hall with a sideways scamper.

She smiled. "It's powerful stuff."

CHAPTER FIFTY

SPECIAL AGENT SKIP Chouw lifted the phone on the first ring. He had been expecting a call from two agents conducting surveillance of the Lotus Blossom Restaurant.

"Chouw here."

"Special Agent Chouw. This is OPUS China Five-Zero."

Chouw sat straight up. His attention fixed as he recognized the voice and code name of the mysterious asset. "Yes, OPUS. What have you got for me?"

"Deng Qin will be leaving the country," OPUS said. "In three days. He will be returning to China and taking something of great value with him. Something classified, very valuable, and of strategic military importance to the United States."

Chouw scribbled a note on a yellow legal pad. "What is it? Classified documents? Software? Military hardware?"

"I do not know. I am sorry. This is all I have."

Chouw continued to press. "How is he leaving? Will he be leaving from Seattle?" There was a pause from OPUS. "Are you still there?" Chouw asked.

"Yes. I have one more thing. This will be my last contact. I have finished my work."

Chouw choked and caught his breath. "Finished your work?"

344

"Yes. I have done what I can do."

At this point Chouw did not know what that meant. He was surprised OPUS continued to engage him in conversation. In the past, all contact had been brief and conversations limited to essential facts. He still didn't know who OPUS was. Could it be he was a confidant of Deng Qin, and a member of MSS? "What do you mean by this?" He prodded. "Are you leaving with Deng Qin?"

"Oh, no. Deng Qin and I will be going our separate ways. We do not exactly see eye to eye on relationships between China and America. Maybe I have grown soft." There was a pause. "Yes, this could be. It is time for me to move on."

Agent Chouw detected a very different voice on the other end. It did not reflect the abrupt and urgent tone OPUS had exhibited in the past, but as OPUS himself had inferred, it appeared softer. Chouw hoped to pursue this conversation further. If just for curiosity.

"So if I may ask, why have you helped us these past few years? You've never asked for anything in return."

The soft voice took time to answer. "As a young boy, in China...Have you ever lived in China, Agent Chouw?"

"No. I was born here."

"Yes, you are very lucky. I am sure you know that. The year was 1950. I will never forget that day. I had just turned thirteen. The Communists came and took our home. They took my father too. They ripped our family apart. We were one of many families displaced by this reign of terror. That was the last day I ever saw my father. I used to hear my mother cry out while I lay in bed. For many years after, I would hear her cries in my dreams. They have since faded. She was left to raise four young children." He paused. "They didn't have to take my father. No child deserves that."

Chouw listened with fascination. He could discern from the voice and the words alone, a deep pain lay within the man calling himself OPUS. He could tell a heart was speaking through a scarred childhood memory. It wasn't a bitter or vengeful voice, rather, resigned with a sense of destiny. "I'm sorry to hear that. A lot of bad things happened to a lot of good people. I am told things have changed for the better, but sometimes, I'm not so sure."

"Yes," OPUS said. "Times have changed. But things have also remained much the same. I still have hope for the future. The world is becoming smaller. China has recognized she must work within the global community, not in isolation. Develop respectful and mutually beneficial relationships with cultures that think differently, with political systems that manage their affairs from a different perspective. I have worked for many years to build stronger bridges between our two countries. I would like to think I have succeeded in some small way. Time will tell."

Chouw asked. "What will you do now?"

"Like so many of those American westerns I have enjoyed at the cinema over the years, I will ride into the sunset atop a weathered saddle and disappear down a long dusty road." Chouw heard a chuckle as OPUS paused. "I want to die with cowboy boots on like that American icon of Western lore, Mr. John Wayne."

CHAPTER FIFTY-ONE

AT DAWN, THE five locomotives pulling a train of railcars arrived at Seattle International Gateway, the SIG yard, across from the Port of Seattle, Terminal Five. The following morning a giant forklift lifted the steel containers that had been dispatched from shippers across the northern plains and placed them one by one onto a fleet of truck chassis. Independent truckers obtained a booking number, hooked their cabs to the chassis and delivered them to the marine terminal on Harbor Avenue, dropping them off in the assigned row. Facing the giant red cranes that towered over the waters edge, they would soon be lifted and stacked upon the deck of *Miss Hong Kong*, in preparation for a journey across the Pacific. Destination: Shanghai.

Container RCQU3054383 was among them.

* * *

AFTER UNWINDING AND recounting the events surrounding the marina incident, Thomas returned to his apartment in the University District and I curled up on Angie's sofa for a restless night of couch-turning.

In the morning Angie woke me up before she left for the veterinary clinic, promising to return during her lunch hour to drive me to the rental car agency. I took this opportunity to make a few phone calls. I first called the rental car company and told them the car I had rented had simply quit running and I had to push it into a parking space on the waterfront. I gave them the location and said I would be by later to pick up another vehicle.

Then I called Jack Buick on his cell. Again, it rang and rang. Receiving no answer, I placed a call to Su Wan Cho. I told him I needed his help. I assured him this would be the last time. It would be easy, he wouldn't have to leave his apartment, but I needed him to do one final thing for me later tonight. Following that I called my ex, Shelly. I knew she would be home and the kids would be out of school for the Christmas break. I just wanted to check on them. They had been on my mind a lot, even with everything going on in my life.

"This is Shelly Beecham," she answered.

"Hey there," I replied.

"Curtis. Why are you calling this time of day? Everything all right?"

"Oh, yeah. For the most part. I just wanted to see how the kids were doing."

"They're fine. You just saw them last week." She hesitated.

I didn't reply.

"I didn't mean anything by that. Actually, I appreciate your concern…your wanting to keep in touch with them."

That was about as good a compliment as I ever got. "So how are you?"

"You know, busy with the kids, busy with work. But now that the holidays are almost over, I feel a load has been lifted. Oh, by the way, thanks for the basket."

"What basket?" I asked.

"The fruit basket you sent."

"I never sent any fruit basket." I paused, my curiosity piqued. "Was there a card with it?"

"Well, yes, but there was no name on it. I assumed you sent it. If you didn't, who did?"

"Probably your office. Your boss. Or do you have a secret admirer?" I asked feigning jealousy.

"I certainly don't have time for a relationship, raising two kids. Hold on a minute. Let me get the card and see what's written on it."

Shelly returned in a moment and picked up the phone. "It's just a card from the distributor."

"Who is it?" I asked, still puzzled.

"The Asia Pacific Fruit & Vegetable Company."

My heart leaped into my throat. My God. They've targeted my family. I tried to stay calm so as not to alarm Shelly, but my words blurted out with heightened urgency. "Listen to me Shelly. Listen carefully."

"What's the matter, Curtis? You sound strange."

"I know who sent the basket. They're dangerous people."

"What do you mean they're dangerous? A fruit company?"

"A lot has happened over the past few days. I haven't told you everything because I didn't want to worry you. There are people who don't want my book published. They're willing to do anything to stop it. Anything."

"Curtis. What are you saying? You're scaring me. What's going on?"

"Shelly. Trust me. It's a long story. I can't tell you much right now except they're extremely dangerous. I've been running from them the past few days."

"Running from them! My God, Curtis. This is crazy. What are you involved in?"

"I know this sounds crazy. But it'll be over in a couple days. I never expected them to find you. I didn't plan on that."

"You don't plan on a lot of things, Curtis. I have two children here. Your children, in case you've forgotten. And you're telling me they may be in danger?"

"Look. You're not in danger. Well, maybe you are. I don't really know. But, I'm not taking any chances." I paused for a moment to think.

"Curtis! What's going on? Does this have anything to do with what happened to your boat?"

"Maybe. Listen. You and the kids are on holiday break, right?"

"Yes."

"Then visit your sister. Take the kids, spend a few days with her."

"Scottsdale? You want me to leave town? Go to Arizona?"

"Yes. I really think it's best. I don't know what these guys will do, but we can't take a chance. Just for a few days."

"You mean I'm going to be on the run? This may be suitable to your out-of-control life, but it isn't the way I want to live mine."

"Please. I know I've hurt you, but I'll make up for it. Please. For the kids sake. Really, I think it's too dangerous for you to stay in Seattle. Please, go see your sister."

I waited for a reply. I could almost feel her glaring at me through the phone.

"Okay," she agreed. "She's been asking me to bring the kids down. She has a pool and I could use a little break from the weather. Okay. But only for a few days."

"Good. Pack right away and catch the first flight possible. I need to know you and the kids are safe. And Shelly, I'm sorry."

"Sure. Don't do anything stupid. And call me."

I hung up, collapsed back into the sofa and breathed out a deep sigh. Those bastards.

I knew I had to get lucky if my plan was going to have any chance of success. It was risky, but I needed to begin putting the pieces into place. I hung around Angie's apartment until she showed up a little after noon, then she drove me to the rental car agency. While she returned to work, I went in search of a new place to sleep. Thomas promised to stop by and pick up my things at the Pink Salmon, and I'd rendezvous with him later. I asked Angie to wait for my call this evening. Tonight we would initiate the first phase of my plan. And if all went well, we'd soon have Deng Qin's balls in a vice, and begin to squeeze.

PART THREE

THE STING

CHAPTER FIFTY-TWO

I PICKED ANGIE up at 10:00 P.M. Told her to wear jeans, sneakers and a dark jacket. We'd been involved in an unauthorized entry twice now, but this would be our biggest challenge and greatest risk, by far.

I had logged onto Google satellite maps earlier in the day and familiarized myself with the layout of Terminal Five. A massive facility of nearly two hundred acres, it was loaded with rail cars, semi-truck chassis, and of course shipping containers. From my study of the terrain I planned my route and selected an access point.

I headed down Fourth Avenue to Spokane Street, then followed it across Harbor Island and exited on Harbor Avenue, along the backside of Terminal Five. That put us some distance from the rows of steel shipping containers at the other end of the massive intermodal yard, but allowed us to leave the car in a remote area with little traffic where we could scale the razor-wire topped chain-link fence.

I killed the headlights and pulled off the pavement among scattered bushes and a few overhanging evergreen trees, stopping against the fence opposite an assortment of rusted containers buried among weeds and debris. The night sky was moonless with heavy cloud cover but the air remained crisp and dry.

Peering through the window, I whispered, "This seems to be as good a place as any." I turned to Angie and tapped her on the knee. "Ready?"

She nodded. I grabbed a small cloth bag that contained the items we would need, then opened the door. Black tape placed over the interior lights prevented unwelcome illumination. I scanned the area, calculating our next step.

I placed my foot on the bumper, climbed onto the hood, then the roof. Angie followed, stepping onto the roof behind me. I threw one of the floor mats from the front floorboard across the razor wire, then put a foot onto the floor mat and tested it for strength. It gave a little slack and a slight wiggle, but seemed secure. I put my full weight on the mat for a brief moment as I leapt over the fence, landing on top of the container on the other side with a soft thud.

I turned and held out my hand. She looked down, placed her foot on the floor mat and tested it a moment before gaining her balance. Looking up, she shifted her weight to one foot, then jumped across, grasping my hand as she landed. We scurried to the front of the container where I handed her my bag. I grabbed hold of the top end of one of the two vertical locking bars, swung my body around and climbed down, using the indented ridges of the container like ladder steps.

I looked up and raised my arms. "Toss the bag."

In a moment she followed my steps and we were both on the ground. I peered around the container, orienting myself. This secluded corner of the property was cast in darkness by heavy shadows from the evergreens that blocked most ambient light. A couple hundred feet ahead lay the exposed area of the rail yard with more than a dozen tracks, some empty, some with rail cars, and light fixtures that threw soft cones of light in a spotty pattern. On the other side of the tracks stood a low office building and beyond that, an area flooded with the ominous yellow light of safety lamps that threw an eerie glow across the yard. In this area, row upon row upon row of steel containers waited to be plucked skyward by the agile fingers of nimble cranes. Thousands of containers, each with its own individual identity code.

We had to locate two of them.

I swallowed. The task before us looked more daunting than I had expected. I wished we had bicycles. And at this point, two Port of Seattle employee ID badges would have provided great comfort.

I searched, looking for any activity. Any security. I observed none, but I could see the movement of cranes against the huge bulk of *Miss Hong Kong* at the opposite end of the yard. I turned to Angie, nodded my head toward the tracks, then started off with a quick dash. Within a minute we reached the first set of rails. I stopped and squatted, glancing to the left and right. Another moment later, I took off again, Angie behind me. We danced our way across three sets of track, until we came to the first train of container rail cars that blocked our path. They provided momentary cover. We climbed over the heavy steel coupling bars and I glanced both ways. It appeared clear. We dashed across another set of tracks and passed between two cars of another train. We repeated this process as we passed through a dozen more trains.

At the last one, we stopped to catch our breath. I knelt down and whispered, "You okay?"

Angie nodded.

I stared ahead. We were positioned behind the building that housed the administration offices. We had to skirt this facility to reach the area where shipping containers lined the dock, within clear sight of *Miss Hong Kong*. Security would be evident from this point forward. I expected roving security vehicles but hoped we wouldn't run into foot patrols or worse, canine units. But this area, though well lit, had a maze of containers to disappear between and hide among.

After studying the satellite maps, I had made a plan for our search based on the location of *Miss Hong Kong* and her proximity to the dock. Terminal Five had berths for three container ships, although there were currently only two in port. *Miss Hong Kong* was on the farthest end. We would begin our search in the area adjacent to her.

We jogged left, past the building, and continued on to an area of many flatbed tractor-chassis waiting for a load. We wiggled our way through them until we faced a long row of containers, lined up like giant loaves of rye bread. This was the first row of about a dozen, each with nearly two hundred containers. I had designated this as our starting point. The area closest to *Miss Hong Kong*, and I hoped, the most likely spot for Deng Qin's container. If we didn't find our prize here, we'd expand the search row by row. It was also the area most visible from longshoremen working the cranes and any of the crew. We had to combine caution with speed.

Running to the first row, we ducked between two containers and crouched. It would be a long night and we had a lot of footwork ahead of us.

"Okay?" I whispered again.

Her chest heaved as she nodded.

"Let's take a minute. Catch our breath." I dug into my bag, pulled out a bottle of water and held it out.

Angie took a sip and passed it back. I took a big swallow.

"Get your ID numbers out." I said. Angie dug into her jeans pocket, and I fished out a folded piece of paper from mine. We were in shadow, but the security lighting that flooded the area allowed me to read the identification codes that had been written on them. One code was for the container of Deng Qin, which was designated for export, the other, a container I hoped had been off-loaded from *Miss Hong Kong* and would be here somewhere, waiting to be picked up and delivered to the Asian Antique Import Company.

I refreshed my memory, studying the four-letter combinations in silence.

After a few moments, I stood up and sidled back to the front edge of the container, sticking my head out, glancing both ways. I turned back to Angie. "You take this side. Walk but keep a quick pace. I'll take the other side. Stay in visual contact with me at all times. After passing each container, look for me. I'll do the same. We can't lose each other. Keep a vigilant eye out for any movement. Any vehicle lights. If you see anything, duck between the containers and signal me. Got it?"

She nodded.

"Scared?"

She nodded again.

"Me too. Let's go."

We headed down the first row in a methodical search. The double doors on the end displayed each container's identification, stenciled in large letters and numbers; a seemingly haphazard alphanumeric code that meant nothing to the average man on the street, but everything to the industry. I gave a quick glance at each container as I passed, concentrating on the first four letters. Unless the first four letters matched, I ignored the seven numbers. I looked down the long row of containers ahead of me and glanced behind as I went. My head turned and swiveled, as I looked for movement. The night remained quiet except for the clanging of cranes against steel containers that echoed across the yard.

If not for our deep anxiety, the search would be a monotonous process. We finished our first pass taking in the first two rows without incident, or success, then moved to the next two.

Halfway down the row, Angie surprised me as she appeared between two containers. She signaled with the wave of an arm. I ducked in behind her.

She pointed in the direction ahead of us. "Lights."

I nodded, then crept between the containers and peered out. A vehicle headed our way, moving at a slow pace. I scooted back to Angie. "Follow me."

We moved toward the back of the container and stood behind it, motionless, our bodies flat against the steel end. My breathing quickened, my heart pounded a little faster.

I peered around the edge with one eye. A security vehicle passed by the narrow space between the two containers. After it disappeared, I ran to the end and watched as it drove down the row. The vehicle made a left turn when it reached the very end.

"Angie," I exhaled in a strong, throaty whisper, while signaling with a repeated flip of my hand. "This side."

She ran to me and we hid ourselves in the same manner, but on the opposite end. I again watched. Within minutes the security vehicle passed. I dashed down and watched as it made a right, patrolling the next row over.

"It's okay. He's gone."

We continued our methodical search, finishing up those two rows then began the next two. A few containers later, I caught sight of the four matching letters, the correct RCQU. My heart leaped. I stopped and fumbled with the note, mouthing the seven numbers as my eyes shot back to the container hoping for a match. They didn't. Disappointed, I moved on.

Two rows and over an hour later I glanced through the narrow space between a couple of containers and caught sight of Angie, jumping up and down, waving both arms.

My heart skipped a beat as I dashed between containers and emerged next to Angie. "This is it."

I turned and stared where she pointed. RCQU. Yes, that's right. I checked my folded piece of paper against the stenciled numbers on the container. 3054383. "Yes!" I exhaled, hardly believing we had found it. Doubt had crept in as the clock had continued to tick.

I set my bag down in the shadows between the two containers, then pulled out a twelve-inch ruler and a roll of masking tape. I handed the items to Angie. "Here." She took them, spun around and began to tape the ruler to the container door next to the letters of the ID code. I grabbed a small digital camera and a flashlight.

I looked around searching for security. Satisfied there were no headlights or movement, I handed the flashlight to Angie and she bounced the beam on the letter and number code on the steel door. I raised the camera and focused, then clicked off two shots, zoomed in and clicked off two more. The auto flash on the camera had been neutralized. I didn't want the intensity of the flash to attract attention.

"Okay," I whispered. "Take a good look. Get your bearings. See where we are."

We both glanced around and noted the space number painted on the ground in front of Deng Qin's container. We'd have to return later tonight. I wanted to be sure we'd find it.

I placed everything back in the bag, lifted it with a tight grip and whispered. "Let's go."

From my earlier research, I had decided we would begin our search for the other container in a different area. I assumed Deng Qin's container would be in an area of export containers, considering their proximity to the ship. The imports would most likely be in a separate area, farther away. We scampered down the row and passed through a number of containers, heading for an area we had passed earlier. The spot where the empty truck chassis were stored.

I had noticed earlier that crane activity had stopped. About midnight the yard had become quiet and the movement of cranes had ceased. Apparently the last shift of the day had ended.

Again, we followed the same procedure, and again, passed through many a row of containers and checked the codes on hundreds of them. I was becoming frustrated. I checked my watch. It was nearly 1:00 A.M. We were both tired. We had been on the property nearly three hours and we still had a lot of containers we hadn't searched. I reminded myself, we don't have all night.

I signaled Angie through the narrow gap between two containers. I stopped and waited for her, stooped down, opened the bag and reached in for the water bottle.

"Doing okay?" I asked.

I looked up, held out the bottle. Her attention was focused on something behind me.

"Here." I jiggled it. Then turned to follow her gaze. We snatched our pieces of paper at the same time, glanced back to the container behind us and checked our ID codes.

"I'll be damned," I muttered. "That's it."

We set up the same procedure as before, taking four quick photos of the ID on Uncle Willie's container. We had located both of them. I had to admit, I wasn't sure we ever would. My long-shot had come in.

After collecting and bagging our materials, we ran for the car, retracing our steps, with more haste and less care then when we came. We reached the chain-link fence, leaped across to the roof of the car, climbed down and jumped in.

My head throbbed, my heart pumped adrenalin and I exhaled in quick breaths. I glanced over at Angie. She had slumped back against her headrest, eyes closed. Her chest heaved.

I cranked the car and pulled out, bumping over the curb as I hit the lights. I turned and headed in the direction of Su Wan's apartment. It was time for him to perform a small, but crucial task before Angie and I returned to Terminal Five, in little more than an hour from now.

CHAPTER FIFTY-THREE

I CALLED SU Wan as soon as we rounded the corner and turned down the street fronting his apartment. It was 2:10 A.M. and I didn't want to wake him any sooner than I had to. The phone rang eight times before he picked up.

"Su Wan. It's Curtis. We're here."

It took a moment for his somewhat groggy response. "What...Curtis?"

"Yeah, we're outside your apartment. Pulling up now."

"What?" He sounded confused. "What time is it? Where are you?"

"It's ten after two. We're outside your apartment. Remember? You were going to help us out. Make a few signs." He was silent and I realized he still didn't get it. "Wake up Su Wan. We're here to make those signs."

"Shit, man," he finally acknowledged. "I thought you were kidding. Are you serious? In the middle of the night?"

"Yes. We have the photos. Two minutes. We'll be there."

I hung up as I pulled into a vacant spot in the parking lot. I awoke Angie with a gentle shake. "Wake up. We're at Su Wan's."

We dragged our tired bodies up the two sets of stairs to Su Wan's and I tapped on the door. It took him a minute, but he soon appeared, wearing sweat pants and a T-shirt. He yawned and rubbed his face, then stepped aside as we pushed our way in.

I pulled the camera out of the bag. "Here. I have four shots of each one. I need two complete sets of both ID's. The ruler will give you approximate scale. Doesn't have to be perfect, but close. Remember, they're ID numbers on a friggin' steel container, not a work of art. Time is important." I handed Su Wan the camera and smiled. "Wake us when you're done."

Angie and I crashed on the sofa, falling asleep even before Su Wan disappeared into the spare bedroom he used as a home office.

* * *

I WAS AWAKENED by a rough shake of my shoulder. "Curtis. Here. It's done." Su Wan stood over me with an envelope. I peered at my watch through half closed eyes. 2:48.

It may have been the hardest thing I'd done in the past twenty-four hours, but I lifted myself up. "Let's see."

We stepped over to Su Wan's dining table and he slid the finished sheets out of the envelope, then assembled them into groups that when side-by-side duplicated the ID numbers on the containers. He had printed out my photos and I checked them against his art.

"Perfect. Great." I scooped them up and placed them back in the envelope. I looked at Su Wan. He wasn't smiling, but I did. "Thanks, Su Wan. Really appreciate this."

I walked to the couch and shook Angie. "Angie. We're done here. Time to go." She squirmed and buried her head deeper into her arms. "Come on. We can sleep later." She opened an eye and scowled. I was making enemies fast.

I grabbed the camera off the table, stuffed it into my bag and headed for the door. Angie followed, dragging herself a few steps behind. I'm sure Su Wan hoped he'd seen the last of me.

* * *

WE WERE PARKED against the perimeter fence surrounding Terminal Five within thirty minutes. The streets were nearly empty of traffic, the night dark and very quiet.

We followed the same procedure to scale the fence, enter and cross the intermodal yard and were soon standing next to Deng Qin's shipping container. I stared at it for a second, wondering what could possibly be inside? To Deng Qin, it must be invaluable. I pulled out the camera and handed it to Angie. I had her take a picture of me standing by the steel doors, holding up the front page of the *Seattle Times*, pointing to the ID numbers, a smile on my face. I then slipped out two sheets of the ID Su Wan had printed on adhesive-back label paper with the ID number for Uncle Willie's container. I peeled off the back of the first sheet containing four letters and slapped it over Deng Qin's code letters. I repeated the process for the seven numbers. I stood back to admire our work. Perfect. We had now changed Deng Qin's container into Uncle Willie's. We scooped up our materials and dashed off to locate Uncle Willie's container, to replace his ID code with Deng Qin's.

* * *

I EXPECTED SOME confusion at the port over the next two days when the loading crew discovered a mix-up in the placement of one of the containers to be loaded aboard *Miss Hong Kong*. Deng Qin's "export" container I had recoded with Uncle Willie's code was now identified as an "import." It would be separated out from the other containers in that area marked for export and loaded aboard a semi-truck chassis, and delivered, according to the manifest, to the Asian Antique Import Company. Uncle Willie's container that I recoded with Deng Qin's export ID would also be discovered to have been placed in the wrong aisle, would be moved to the proper area for export and loaded aboard *Miss Hong Kong*. Though I hoped to avoid this. Over the next twenty-four hours my plan would be to enlist the "reluctant" cooperation of Deng Qin, and have him see to it that Uncle Willie's container is *not* loaded aboard *Miss Hong Kong* but delivered to Uncle Willie's warehouse in the International District. Timing was tight. I hoped my luck would hold.

* * *

AFTER A FEW hours sleep, Angie dragged herself out of bed, showered, dressed and drove to the import company. It had been a long, tiring night, but she had to arrive early to meet with her father. It was time they had an important talk.

"Hello, Father," she said as she peered in the doorway of his office.

Wung Hu looked up and smiled. "Angela. How wonderful to see you. Come in. Come in. Have a seat." He rose up and pulled a side chair out for her. "Your visits have become much more frequent these days."

Angie closed the door behind her as she stepped to the chair and sat down. "Father. I have something very important to discuss with you."

"Yes, yes. What is it, my dear?"

"I guess I don't know where to start." Angie squirmed and tugged at her short skirt. She had taken a few days off due to the events she had been involved in with Curtis, using the holidays as an excuse, so she was not in her usual white uniform. "Father, there have been things going on in the Chinese community that I have become involved in. It's become kind of a messy situation." She hesitated, thinking through her next words.

"There are many good people in our community, but, as you know, there are some who aren't. I know you immigrated to America with, well..." She paused. "Well, with certain arrangements made by the Chinese government. I understand all that. I think a lot of good has come from it. You know, working to create a better understanding between our two countries. And of course, your children have benefitted. But there's also some bad that has come from it." Angie waited to see her father's response. He nodded but kept his look neutral.

"We don't know what has happened to George, but I believe it has something to do with the bad element within our community." Angie hung her head. "I just don't know. But I think there may be a way to help George. It may be the only chance we have."

"What are you saying, Angela?" Wung Hu asked, alarmed. "Do you know something?"

Angie spent the next twenty minutes telling her father what she knew. How she met Curtis. The white van and the two hoods, and what she could of her relationship with Sayonara, Sayonara's involvement with MSS and her recent murder. Wung Hu listened in silence. He never interrupted, but it was obvious to Angie that the confession shocked him.

"Father. You have said nothing."

Wung Hu shook his head. "I am stunned. My little Angela mixed up in this? Is this all true?"

"Yes, Father. It's all been to try to find George. I will do anything to find him. I can't just sit back and hope for the best."

"I understand," Wung Hu said. "You are doing what you can. And I have really done little. What kind of father am I?" He sat, head down, wringing his hands.

Angie got up, circled the desk, leaned over and hugged her father. "There was not much you could do, Father. If you did, things might have become worse. You had the rest of your family to think about." She stood and leaned against the edge of his desk. "But now there is something you *can* do." Wung Hu looked up with an expression of concern but a sparkle of hope in his eyes. She paused for a moment. "There will be a shipment arriving here, at the warehouse. Remember that shipment you told me about arriving on the *Miss Hong Kong*? You gave me a copy of the manifest."

Wung Hu nodded.

"When the container arrives, it will appear to be yours, with the proper paperwork and identification on the container, but the contents will not be yours."

Wung Hu squinted and tilted his head. "What are you saying?"

"Inside the container are stolen goods," she continued, watching her father's reaction. "Highly classified American military secrets of some sort. A high-level Chinese spy working with MSS by the name of Deng Qin has stolen this stuff from the U.S. Government. When it arrives, I need you to give the authorization to reroute this shipment to a different address." Angie pulled a piece of paper from her pocket and held it out. "This address."

Wung Hu's mouth dropped, his eyes opened wide, his head jerked back and forth in small quick movements. "No! No! No, Angela! What are you telling me? Stolen secrets? MSS? This is most dangerous. These people are…" He lowered his head and held it in his hands, still shaking back and forth. "No. No. How can *you* be involved with these people? I don't want to hear this."

"Father. I understand how you feel. But it's true. This shipping container will be delivered here today or tomorrow. It can't stay here. Deng Qin can't find it here. Do you understand? It needs to be sent to this other place, away from here. It can't be linked to you or Uncle Willie. A day or so after that, the container with your merchandise will arrive." Angie bit her lip. She hoped Uncle Willie's container would arrive. If everything worked out it would, but there were still a lot of "ifs." "Father. Can you do this? For me. For George."

Wung Hu looked up. "My Angela. You are dealing with very dangerous men. You can bring danger to you and everyone in your family. You know this?"

"Yes, I do. But I need to help George. Even if it means

putting myself in danger."

Wung Hu was quiet for a moment. "And you are asking me to help the American government? To betray those of China?"

"This is different, Father. These are bad people. It doesn't matter if they are American or Chinese. They are bad. They did something to George, I know it. They killed my friend. These are not people we should protect. We must do the right thing."

Wung Hu stared at Angie. He looked at her a few moments in silence, in deep thought, then reached out with his hand and laid it on hers. "You are certain this is the right thing?"

"Yes, Father. We *must* do this." Angie studied her father's face. She could see torment and anguish within him. A struggle not so unlike one between a fire-breathing dragon and an eagle armed with talons.

Wung Hu swallowed. He paused, looking into Angie's eyes. "I love my country. I miss China everyday. And I hope someday I may return to my home. But America has been good to my family, to my children. My children are strong and bright and sometimes an old man can learn from his children. You are right, Angela. These are bad men. I will do as you say."

Angie knelt down by her father and threw her arms around him, tears running down her cheeks. "Thank you, Father. Thank you."

* * *

FOR NEARLY TWENTY-FOUR hours I had been living in my car, parked against the curb just outside the gates to Terminal Five, staring through binoculars, observing every truck loaded with containers as they exited. It was exhausting work. Less strenuous than the all-night marathon through the container yard, but tiring nonetheless. But my perseverance paid off as my gaze fell upon container RCQU3054383, sitting on the bed of a silver Kenworth.

The semi-truck coughed black exhaust and popped through a series of gears as it rumbled along Marginal Way, picking up speed, heading for Spokane Street on its way to King Street and the Asian Antique Import Company.

I watched as it passed, then picked up my disposable phone and called Angie.

"Angie. I just saw it. It's heading down Spokane Street."

"Okay," Angie replied. "I'm ready."

She hung up. I pulled out and began to follow at a distance. The semi-truck turned onto King Street, two blocks from The Asian Antique Import Company. I pulled to the curb and watched, undetected. It stopped alongside Uncle Willies office in a loading zone. I saw Angie walk out the front door with a middle-aged Asian man, who I assumed must be her father. The man stopped in the doorway and stood while she approached the semi.

* * *

ANGIE PULLED OUT the copy of the manifest her father had provided and waved it at the driver, her head tilted up to the cab. "Hello!" The driver leaned over and peered out. "There's been a screw-up with the paperwork," Angie shouted over the idling diesel. "We need to have this delivered to our other warehouse. She held up the manifest and the corrected form with the adjusted address. The driver reached down and took it, his eyes scanning the form. He glanced at Angie.

"I didn't know anything about this." He scowled.

Angie used her most persuasive tone. "I know. I know. It's not your fault. But someone's gonna answer for this."

The driver glanced again at the paperwork. "Where's seven four three two South Hampton?"

"A few blocks down the road. I'll lead you."

"Then let's get on with it, lady. I ain't got all day."

Angie turned and dashed for her car. She pulled out, passed the front door of the import office and waved to her father who had remained in the doorway. She led the reluctant driver down King Street to Sixth Avenue, then a couple of miles farther to Hampton and Sayonara's warehouse. It was located within an industrial district filled with warehouses, distribution centers and light manufacturing facilities, so semi-trucks and flatbed trailers with containers were a common sight. Deng Qin's container with Uncle Willie's ID numbers would remain inconspicuous among the hundreds of others in the area.

Angie pulled up in front of Sayonara's warehouse-turned-sex-den, and parked, jumping out to point in the direction she wanted the trailer left. The driver swung the bed of the truck around and with masterful precision backed it down a gravel drive that ran between Sayonara's warehouse and the brick building next door. He unhitched the trailer from his cab, then handed Angie his paperwork. She signed it and smiled. "I'll put in a good word for you."

He frowned, snatched the paperwork, turned and left without a reply.

* * *

I PULLED UP as soon as the truck cab drove off in a huff of exhaust and a spin of gravel.

"Real friendly sort," Angie said as I stepped out of my car.

I glanced over my shoulder as he rambled down the road, then shuffled up to Angie, a big grin splashed across my face. I dipped down, bending at the knees, threw my arms around her and lifted her high into the air, spinning the two of us in a clumsy celebration. Two, maybe three, tight little circles. "We did it, Angie! Praise the gods and our guardian angel, Sayonara. I can't believe we pulled it off, but we did. We really did!"

I set her down, exhilarated, but a bit winded. She smiled with a sheepish grin. "Yes. We did, didn't we."

"Yes! Yes, we did!" I brushed her hair back and stared deep into her eyes, beyond the sparkle, looking for that something special, hoping it was there, lying in wait, before letting her go and allowing my excitement to subside.

"Enough celebrating," I said. "Let's see what we've got."

Returning to the car, I grabbed a pair of bolt cutters and the camera and walked back to the container. I held out the camera. "Hold this." Gripping the bolt cutters around the lock, I pressed the handles together. After a few moments of grinding under heavy pressure, the lock snapped. I set the oversize snips down and removed the lock, tossing it to the side. I pulled the locking bar up, slid it to the side and pulled on the door. It swung open and I gave it a shove, pushing it back. We stood staring. A single large crate covered with a tarp nearly filled the container end to end.

"What is it?" she asked.

"I don't know. Let's get the tarp off."

Within minutes we had unsnapped the restraints and yanked. The tarp tumbled toward us and fell into a heap at our feet.

I stared at the crate. I had to open it, but how? Then I remembered my car, the rental. I checked the trunk and found a lug wrench with a tip on one end made for popping off hubcaps. I went to work and eventually pried the end of the crate loose. It dropped downward and I pressed it flat against the floor with my foot. It screeched and strained against the last few nails attached along the bottom.

My mouth dropped open. "Damn. It's an engine of some kind. Maybe an aircraft engine. It's huge."

"Is it important?" Angie asked.

"It must be. It's a friggin jet engine." I moved closer and stuck my head in. Silver in color, it had a metallic exterior that appeared to be aluminum or some alloy, and was cylindrical in shape, tapered at one end like a bullet. It was held up by two steel arched-girders attached to two steel rails that in turn were supported by four heavy-duty tires.

"My guess is it's top-secret. Maybe a new model. Probably designed for a military fighter aircraft. But I really don't know much about this kind of stuff."

"Let's hope whatever it is, it's important to Deng Qin."

I smiled. "Oh, yeah. You can bet it is." I patted the metal beast with a gentle touch. "Get the camera. Let's take some nice photos to send to Deng Qin. It's time *he* felt a little pain."

CHAPTER FIFTY-FOUR

AFTER CLOSING UP Deng Qin's container and securing it with a new lock, Angie and I drove our vehicles back to Uncle Willie's warehouse where she left her car. She slipped into my passenger seat and we headed to a neighborhood pharmacy with a photo-processing department. There we downloaded the photos of me holding that day's newspaper in front of Deng Qin's container, as well as the ones of me and his prized jet aircraft engine. We printed out two copies of each, purchased a pack of manila catalog envelopes and stuffed one set of the photos into one of the envelopes. I wrote Deng Qin's name on the outside and sealed it. We then drove to the Bamblue Club, and paid the eye at the door fifty dollars to hold the stuffed envelope for a later pick-up.

I had reviewed my plan with Angie. Our most important objective was getting George back safely. We both believed Deng Qin had played a part in his disappearance and knew he wouldn't cooperate with us unless we had some leverage. His container provided that. But I had to be convincing in my conversation with him.

To keep my advantage I couldn't appear weak, some wannabe hero trying to save a friend. From what I knew of Deng Qin, he wouldn't understand anyone incurring all this risk just to save the life of another human being. I needed a better motive. Something he would relate to. He had to believe he was dealing with an unscrupulous scumbag who was as unconscionable as he was. I needed to appear to be an extortionist, a greedy blackmailer looking out for my own interests, working outside the law, *not* with the FBI. I had to ask for something more than just George's return. To be convincing, I had to exact the extortionist's universal demand: Money. This, Deng Qin would understand.

But if I actually accepted money from MSS in exchange for the stolen military property, I could be putting myself into serious jeopardy with the Feds. Up until now, I'd only been dancing around first amendment issues with the FBI. By stealing Deng Qin's container and then demanding and receiving money in exchange, I would be elevating my involvement and my culpability. I didn't want to end up sharing a jail cell with Deng Qin.

The amount of money I would demand had been thoughtfully calculated. It had to be an amount Deng Qin could get his hands on within our short time frame, but most important, an amount the FBI would be willing to front me. It would be tricky. I had to play this out carefully and make sure my plan worked to perfection.

Sitting in the car in the alley outside the club, I reached for my disposable phone while Angie dug into her purse for Sayonara's. I leaned over and squeezed her arm. She looked up, gave me a thin smile. I smiled back, feeling very anxious. She scanned Sayonara's phone searching the contacts, stopping when she found Deng Qin's number and held the phone up so the digital display faced me. I dialed his number. It rang twice then someone picked up.

A voice uttered something in what I assumed to be Chinese.

I forced my voice to sound confident, authoritative, anything but how I felt. "Is this Deng Qin?" I asked.

"Yes. Who is this?" he replied in English.

"That's not important. What's important to you is that I have your shipping container."

There was a moment of silence. "Who are you?" the voice demanded. "What are you saying?"

"Deng Qin, I know about the stolen jet aircraft engine. It's not at the container port anymore. I've got it. It's in *my* possession."

The phone exploded with a stream of rapid-fire obscenities and questions. First he relapsed into Mandarin, then he reverted back to English. "What do you know of *my* container? Who are you? How did *you* get my number?"

I couldn't get a word in as Deng Qin went on a tirade of uncontrolled anger. I waited for him to calm down, though I rather enjoyed hearing him begin to unravel. I held the phone out to Angie. Having broken the tension with his outburst, she grinned, her hand covered her mouth. I knew as he lost control I would gain it.

He finally paused long enough for me to respond. "Slow down, Deng Qin. You're upset, and that's understandable. I would be too if someone ripped me off. But I really don't want your stuff. I'm just holding it for safekeeping. We both know the FBI would like to get their hands on it."

"You bastard. I do not believe you. *You* are lying. I will find you and tear your heart out and feed it to the snakes. You will *never* be safe."

"You just worry about your prized cargo, Deng Qin. You don't have much time if you want to see your container on board *Miss Hong Kong* when she sails."

He was slow in answering and his voice had lowered. "I do *not* believe what you say. It is impossible. I do not understand your motives at all."

"Listen, Deng Qin. I know the content of this container is valuable. I'm sure you've invested a lot of time and money in it.

My timetable is tight, so you have to act quickly. Send someone to the Bamblue Club. You know where that is. The ticket taker will have an envelope for you. The photos inside will prove I have your container. I'll call back in one hour."

"You excrescence of a whoring mother—"

I hung up and stared at the phone for a moment, took a deep breath, then turned to Angie and grinned. I harbored a fair amount of apprehension and anxiety, but the plan was moving forward. The vise was tightening.

* * *

WE HAD AN hour to kill, so I drove with no particular destination in mind. We ended up at the Washington Park Arboretum, a botanic garden near the University, sitting in a parking lot surrounded by nature. In contrast to the craziness swirling around us, an unexpected calm encircled us: lush evergreens, azaleas, rhododendrons and a variety of bare deciduous trees hibernating until spring. A few joggers bundled in ski caps, gloves, thick sweaters and warm-ups passed under the canopy of branches that enclosed the winding road in front of us.

At the appointed time, I pulled out the phone and dialed Deng Qin. He picked up on the first ring.

"You bastard," Deng Qin jumped right in where he left off. "I don't know how you did this, but you are a dead man. Do you *hear* me? You are dead to your family. I will hunt you down. You will feel the power of a thousand dragons tearing at your throat. No one does this to *me* and lives to breathe another day."

"Nice photos, huh?" I was gaining confidence and getting pure pleasure out of torturing Deng Qin, knowing the pain and suffering he had caused. "Now, are you ready to get down to the business at hand?"

He was slow to answer. "What is it that you want from

me?"

"Three things. Things you *will* make happen if you ever want to see your container again. First, I want George Hu. He's disappeared and I know you know something about it. His family wants him back, safely."

"Humph! I do not—"

"Hold on, Deng Qin, let me finish." I paused to make sure he was listening. His heavy breathing told me he was. "Second, there's a container sitting at Terminal Five at the port. It has your container identification number on it, but the contents belong to someone else. There's been a little mix-up, which the port is still scratching their heads over. I understand it happens occasionally." I winked at Angie. "I'll give you the local address where you can have it delivered. The authorities believe it belongs to you so they'll do whatever you say. Third, I need a deposit in the sum of two hundred and fifty thousand dollars, American, wired to a certain bank account. I'll provide the wire instructions."

"You are a dog's piss!" he screamed. "This is not possible! This is outrageous! You do not know *who* you are dealing with. This is blackmail. Extortion. *I* will not have it!"

"Call it what you want. But you don't have any options. I understand your ship sails in twenty-four hours. That's our timeline. I get what I want. You get what you want. Otherwise, I'll turn the container over to the FBI, and we both lose."

"I will find you first," he threatened. "You will not see the sun rise on the day I sail."

"Think about it, Deng Qin. You have twenty-four hours. That's not much time." I glanced at my watch. "I'll call back in one hour for your decision. And Deng Qin. If you go to the port to report your stolen container, or try to track it down, I'll be forced to contact the FBI. You don't want to have to explain why you have a stolen aircraft engine in your possession."

I hung up, knowing Deng Qin would not be cooperative initially. He would resist working with me until he exhausted all attempts to find me and his container. But he had little time to make a successful counterattack. I had to keep the pressure on.

I looked at Angie as I lifted the phone and started dialing. "I'm gonna try Jack Buick again. I've tried a couple times, but I still haven't reached him."

I let it ring a dozen times. He didn't answer.

"Have you tried his office?" Angie asked.

"No. Just his cell." I looked at my disposable phone, then up to Angie. "Let me use your cell, I need to save my minutes." She handed me her phone, I dialed information and they connected me.

"Good afternoon. Kaleidoscope Book Publishing. How may I help?"

"Mr. Jack Buick, please."

"I'm sorry. Mr. Buick is no longer employed by Kaleidoscope Book Publishing."

"What? He's not there anymore?" At that moment the wind went out of my sails, and I felt the first crack in my confident exterior.

"That's right. Is there someone else you would like to speak to?"

I stuttered. "Ah, wait. He's my editor. I'm working with him on a manuscript. What do you mean? Where is he?"

"I'm sorry, sir. All I can say is that he's no longer employed here."

"But my book? We're in the middle of my book."

"Yes, I'm sorry. I can have you speak to one of the vice presidents if you'd like."

"Did he leave a number? Is there some place I can reach him?"

"No, I'm sorry." The phone went silent for a moment. "You're one of his writers?"

"Yes, Curtis Beecham."

There was a pause. "You're not alone, Mr. Beecham. I've had calls from other writers as well. I don't know what got into him, but he seemed very different the last few times we talked. He wasn't himself. Something seems to have made him quite upset. I haven't seen him of course, we've only spoken on the phone. He emailed his resignation and said he would have somebody stop by and clean out his personal items from the office."

"He's gone then?"

"I'm afraid so."

"What about my manuscript? Won't one of the other editors take it on? Can't I work with someone else?"

"I'm sorry. Editors have an independent relationship with their authors. Unless Jack has passed the manuscript on to another editor who expressed an interest in the project, I'm afraid it's dead. You'd have to submit your manuscript again for consideration. You might get lucky, but most editors are pretty busy with their own writers. Now, if you could only get hold of Jack and get him to recommend you. You know, pass your name along."

Somehow I didn't think that was gonna happen. "Thanks anyway."

I hung up. Dazed, I turned to Angie. "Did you hear that?"

She nodded.

"Why did he resign so suddenly? Why doesn't he answer his phone? Damn him."

The news of Jack quitting hit me with the suddenness of a lightning strike out of a clear blue sky, and the consequence of his abrupt departure set in. As far as my writing career was concerned, I was back to square one. I would have to search for a new publisher. After what I'd been through, I was really pissed. Jack could have handled this better. Angie reached over and rubbed the back of my neck as I stared out the window and my mind drifted. I had to get beyond this disappointment. I couldn't have distractions.

With time to kill before our next call to Deng Qin, we left the car and took a stroll through the arboretum. A short emersion in the uncomplicated purity of nature might clear my head and help me regain my focus.

* * *

AN HOUR LATER we returned to the vehicle. I picked up the phone once more and dialed.

"Nothing has changed, you infected pus on a bitch dog," Deng Qin blurted in true form. "I will find you. You cannot blackmail me and get away with it."

"Deng Qin," I said. "You're not in any position to delay. Your package is very valuable. You've already made a huge investment. You've put too much time and money into planning this. Don't waste it. If I have to turn your package over to the FBI, the chance of you ever getting another opportunity is zero. You and I know this is your only shot. Don't let it slip through your fingers. And listen, you might be thinking about buying time so you can search for me and find your container. Taking the next boat. Don't even think about it. The longer your container sits on U.S. soil, the greater the chance the FBI will find it. I'm sure they're aware of the theft by now. They could be closing in."

There was silence. He had to know I was right. He didn't have any options. His best chance would be to deal with me, and then kill me *after* he had the container in his possession. My best chance would be to keep that from happening. The game was on.

I needed to force his hand, make him commit. "Listen, Deng Qin. If you're *not* interested, I can always—"

"George Hu...he's...he's in China," he blurted with a bit of reluctance. "A Son of the Red Dragon, he had this sudden interest in visiting his ancestral homeland."

Angie stiffened and took a deep breath. I reached over and grabbed her hand. "What! Now *you're* bullshitting me Deng Qin. You have him. I know it. He had no interest in going to China. Not now. He would have told his family if that were true. You're lying."

"I had nothing to do with it. If it were up to me I would have…"

Angie's grip tightened as he spoke. I glanced her way. Her eyes glistened. She turned her head and stared out the window.

"What Deng Qin? You would have what?"

"It does not matter. He was a traitor to China. He talked too much. He needed to be silenced, but it was not up to me. Now he is a guest of my government."

"That's kidnapping. He's a U.S. citizen. You can't do that." Even as I said it I felt hopelessness begin to overcome me. I've heard of such things happening. There would be no way to prove George didn't go of his own freewill. My head dropped and I stared down, not wanting to face Angie.

"And what about theft and blackmail," Deng Qin responded. "You don't seem to be one to worry about what side of the law *you* stand on. You are scum. George was scum. We deal with scum in our own way."

"You son of a bitch," I fired back. "You haven't heard the end of this. You've made a big mistake."

"No, it is you who have made the mistake. George will pay and you will pay. Just as your friend Jack Buick paid. No one gets away with fucking with Deng Qin."

I lost my breath for a minute. "Jack? Jack Buick! What do you know about Jack Buick?"

"Just another incompetent fool who thought he was smarter than Deng Qin. He found out different."

"What does he have to do with *you*? Where is he? What did you do to him?"

Deng Qin chuckled. "He is resting. Peacefully."

I choked. "You killed him?"

"He will not be fucking with Deng Qin *any* longer."

I felt my body go numb. I dropped my hand holding the phone into my lap and stared out the windshield. It was an understatement to say my conversation with Deng Qin was not going well. Control had shifted. My confidence had fallen flat and I realized more than ever whom I was dealing with, and how dangerous this had turned. I fought to regain my strength and check my emotions.

I lifted the phone back to my ear and asked in a subdued tone, "What did Jack do?"

"He was a traitor. He tried to play me against the FBI. I am too smart for that. He was willing to give you up too, for a price. He ended up as a traitor should. You should thank me for that."

"Dead," I added.

"Just as you will be, if you do not return my container," Deng Qin growled.

Finally, I had first-hand proof Jack had betrayed me. He sold me out, put my life in danger. My stomach began to churn, an acid taste rising up, my mouth feeling gummy. I fought to regain my composure and return to the issue. "Listen. I'm not budging on George. I need him back, alive. Start making phone calls. I need to know he's alive."

"That will not happen. He is in China. He has a lot of explaining to do. If he is lucky, he may be allowed to return to your hypocritical America someday. But, do not expect that to happen anytime soon."

I felt helpless. If what Deng Qin said were true, there would be no way of getting George back, at least not without the help of the State Department and the cooperation of both governments. "What assurances can you give me that he's still alive?"

"If he were dead, you would have already found his body parts scattered in a very public place. The Chinese community must be aware of such transgressions. A deterrent you might say. Now, enough of this George. Where is *my* container?"

"Listen. George is still my priority. I need some indication George is still alive."

"We will see." Deng Qin paused for a moment. "As for your second request, if things are as you say, I can have the container you desire delivered to the address you provide. But I *cannot* get two hundred and fifty thousand American dollars."

"The money is non-negotiable," I said. "To a great country like China, this is not so difficult. And for such a valuable package, two hundred and fifty thousand is an afterthought. I know you can get the money. I know you have resources. And I know you'll need more than an hour to arrange this. You have until morning. I'll call at ten a.m. and provide the wire transfer number. When everything has been arranged, you'll have your package. I hope you understand the urgency. Remember, you will never see your container without confirmation that George is alive."

I hung up without waiting for a reply. I turned to Angie and squeezed her hand. I wiped at a tear that left a path on her cheek glistening against the soft sunlight filtering through the forest canopy. "I'm so sorry, Angie. But I know he's alive, and we *will* get him back. You must believe that."

"We must, Curtis. We must. I can't imagine what he's going through right now."

She buried her head in my shoulder and we sat without saying a word for a time. I stared out the window, thinking, rebuilding my resolve, when she lifted her head, wiped her eyes and broke the silence. "I'm sorry about Jack. His betrayal, I mean."

"Yeah. I guess I just can't believe it. Jack. My editor. He sold me out. And now he's dead."

"Do you believe he was the one who tipped off the Hoods about your arrival on Magnolia that night?"

"I've given it a lot of thought. At first I told myself no. It couldn't be. Now, I have to believe he did. Jack was the only other person besides us that knew I was returning that night. It makes sense. It's just hard to accept."

"I know. You trusted him. You had no reason to believe otherwise."

"I did trust him. Now, I have to move on." I glanced at Angie. "I have more important things on my mind, than Jack."

CHAPTER FIFTY-FIVE

AFTER MY CALL with Deng Qin I felt I had lost some control. Control gave me confidence. Without confidence in my plan, I would be on shaky ground. And if the ground started moving beneath me, I could make a deadly mistake. Deng Qin was an experienced and seasoned adversary. I, on the other hand, was nothing more than a novice, a rookie at this game. I had to make up for my shortfall by playing smarter. My life depended on it.

I had not expected Deng Qin to tell me what he had. George, in China. Jack, dead. But it appeared Deng Qin was willing to deal. I hoped he understood I would not back down. I needed him to satisfy all three of my demands.

After digesting my phone call with Deng Qin, I placed a second call. This one to the FBI.

"Mr. Jengwi. This is Curtis Beecham."

A slight pause. "Oh, yes, Mr. Beecham. I don't suppose this is a social call, is it?"

"No. But I'll make it worth your while."

"Go on."

"The last time we talked I told you about Miss Hong Kong. I said she would be involved with a theft of military secrets. Something big. Highly sensitive."

His response came with slight hesitation. "Ah, yeah."

"Well, I was wrong, in a way. It *is* Miss Hong Kong who's

involved, and who will be carrying a package. But she's not a beauty queen. *Miss Hong Kong* is a container ship."

"A container ship? Son of a bitch! *Miss Hong Kong* is a fucking container ship?"

"Yeah. Do you know a guy by the name of Deng Qin?"

His voice raised a notch. "Yes. What do you know of him?"

"A real badass, Mr. Jengwi. And, as you probably already know, a senior spy with MSS. He's the one involved with the stolen merchandise. The sensitive military hardware. And he's shipping it to China on the *Miss Hong Kong*, I might add."

"Yeah. We figured he was involved in this," Jengwi said, speaking slow, pausing, apparently digesting my revelation and recognizing I had just provided the last piece to the puzzle. "This all fits with what we know. But, shit, Beecham, we were chasing a damn beauty queen. That was all your doing."

"Hey, I got a tip from a reliable source. I was given the name Miss Hong Kong and made an assumption. I had no idea."

"Yeah, and your fuckup has cost the FBI valuable time and money. Time I could have spent tracking down this theft."

Agent Jengwi was upset and I couldn't blame him, so this seemed the ideal time to play my cards. "Well, what if I could get my hands on the container. Deliver both the stolen goods and Deng Qin to you. Would you be interested?"

"What are you talking about, Beecham? What *do* you know?"

"I have some friends who might be able to locate this container. With a little incentive they might be able to produce it."

"Incentive? How about 'we won't throw your ass in jail'? That enough damn incentive for you?"

"Hey, listen. I'm just the middleman. I'm dealing with some unscrupulous characters here. They need compensation.

I know the FBI pays for information. You know, reward money."

"Listen. You're in deep and you don't know who you're dealing with. We know this Deng Qin. He's a dangerous guy. If you know something, you'd better start talking. Fast."

"Look, I'm telling you what I know. I might be able to arrange to have this container turned over to you. In less then twenty-four hours *Miss Hong Kong* is sailing, destination, China. She's carrying over two thousand containers. Deng Qin's may have already been loaded. It could be buried deep within her hold by now. We don't have time to debate patriotic obligations or legal ramifications. We have to move quickly. Can you arrange for compensation or not?"

The phone was silent for a moment. "What kind of compensation are you talking about?"

"I need a boat. My boat was mysteriously blown to hell. Maybe you remember something about that."

"Yeah, a real touching story," Jengwi replied.

"I understand the government has a small fleet of vessels they've confiscated from drug busts. I'd be glad to take one of them off your hands. Something that's seaworthy and big enough to live on. I'm sure the maintenance and upkeep is a terrible drain on the taxpayer. You'd be doing the country a favor."

"I thought this compensation was for your damn friends. These unscrupulous characters you spoke of."

"They're very generous though. They know how much I miss my boat."

"Yeah, right. That it?"

"Not exactly. I'll need a little cash. I think when this goes down I'll have to disappear for a while. The Chinese are not going to be too happy with me, and I'm sure Deng Qin has a good memory and a long reach."

"How much?"

"Two hundred and fifty thousand."

"What? No way!"

"Listen, it has to be this way. Consider it a loan."

"A loan?"

"Yes. A government loan. It works this way. The FBI compensates me with two hundred and fifty thousand dollars. Meanwhile, the Chinese government will be making a deposit of two hundred and fifty thousand dollars into the Federal Treasury. You might say they're going to pay off this loan for me. In the end, there's no money out of Uncle Sam's pocket."

"What in hell are you talking about?"

"It's complicated, but I assure you it will work out just as I say. You'll have to trust me on that."

"You're telling me the Chinese government is just going to give Uncle Sam two hundred and fifty thousand dollars for no reason, with no strings attached."

"Exactly," I confirmed. Although I admit, that was a little white lie. There were strings attached, of course, like returning Deng Qin's container with the stolen military property. Classified material the Chinese wanted very badly. I knew Agent Jengwi was smart enough to figure that out. I just didn't want to be too specific.

"I just trust you with two hundred and fifty thousand dollars of taxpayer money and provide a fast boat for you to disappear with," Jengwi added with a bit of cynicism.

"I suppose it sounds like that, but it's for a good cause. Securing America's military secrets, breaking up a spy ring and arresting a murderer."

"Murderer?"

"I'll fill you in on that later. Oh, and one more thing." I paused, waiting for a reaction, but Jengwi remained silent. "There's an American citizen in Chinese custody in Beijing. He was kidnapped right here in Seattle by Deng Qin and quietly taken out of the country. I want you to arrange with the State

Department to have him returned."

"An American citizen kidnapped in Seattle? Now he's in China? Who is it? What the hell are you involved in, Beecham?"

"I'll provide his name later. But he *isn't* involved with MSS or the stolen goods. And, remember, *I'm* not involved either. It's those unscrupulous friends of mine."

"Dammit. Now listen to me Beecham. I've had enough of your spy games. Now, you're attempting to extort the Federal government. You're no match for MSS or the FBI. You're gonna get burned. I'm *not* letting that stolen container leave the country. With or without your help."

"With all due respect, Agent Jengwi, you do need my help. And that of my friends. This is big. I promise you this is really big. We don't have much time. As I mentioned, the ship sails in less than twenty-four hours."

Jengwi broke in. "If I don't have that container in my possession, that ship's *not* going anywhere, I assure you of that."

"Agent Jengwi, I know as soon as we hang up you're going to be tempted to disperse your team to the port, flash your ID's and throw your weight around searching for that container. You're gonna do everything in your power to bring Deng Qin down and recover the merchandise. If you do, you can guarantee Deng Qin will hear about it. You'll spook him and he and that container will disappear for good. Remember, that ship is owned by China Lines, as in 'Chinese'. We can't trust anyone. If you play it cool we can pull this off. This is a game of chess. It requires finesse. The muscle will be needed later. That's where you come in."

"Are you telling me how to run a goddamn investigation, Beecham? You're pissing me off, and that's not a good place to be."

"Look. This is really the only way it can happen. If I don't deliver, you can take down the ship and the entire container yard. That's your ace in the hole. I'll call you in the morning. That's D-Day. It's all going down tomorrow. Make sure you've arranged for the compensation we've agreed on so we can get Deng Qin and the stolen container."

"I didn't agree to any damn com—"

I hung up and exhaled a deep breath. I knew Agent Jengwi would be fuming. With the remaining time he had he'd be pursuing his own investigation like there was no tomorrow, and in truth, there wasn't. He wouldn't settle for sitting on his hands, waiting for some flake writer to deliver a spy ring. He'd be racing around like a man with his hair on fire. I only hoped whatever he did, he wouldn't do something to alert Deng Qin. The success of my plan, and my life, depended on it.

Mentally exhausted, I felt I had done all I could today. I needed to lie low and wait until tomorrow. I turned to Angie and gave her a hug as I whispered in her ear. "I need you strong, Angie. We're gonna get George back. He's alive and we're gonna bring him home."

CHAPTER FIFTY-SIX

WE HAD REACHED such a critical point in our plan I thought it unwise for Angie to return to her apartment. Knowing Deng Qin now had a connection between us and George Hu, he might suspect his sister's involvement. I called Lieutenant Sam Watkins with SPD and gave him a brief update, telling him only what he needed to know. I told him tomorrow would be an interesting day for the both of us. I would have something concrete for him on Sayonara's murder. Explaining the potential danger to the Hu family, I asked if he would post a squad car in front of Wung Hu's house throughout the night just to be on the safe side. He agreed.

Angie drove with me to my new digs, a chain motel in the east side community of Bellevue. I wanted to put a little space between me and the unbalanced Deng Qin. I wanted to sleep on clean sheets and enjoy a little luxury for a night. Not that I planned on "going out" in style, but that grim possibility remained in the deep recesses of my mind. We both needed a good night's sleep.

I had grown close to Angie. She was beautiful, sweet and strong. We had shared a lifetime of emotions and I felt my heart kick into another gear when I looked at her face. I wasn't sure if it was due to the emotional stress we had been under or the fact we had been putting our very lives on the line together, supporting each other when one of us hit bottom.

I felt I might be falling in love with Angie, but tonight would not be the best time to begin a relationship, considering the task facing me tomorrow. I needed to be clear headed and unencumbered by a romance. I didn't know if she felt the same way, although I sensed she might. Like I said, we both needed a good night's sleep. I booked separate rooms.

* * *

THE NEXT MORNING Angie and I headed back to Seattle where I would drop her off at Uncle Willie's warehouse. She would remain there as my plan unfolded. I had Angie drive so I could concentrate on making a couple of phone calls. I dialed Deng Qin as we crossed the I-90 bridge and prepared myself for his usual outburst—threats of death and doom. According to him, diving into a wood chipper would be a more humane death than the one he had planned for me. I tried not to think about it. I dialed. He picked up, but for the first time he didn't answer immediately.

"Deng Qin?" I asked.

"This is Deng Qin." His voice, so calm and cool, nearly unnerved me.

I preferred him screaming and out of control, but cooperative. I got right to the point. "Do you have a confirmation from George?" I asked.

He was slow in answering, reluctant, but resigned. "George Hu will be sending an email message to his sister. He will put something in this message that only she will understand. By that she will know he is still alive."

"And the money?"

Again a pause. "I am ready with the money." Then his voice rose, but he remained a shadow of his former belligerent self. "What assurances do I have that you will deliver the container? How do I know you are not setting *me* up with the

FBI?"

"You don't." I had to reassure Deng Qin. I didn't want him getting cold feet at this late hour. He had to be convinced I had as much to lose as he did. "But if I were working with the FBI, I sure as hell wouldn't be asking for money. I could have just used the container for bait. If they catch me taking money from you I'll be arrested for accepting an illicit payment from a Chinese agent. That's a felony. The Internal Revenue would be after me. I'll have U.S. government agents coming at me from all directions. I have as much to lose as you do. But I understand your concern." I explained my plan to him and he agreed. He didn't have much choice. Time was short.

I looked over and shared a nervous smile with Angie as we wound our way through the International District. My plan was beginning to unfold as I hoped it would, but it was too early to begin celebrating. After hanging up with Deng Qin, I made another call.

"Supervisory Special Agent Lou Jengwi here."

"This is Curtis Beecham."

"Mr. Beecham. I wasn't certain I'd ever hear from you again. That's some wild scenario you came up with yesterday. If it's true, you could be putting yourself in a risky position, or is this just more of your fantasizing, a novel you're playing out?"

"You don't believe me? You're going to let Deng Qin and his stolen cache slip through your fingers because you're reluctant to believe me?"

"Yours is a crazy ass story, Mr. Beecham. But, let's just say I know enough to believe some of what you've told me may be true. I've known all along you've been involved with the Chinese in some way. I'm still not convinced what side you're on, or if you have some kind of death wish. But due to the fact we're running out of time, I'll play your game. If you're lying to me Beecham, you're gonna be looking at the inside of a cell block in a Federal pen. Maximum security. You'll be sleeping and showering with some *real* unscrupulous characters. Your asshole's gonna get mighty sore."

"I get it. It'll work out, just as I said. Now, I get a boat, two hundred and fifty thousand dollars, and assurances that the State Department will see the kidnapped citizen is returned from China. You get the recovered container with the stolen military hardware, two hundred fifty thousand from the Chinese government, and Deng Qin with his hands dirty. Once you have him he'll most likely lead you to other contacts in MSS, and provide you with a wealth of valuable information. Are we in agreement, Agent Jengwi?"

"I've made the arrangements," Jengwi replied. "Of course we can't guarantee we can get this citizen back from China. That's out of my control. But we'll look into it and see that all efforts are made on his behalf. We have a small fleet of confiscated boats in San Diego. You can pick out whatever suits you. The money can be wired as you wish."

"Good. Here's how it's going to go down."

I gave SSA Lou Jengwi what information I wanted him to have regarding the plan to apprehend Deng Qin and the FBI's part in it. I also gave him the wire instructions for transferring the funds into an account I had set up in the Cayman Islands from an on-line site. With some reluctance, he had agreed to my plan but I'm sure he was not at all happy about taking directions from a writer, an unpublished one at that. But the chance to catch Deng Qin with the goods made my offer too irresistible.

When all is said and done, providing the outcome is favorable, my part in the success of apprehending Deng Qin would no doubt be relegated to a small bit part and buried under an avalanche of Bureau files.

"Are we in agreement?" I asked.

"Yes. But If I get any sense something's not right, if I hear even one damn squeak that tweaks my better judgment, I'll shut this fucking operation down and take this city apart piece by piece until I find you. Remember that." He paused a moment and his voice calmed. "By the way, I spoke to your editor a few days ago."

"You did?" This caught me off guard. "What'd he say?"

"Sorry to tell you this Mr. Beecham, but he had a change of heart. Must have been struck by a sudden bolt of patriotic fervor. Wanted to help us. If I were you I wouldn't count on him in the future. Very fickle guy."

Deng Qin had already divulged Jack's involvement and shared his deceit, but hearing it again from an FBI agent, really hurt. I had depended on Jack. Thought he was part of my team. But Jack was more interested in taking care of Jack. He took a fatal gamble and lost. I only hope I don't draw the same hand.

"Yeah," I said. "Turned out he had different objectives than I did. But he's not my editor anymore." *Yeah,* I thought, *Jack Buick won't be anybody's editor.* I didn't want to get into the issue of Jack's demise with Agent Jengwi, so I dropped it.

"Oh, you have a new one?" he asked.

"Working on it. I'll send you a press release."

"I'm sure you will."

"Oh, by the way, Agent Jengwi. Do you know what's in Deng Qin's container?"

"No. Want to share what you know?"

"Yeah. I suppose you should know what makes Deng Qin's heart flutter, and what it is you're going to have to find a good home for when this goes down." I said. "My unscrupulous friends tell me it's a jet aircraft engine. Maybe a secret prototype. Most likely highly classified. And certainly not meant to end up in the hands of the Chinese."

* * *

WE PULLED UP at Uncle Willie's import office and I

slipped out of the car and walked around to Angie's side. She stepped out and I held her tight for a few moments, smelling her hair, her breath. Then I backed off, gazed into her eyes, lifted her chin and kissed her. She kissed me back, pressing her mouth hard against mine, sending a wave of warmth through me and stirring deep feelings I hadn't felt for a very long time. She drew back with one final touch of her lips and I stroked her cheek. Giving her a confident smile I returned to the car and closed the door. If things worked out, I'd see her later. If things didn't work out, I might never see her again.

I drove toward Sayonara's warehouse. The time had arrived to close the vise.

CHAPTER FIFTY-SEVEN

AFTER STOPPING AT Sayonara's warehouse to unlock the container, I drove around the block and turned down an alley behind an older two-story brick building. The brick building ran the length of the entire block and created a lengthy barrier between Sayonara's warehouse across the street and the alley that would serve as my escape route. There were a few cars parked in the area, but no one in sight. I slowed and stopped along the brick wall near a metal ladder that led to the roof.

I slung my computer bag over my shoulder and worked myself up the ladder. The roof was flat with a black tar surface surrounded by a brick wall three-foot high. I walked over to the front side of the building and glanced around. I had a perfect view of Sayonara's warehouse and the container parked along the right side, resting on a truck chassis. There was light vehicular traffic, but no pedestrian movement.

I pulled out my phone and computer. During a scouting trip a few days earlier I discovered an Internet start-up company was housed in the building beneath my feet and would provide the complimentary wireless service I would require over the next few hours. This wasn't so unusual in a community that entertained the headquarters for both

Microsoft and Amazon.com and the hundreds of spinoff companies they had fostered over the years.

I looked at my watch. 9:48 A.M. I opened my computer and checked for an Internet connection. Within moments I was linked to my email account. Twelve minutes later I placed the call.

"Deng Qin," a voice answered.

"Send your man," I told him. "Remember. One man. He can view the merchandise and call you to confirm. If I see any attempt to remove the container before I have George's confirmation and possession of the other container and the money, I will notify the FBI and Seattle PD. They will be on you like sticky rice. Do we understand each other?"

"Give me the location," Deng Qin snarled.

"Seven four three two South Hampton."

"Where is that?"

"I'm surprised you don't know."

"Why should I?"

"It's Sayonara's warehouse."

The phone went silent. I sensed Deng Qin had built himself up to slow boil. I hoped his agitation over this whole incident would dull his senses and cloud his professional judgment. I wanted him to remain a little off balance.

"If you are fucking with me, you will pay dearly."

I hung up. It was now a waiting game.

* * *

MY DISPOSABLE PHONE wouldn't accept incoming calls, so Angie couldn't call, but she had been instructed to email me as soon as she heard from George or the container arrived at Uncle Willie's. I kept a close watch on Deng Qin's container. Someone would arrive soon and I didn't know who it would be, or how he would arrive. I didn't trust Deng Qin any more than he trusted me. If he tried to take the container before he had met my demands, I would summon SSA Lou Jengwi, and he and his band of merry men would swoop down from their hidden location within minutes. My advantage turned out to be the size and bulk of the container—not something easy to hide or quick to remove.

* * *

TWENTY MINUTES LATER a black sedan, driving at a slow, deliberate pace, approached. The windows were tinted, dark, I couldn't see in. The vehicle hesitated in front of the container, then drove on to the end of the block where it turned around and headed back, parking on the gravel in front of Sayonara's warehouse. I lay flat on the roof and watched through a drainage outlet in the wall. An opening the size of a mouse pad, it provided a perfect view across the street and allowed me to see but not be seen.

A man dressed in dark slacks and a trench coat, with black hair and Asian features, stepped out of the sedan. He looked up and down the street then glanced around, studying the building in front of him and the container off to the side. He strolled up to the warehouse, his hands stuffed in his coat pockets, then reached out with his right hand and checked the door, finding it locked. He glanced up and down the street again before walking toward the container, then disappeared behind it. I could see the top edge of the steel doors swing open. A moment later they closed once again and the man circled the other side. He pulled out a cell phone, dialed, and held it to his ear as he continued to survey the area. A moment later he returned the phone to his pocket, walked to his vehicle, pulled the handle, sat down and disappeared behind the closed door.

I dialed Deng Qin.

"Satisfied?" I said.

"Yes," he answered.

"Bank of America." I gave him the number SSA Jengwi had given me of the account the FBI had set up for this transaction. Then I gave him the address of the Asian Antique Import Company where he would deliver Uncle Willie's container. "I don't have to remind you. I don't want to see any movement with that container until I confirm everything. I'll call you when I have confirmation. When will we receive George's email?"

"I will contact the authorities. It should happen very quickly."

"When will the other container arrive?"

"It is on the way now."

I hung up and checked my email, anxious, nervous, but knew it was too soon to have heard from Angie.

I glanced back to the black sedan. I kept my gaze on it, watched, waited.

The day had dawned with a sharp chill, but only a slight chance of rain. A stiff breeze swept in across Elliott Bay, and the usual low-hanging clouds formed a gray ceiling as they tumbled and rolled in a constantly changing pattern. I checked my email. Nothing. Eight minutes later I checked it again. A message arrived from Angie. I exhaled a deep breath as I read her brief confirmation. George *was* alive. I had told her not to forward his email; I didn't want my hard-drive to have any traceable link to Chinese computers. For the moment, I breathed easier. If George was alive now, I had to believe he would remain safe once the Chinese realized our government knew of his situation. Negotiations could then begin in earnest.

Anxiety surrounded me like a cold blanket. Sitting and waiting, counting the minutes was nerve-wracking. Completing these transactions would take time, and that allowed my mind to think about everything that could go wrong. I thought about SSA Lou Jengwi. I knew he'd be pacing and swearing, unhappy that on such a major operation, he was not in complete control.

I looked at my watch. 10:43. With an eye on the sedan, I went to the Internet and brought up my account. Nothing.

I sat back and took a deep breath, trying to slow my breathing and remain calm. It's too soon I told myself. I watched the sedan. Fifteen minutes or so passed. Then thirty. I checked my email for what seemed the millionth time. "Yes!" I exhaled. Again, Angie had sent a confirming message. The container had arrived at Uncle Willie's at 11:10. The semi-truck driver was unhooking the chassis as she sent the email.

Two of my three demands had been fulfilled. But these were the easy ones. The question remained. Would Deng Qin follow through with the wire transfer, or does he have a trick up his sleeve? Was delivering Uncle Willie's container a diversion? Am I missing something? Doubt began to creep in. He could simply be pacifying me. I didn't trust him. I checked the sedan. It hadn't moved. No one else had come sniffing around. I now had only to wait for confirmation from Agent Jengwi that the wire transfer had been completed.

The overcast sky became thicker and darker as the cloud mass continued to build. The breeze picked up and cut with a sharp edge through vulnerable gaps in my clothing. I tugged on my parka and pulled the hood over my head, cinching the string running through it.

The sound of voices drifted up from the backside of the building near my car. Startled, I poised for a quick exit. Laughing. A woman's voice. Then doors closed, a vehicle engine cranked over, drove away. I exhaled a deep breath and collapsed back into a seated position.

I checked my email again. I tried to relax, forcing myself to be more systematic—a quality I had never embraced—putting myself on a schedule. I would check my account every ten minutes. I looked at my watch. 11:30.

Still nothing.

I glanced through the peephole. I waited. Ten minutes. Then twenty. Then thirty. Forty minutes went by.

I heard the low rumble of a motorcycle and glanced through the peephole. Damn. A motorcycle cop. He slowed as he passed the container, glanced back and forth from one side of the street to the other. He appeared to be searching for something. Vehicle license plates perhaps. The officer stopped, balanced his idling machine with firmly planted boots and pulled a small notebook from his jacket pocket. He flipped a few pages, glanced at the line of cars parked in front of the brick building, then returned the notebook to his pocket and continued motoring down the street until out of sight. A slow exhale escaped my lips. I sat back and rested against the wall. My shoulders had tensed and tightened. I tried to work out the kinks, but my muscles, taut with stress, wouldn't respond in the cool air.

Another ten minutes passed. I checked my account again. I clicked on my inbox. I heard a low beep. I stared, my heart making a jump-start, as a message popped up from Agent Jengwi.

> SEATTLE OFFICE OF THE FBI HAS RECEIVED AN ALERT. HIGHLY SECRET PROTOTYPE MILITARY AIRCRAFT ENGINE HAS TURNED UP MISSING FROM UNITED ELECTRIC AIRCRAFT ENGINE IN NEW LONDON, CONNECTICUT. BEECHAM, YOUR ASS IS ON THE LINE. YOU HAVE UNTIL 2:00, BEFORE I CALL OUT EVERY LAW ENFORCEMENT OFFICER IN THE CITY AND BLANKET THE PORT AND EVERY NEIGHBORHOOD SURROUNDING IT.
>
> SUPERVISORY SPECIAL AGENT LOU JENGWI

I exhaled and checked my watch. 12:23. "Damn! An hour and a half." I studied the screen a moment, then looked over and stared through the peephole. "Come on, Deng Qin." But I knew, even if Deng Qin had made the transfer of funds, it was up to the financial community as to how quickly the transaction would be completed. I hoped this one received priority status. I glanced again through the peephole. The black sedan remained in position.

I thought of Angie. This relieved some tension. I thought about the kiss. She had kissed me. Thoughts of Angie helped pass a few moments as I continued my vigilance.

I had been watching for a moment when a white van drove by, hesitating as it passed Sayonara's warehouse. My inner alarm sounded. There was no identification on it. I had no reason to be alarmed, but something made me take notice. What was it? I stood up and risked looking over the wall, watched as it continued down the street and turned the corner. I crept back to the alley side, squatted down behind an air conditioning duct that dropped over the wall and peered beneath it. The van rounded the brick building, turned into the alley and headed my direction. As it neared, I saw two figures through the windshield. Hooded jackets covered their heads. Shit! Deng Qin has sent his Hoods. While he appears to be playing the game, he's trying to make an end run. He must have figured I'd be somewhere within eyesight of Sayonara's warehouse, and he's looking for me. He may or may not be wiring the money. Either way, he means to find me.

The van stopped directly below, next to the ladder. My heart raced. I'd waited long enough. I scooted back to the front wall, grabbed my computer and stuffed it in the case. I scanned the roof looking for an escape. At the far end I noticed a small brick enclosure that appeared to be a roof access. I ran hard toward it, needing to reach it before the Hoods caught sight of me. One side held a steel door with a small louvered ventilation window near the top. I tried the doorknob. The door swung open.

I glanced back toward the ladder. The top of a hooded head bobbed as it appeared over the wall. Adrenaline rushed through my body. I stepped over the twelve-inch threshold and closed the door, clicking it shut. A bare bulb at the top of the stairs provided a source of light that faded as the steps dropped into near darkness. Did they know I was here? Had they seen the door closing?

I fiddled with the doorknob, tried to lock it. It was inoperable. I looked around for something to jam against the door but found nothing. I headed down the concrete steps, not knowing where they led, or if I had a clear escape. I reached the steel door on the second floor and twisted the doorknob. No movement. I kept my feet moving, taking two steps at a time on my downward flight.

The stairwell fell into darker shadows as I descended. I grabbed the knob on the first floor and turned it. Locked. I pulled harder. Nothing. Reality shot through me with a pang of fear. I was sealed inside the stairwell with only an unlocked door on the roof between me and the Hoods. If they knew I was here they'd be coming. I was trapped. There was no way out.

I balled my hand into a fist intending to pound against the steel. Call for help. Draw attention. I stopped myself in mid-motion, hesitating. The only attention I might draw might be unwanted. Might be the Hoods. Should I risk it? I wavered. I had no way of knowing if there would be someone on the other side.

Bare concrete walls surrounded me. I spun around, frantic, looking for any help, as my eyes adjusted to the dim light. I caught a glimpse of a good-sized wrench tucked behind an iron pipe attached to the back wall. I grabbed the tip and wiggled it free. I took a firm grip with a tight fist, slapping the rusted metal surface against my open palm. Hardly any defense against two armed thugs, but it was all I had. If I surprise the first one, get his gun, maybe…

I ducked down and scooted under the steps, finding the tightest spot where shadows were deepest. I crouched with my back against the cold wall, my breath coming in quick gasps. Within moments a rattle echoed throughout the corridor. It came from upstairs. The steel door that led to the roof. A harsh light flooded in, erasing the deep shadows. The movement of a silhouetted shape flashed against the floor. A blur. Then footsteps. A quick slapping sound echoed with a two-step rhythm. It became more pronounced. Louder. Closer. I pressed back against the wall and held the wrench with a tight moist grip, ready to spring.

I tensed my body, my arm cocked, waiting for the precise second when sneakers, jeans, then a hooded-face would emerge in the sharp angular light beyond the shadow where I remained in hiding.

I lifted up, prepared to spring, as a shrill voice broke the silence, startled me, like a chilling prelude of the inevitable. It came from above, sharp, jerky syllables in Chinese. The garbled words ricocheted against the walls. The footsteps slowed, then paused. The sound of a second voice, louder, nearly within my grasp, called back, in a rapid-fire Chinese echo. The footsteps, a faint heartbeat away, shuffled against the concrete, eking out a subtle squeak from rubber soles, then the slapping began again, moved away, became more distant. A door slammed at the top of the stairwell, reverberating like distant thunder. The tomb once again became pitched in shadows, filled with silence, broken only by my heavy exhale. I had been holding my breath far too long.

I heard no sound but my breathing. I remained frozen, unable to move. The silence continued. My legs began to cramp from my confined squat. After what seemed an eternity,

I gained the strength to lift my arm and check my watch. I couldn't remember when I had checked it last. It had been twelve something, but I couldn't remember exactly. In the deep shadows the lighted display read 12:47. There had not been any sound from above for some time, but I wasn't ready to show my face just yet.

I thought about calling Deng Qin, giving him my heart-felt sentiments for breaking our agreement, but if he knew I had seen the Hoods, he would know I was nearby. And a threat. They'd be back. I had to ignore this little breach of mutual trust on his part. I shouldn't have been surprised. But I also should have planned more carefully. I should have had another escape option. I had made a mistake. I had better not make another. This one was near fatal, the next one very well may be.

CHAPTER FIFTY-EIGHT

AFTER THE ENCOUNTER with the Hoods, my nerves were frayed. My hand had cramped from gripping the wrench, which I set on the concrete floor. I crawled out from the shadows, sat down on the step and pulled out my computer. It took another few moments to gather myself before checking my email. I stared at the screen a moment before it registered. I had no new messages. Another ten minutes went by. Then twenty. The tension of the encounter had begun to subside. My mind became sharper.

The stairwell remained quiet, but I was reluctant to return to the roof. If Deng Qin didn't find me he might try something. He might remove the container, and if I remained in the stairwell, I'd never know. But the risk of exposing myself was too great. I decided to remain in place and wait a bit longer, hope I would soon hear from Agent Jengwi.

I returned to my routine of checking email every ten minutes. I became consumed with concern, a sense of foreboding hung over me. Is there time? Would Deng Qin come through? Jengwi had given me until 2:00. Would that be enough? Damn. I wish Jengwi hadn't received that alert bulletin. He was already nervous about relying on my plan, and that put him over the edge. Come on Deng Qin. Where's the money? I checked a few more times. Nothing. Another ten minutes, nothing. Ten more minutes. I looked at my watch. 1:52. Time was almost up. There was nothing I could do but wait, and hope. Ten minutes went by. Then another ten. It was after 2:00. I checked my email once more. I heard a beep. One new message. I stared.

> FUNDS IN THE AMOUNT OF $250,000 CONFIRMED. CALL ME IMMEDIATELY.
> JENGWI

I continued to gape at the computer. I took a few deep breaths, not believing what I read. The fear I'd felt the last hour or so had drained me. I didn't have the energy to be excited. Though filled with relief, my pulse continued to race. Thank God. I read it once more. Yes, yes, yes. He did it. Now let's see if Deng Qin will be drawn into the trap. He's done everything I demanded. Why wouldn't he?

I pulled out my phone and dialed, then put it to my ear. Nothing. I lowered it and studied the digital display. NO SERVICE. Shit! Not now. I shook the phone. "Cheap piece of crap," I mumbled. Wait. It must be this stairwell. Or maybe there's some kind of interference from the Internet company. I glanced up the stairs and a feeling of anxiety came over me. I couldn't put it off any longer. It was time to crawl out of the tomb.

I bagged my computer, crept up to the top landing and placed my ear against the door, listening. Hearing no sound, I stepped up on an exposed pipe and peered through the slatted opening. I could see nothing through the limited portal. My breathing accelerated. I took a firm grip on the doorknob, took one deep breath, then pushed the door open with a shove and stuck my head out. I glanced back and forth with a quick glance. No one. I waited a moment before stepping out, exposing myself. I kept my ears alert and my eyes scanning three-sixty as I scooted along in a low crouch to the edge of the roof where the ladder dropped down to the alley. I peered over, my heart racing.

The white van was gone. I glanced up and down the alley until satisfied they had moved on. I breathed out a deep sigh of relief. My legs, feeling the stress, nearly buckled beneath me. I crept back to the front wall, slumped down in a total collapse, and peered through the peephole. I almost believed the container might disappear as the money appeared. It hadn't.

Deng Qin had played his ace and had drawn a joker. I knew there was still danger, but I was gaining confidence as the end appeared near. A smile crept across my face as my excitement grew, but I had to keep my emotions in check. I retrieved my phone from my pocket. Finding I had service, I dialed.

"Deng Qin," I said. "It's all yours." I hung up without waiting for a reply. This would be the last time I would talk to him and I wanted to have the last word.

I glanced back to the computer once more and stared. Deng Qin had satisfied my three demands. He had wired the money. A tinge of excitement crept in, overcoming the initial shock and a lifetime worth of angst and anxiety.

But it wasn't over. Not just yet.

Within a few moments I heard the low rumble of a semi-truck. Deng Qin must have been nearby. I wondered if he'd been waiting in the same parking lot as Agent Jengwi. The two of them and their goons, sitting side by side in their tinted sedans, impatiently making calls and checking email, waiting for the green light. They may have even shared a bag of fortune cookies. I wondered what their fortunes would have told them on *this* particular day. I chuckled at the thought. It provided a brief moment of much needed relief.

I peered through the peephole. A silver import leading a semi-cab drove up and parked next to the black sedan. Two men stepped out of the silver car as the man from the sedan joined them. They walked to the container. The semi swung around and began backing up. With respect to a deceased friend, I whispered, "*Sayonara* Deng Qin, you bastard."

I picked up the phone and dialed. SSA Lou Jengwi answered from the hidden location where he had been waiting for my call.

"Yes," he replied, sounding anxious, breathing heavy.

"They're here. Three guys. Two cars, one black, one silver. One semi-truck cab. They're all yours."

"Address, Beecham," he barked.

"Seven four three two South Hampton. Two blocks away."

"Shit!" I heard as he hung up.

I knew he'd soon be tearing around the corner, tires squealing, guns pulled, badges flashing. This I had to see. I checked my watch. 2:24. I stared through the peephole. The three men had gone to the back of the container and opened the doors. Moments later they closed them. The truck driver had jumped out to hook the chassis to his cab.

Before I saw them I heard the sound of vehicles accelerating. In my excitement, I lifted myself up and peered over the wall. Two dark sedans approached from one end of the street. Another one came from the other direction. A gray van followed. 2:27. They're good! Tires screeched as they slammed on brakes and skidded to a quick stop at various angles, facing the container. One vehicle hit the gravel and slid, kicking up a cloud of dust.

Doors flew open from the van as four armed agents jumped out in full SWAT gear brandishing automatic weapons. The suits in the cars wore bulletproof vests with large white letters on the back identifying them as FBI. They poured out and scattered, finding cover behind the barricade of stopped vehicles. Outstretched arms gripped handguns. Within seconds they had the area covered.

The truck driver dropped to the ground and laid flat on the gravel, his arms and legs splayed. The three Asian men in dark coats ducked behind the container as the first cars skidded to a stop. Excited shouts in Mandarin were heard coming from their direction.

An agent behind one of the sedans raised a bullhorn. "This is the FBI. Drop your weapons. Step out with your hands up." The voice sounded all too familiar.

Two FBI agents and two members of the SWAT team took off in a low crouch toward the left side of Sayonara's warehouse. They gave a quick glimpse into the black sedan as they passed, then disappeared around the corner. At the same time one of Deng Qin's men dashed out from behind the container in a beeline for the rear of Sayonara's warehouse, unaware he was running directly into the path of the agents circling from behind.

The bullhorn sounded again. "Drop your weapons. You're surrounded. Step out with your hands up."

The two Chinese who had remained behind the container bolted in a quick retreat, took a few steps, then froze, threw their hands up and dropped to their knees. The four agents that had circled the building appeared from behind it, their weapons drawn, led by the third member of Deng Qin's team who had bolted minutes earlier, his arms cuffed behind his back.

The agents scrambled from behind their vehicles and converged on the two kneeling men. The agent with the bullhorn, following a few steps behind the others, ran over and disappeared behind the trailer. The steel doors opened, then closed. A few moments later he reappeared. It had been a while, but I couldn't forget that face. Supervisory Special Agent Lou Jengwi.

Agents handcuffed the two guys on their knees and Jengwi glanced about while talking on his cell phone.

I waited until he finished, then I dialed.

He spoke first. "Curtis. I assume you've been enjoying the excitement."

"You bet. I've been looking forward to this."

"Where are you?"

"Turn around and look up."

Jengwi turned toward me and I gave him a thumbs up. "I guess that takes care of Deng Qin."

He paused. "Deng Qin isn't here."

"What! What do you mean he isn't here? You didn't get him?" My heart raced. "Deng Qin's still out there?"

"No. We got the son of a bitch all right. He just wasn't at the warehouse. He sent his flunkies. Kept his distance. But we've been watching him for some time now. Soon as we got your call, we had a team take him down. He was in shock I'm told. Never expected it. I haven't seen him myself. I'll get up-close and personal later."

I settled down once more and took a deep breath. "Give him my regards. And tell him the writer says, 'Thanks for covering my loan.' "

I hung up and watched as agents led the three captives to the FBI van, climbed in and drove off. A small crowd began to form on this side of the street as a white sedan arrived and two men in suits climbed out. Joined by Jengwi, they walked to the back of the container. The truck driver once again hitched the chassis to the cab and minutes later pulled out with an FBI escort.

I threw my computer into its case and headed back across the roof. Then I remembered something, stopped and dug into my pocket, retrieving Sayonara's phone. I laid it down on the roof before heading to the back wall.

I scrambled down the ladder and trotted to my car. My heart pounded with excitement, my hands shook with relief. I took a deep breath and exhaled. The finality was setting in. It was over. I fumbled for the keys, cranked the engine and backed out. I bounced down the alley and turned onto Fourth Avenue, heading for Uncle Willie's warehouse.

As I drove I dialed the Lieutenant's direct line. "Lieutenant Watkins, Curtis Beecham."

"I've been waiting for your call, Mr. Beecham."

"It's over," I began. "The FBI just arrested a Chinese agent by the name of Deng Qin. They'll nail him on various Federal charges. They don't know about the murder of Sayonara. I'm handing that over to you. Don't know who has jurisdiction, but you can now dance that tempestuous tango with the FBI you spoke of. I'm betting they find a gun on Deng Qin. And I'm betting you'll get a ballistics match to the bullet that killed Sayonara. You should also check out the warehouse at seven four three two South Hampton. It belonged to Sayonara. Sayonara met Deng Qin there for paid sexual favors. You'll figure that out when you see the place. There might be some evidence there. Check the bathroom. Across the street from her warehouse is a two-story brick building. On the roof is a cell phone. It belonged to Sayonara. She used it to contact Deng Qin. Again, evidence you might be able to use."

"Mr. Beecham. I don't know what you've done or how you did it, but I promise you, we'll get Sayonara's murderer." He paused. "And hey, stop in sometime. I'll buy you a cup of coffee."

"Thanks, but no thanks. I've seen the inside of your office one too many times. Besides, I hear cop brew tastes like watered down motor oil." I heard a hearty chuckle as I hung up.

I made one last call. Angie picked up on the first ring. "Curtis?"

The sound of her voice sent chills down my back and little goose bumps dancing up my arms. A wave of relief swept over me as my face felt a warm flush and my eyes became moist. My body morphed into a state of mush, my strength zapped. I slipped lower into the seat, barely able to mouth the words: "It's over Angie. It's finally over."

EPILOGUE

Puerto Vallarta, Mexico

I NEVER KNEW how vivid and intense a sunset could be when setting over the *warm* Pacific Ocean. I lounged across the padded bench seat on the stern of my classic 1940 Chris-Craft cabin cruiser and stared, mesmerized, across the small marina through a collection of tall masts and fluttering insignia. The sun kissed the horizon and a red glow radiated outward in a subtle arc, a masterpiece created from a fine airbrush in the hand of nature. Not a cloud made its presence. The sky behind had begun to turn a deeper shade of blue. A lone pelican stood on a tall pylon in reverence, or so it seemed, observing the same stunning display. The water lapped in silence, broken only by the sudden bob of a small fish breaking the surface for a delectable water bug.

It had taken me two lazy weeks to work my way down from San Diego to Puerto Vallarta in the new boat I had selected from a collection of confiscated yachts previously owned by drug lords. SSA Lou Jengwi had kept his word about the boat and the money. After all, it didn't cost the government a thing. This vintage yacht met all my requirements, and had been well taken care of thanks to her former owner and the illicit drug money he had accumulated. She was a piece of history, in pristine condition. A length of forty-four feet, configured into two cabins, two baths and a galley, she was the perfect size. The only modification necessary was on the aft end, where I had a talented sign painter hand-letter, *Margaritaville Too* across the stern.

Other than George's fate, things had turned out even better than I had planned. I kept up on the latest developments with the Deng Qin spy ring case over the Internet. In addition to charges of espionage and theft of classified military hardware, they had confiscated his gun and had enough evidence to build a strong case against him for the first-degree murder of Sayonara. They had not found Jack Buick's body, so until investigators had more evidence, Deng Qin had not been charged with his murder. Due to the seriousness of the charges, Deng Qin had plea-bargained with the District Attorney, giving up numerous contacts and information about his operations to the FBI in order to avoid the death penalty. Arrest warrants were issued in Seattle, New York and New London, Connecticut for numerous accomplices. The MSS spy ring had been broken.

With my support and encouragement, the Hu family had continued to press the State Department to do more to seek the return of George Hu. Because of that, along with pressure from the FBI provided by SSA Lou Jengwi and his superiors, they had opened dialog with the Chinese government. But the best news coming out of Washington, D.C. concerned the Vice-President and a trade conference scheduled for Beijing in April. Reports were that efforts would be made to put George Hu on the agenda.

I was told, don't get too hopeful, it might take a while. Then again, it might not. One never knows when dealing with the Chinese. My thought was, nor does one ever know when dealing with American politicians. George's freedom may even cost our negotiators future concessions on some trade issues. That's how these things work, they tell me. Political ballet. And, of course, both sides want to be the prima ballerina.

When thinking of George, I still have a knot in my throat and a twinge in my heart. I promised to never give up in my efforts until he is once again reunited with his family.

I lifted myself up, stretched out my stiff joints, then shuffled up the dock to the marina where I slipped my phone card into the slot on the public phone. I wanted to talk to my kids back in Seattle. Shelly picked up on the second ring.

"Hey, it's me," I said.

"Oh, hi. How are you?"

"I'm fine. Just wanted to say, hi."

"Everything okay?"

"Yeah. It's great."

"Where are you?"

"Puerto Vallarta. Got here two days ago. It's beautiful. You should see it."

"Sure, maybe someday. How's the boat?"

"Love it. It's everything I ever dreamed."

"That's nice."

"How're the kids?" I asked.

"Good. Doing good." She paused. "I'll put them on."

"Thanks."

After talking with Teri Lynn and Michael I asked to speak to their mom again.

"Hey, I'm going to have to stay away for a while. I won't have a chance to see the kids anytime soon. I'm gonna have to lay low. Deng Qin's going away for a long time, but he might have friends looking for me. I don't want to take a chance, so I'm gonna disappear somewhere in the Caribbean. I'll see that the kids are taken care of though, don't worry about that. And I'll call when I can. But I want them to know I still love them. Would you let them know that? You know, every once in a while."

"Sure, Curtis. You take care of yourself. Be safe. And don't write any more spy novels. It's much too dangerous."

"Yeah, it is, isn't it?" I allowed myself a slight grin before getting more serious. "With all the trouble the book has caused, I'm having second thoughts about publishing it. Two people are dead, one kidnapped and left in some Chinese prison and my family threatened. It's caused too much pain for the Hu family. I think I just want to put it aside and get on with my life. Write something a little more on the safe side. Like books for teens. I'm thinking something along the lines of two kids who find adventure in an undersea world in the Caribbean. You know, Harry Potter meets Aquaman. Something like that."

"Ah, yeah, Curtis. That'd be nice." She paused. "Well, take care of yourself. And when you can, let us know you're okay."

I had one more question before I let her go. "Say, have you had a chance to see Dad? Take the kids?"

"Yeah, Curtis. He told me he appreciated you stopping by before leaving town. Checking on him."

I thought back, remembering that visit. Knowing it would be the last time I'd see him for a while. "I kinda told him all that had happened. He said he saw something about it on the news. Was surprised to hear I was involved. I'm not sure if he thought I was foolish or what."

"No, Curtis. He didn't think you were foolish at all. He told me he was mighty proud of you. Said he knew all along you had it in you."

"Really? He said that?" I paused a moment. I think the breeze blew a speck of sand into my eye. It watered. I wiped at it. "I'd call him, but I know he doesn't answer his phone. Say, Shelly, would you mind dropping by once in a while? Checking in on him?"

"Not at all Curtis. I know he loves to see his grandkids,

even though he tries not to show it. And in his way, I think he likes me too."

I hung up and leaned against the weathered wood siding of the building, rerunning in my mind that last bit of conversation I'd had with Shelly. The sun had disappeared and the night sky was rushing in like a new tide. Two seagulls squawked and fought over a fish head tossed by a local fisherman. I shuffled back to the *Margaritaville Too* and collapsed on the padded bench seat once again, while I listened to my man Jimmy strum a few notes of "Cheeseburger in Paradise."

"Would you like a margarita, *señor?*"

Pleasantly whipped from my daydreaming, I turned my head as Angie emerged from the cabin door holding two salt-rimmed glasses bearing a slice of lime garnish. A bright red hibiscus sprouted from a crease in her jet-black hair, petals caressed her pale cheek, her slender frame draped with a shear, swim cover-up. Her eyes sparkled and her face lit up with a sly grin. Handing over a glass, she slipped in beside me, tucking her bare feet underneath. Our eyes locked, we tipped our glasses. A little salt settled on her lip.

I leaned in and removed it…with a delicious kiss.

ACKNOWLEDGEMENTS

My special thanks to Deborah J Ledford and Virginia Nosky, two accomplished authors in their own right, who both inspired me with their encouragement and guided me with their knowledge of the fine art of writing. To Deborah as well, for her critical assistance in turning my manuscript into a published reality. To Deborah, Virginia, Art Kerns, Judy Starbuck and Val Philstrom for the many hours they dedicated to the editing process and turned my first, second and 29th. draft into a polished manuscript.

ABOUT THE AUTHOR

Mardi Lynn Roselius' publishing credits include two novels, two memoirs, numerous short stories in Sisters in Crime anthologies, and articles in *Caribbean Travel & Life* magazine and the *Mystery Readers Journal*. She lives in Sarasota, Florida with her spouse and their adorable Yorkies.

Made in the USA
Columbia, SC
22 March 2020